THE ISLAND OF THE
SEVEN★KINGS

KEN STEPHENSON

authorHOUSE®

AuthorHouse™
1663 Liberty Drive
Bloomington, IN 47403
www.authorhouse.com
Phone: 1-800-839-8640

Published by AuthorHouse 1/25/2012

ISBN: 978-1-4685-4370-4 (sc)
ISBN: 978-1-4685-4369-8 (hc)
ISBN: 978-1-4685-4368-1 (e)

Library of Congress Control Number: 2012900731

FOREWORD

In an age before there was a man to measure time, Idos, the creator god, searched the universe for the perfect place to establish his domain. When he found his place in the universe, he removed everything from it and placed seven stones in the center of it and he created Astral, the god of the stars to guard his domain and protect it from the chaos of the universe. Now Astral loved Idos seeing his plan for his kingdom was perfect and she set her heart to serve Idos faithfully and be council to him and Idos gave her dominion over all the stars that surrounded his domain. Together they built a home for Idos and one for Astral also amongst the stars from which he could survey his whole domain but there was darkness across his domain save that which emanated from Idos and Astral.

Then Idos created Ratton, the god of the sun, and he took Ratton and Astral to the seven stones and Astral took the six stones that Idos gave her and placed them wherever Idos instructed her across his domain. Together Idos and Ratton hallowed out the seventh stone and made a home for Ratton there setting it on fire and the light from Ratton's home could be seen across the entire domain of Idos. Now Ratton loved Idos seeing his plan for his kingdom was perfect and he set it in his heart to serve Idos faithfully and take council with him and Idos gave him dominion over everything that the light of Ratton shined on in his domain.

Then Astral returned to her home in the stars and Idos departed from the home of Ratton and traveled to one of the six stones Astral had placed for him and he created Terrat, the god of the earth. Together Idos and Terrat hallowed out the stone and created a home for Terrat in it and Idos spoke these words. "This shall be called Earth for it shall be the womb of my creation." And Idos called to Ratton mightily and Ratton sent Terrat fire and he placed it in his hearth at the center of the earth and great volcanoes erupted over the face of the earth and heavy black clouds covered the whole earth. Now Terrat also loved Idos seeing his plan for his kingdom was perfect and he set his heart to serve Idos faithfully and take council with him and Idos gave him dominion over the whole earth.

Then Idos called to Astral mightily and she sent him water from beyond the stars until the whole of the earth was covered even unto the tops of the volcanoes and Idos created Aquino, the god of the sea. Together Idos and Aquino labored to build a home for him in the sea. Now Aquino also loved Idos seeing his plan for his kingdom was perfect and Aquino set his heart to serve Idos faithfully and take council with him and Idos gave him dominion over all the seas and lakes and rivers in the earth.

Then Idos departed from the home of Aquino and rose up above the sea and he called mightily to Aquino and Terrat and to Ratton also and together they caused a great wind to blow over the waters and clouds formed above the waters of the deep. Then Idos created Atmon, the god of the sky and together Idos and Atmon labored together and built a home for Atmon in the clouds. Now Atmon loved Idos seeing his plan for his kingdom was perfect and he set his heart to serve Idos faithfully and take council with him and Idos gave him dominion over all the sky.

Then Idos departed from the home of Atmon and raised high above him and he laid his hand against the earth and it began to turn. Now the days began and the earth was dark where Ratton's light could not shine so Idos created Lumirus, the god of the moon and together they labored and hallowed out a lesser stone and made a home for Lumirus in it calling it the moon. Now Lumirus loved Idos also seeing his plan for his kingdom was perfect and she set her heart to serve him faithfully and take council with him and Idos gave her dominion over all the places where Ratton's light did not shine.

Then Idos departed from the home of Lumirus and called mightily to all who took council with him and Aquino gathered the waters of the deep together as Terrat pushed up the dry land and Atmon shaped and sculptured the earth with a mighty wind and when they had finished Idos descended to the earth in a high mountain and created Orig, the god of living things on the earth. Together Idos and Orig labored and built for him a home in the mountains. Now Orig also loved Idos seeing his plan for his kingdom was perfect and he set his heart to serve Idos faithfully and take council with him. Idos stayed in Orig's home and they created all the seeds for all that live in the earth and the sea and the sky and Idos revealed to him also the seeds of man which he had brought from beyond the stars and he gave to Orig these seeds also save eight which he kept for himself. Eight seeds Idos kept for himself, four male and four female and he kept also for himself the seeds of the dragon in which Idos found great joy. He took those seeds also to himself saying "These are the pride of Orig and they shall be called the Sword of Idos for they shall be a tool and a teacher to my people." Then Idos sent Orig out to scatter the seeds which he had in his hand over the whole earth and in the seas and in the air also warning him to save a few seeds in reserve and life sprang forth over the whole earth but not the seed of man. Now when Orig had finished, Idos left Orig's home and found a place in the center of the ocean and called mightily to all that took council with him. Terrat raised and Island from the bottom of the sea and together they labored to make it as a paradise and surrounded it with great mountains on three sides. Idos gave Orig the seeds of the dragon and the eight seeds he had kept for himself and Orig spread the seeds of life over the island. They labored together for seven days to make it perfect and life sprang up in abundance on the island but not from the seeds of man. On the seventh day, Idos rose up above the clouds and began to circle the earth and his spirit was in the light that radiated from him intensely so that no living thing that had eyes could turn their face to him and as he passed over, the seeds of man sprang up in maturity. Idos came to the island and raised up those eight seeds lastly saying. "In these people, I shall place not only my spirit and my truth but my law also for I shall establish my government in them. They shall live in peace for a thousand years and all the earth and the gods that live in her and above her shall be their teachers." Idos lived among his chosen people for seven years and answered whatever inquiry they made of him and the people flourished and multiplied and built a city and named it Mesina. In the seventh year, Idos gathered his chosen people together in the city and gave them his blessing. "I shall not dwell among you but return to my own house. Fear not for my promise is with you and my spirit and my truth also. I place the whole of my creation at your feet and give you this island for your home and all you desire shall be in your hand. Embrace faithfully the government I have taught you and hold fast to my commandment that you love one another as I love you also for I shall never forsake you or abandon you. If you are righteous, I shall gather you to me and the unrighteous also after they have paid for their unrighteousness. Have no fear for tomorrow even as my purpose for you is hidden from you now but all things will be revealed to you in their season." When he had finished speaking, he transformed into a great golden dragon and rose up from the city of his people and returned to his home in the stars.

This is the truth Idos revealed only to his chosen people and it was passed from generation to generation as the sons and daughters of the Great Father grew mightily on the island.

C A L E N D A R

———✸———

Season	Weeks	God	Corresponding Dates
Idos	3	Idos (Creator)	26 Feb – 19 Mar
Orig	7	Orig (God Of Life)	20 Mar – 7 May
Ratton	7	Ratton (God Of The Sun)	8 May – 25 Jun
Terrat	7	Terrat (God Of The Earth)	26 Jun – 13 Aug
Atmon	7	Atmon (God Of The Sky)	14 Aug – 1 Oct
Aquino	7	Aquino (God Of The Sea)	2 Oct – 19 Nov
Astral	7	Astral (God Of The Stars)	20 Nov – 7 Jan
Lumirus	7	Lumirus (God Of The Moon)	8 Jan – 25 Feb

CONTENTS

❋

THE SONS AND DAUGHTERS
OF THE GREAT FATHER

It is a most glorious morning outside the castle of the Great Father. It is the third week in the season of Lumirus and the warm sun glows brilliant as it rises over the eastern mountain range. The seven young dragons stretch skyward from their perspective perches to bask in the warm rays and their multicolored scales glisten reflecting the suns light. Each messenger stands close by, awaiting the news that will surely come today as this is the last day of the Festival of the Great Father. Today a new Great Father will be elected from the elders of the mountain castle they call Castle Paternus and when it is announced, the messengers will mount their young dragons and spread the news across the island as has been done for all recorded history on the island of the Great Father.

The messengers are a proud group of young men and women, and most of them are in their second tour as dragon riders. It is a great honor to deliver this message to your city. Two tours is usually the limit for any given messenger as each tour lasts until their dragon matured prior to age 8. To ride a dragon past the age of its adolescence is certain death as they develop the fiery glands on both sides of their mouths and will turn on a rider and set him on fire once they matured regardless of the bond they share. The dragons have occupied the island long before recorded history and live and breed in the mountains that surround the island of the Great Father. They are the protectors of the mountain passes on the island and the descendants of the Great Father had suffered harsh lessons before they learned to share the island and live in harmony. The flat land belongs to the sons and daughters of the Great Father but the mountains belong to the dragons. A young dragon is the fastest way to travel to each of the seven cities on the island and they could be harvested before they hatched and trained by a skillful rider to do his bidding until he matured. A skilled messenger could cross the entire island in a matter of hours where a horseman might take several hours just to get to the next city. Each city has an office of scribes that collects news and stories about the events in their city and makes 6 copies that the messengers will carry at first light each day and distribute throughout the kingdom. This way any citizen in the kingdom can obtain a copy of this 7 page scroll and read what had transpired yesterday all over the kingdom. Therein, the messengers had become a favored sect in the culture of the Sons and Daughters of the Great Father and were honored as royalty.

A mature dragon is especially deadly with the exception of mating season which lasted a week in the first full moon of the spring. Mating between dragons is a very delicate event that requires a female mature dragon to lie on her back and submit to the male dragon with her wings spread out over the surrounding grasses. Mating and death are the only times you ever see a dragon on its back. When the male dragon mounted her, both would place the sharp talons of their front feet on the others chest and gently grip the other until the mating ritual was completed. The female might lay as many as three eggs surrounding the spot where she mated before setting the grass on fire around her eggs to mark her nest. Neither she nor the male will return to that spot until after the mating season is over and the eggs hatch. Once hatched the parents return and feed a single live fish to two of the hatchlings. If the female laid 3 eggs, one of the hatchlings will perish as the parents only bring one fish each. Young dragons stay with their parents until maturity. It is during this week of mating that the sons and daughters of the Great Father take to the sea and sail around to the northern coast where the entrance to the valley of dragons is. For that week the dragons are passive and completely occupied in the mating trance. Each kingdom sends a perspective dragon rider pushing large carts to harvest a single white dragon egg along with the bones from fallen dragons. Dragon bones are much denser than any of the wood the Sons of the Great Father can harvest and are seemingly impervious to decay. They look for the burnt grass and deposits of three eggs. If the dragon egg is yellow it was too young and if it is brown it was too old so only a white egg will hatch with satisfaction. Once each messenger secured an egg, they will set sail to return to the coastal city of Sandista where they await the birth of their dragon. When the dragon hatched, the messenger will present a live fish to the dragon thereby bonding with him until the dragon matures. Dragons grow fast and usually before the moon completes three cycles, a messenger is able to mount his dragon and fly back to his own city. Before he left Sandista, the likeness of his dragon was tattooed on his forearm and the headmaster at the Academy of Dragon Riders awarded him the title "Count or Countess" if it was his or her first tour. So one would know by his title and his tattoo, that Count Brandon of Red Oak was a messenger from Castle Red Oak.

Messengers can also be called to protect the Sons of the Great Father. Even a young dragon developed deadly talons and fearsome canine teeth that can rip though armor and flesh easily. All the cities on the island of the Great Father make the trip to harvest eggs each year so each city has 6 or 7 messengers at any given time. Just before a messenger's dragon reached maturity, he will be flown to the mountain pass that leads to Castle Paternus and released to join his brothers and sisters in the mountains. A new messenger might start as early as puberty, or 13 years, if he or she is physically capable of handling a young dragon. Early in the history of the Sons of the Great Father, many riders perished falling from their dragons once they reached high speeds but the advancements to the harness now made it virtually impossible to lose your seat even during wild high speed maneuvers. Two tours as a messenger are common but occasionally, if a rider was small in stature and very skilled, a third tour could be accomplished. Countess Rebecca of Gardinia was the only living messenger to have three dragons tattooed on her forearm and she now presided as Head Master over the Academy for Dragon Riders at Sandista.

The festival had been a week long and emissaries from all seven kingdoms had come to participate and celebrate the Great Father's 60th birthday and select a new Great Father. This was the way of the people from ages past as given to them by Idos. Each of the seven great cities had, in their own time, the Festival of Royalty on the 25th birthday of their King or Queen. All children are educated in the general arts of the people from age 13 to 17 in their perspective cities academies. The people of that city selected a virgin girl who is of age for conception and a graduate of the city academy. Only the most beautiful and talented girls who show great promise and physical skill can win the honor of Maiden to the Crown. It is the most prestigious position a daughter of the Great Father can achieve. A narrow wreath is tattooed around both her wrists decorated with the flower of the city she represents to identify her for life as royalty from that city. For the rest of her life, she will be held in high regard across the island and especially in her own city. Once selected, she will go to live in Castle Paternus in the Hall of Maidens where she is educated in the romantic arts for seven full weeks.

The romantic arts are taught by the Nursery Maidens and they are assisted by seven eunuchs who were altered and certified by the Academy of Medical Arts. Eunuchs are all graduates of the Academy of Medical Arts and considered royalty for their dedication and sacrifice to the kingdom. The romantic arts teach the Maiden to the Crown to focus her energy on the passion between her and the Great Father which is considered most important because the strength and wisdom of her child is believed to be directly related to the level of passion between her and the Great Father at the moment of conception. The school is highly mysterious and secretive and discussion of the nature of the classes is strictly forbidden. It is believed that the techniques taught by the Nursery Maidens can even affect the sex of a child at the time of conception. At the end of seven weeks, the Great Father will visit her in her chambers and lay with her until he impregnates her. Once impregnated, the Great Father will visit her no more. Her first child will be the heir to her cities throne unless the council has directed that a male child is required. To maintain the lineage to the Great Father, 4 of the 7 cities must always be ruled by a King. However, the council has not found it necessary to make a directive of this nature since the establishment of the School of Romantic Arts in the Hall of Maidens. It is one of the mysteries that are guarded by the Nursery Maids in the Hall of Maidens and a contributing factor as to why they and the Maidens to the Crown are held in such high esteem.

If a child is not conceived in the first two years, a new Festival of Royalty is announced in that city and the Maiden to the Crown is replaced. However, no women selected as Maiden to the Crown ever loses her esteemed stature and enjoys the benefits of that title for life regardless of whether they conceive a child or not. They are always the most sought after and desirable women in the kingdom. Their education is second only to a King or Queen and only a Maiden to the Crown receives training in the romantic arts in the Hall of Maidens at Castle Paternus. Once the baby is born and celebrates his or her 1st birthday, the Maiden to the Crown is free to devote her life to whatever endeavor she chooses. It is tradition and custom that she return to her city. The child is referred to as "Prince or Princess" and raised at Paternus by the Nursery Maids who all become the child's mother equally and are referred to as such. The biological bond between the Maiden of the Crown and the child is by no means considered superior to that of any other Nursery Maid. Some of the Maidens to the Crown elect to stay at Castle Paternus and serve as Nursery Maids and enjoy the other pleasures implicated with the Hall of Maidens but they are encouraged to return to their city at the child's 1st birthday and let the Nursery Maids nurture the children in the traditions and customs of the crown. She may choose to continue her education at any of the city academies but she will always retain the title "Maiden" and be considered part of the royal family. A Maiden to the crown is the only woman who can choose her spouse and once her selection is made, she cannot be refused.

All children are taught to read and write prior to puberty but childhood is considered a sacred time to be enjoyed. No child begins a formal education before puberty and is encouraged to just enjoy the adolescent period of his or her life. They are taught to read and write early in the home but no standard of education is imposed prior to puberty. Children are encouraged to pursue their own desires and enjoy the pleasures of youth. At 13 they may choose to enter into formal education at any of the cities academies to pursue a degree which normally takes 7 years for any discipline. A prince or princess is educated quite differently. While many of the classes at all the academies are similar, each city academy has its own unique degree program. The prince or princess is educated at each city's academy for a period of one year in turn starting at puberty or 13. During their seven years in school, they live in each of the city castles where that discipline is taught for a year and thereby not only achieve a well rounded education in the basics of all the disciplines but earn the respect of all the Sons and Daughters of the Great Father attending classes along side them.

Sporting events are highly regarded throughout the Kingdom and at the Academies. All sporting events are identical throughout the kingdom and the city academies compete against each other year round in a variety of athletic endeavors. The festival of Games is held in two parts each year at Castle Gardinia to decide the island champions for that year.

As the moon completes its first cycle in the spring, the summer games are held and each academy sends their teams to the arena in Gardinia to compete in the outdoor games. The men and women compete separately in the races and other events but all points are accumulated toward their city academy equally. The great swim across Lake Willow is always the first contest after the opening ceremonies. One contestant from each city academy begins at the far end of the lake and points are awarded for the first three that complete the swim. A high platform and bleachers are located at the south of Lake Willow where the diving championships are contested at the conclusion of the great swim. There are several relay races to test each academy and the teams compete in individual foot races of seven different lengths from 100 paces to the grueling race around Lake Willow at the culmination of the games. The Great Father presides over the closing ceremony and awards the ultimate prize of Champion of the Summer Games for the city academy that has accumulated the most points. The festival will continue for the next week in each city as they honor their individual champions and hopefully the distinction as City of Champions for the summer games.

The winter games are much different and divided into three sections. The games open with the great race of the messengers whereby each city enters its most skilled dragon rider to start together from the arena and retrieve a flag from each of the six other cities on the island and Castle Paternus during the race before returning to the arena in Gardinia. Each rider can choose his or her own course but must return with seven flags. It is a grueling race for each dragon and its rider. Dragons do not sweat and they will overheat if not watered and rested at proper intervals so it takes a tremendously skilled rider to care for his dragon and win the race. The race begins as the sun rises and typically finishes just before the sun sets.

While the messengers make their way around the island, the second section of the games begins and the women compete in seven events of gymnastics over the next three days to accumulate points for their city academy. They are awarded points by a judge sent from each of the cities who is usually a previous champion of that event. They are graded on strength and style and grace on each event. Each academy may send as many members of a team as they choose but only one girl can compete in each event. Team and individual champions are awarded.

While the women's gymnastics competition is going on, the men compete in a wrestling tournament that covers the same three days. Each academy sends a team of seven men to compete in seven different weight classes. The contest is simple and judged by a single referee. While no strike of any kind is permitted and the head and groin cannot be targeted, the contestants wrestle until one man submits to the other. Team and individual championships are awarded as with the women's contests.

The third and final section of the winter games is the great equestrian challenge where the men and women can compete side by side. Horses are a valued commodity on the island. The equestrian track is one mile in circumference and there are three races. The open single is one rider from each academy and they race a single lap. The team relay is four riders and they must pass a baton within a designated area and make four laps. The culmination of the winter games is the chariot race where a single driver steers a team of four horses around the track for seven laps. Each of the seven chariots is the pride of its city and the craftsmanship is always evident and plays a big role in the success of the driver. The skill of the driver and the team's endurance is severely tested in the seven mile race. The Great Father is always present for the race and presides over the closing ceremony as the Champion of the Winter Games is announced. The celebration spills out to each of the seven cities on the island over that next week as they honor their individual champions and hopefully capture the coveted distinction as City of Champions for the winter games for that year.

Not until they have completed the seven years of study at the various academies may a Prince or Princess select a spouse. The last year of a Prince or Princess's education is always done in the city they will rule as King or Queen. It is a long standing tradition that the wedding of the Prince or Princess occurs in conjunction with the completion of their education. It would reflect a lack of character for a Prince or Princess not to have selected a mate prior to his or her graduation having spent a year at each of the cities in the kingdom. A Prince or Princess usually lives in the castle with his or her spouse and has 3 to 5 years to tutor under the outgoing King or Queen before they take the throne. The King or Queen's spouse has no authority in the governing of the city but they may run for a position on the city council regardless of what city they were born in. The King or Queen presides over a seven member council that is elected by popular vote to a 4 year term by the residents of the city. Elections are held every two years. The offspring of any of the royal family are considered the same as all the other children in the kingdom.

On the 49th birthday of a city King or Queen, that Prince or Princess will replace the current city King or Queen at a ceremony called the Festival of Kings. The outgoing King or Queen becomes an elder at Paternus and assumes the title of Chancellor and is eligible to vote on any issue facing the supreme council. However, only seven chancellors are selected to serve on the supreme council. In addition, any male Chancellor may be selected as Great Father. This is the lineage of the Great Father who is head of the council that governs all the seven cities of the Island of the Great Father. All the Great Fathers were once city kings and he has the power to veto any decision by the supreme council and force them to come to 100% agreement to override his veto. So when you speak of Chancellor Mica of Archemeius; you know he was once King of the city of Archemeius. Only royalty may enter Castle Paternus without invitation.

Castle Paternus is not a city to itself but the seat of the government and built from solid stone mined from the mountains on the island. It was built on a great plateau atop the mountains on the northeastern side of the island. Long ago, the great dragons that patrolled the mountains had come to accept the existence of the castle as the Sons and Daughters of the Great Father constructed it and soon ceased to attack the inhabitants of the plateau. The dragons seemed to concede that it was flat ground and relinquished the territory to the Sons of the Great Father. Even so traveling through the mountain pass remained deadly and many a party attempting to get to or from the plateau met horrific deaths when they encountered a dragon on the mountain pass. A tunnel was proposed though the mountain and after many years of backbreaking work, it was completed by the engineers from Mesina. Nearly 10 miles long, it slopes gently downward from the plateau through the mountain and into the forest just east of the great freshwater lake called Willow Lake. Not a soul has been lost to the mountain dragons since the completion of the tunnel. It has been widened to accommodate a horse and carriage by the engineers form Mesina using great redwood beams to prevent a collapse.

Castle Paternus is a magnificent tribute to the majesty of the Sons of the Great Father. The entire castle is covered in thick ivy from planters on narrow ledges on the outside of each floor. Great redwood beams support seven floors in the massive castle brought from Castle Red Oak. The two large doors at the entrance and all the window shudders were inlaid with gold leaf and the frames were ordained with silver from the mines at Castle Mesina reflecting the sun brilliantly. A wide moat 8 feet deep surrounds the entire castle fed by a mountain spring at the rear of the castle and a 10 foot redwood double fence encloses the moat with gates on the inside only, except for the main gate. The engineers from Mesina had constructed a magical system of pumps using the energy from the moving water in the moat to pump it all the way to the top of the castle. Great metal tubs were fashioned atop the castle to collect the water and fires constantly burned under them to provide hot water to every room in the castle though a series of pipes and valves. The seventh floor is the roof and that is where the messengers had built their perches. The fires under the tubs make it easy for a young dragon to find his perch even at night. Not all the tubs are heated and some are used to wash the sewage and waste from the privacy rooms the engineers had constructed on every floor. The sewer ran through a larger pipe and was buried all the way out of the castle and off the eastern edge of the mountain with the overflow from the moat.

Countess Regina of Red Oak exited the privacy room still buckling the leather britches she wore under the pleated red skirt when she rode. She was in a hurry to get back to the balcony on the fifth floor where all the other messengers were waiting. She tugged at the two large iron rings under her arms that were woven into her riding vest to straighten it out. The metal rings were what the riders used to secure themselves to their dragon's harness. Countess Regina was only sixteen but she had won the race of the messengers at the last winter games and was consequently rewarded with the privilege of delivering the news about the selection of the Great Father to Castle Red Oak. She rejoined the other riders and went to stand beside her new friend Count Cameron of Mesina at the railing of the balcony. He was gazing over the courtyard below watching the workers at the gate. The huge ramp at the main gate was always down except for once each new cycle of the moon when the engineers tested it. Two new great towers were being erected on either side of the gate to support the newly developed cannons from Castle Green Stone. Count Cameron was also on his first tour being only 18 and Regina had barely beaten him at the games. All the other messengers were much older than them and in their second tours. Cameron was tall and lanky for a messenger and Regina had to look up at him. She was impatient at the selection process for the Great Father. "Jeeze, do you think they will take all day?" Regina asked still tugging at her vest. "It's not a race." Cameron chuckled looking down at her. She tugged again at her riding vest but it was still uncomfortable. Cameron frowned at her seeing her discomfort and turned her around. The lacing on the back of her vest was a tangled mess. "Heavens...., who laced this for you?" Cameron asked as he began to undo the leather straps. "I was in a hurry." Regina protested but she allowed him to help her. "You're always in a hurry." Cameron giggled as he rewove the leather straps back through all the loops in the vest. "One of these days your haste is going to get you in trouble." Cameron said as he pulled the strap tight and tied it. "Well at least you got the britches right." Cameron chuckled again pulling on the two rings woven into the thighs of her thick leather pants. "I can see those." Regina replied turning to smile at him. The vest now fit snug and comfortable and Cameron looked back over the railing at the workers. Regina felt more comfortable around Cameron than the other messengers and felt they had more in common. In beating him at the games, she had almost pushed her dragon to the point of overheating and it was Cameron that had saved her dragon's life when he helped her cool him back down. Her dragon was on the verge of collapse after the race and she feared she had pushed him too far. A dragon usually shies away from water but Cameron had led her dragon deep into Willow Lake and the cool water probably had saved him. Regina had renamed her dragon Waterbird after that as he seemed to have no fear of the lake and often wanted to land in the water and enjoyed it particularly after a long ride. After that experience, Regina felt there was something much different about Cameron than any other boy she knew. She admired him and he did not tease her mercilessly as the other riders did. "Have they brought the cannons to Red Oak yet?" Cameron asked her admiring the new towers beside the gate. "No." Regina replied. "I think we will be the last city to get the cannons. I don't think they even have a plan for where to put them." She added. "They have almost finished all the emplacements around Mesina. Red Oak would be next is my guess." Cameron replied. Suddenly the large oak doors opened and Chancellor Ellis stepped out smiling a broad smile. "Chancellor Alexander of Mesina has been elected to Great Father." He announced to the gathering of messengers on the balcony. "Now go….., and spread the news to the castles of the seven cities." He added and all the messengers began to scurry up the stairs to the left and right to the roof. "Congratulations!" Regina shouted as she watched Cameron buckle himself in to his young red and brown dragon. There were 14 perches atop the roof at Castle Paternus but only two launch platforms so Regina followed Cameron and Lightning moving toward the platform in single file. "Lightning is ready to fly." She giggled watching Cameron's dragon stretch his wings as they moved toward the launch platform. Cameron had named his dragon Lightning before he had hatched hoping he would be fast. Lightning was a year older than Waterbird but they were about the same size. The dark green and blue tattoo on Regina's forearm matched Waterbird's colors perfectly. Cameron beamed back at her knowing it would be a great honor to all the inhabitants of Mesina that the new Great Father was from their city. "You should come to Mesina tonight. The parties will be crazy fun this week." Cameron replied as he reached the end of the platform and tightened his grip on Lightning's reigns. He lowered his head behind Lightning's ear and let out a loud whistle urging the dragon to jump. Lightning spread his wings the full 10 feet of his wingspan and dove from the platform letting out a shrill whistle of his own. They disappeared beyond the platform before reappearing very close to the ground some 400 paces to the northwest and Cameron had Lightning in a full stretch climbing skyward. His legs tucked under him, Lightning pumped his massive wings accelerating and climbing toward Mesina like a giant arrow fired from the ground below. Regina smiled. To Regina, there was only one thing more exhilarating than watching a messenger take flight as she urged Waterbird to the edge of the platform. As she peered over the edge of the castle to the ground seven stories below, she wrapped the reigns one more time in her hands and pressed her body hard against Waterbird holding tightly to the harness. She took a deep breath as the wings of her dragon stretched out on both sides of her and whistled into Waterbird's ear. He leaped off the platform and they began to fall. Waterbird turned his body straight down as he pumped his wings once accelerating their decent. As they neared the ground, the young dragon again stretched his wings and pumped increasing their speed as he leveled off precariously close to the ground. Regina whistled again pulling the reigns to guide Waterbird toward Castle Red Oak as they climbed skyward. She had to match her breathing with the strokes of Waterbird's wings as he accelerated because the tremendous pressure Waterbird created when he pushed forward was too intense to allow Regina to take a breath. Regina had blacked out before on takeoff with Waterbird from the intensity of their acceleration but she had, since that time, learned how to control her breathing. On flat ground a dragon would have to run a long ways to build up enough speed to fly but diving from altitude was definitely the most exhilarating thing Regina had ever experienced in her young life. Waterbird quickly crossed the plateau and soared over the trees and Regina could see Lake Willow and Castle Gardinia below.

Castle Gardinia was the most beautiful of all the cities the sons of the Great Father had built. It was 60 miles north of Castle Green Stone and located in the center of the island on the great plain surrounded by lush fields of vineyards and crops of all kinds. The Academy of Agriculture and Animal Husbandry was centered there and the surrounding villages tended the fields and raised horses and cattle and sheep and a myriad of other domesticated animals. Castle Gardinia was not made of stone but rather constructed of the large red oaks. It is open and airy being only two stories high but much wider than the other castles and filled with garden rooms and great pools filled with tropical fish. The royal throne room sits in the heart of the castle between two of these pools. A wide staircase climbed to the second floor behind the throne that led to the halls to the guest quarters and Royal quarters. Behind the stairs is the kitchen enclosed by redwood walls and the rest of the first floor was separated into rooms by large flowing multicolored curtains which hung from the ceiling. On the north side is a banquet room and the south side is the concert hall and a library. Each room on the second floor had only three walls with a door facing the hallways in the center and great curtains of varying density hung all around the outside of the rooms. The moderate climate on the vast plain made this design very light and airy as the temperature stayed in the mid 70s year round. It is only necessary to close the heavier canvas curtains when the rains came and much lighter curtains could be used most days. Castle Gardinia is renowned for its hanging plants which are filled with lush flowers of every color and description. Located atop a natural spring, the main fountain at the center of the city was where everyone drew water and the engineers had designed a most elaborate irrigation system that spread to the vineyards well outside the city. Queen Pamela was in her 4th year as ruler of Castle Gardinia and considered one of the most beautiful and wise Queens the kingdom had ever known. She and her husband Leland who was a member of the city council were attending the Festival of the Great Father at Paternus also. Regina turned Waterbird northwest once they got atop Castle Gardinia and proceeded across the vast fields of corn and wheat that lay between the city of Gardinia on the plains and the forest's edge. Regina turned Waterbird to follow the highway.

Another 50 miles west and nestled in the forest southwest of the plains was Castle Red Oak. The Academy for the Medical Arts is centered there. The surrounding villagers made their living working in wood and supplying timber to the island. Their villages were occupied by skilled hunters and trappers providing much of the venison and other game meats the sons of the Great Father enjoyed. The city was surrounded by a six foot redwood fence merely to keep the forest animals out of the city. Bears and other smaller wildlife fill the forest around the city and could be quite a nuisance to the merchants and shop keepers. Red Oak was filled with great woodworkers and their castle reflected it. Regina gave two short whistles as the top of Castle Red Oak came into view above the trees signaling Waterbird to land. The castle is six stories high and each tree was cut and meticulously crafted and designed to construct seamless walls throughout the castle. Two large doors opened into an ornate banquet hall on the first floor and a wall separated the kitchen at the rear of the castle on the south wall. Two staircases bracket the kitchen and lead to the second floor and the Royal Court where the King's throne is against the north wall. A large conference table is in the center of the room which doubles as a dining table. Another set of redwood stairs spiral up to the third floor on each side of the throne. Several guest rooms surround a concert hall and library with the stairs to the fourth floor on the south wall. There is no wall on the north side where a grand balcony overlooks the city. A single spiral staircase is centered in the balcony and climbs to the balcony on the fifth floor where the Royal quarters are. The large tubs are located on the roof and are fed water from a pool behind the castle by the buckets on the pulley system. The three perches for the messengers were also on the roof and this is where Regina would land with Waterbird. The servants of the castle live in cabins at the rear of the castle. King Raymond has ruled from Castle Red Oak for 18 years and he and his wife The Maiden Ruth of Archemeius are attending the Festival of the Great Father at Castle Paternus.

Waterbird circled the top of the castle and slowed as they approached the perch. Four members of the city council stood atop the roof and braced themselves against the wind Waterbird created as he hovered over the perch. He came to a complete stop and stretched out his back legs finding the perch with them first before folding his wings at his side and extending his front feet. Regina unbuckled the four rings of her harness quickly and jumped down from Waterbird as he began to drink from the water in the trough in front of the perch. "So what message do you bring us from Castle Paternus Countess Regina?" One of the councilmen asked. Regina smiled broadly as she was still enamored by the sound of her royal title. "Chancellor Alexander of Mesina has relinquished his title and accepted the position of Great Father." Regina replied with as much majesty as she could muster. All the councilmen beamed and smiled broadly nodding their heads. "Chancellor Alexander is an excellent choice and he is only 53 giving us a Great Father that will rule for seven more years." One of the councilmen replied. "We should go directly to the balcony and make the announcement." Another councilman suggested and Regina followed them down the stairs. "You have done another great job Countess Regina. Please join us on the balcony." The councilman said smiling at her as they walked down the stairs. Regina was stunned that the councilman had invited her to join the council to address the city. Two servants of the castle quickly grabbed her and undid the tight bun she had tied her hair into brushing it out over her shoulders. Regina pulled at the vest straightening it out as one of the servants placed the dark green sash of the royal messenger over her shoulders and hooked the clasps in the front. One of the councilmen was already addressing the people in the courtyard below. They hurried her to the railing between all the councilmen of the city and a great roar rose up from the courtyard below when she got to the railing and they saw her. Regina was flabbergasted and a bit fearful. The courtyard was completely full below and they got quiet as the councilman beside her raised his hand. The councilman on the other side of her leaned down and whispered in her ear. "Give them your message from Castle Paternus just as you told us." He encouraged her and Regina cleared her throat nervously. "Speak loudly Countess, so they all can hear you." He added smiling at her. The whole city was dead silence as they waited. Regina took a deep breath gazing over the crowd. "Chancellor Alexander of Mesina has relinquished his title and accepted the position as Great Father." Regina shouted and the crowd erupted into cheering again. Great trumpets blasted from the balcony on the fourth floor below them as music began to fill the courtyard from the orchestra located there and the people in the courtyard began to dance. Regina was a little awestruck at the response and the grand pageantry of it all. "What a fine messenger you have turned out to be." One of the councilmen said beaming at Regina. All the men and women of the council came over to her and praised her for the job she had done and Regina felt as proud of herself as she ever had.

One of the councilwomen pulled Regina back from the balcony railing and the servants came back to her and began braiding her hair to ride again. "Do you need to eat something or can you deliver another message?" The councilwoman asked handing her a cup filled with a non-alcoholic cherry wine. Regina took a big sip of the wine. "Where am I going?" Regina replied accepting the task enthusiastically. "It's still part of the formal celebration between the cities. You can eat before you go if you need to." The councilwoman said showing concern. "If I eat just before I fly, I may lose it when Waterbird takes off anyway." Regina admitted and the councilwoman laughed and smiled at her. "We need you to take our gift to the council at Mesina to honor the selection of one of their citizens to Great Father. You will present it to the head of their council and I will school you on just what to say when you present it. One of the servants will meet you by the perch and prepare you before you go into the council chambers." The councilwoman said as she pushed a beautifully wrapped package into a canvas pouch and handed it to Regina. "Be bold and courteous Countess Regina!" She challenged her fearlessly. "You will be our only representative to their council for this ceremony and it is important." She added with a smile. The councilwoman led Regina back to the roof and they sat beside Waterbird for a long while practicing the short speech she would deliver at Castle Mesina until the councilwoman was satisfied. "How great is it to be a messenger?" Regina thought to herself. She would get to participate in not one but two ceremonies in two different cities. Only a messenger could do that on the same day.

Waterbird appeared to be sufficiently cooled from the first flight so Regina climbed back up and buckled herself in after securing the pouch to the dragon's harness. "It's time to go back to work Waterbird." Regina sighed gripping the reigns again as he stepped off the perch and she guided him to the launch platform. Waterbird let out a soft whistle and Regina smiled. "That's right; we're going to fly again." Regina replied answering him. As they got to the edge of the platform, Regina doubled the reigns in her hands again and whistled loudly in Waterbird's ear clutching hard against him as he jumped. Taking off from Castle Red Oak was more difficult as it was surrounded by trees but Waterbird knew just where to turn and Regina needed only to be able to respond with him until they cleared the trees. They headed straight north to the highway intersection and Regina whistled a long blast as they cleared the forest urging Waterbird higher into the sky. They glided effortlessly on the breeze with the forest on the left and the great plain to the right following the highway below.

The largest of the seven cities is Mesina. It is 70 miles west of Castle Red Oak down the highway and more than 100 miles west of Gardinia across the great plain. Stonecutters and miners occupy its villages providing much of the metal from the ore in the surrounding mountains. The academy of Design and Architecture is centered there in an elaborate fine school cut out of the side of the mountain. Work never ceases on the school as they burrow deeper and higher onto the mountain. All of the highways and many of the structures on the island are a direct result of the hard work of the people of Mesina and they are a very proud people indeed. Mesina is the oldest community in the kingdom and a wall 20 feet high surrounds the entire city on three sides connecting to the mountains to the northeast. The highway to Mesina winds through the forest from Castle Red Oak into the gate at the south end of the city. The highway circles around in front of the Academy and the Castle and on into the city. Every fifteen paces atop the wall around the city, one of the newly designed cannons are now perched to guard the city. Like the Academy of Design and Architecture, Castle Mesina is cut right into the mountain. There is a great balcony on each of the seven floors that overlook the entire city. All the floors in the castle are made of the most beautiful marble and alabaster. All the staircases and balconies are lined with finely crafted oak railings. The first floor is completely open and is a grand concert hall. Two magnificent fountains extend eastward 30 paces on either side of the large grass covered yard in front of the castle. Their water level is maintained by some magic of engineering by the servants of the castle. Seven huge oak trees provide shade to the front yard planted three on either side just next to the fountains and one at the east end of the yard. Huge stone pillars support the second floor some 20 feet above the concert hall and the stairways on both sides of the castle circle up to the second floor and meet at the rear of the concert hall. This stairway there continues all the way to the seventh floor. The second floor is where the throne room is and the council chambers surrounded by several rooms. The third floor is the kitchen and great dining hall. It is built like a tavern with a bar and a huge dance floor on its balcony. The fourth floor is divided into the library and servants quarters with the library facing the balcony and the servant's quarters against the mountain. The fifth and sixth floors are both quarters for the Royal Family. The seventh floor, or roof, is completely open for access by the dragon riders. This is where Regina steered Waterbird. The mystery of how the engineers provide water to Castle Mesina is a well guarded secret and only the engineers can enter the enclosed room where the large metal tubs are kept on the seventh floor. Queen Elizabeth has ruled over Castle Mesina for 19 years and she and her husband Michael the Count of Mesina are attending the Festival of the Great Father at Castle Paternus.

Regina always had trouble landing at Castle Mesina because Waterbird liked to circle a perch to slow down before landing and he couldn't do that at Mesina because it was built into the mountain. Regina pointed Waterbird's nose to the perch and whistled twice and he began to slow up awkwardly and abruptly. He struggled to get his back feet on the perch and whistled somewhat irritated as his front feet stretched onto the perch. Immediately he started to drink the sweet cool water from the trough as Regina unbuckled from the harness. "You're such a crybaby." Regina teased him. "When are you going to get comfortable landing here?" She giggled and jumped down as Waterbird snarled and whistled at her. She reached up to retrieve the pouch attached to Waterbird's harness. "Maybe you should bring him in from the north like I do Lightning." A familiar voice chuckled from behind her and she turned her head to see Count Cameron with two of the servants from Castle Mesina. Regina had never seen Cameron with his hair down on his shoulders and she thought how striking he looked all decked out in his royal sash and the formal uniform. "You know I'm not used to following you but I might try that." Regina laughed teasing him.

Cameron just scoffed at her joke and waited for her to step off the perch. "You're going to make the rest of us look like ruffians dressed like a fairy prince." She laughed teasing him again and Cameron took her hand to help her off the perch. "I'm in charge of greeting all the messengers and announcing them to the council." Cameron replied a little embarrassed by her comment. "We're going to wait until all the messengers are here to start." Cameron said grinning nervously at Regina as they walked to the stairs and the servants followed them. Regina thought it was odd he didn't let go of her hand as they walked down the marble stairs but she didn't protest…., after all they were friends. "Who else is here?" Regina asked as Cameron opened the door to the first room off the hallway on the sixth floor. "You're first as usual." He chuckled. "Lady Marian will help you get ready and then you can join me behind the council chambers." He added as one of the servants started to undo the braid on her hair. "This is your first formal isn't it? She has a formal uniform for you too." He laughed as he backed out the door and closed it.

Lady Marian looked to be just 12 or 13 years old and she finished undoing the braid before she opened the large closet in the room. There were formal messenger uniforms from every city in the kingdom there. Marian was very shy and barely looked at Regina as she pulled one of the dark green uniforms from the rack. "Why are *you* so nervous Lady Marian? Is this your first formal ceremony too?" Regina asked smiling at her trying to make her feel at ease. "You are the Countess Regina of Red Oak and the champion of the winter games." Marian replied still staring at the floor. "I never imagined Count Cameron would select me as your servant for the festival. Everybody knows you." She added holding the uniform up to size it against her frame. "How old are you?" Regina asked lifting her chin to smile into her eyes. "I'm 14." Marian replied smiling back nervously and Regina giggled. "Well I'm just 16 so I'm going to need your help to make this formal thing work." She laughed pulling a smile from Marian. "We girls have to stick together." Regina added and Marian giggled and turned her around to undo the laces of her riding vest. "Tell me about your family." Regina asked. "My father works at the mine and is a senior bowman with the league of hunters and my mother is a seamstress and takes care of me and my brothers." Marian replied. "And how old are your brothers?" Regina asked. "Benji is 10 and Mason is 12. My father is going to take us camping and hunting at Lake Willow after the festival." Marian replied excitedly. "You said Count Cameron selected you as my servant for the entire festival?" Regina asked. "Yes mam. I'll be by your side for the rest of the week if you decide to stay for the whole festival." Marian replied as Regina pulled off the heavy leather vest and dropped it on the bed. "Oh I can't do that. I have to get back to Castle Red Oak." Regina said sitting on the bed to remove her boots. "I think Count Cameron was hoping you'd stay." Marian giggled bashfully. Regina looked at her frowning. "You need to curb your tongue Marian. Count Cameron and I are just friends." Regina chastised her standing to unlace the leather britches. Marian looked at the ground again. "I'm sorry. That's sad." She replied. "Do you want to take a bath?" Marian asked quickly changing the subject. Her demeanor puzzled Regina. "No, I don't want to take a bath. I bathe before bed. You don't have to feel sorry and why is that sad?" Regina demanded folding her hands across her chest. "Oh I'm not sorry for what I said. Count Cameron asked me to encourage you to stay. I feel sorry for Count Cameron. It's sad because he obviously wants to be more than your friend." Marian sighed as she pulled a bottle of perfume from the chest by the bed and sprayed it on her wrist. "You like this one?" She asked holding her wrist up to Regina's face. Regina sniffed the perfume not really interested in what the scent was as she pulled off the britches. "That's fine." Regina replied acknowledging the perfume. "Count Cameron told you to tell me all this?" Regina asked still perplexed as she removed her shirt. "Oh heavens no!" Marian chuckled bashfully again. "But he talks about you all the time and I assumed when I saw you holding his hand you liked him too." Marian said as she began to spray the perfume all over Regina. "Jeeze Marian, that's enough!" Regina protested but Marian continued to spray. "If you're not going to bath, you need more." Marian replied but ceased her assault with the perfume bottle and instead started to polish Regina's boots. Regina pulled on the bright red shirt and buttoned it up to her neck turning the round collar up as she contemplated what Marian had said. "I think your fantasies are getting the best of you Marian. Count Cameron has never said anything like that to me and I'm not ready for a boyfriend." Regina stated emphatically. "Count Cameron and I are just friends." She added and Marian just smiled handing her the uniform pants. These britches were much lighter than the leather pants for riding and the rings woven into the thighs by a decorative red cord were jeweled. All the straps and ties on the uniform were red she noticed when she picked up the vest and pushed her arms through it. Marian stood up and Regina turned her back to her to let her tighten the straps on the vest. Regina didn't like the way it felt at all. The vest was cut to emphasize the fact that she had breasts rather than hide them like the heavy leather vest did.

Regina felt very uncomfortable looking at her image in the mirror. The uniform accented all her curves and when Marian pulled the cord tight to tie it in the back the vest pushed her breasts up. "Is it supposed to look like this?" Regina asked displeased with her image in the mirror. Marian came around in front of her and shook her head. "No." She replied as she unbuttoned the top buttons of the shirt and folded the collar back down on her shoulders. "It's supposed to look like this." Marina sighed smiling at Regina and stepping to the side so she could see her image in the mirror again. Regina's face turned red seeing the tops of her breasts pushed up by the tight vest and exposed by the way Marian had folded the collar back. "Are you kidding me? Give me the sash!" Regina protested and Marian picked it off the bed and hung it over Regina's neck. Regina kept pushing it to the center but it wasn't going to cover what she wanted it to. "You look magnificent." Marian ventured cautiously. "I could put you in a men's uniform but after all….., you are a girl." Marian added with a smile. Regina was conflicted. She was very proud to wear the uniform of a messenger and represent her city but it was much different than anything she would choose for herself to wear. Marian draped the cape over her back. It was long and dark green with a red lining. She opened a drawer and found a replica of the medal she had won at the winter game and tied it around Regina's neck so that it lay on the bare skin between her breasts. Marian had a high shine on Regina's boots and she pulled them on last tucking the pants down into them before lacing the tops tight around her calves. "It doesn't look that bad I guess." Regina sighed reluctantly. "You are the Countess Regina of Red Oak, champion of the winter games and one of only two women messengers. The other wasn't even invited to a ceremony. You should be proud to be a woman and you look stunning. I'm proud to be your servant." Marian said bowing before her. "Thank you Lady Marian. You've done a good job." Regina replied still feeling a little odd. "Do you want to practice your presentation?" Marian asked as she stood back up. "Can you get me something to drink, maybe some cherry wine? My throat feels dry." Regina asked and Marian dashed out the door leaving her alone.

Marian ran all the way down the stairs to the third floor and the bar against the back wall. "Countess Regina of Red Oak requires cherry wine." She panted breathlessly to the bar tender Miguel. "Does she want the mild wine or the fermented version?" Miguel asked. Marian dropped her head frustrated that she hadn't thought to ask. Miguel recognized her dilemma. "Is she just thirsty or does she want to calm her nerves?" Miguel asked sympathetically. "I think both." Marian replied still trying to catch her breath. "You should know to ask." Miguel chastised her. "I'm going to give you two glasses. The left is mild and the right is not. You can drink the one she doesn't because you're going to pay me for that one." Miguel said pushing the glasses toward her after he filled them. "Don't run because you'll spill them and I'll have to charge you for both of them." Miguel chuckled as Marian turned to leave. Marian swore under her breath at herself as she made her way back to the sixth floor. She knew she would get a bonus from Count Cameron if she took good care of her charge but if she kept making mistakes like this she might not get it or it could cost her more than her bonus. She set the mild one on the bench beside the door to open it and reminded herself which was which as she returned to Countess Regina. She was hoping the Countess would take the fermented one because she wasn't about to drink it herself with all the responsibilities she had in front of her.

"This one will calm your nerves and this one will just quench your thirst." Marian announced praying to herself that Countess Regina would take the expensive one. "I shouldn't drink too much before the ceremony but one glass couldn't hurt." Regina said smiling at Marian who sighed with relief. Regina sipped the sweet wine and Marian listened as Regina practiced her presentation a few times. "You're going to do a marvelous job." Marian said feeling confident and took a big gulp of the glass she still had. She almost gagged and her eyes filled with tears as she realized what she had done. "Left right DAMMIT!" She cursed herself again under her breath. "What's the matter Marian?" Regina asked and Marian was paralyzed afraid to admit her mistake to the Countess. Now she would have to pay for both glasses and when Count Cameron heard of her mistakes she would be in trouble. "I gave you the wrong glass." Marian admitted reluctantly and began to cry. Regina walked to her and took the glass from her and sipped from it. "My, that is a bit stronger." Regina sighed exhaling dramatically. Marian looked devastated and she felt sorry for her. Regina lifted Marian's chin to look in her eyes again as she took another sip of the stronger wine. "I think you were just looking out for me. At any rate, I think we should keep this between us girls." Regina said with a grin. Marian was ecstatic and wanted to embrace her but knew that would be improper. "No wonder Count Cameron fancies you, you are so kind." Marian replied bowing before her again. "Please don't start with that again. I'm already nervous and if you keep that up I won't be able to look the Count in the eyes." Regina giggled and took one more sip from the glass. "Speaking of which; we should probably go to join the others." Regina said taking the beautifully wrapped package out of the canvas bag and handing it to Marian. Regina decided to take the glass of wine with her as they left to join Count Cameron and the other messengers.

Marian led Countess Regina down the stairs to the second floor and the large room behind the council chambers. Regina felt much less self-conscious about her uniform as she gazed at the other female guests in the room. All the women there wore gowns that made her uniform seem very conservative in comparison. Count Cameron was with four of the other messengers and he looked very nervous as he conversed with them. Each messenger had a servant standing behind them with a package and Marian moved behind her as they joined them. They all stopped talking when Regina drew alongside them and Count Cameron had a peculiar look on his face as he stared at Regina. "Did I miss something?" Regina asked breaking their silence and Cameron shook his head as if waking from a day dream. "I'm sorry; you all know The Countess Regina of Red Oak." Regina shifted her glass to her left hand and shook hands greeting each rider in turn. Count Michael of Gardinia, Count Daniel of Grace, Count Arthur of Archemeius, and Count Anthony of Greenstone all shook her hand and smiled graciously. "Where is Count Andrew?" Regina asked. "He's still upstairs changing. He had the longest ride from Sandista you know." Cameron replied. "Yea but he had the shortest ride from Paternus." Regina giggled. "He should have beaten us all." She laughed and they all did. "I think he ate before he left Sandista." Arthur laughed. "Andrew is always eating. I feel sorry for Crimson." Daniel added referring to his dragon and everyone laughed again. "So who is going to go first Count Cameron?" Anthony asked sipping from his glass. "I thought it would be appropriate for our Champion to go first and then the rest by age." Cameron replied. "Fine, that makes sense." Anthony replied obviously disappointed. "What's wrong with that?" Cameron asked. "Well that makes me last again and unlike SOME of you; I have a young admirer waiting at Castle Green Stone for me to return and enjoy the festival with her." Anthony said emphatically. "We all have someone waiting at home." Daniel replied and looked at Regina grinning. "Well other than our Champion I guess. Tell us Countess Regina; is there a lucky young man waiting for you to return to Red Oak?" He snickered and Regina turned red. Regina took another sip of her wine and frowned at Daniel. "Is this going to be the topic of conversation whenever we get together? How is it I always *hear* about your girlfriends but never *see* you with one?" Regina replied grinning back at

Daniel. It was Count Daniels turn to turn red as everyone chuckled. "She didn't answer the question. I guess that means no." Daniel shot back just as Count Andrew joined the group. He greeted everyone and shook hands. Cameron turned to his servant and whispered and he ran into the council chambers. "Ok, now that everyone is here, this is what happens. I will announce you and then you walk down the center isle to the first step in front of the throne. Make your presentation and one of the councilmen will walk down and take your gift and unwrap it showing it to the crowd before he hangs it on the railing. Then you take your seat on the first row on the left and I will announce the next messenger." Cameron said nervously. "Any questions?" Cameron added looking at Regina. Everyone shook their heads no and Cameron took one last sip of his wine as Marian handed Regina her gift and took the glass from her. Cameron took Regina's arm and led her to the doorway to the council chamber. "Just keep your head up and have fun." Cameron said smiling at Regina and nodding to the doorman. The trumpeters along the back wall sounded seven blasts on their trumpets and the crowd got quiet turning in their seats to look back at the door. "Ladies and Gentlemen; I present to you, the Champion of the Race of the Messengers at the Winter Games, The Glory of her city in the forest, The Countess Regina of Red Oak." Count Cameron shouted and everyone began to applaud and cheer. It took Regina completely by surprise and she had to focus hard to take the first step. Each row came to its feet as she passed them. She smiled nervously at the crowd and stepped quickly toward the first step trying to walk as dignified as she could. It was almost too much for her to bear and she felt so proud. When she got to the first step one of the councilwomen raised her hand and the crowd fell silent. Countess Regina bowed low before she began to speak loudly and boldly. "I bring you greetings from King Raymond and the city council of Red Oak. They congratulate you on the great honor of having one of your own selected as Great Father. It is my pleasure and my great honor to present this token of respect and a seal of the bond between Castle Red Oak and Castle Mesina." Regina concluded as the councilwoman approached her and Countess Regina bowed presenting the gift to her and the councilwoman took the package from her. She pulled the ribbon and the wrapping fell away as she hung the beautiful banner over her arm and presented it to the crowd. Again the crowd rose to its feet and cheered as the councilwoman displayed the banner. It was as tall as a man and dark green with gold weave fringe and a gold seal in the middle with the words "Home of the Great Father" embroidered below the seal. The councilwoman smiled and nodded to her and Countess Regina bowed low again before she retired to her seat on the left side.

Each messenger in turn did basically the same presentation and Regina was relieved to see each one of them sweating as she was after their presentation. Now Regina's nervousness faded and she began to enjoy the ceremony. She looked back several times at Count Cameron feeling sorry for him because she knew he was probably sweating through all the presentations. After Count Anthony made his presentation, the councilwoman thanked the messengers and made a short speech about the city pride and the new Great Father before inviting everyone to join in the festival at Mesina. As the messengers exited the council chambers, their servants returned to their sides and Count Cameron called them all together. "You all have to come up and let me buy you a drink." Count Cameron said excitedly obviously relieved that the ceremony was over. "Thank you Cameron but I want to get home before the sun goes down." Count Andrew replied as they headed for the stairs. "Oh come on Andrew; one drink to let me show my appreciation for making me look good." Count Cameron laughed pleading with him. Regina followed them all up the stairs unsure of whether to stay or get back to Red Oak in time for dinner. Her family would certainly understand if she chose to stay in Mesina for the celebration but she was pretty hungry. "Ok, I'll stay for one drink if everyone else is." Andrew sighed and Cameron put his arm around his shoulder and hugged him. "That's the response I need to hear from my friends." Cameron laughed and he sent his servant ahead of the group to prepare a table. He waited on the stairs until Regina caught up to him. "Why are you lagging back here behind everybody else? Are you tired Countess Regina?" Cameron asked grinning at her teasing her. "No, I'm hungry. Unlike Andrew, I missed the midday meal today to get here on time." Regina said loud enough for Count Andrew to hear and the group laughed at her inference. Now Regina was the youngest of all the riders and Andrew was one of the oldest. He had found sport in teasing her from her first day on assignment as a rider. At first Regina had not known how to respond to Andrew's teasing as he was her senior but soon she learned to give as well as take. Lately it had become a sport that she too enjoyed being careful to still show respect to her senior. Andrew turned and frowned at her playfully. "Someday, when you're older, you'll learn that endurance is as valuable a trait to a great rider as speed." Andrew replied jovially and everyone laughed. Count Andrew was by no means fat but he was the biggest rider in the group and he was the oldest at 26. He was going to have to retire his dragon this year because it was approaching maturity and this would most likely be his last tour as a rider. No one talked about that but everyone knew that would be a very sad day for Count Andrew and all his friends. He would most likely go to Castle Green Stone to study at the academy of combative arts and join the elite guard but tonight he was going to have one more drink with the other riders chosen to represent their cities at Mesina's festival. "Good, so you'll let me buy you dinner tonight and dine with me?" Cameron suggested taking Regina's hand again hopefully. "Careful Count Cameron; you'll give your intentions away too early I fear." Arthur laughed teasing Cameron and he turned red from embarrassment at Arthur's comment. "I could imagine a worse companion for dinner." Regina scoffed directing her comment to Arthur playfully and the party laughed at Arthur's expense again. "You are better off avoiding verbal combat with Countess Regina Arthur. Her wit is as quick and deadly as her riding skill." Count Daniel interjected poking Arthur playfully as they sat down at the table. Regina looked at Marian as she took her seat next to Count Cameron. "You can retire for an hour or two and have some dinner yourself if you want." Regina smiled and Marian bowed graciously before she disappeared into the crowd. There were six mugs in the center of the table and one glass. Cameron grabbed a mug and the glass and set the glass in front of Regina.

"I kinda figured you'd prefer the wine." Cameron smiled. "Are you satisfied with Lady Marian?" He asked sipping his beer. "She's perfect." Regina replied and took a sip of the wine feeling a little uncomfortable that Cameron was focusing all his attention to her. "Why did you name your dragon Treetop Count Daniel?" Regina asked turning her gaze to Count Daniel. The other riders all laughed as well as Count Daniel. "Yes tell her Daniel." Count Arthur laughed poking Daniel playfully. Daniel smirked at Count Arthur as he stood to talk. "After I finished the bonding cycle at Sandista, I mounted him to go to Castle Grace for the first time. As you know, there are few trees in close proximity to the perches at the school so we had no problems with takeoff or landings there. I followed the coast passed Castle Green Stone and flew all the way to Castle Archemeius on the first leg. He responded very well to all the commands, banking left and right and climbing and descending and landed perfectly atop Castle Archemeius when I gave the double whistle command. I rested him and watered him there for a good half hour so he wasn't tired or overheated but when we got to Castle Grace, I guess he just got confused." Daniel paused shaking his head in disappointment as Arthur and Cameron began to chuckle knowing the story. When I turned his head facing the perch and gave the double whistle command to land he picked out a tree instead and managed a quite precarious perch on top of one of the trees." Daniel concluded and all the riders laughed. "I couldn't get him to take flight again until the branch broke and we damn near hit the ground before he recovered and I could get him back above the trees. He was still confused by the trees but our second attempt was more successful and that is when I named him Treetop." Daniel concluded. Regina was laughing so hard her sides hurt. They all had experienced similar problems early on with their young dragons but luckily Waterbird had never tried to land in a tree. None of them liked to admit to losing control of their dragons but it happened to all riders at least once. Count Andrew stood after he had finished his beer. "While I appreciate your hospitality Count Cameron, I must get started if I'm going to get back to Sandista tonight." Andrew said and Arthur and Daniel stood up with him. "I was serious. You all made me look good today." Count Cameron said hold his mug up saluting them.

The trio climbed the stairs together with the servants to go change back into their heavy leather riding uniforms. "If you're going to fly the coast we can go in formation to Castle Grace." Count Daniel suggested. "An excellent idea, I'll meet you by the perches." Arthur replied ducking into a room with his servant. As he finished changing into his leathers, Count Andrew turned to his servant. "Marcus, I don't know what bonus Cameron will give you but you have been a great help to me for the ceremony and I appreciate it." He said pulling a ten mark gold coin from his purse and handing it to him. Marcus was stunned by Count Andrew's generosity as it was as much as he expected to get from Count Cameron. He bowed low before the Count. "It has been my honor to serve you sir and I thank you." He replied and he followed the Count to the roof. Crimson was the name Andrew had given to his dragon because his scales reflected bright red in the sun. The young dragon whistled excitedly when he recognized Count Andrew approaching in anticipation of a flight. Count Andrew had been riding long enough to know that a dragon enjoyed the ride at least as much as any rider did. Crimson shook his head as the last rays of the sun glistened and sparkled off his body. It pained him to think about turning Crimson loose almost as much as the thought of leaving the dragon riders after he did so. He had had two tours on fine dragons and his time was too quickly coming to a close. Count Andrew had to inspect Crimson every morning and the fiery glands were developing quickly inside Crimson's mouth. He and Crimson had certainly developed a close bond but Andrew had no delusion about what would happen once Crimson matured. He knew he was expected to release Crimson in the mountains on the trail to Paternus before that happened but Count Andrew harbored a secret and was banking on it to save himself and Crimson from that day.

He mounted Crimson and waited for Count Arthur and Count Daniel to do the same. "We'll let Daniel take point and we can fly in tandem behind him." Andrew suggested as Arthur hooked into his dragon. "Are you flying straight though to Sandista or stopping to have a beer with me at Archemeius?" Arthur asked. "I like the beer at Archemeius. Especially when it's your coins that purchases them." Andrew laughed and Arthur smiled. "I will purchase you a beer at Castle Archemeius, but only if Crimson attains footing on his perch before Emerald does." Arthur challenged him as Daniel joined them. Count Daniel turned and flipped a coin to his servant before mounting Treetop and buckling in. "You're on point." Arthur called to him and Daniel smiled and nodded urging Treetop toward the launch platform. Treetop reminded Arthur of his first dragon being white with yellow highlights. Arthur spurred his green dragon and followed Daniel and Treetop closely and Andrew urged Crimson in behind both of them. There was no hurry now. The race would not start until they reached Castle Grace so Andrew watched leisurely as Treetop bounded from the platform and spread his wings. Count Daniel circled back toward the launch and did a complete roll as he flew in front of them blocking Arthur from taking off. "What a show off!" Arthur chuckled before he whistled and Emerald dove from the platform. Andrew looped the reigns and pushed tight against Crimson staring over the wall. He whistled and the air rushed by his cheeks as Crimson fell from the Castle. A great pump of his wings and the young dragon turned skyward as Andrew clung tightly to the harness and pointed Crimson's head toward the other two dragons. He closed quickly and Andrew whistled 3 times signaling to Crimson to follow. They made a perfect triangle against the setting sun being careful not to steal the air from each other. When Treetop glided with his wings spread out wide to each side the other two did likewise and when he pumped his wings to accelerate, Crimson and Emerald seemed to anticipate intuitively and followed in perfect synchronization. They flew high, heading straight south from Mesina over the forest and continued to climb as they approached the mountains. Soaring solo was exhilarating but nothing compared to letting the dragons use their natural instincts and experiencing how they communicated and responded to each other in formation flight. Daniel was on point because Treetop was most familiar with the path through the mountains to Castle Grace. It made Andrew smile to feel Crimson bank and turn with the other two dragons as they navigated the pass without a command from him. It was almost as if Count Daniel was steering all three dragons.

A winding road leads south from Castle Red Oak through the forest and into the mountains but it is miles south of where the trio crossed into the mountains. Some 40 miles of treacherous highway climbs into the mountains and ends at Castle Grace which is the center for the Academy of Theater and Music. The great western mountains split into two steep ranges and Castle Grace is located at the southern end of the long narrow valley that is heavily forested and very marshy and wet year round. No roads go north from here but many of the sons of the Great Father have ventured all the way to where the mountains close in again to go hunting and reap other rewards from the fertile valley. Great waterfalls cascade down the cliffs on both sides of the narrow valley. It is called the Valley of the Cats as large tigers and black panthers also hunt that valley. Great herds of wild boars roam the valley and can be equally dangerous to a lone hunter. The pelt of a tiger or panther is a prized trophy but only one big cat is allowed to be hunted each fall and only a citizen of Castle Grace or its villages is eligible for that lottery.

Castle Grace blocks the entrance to the valley and keeps the large cats from leaving the Valley of the Cats and over populating the island. It rises out of the marshy forest and connects to the high cliffs of both mountain ranges before they separate around the valley that spreads out northward. The community surrounding Castle Grace is one of the oldest on the island second only to Mesina. The castle is seven stories high and towers over two great archways on the east and west sides of the castle. Under the archways are the cities gates made of thick redwood and always open. Two great waterfalls, one from the eastern mountains and one from the western mountains, fall into a large fountain just north of the gates and the castle creating a moat. The cobblestone road turns east and west past the stables and into a garden. Twin bridges allow travel over the moat that drains from the center between the bridges northward through the city by a canal. Large wooden bridges cross the canal connecting the shops and houses in the city on the east and west sides. The entrance to the castle is on the north side in the center of the garden between the bridges. The two huge elaborately designed oak doors in the castle were closed signifying the King was not currently in the castle. Through those doors, the first floor was dominated by the throne room in the center. Solid stone walls separated it from the armory on the west side and the library on the east side. A solid marble stairway curled around the Royal throne on the south wall leading to the second floor. The second floor is the barracks for the castle guard and two large cannons face southward on balconies guarding the pass. The stairway to the third floor is on the north wall. The balcony on the third floor extended over the garden and the great concert hall was at the center of the third floor surrounded by rooms that provided quarters for the musicians and actors that performed there. It is a grand balcony with an oak staircase that led down into the garden below. The musicians played daily on the balcony and it could be heard across the entire city. From the concert hall, another marble stairway leads to the fourth floor and the guest rooms that line a wide solid marble hallway. At the end of that hallway, the stairs climbed to the fifth floor where the kitchen and a great dining hall were surrounded by the servant's quarters. Another marble staircase leads to the Royal quarters on the sixth floor from the dining hall. The seventh floor, or roof, is where the dragon rider's perches are and the constant breeze that blows there made it possible for the engineers to construct a great windmill that pulls water from the garden below to fill the large metal tubs. The fires burning under the tubs to heat the water make it easy for the dragon riders to find their perch even at night. Two more cannons face south atop the castle guarding the only entrance to the valley. Kevin has been the King of Castle Grace for 20 years and he and his wife, The Maiden Elisha of Mesina, are attending the Festival of the Great Father at Paternus. As the fires atop Castle Grace came into view, Count Daniel looked over his shoulder and waved first to Arthur and then to Andrew.

CHAPTER 2

※

ANDREW'S FALL

They were cruising a mere 40 miles an hour when Andrew leaned forward and whistled giving Crimson the command to break formation and they began to climb above Count Daniel and Treetop. Abruptly Arthur and Emerald turned due east and Andrew heard Arthur's command for maximum speed to Emerald as they passed underneath him. As they quickly disappeared up the valley, Andrew chuckled to himself. Arthur was going to try to navigate the mountain paths to Archemeius to beat him. Andrew couldn't believe Arthur would make such a mistake in a race. He urged Crimson over the mountain range still heading straight south until he got on top of them. Every rider knew that valley level air was much denser than mountain air and a dragon could fly much faster at high altitudes. Andrew could not imagine what Arthur was thinking but it made him nervous the more he thought about it. Maybe Arthur had discovered a new short cut. As the white sands of the beach came into view, Andrew pointed Crimson's head due east and clung tightly before giving the command for maximum speed. Crimson began to pump his wings ferociously and the wind against Andrews face rushed by ever faster and faster with each blast from Crimson's wings until all he could hear was a powerful roar. Andrew hunkered down watching the horizon and gently spurring Crimson for more speed as the world flashed by. The city complex surrounding the castle came into view quickly and Andrew turned Crimson's head towards it very gently. Crimson knew where the perches were having been to the castle on numerous occasions.

If Andrew could make him understand they were the objective he felt he could give the command to land back here and Crimson would continue at maximum speed until he had to slow to land. Crimson's natural instincts would be better than his. Gently he kept adjusting Crimson's head until he could see the top of Castle Archemeius. He could pull back on the reigns and Crimson would slow but he chose not to. He wasn't sure with the roar of the wind if Crimson would even hear the command. He leaned as far forward as he could fighting the tremendous rush of air and whistled two blasts before clinging tightly again against the young dragon. Crimson didn't respond. He either didn't hear or he understood. Andrew decided to bank on the latter as he watched them close the distance to the castle with unnatural speed. He considered that the worst thing that could happen was they would overshoot the castle and have to circle back. Crimson's nose was pointed right at the top of the castle and Andrew got suddenly very nervous heading straight for the wall behind the perches. He gripped the harness on Crimson with all his might as his dragon suddenly spread his wings and turned in mid air to capture as much air as he could. Andrew couldn't see the castle anymore over Crimson's head because he was standing straight up. The force of them stopping was crushing Andrew against Crimson's back. As they came to a stop Andrew was mashed tremendously hard against Crimson's back and lost his grip on the harness when Crimson began to fan his wings to hover. If not for the iron rings clipped to his vest and britches he most certainly would have fallen off the castle. Crimson's back legs pounded against the perch and he fell forward catching himself with his front feet before they stumbled off the perch and onto the roof. Andrew sat up gasping for air. He felt like his chest had been crushed and he could not breathe. Two servants ran to him and unbuckled him from the harness pulling him from the perch. "Go for a medic." One servant said urgently. "Small breaths Count…., re-expand your lungs slowly." He said cradling Andrew in his lap. Andrew heard his advice and tried to heed it. Each small breath brought him closer to recovery but the pain in his chest was unbearable. Soon though; he felt his lungs expanding and collapsing more normally. "What horrific news do you bring us that requires such a landing?" The servant asked and Andrew felt the rush of air as another dragon landed on the perch above him. He tried to stand but the pain in his chest was too intense and tears streamed down his cheek as he fell back against the servant. "What the hell happened here?" Count Arthur shouted jumping down beside Andrew and the servant. "I saw the whole thing. He had his dragon at maximum speed less than a hundred paces from the castle. I've never seen a landing like that before." The servant said nervously. "And you'll never see me do it again." Andrew winced in obvious pain. "I sent for a medic." The servant said laying Andrew flat on the roof. "Let's bare his chest and loosen his clothes." Arthur suggested beginning to undo the vest. "Oh don't touch my chest." Andrew groaned as Arthur slowly folded back the shirt revealing the growing purple bruises from his neck to his stomach. "Good lord man what have you done?" Arthur said as the servant returned with the medic. "That's not good. We need to move him to a bed or better yet take him to a bath tub." The medic said. The four men picked Andrew up and carried him down the stairs to the first room with a tub and laid him in it. The pain in his chest was so intense that Andrew lost consciousness. The medic opened the cold water valve and the tub began to fill. "I can't tell if anything's broken. It doesn't look like it but you're certainly badly bruised. The cold water should minimize the damage if the bleeding under the skin will stop." The medic said shaking his head. "What else can we do?" Count Arthur asked extremely concerned. "He's not spitting up blood yet. We have to pray he doesn't and keep his body in cold water. We'll know in a couple of hours if he has done something fatal or if it's just superficial." The medic replied. The servants removed Count Andrew's clothes and Arthur pulled up a chair beside him. He was scared and overwhelmed with emotion for his friend. He couldn't believe this was the result of their stupid race. "You stupid idiot. If you die on me, I swear I'll kill your damn dragon and bury him on top of you." Arthur whispered as the tears streamed down his face. Andrew opened his eyes straining against the pain in his chest to look at his friend. "You wouldn't dare kill Crimson." He winced and Arthur looked back at him sympathetically. "You better survive and make sure I can't." Arthur whispered again. "What the hell happened?" He asked. Andrew lifted his chin and grimaced trying to smile. "I learned a new trick. You probably shouldn't try it though. I gave Crimson the command to land as soon as I saw the castle and then let him go." Andrew said closing his eyes trying to relax in the cold water. "That's just crazy." Arthur replied seriously and Andrew's chuckle turned quickly into another painful grimace. "You think so?" Andrew replied and tried to focus on something other than the pain in his chest. The medic came back over and leaned against the tub. "Can you piss?" He asked and both Counts looked at him puzzled. "I want to see if there is blood in your piss. If you can, just do it now." He explained and watched the water between Andrew's legs. Andrew tried but he couldn't and looked up at Arthur. "You owe me a beer." He gasped uncomfortably at Arthur. "Bring me a beer so I can piss." Andrew winced and Arthur turned to one of the servants. "Bring us all a cold beer." He commanded. "And send another messenger to Mesina to let them know what has happened." He added. "NO! Not yet." Andrew protested. "If this turns out to be a bruise, I don't want to spoil anyone's festival." Andrew suggested pleading with his friend and the servant looked to Arthur. Arthur waved him off. "You know I'm going to tell them about your stupid trick regardless." Arthur said chastising him and Andrew smiled through his pain. "It could be done successfully you know. It might turn out to be a valuable trick but we need to increase the padding in front of the rider." Andrew suggested. Arthur looked down at Andrew's chest which glowed purple from his neck down his chest to just above his stomach. The medic put his hand against Andrew's stomach. "Can you feel my hand?" He asked Andrew and he shook his head yes. "Is there any pain there in your gut?" He asked and Andrew said no. "That's a good sign. Can you taste any blood in your mouth?" He asked. "My mouth is very dry." Andrew replied and closed his eyes again. "It's important that you stay awake Count Andrew. You're head probably took a pounding too." The medic said and pulled a vial from his bag. "I want you to drink this. It will pacify some of the pain." He added and held it to Andrew's lips as he sipped it. The servant came back with a tray and several mugs. "Lord, give me one of those. Your medicine is nasty!" Andrew said looking at the servant with the tray.

Arthur sat with Andrew for the time that the medic had designated and they found no blood in Count Andrew's urine. They were all relieved when the medic said that the servants could move Andrew to the bed. "You're lucky Count Andrew. I'm fairly certain your wounds are superficial. You probably have a few cracked ribs and it will take some time to heal but you will recover." The medic concluded. "How long before I can travel?" Andrew asked. "That's entirely up to you but my guess would be a week at least and definitely no flying for at least two maybe three." The medic replied. "Drink the rest of this vial when you retire and sleep tonight. I will check on you tomorrow morning." The medic said smiling at Andrew before he left. Andrew sighed deeply still feeling a lot of pain when he filled his lungs and shook his head at Arthur. "Looks like I'm going to be your guest for a while. Whose quarters are these?" Andrew asked. "It's one of mine." Arthur replied sipping his beer. "**One** of yours….., a single man with multiple rooms?" Andrew responded impressed by Arthur. "I've been here a long time." Arthur replied smiling at him. "This is Jerome." Arthur said presenting one of the servants to Andrew. "He'll be your charge or you'll be his," Arthur chuckled, "until you feel well enough to travel." Andrew smiled at Jerome who appeared to be 18 or 19. "How do you feel about being my nurse maid for a week Jerome?" He asked. "It will be my honor sir and I'm sure quite profitable since you're such a valued friend of Count Arthurs'." Jerome smiled. "Young and ambitious; a perfect companion to pass the time with while I heal." Andrew chuckled softly trying not to move his chest. "I'm starved Jerome. Maybe you could find some fish or veal for me in the kitchen and come back and dine with me before I retire." Andrew suggested and Jerome left quickly on his task. Andrew turned to Arthur. "You have friends that are waiting for you, probably some young girl that finds you irresistible." Andrew smiled. "You should go join them while the night is still young or you could stay here and make me feel guiltier than I already do." Andrew suggested and Arthur scoffed at him. "You shouldn't feel guilty. It was an accident. Any one of us could have made that mistake." Arthur said and Andrew held up his hand to cut him off. "We've both been riding long enough to know that trying a high speed maneuver like that without thinking it through is just stupid. I'm lucky to be alive and I'm embarrassed by my own stupidity. Please don't compound my embarrassment by coddling me and ruining your time at festival." Andrew pleaded. Arthur wanted to stay by his friend's side and dine and drink with him until he retired but he knew Andrew and he would feel worse if he didn't leave. "All right then, if you don't want to drink with me, I'll go find someone that will. You're sure you'll be alright with just Jerome? I can send more servants if you want." Arthur suggested. "Jerome and I are going to eat and have one more beer and then I'm going to drink this potion and retire. I hurt and I'm too tired for much more than that." Andrew admitted. "Ok then; I'll see you tomorrow morning. Sleep well Count Andrew." Arthur said and stepped out of the room and leaned over the balcony. He watched the water fall down to the fountain on the first floor. Arthur felt the waterfall that fell into the heart of the castle made Castle Archemeius the most beautiful in the kingdom. He went into the room adjacent to where he had left Count Andrew to change out of the heavy leathers into a cotton shirt and pants that would be more comfortable. He would ride no more tonight.

Castle Archemeius is maybe 30 miles from Castle Green Stone along the coastal road. White sand and tall palm trees lined both sides of the coastal road that lead to Castle Archemeius. It is a strong fishing community building a vast fleet of fishing boats and other sailing vessels around a fine harbor. Arthur's family was all fishermen but he had become enamored by the dragon riders at an early age. The engineers are in the process of fitting some of the larger ships with the great cannons. The Academy of History and Mathematics is located between the castle and the sea and many of the royal family had great houses with glass walls facing the southern ocean. Arthur hoped to build one there one day.

Castle Archemeius was built right into the mountain and a waterfall fell into the center of the castle and a grand pool. The first floor was the Kings court and his throne faced the grand pool with its back to the mountain wall. Two large circular staircases bracketed the King's throne inside the castle to the second floor where a great balcony circled the waterfall inside the castle. The kitchen is on the south wall on the second floor and fine oak tables filled the balcony facing the waterfall. A large door on either side of the kitchen leads to a grand covered balcony outside where the musicians had set up and were playing for the whole city to hear. The twin spiral staircases continued to the third floor and another great balcony inside the castle. There were 14 rooms off the balcony. Seven servant rooms on the west and seven guest rooms on the east are separated by a wall between the spiral staircases. The stairs continued to the fourth floor where the office of messengers is and there is a library on each side of the stairwell. The Royal Families quarters are on the south wall. The Kings quarters had a large balcony that faced the southern ocean and overlooked the whole city with a beautiful view. The fifth and sixth floors were smaller and their balconies circling the waterfall inside the castle were narrow but all the rooms had large windows that faced the ocean and the city. Arthur had talked the council into letting the messengers have some of these rooms and he had charge over them. The grand metal tubs were located on the roof and captured water from the waterfall. King Thomas and his wife Marion were attending the festival at Castle Paternus. King Thomas was now 35 years old and in his 15th year as King of Castle Archemeius. Marion was also a member of the city council at Castle Archemeius and was an invited guest to the festival of the Great Father not being a member of the Royal Family. Count Arthur had always thought it was odd that the spouse and the offspring of the King or Queen were not held in higher regard in any of the cities in the kingdom.

Arthur was 25 now and he had released his first dragon over a year ago before he got Emerald. It had been heartbreaking to take Arch Angel, his first dragon, into the mountains and remove the harness from her. He had ridden her for seven long years and he wondered about her often and how she was living in the mountains with her brothers and sisters. Finding and training Emerald had helped heal the pain of separation he had felt but every once in a while he would catch a glimpse of a pure white female dragon when he flew over the mountains and wonder if it was Arch Angel. He, like every other rider before him, wished he could find a way to teach a dragon to overcome the natural instinct to turn on his handler at maturity. But he knew every rider that had attempted that had met a fiery death at the hands of his own dragon. He also knew it would be his responsibility to return Count Andrew's dragon to Castle Sandista tomorrow. A dragon needed to be around handlers he knew and trusted to eat properly and two or three weeks would be too long for Crimson to be away from his home perch. Arthur would ride Crimson to Castle Sandista tomorrow and take a carriage back.

Arthur could hear the music coming from the outside balcony on the second floor beyond the kitchen as he walked down the staircase after he changed. He knew he would find his friends either at the tables in the dining hall or on the lawn below the balcony where the musicians played. As he got to the second floor, he saw his friends at a long table obviously still dining. Councilman Trent noticed him first and waved him over to the table. Councilman Trent was a jovial older gentleman and his round face revealed his fondness for good food. There were three other riders and two other councilwomen but it was the Maiden Melisa of Archemeius that Arthur was most happy to find at the table. Two of her four servants accompanied her. A Maiden to the Crown was allowed up to seven servants all paid for by the crown but Melisa was most conservative. She smiled brightly at him when their eyes met and Arthur felt a warm stab of nervous excitement as he gazed at her. Melisa wore a red strapless velvet gown with white flowers embroidered down both sides. She had a crown of white flowers in her blonde hair which fell across her bare shoulders down just above her waist. The tattoos on her forearms that identified her as a Maiden of the Crown were far and away the most beautiful in the kingdom by Arthur's account. They extended from her wrist to her elbows and every know flower of the kingdom was perfectly represented in the design. Arthur was hard pressed to turn his gaze from her. "Is it true what we heard about Count Andrew? How does he fair?" Councilman Trent asked with much concern as Andrew shook his hand. "Please tell me your friend is ok." Maiden Melisa said obviously very concerned herself. One of the other riders vacated the chair next to Melisa and held it open for Arthur. "I think he will be ok with time. He had a terrible accident and will probably have to rest here for two or three weeks." Arthur replied taking his chair. He surveyed the table covered with fish and venison and vegetables of all kinds. "I left my servant, Jerome, with him as he chased me away wanting to recover in solitude tonight." Arthur reported. Melisa's expression turned pained. "He must be in terrible pain. Should we go up now to wish him a quick recovery or wait until tomorrow?" Melisa asked. "Please tell us what happened to him?" Count Richard pleaded with concern. "I was going to dine with him but truthfully the accident is not only painful but embarrassing to him. I know he would rather tell you about it himself tomorrow." Arthur replied. "As for me I'm very hungry and his accident has made me acutely aware of how much I value my friends." Arthur concluded smiling into Melisa's beautiful blue eyes. She laid her hand on Arthur's arm and kissed his cheek. "Your occupation leaves us all frightfully concerned when you fly. You must take me with you to see Count Andrew tomorrow." Melisa pleaded and Arthur placed his hand over hers appreciative of her concern. "I must take his dragon back to Castle Sandista at first light. I fear I won't be back until late tomorrow even if I secure the fastest carriage for my return. Maybe Councilman Trent will be kind enough to escort you?" Arthur suggested turning his head to the senior councilman. "I would be most honored to call on you after breakfast to go visit with Count Andrew." The councilman replied and Melisa smiled at him but looked dejected. "And what is to become of our picnic and the other festival activities we planned for tomorrow?" Melisa asked and Arthur could see the disappointment in her face. "You know I would much prefer your company but this accident creates a situation that requires my immediate response. I should be on my way to Sandista now but I wanted to see you first." Arthur said trying to apologize to her. "Any dragon rider could take Crimson back to Castle Sandista." Maid Melisa pouted showing her disappointment at losing a whole day they had planned together. "Would you fancy a man who would pass his responsibilities to a subordinate and ruin that man's plans for his own pleasure? You know I will execute my duties and return to Archemeius as quickly as I can to make it up to you." Arthur promised and kissed Melisa's cheek before he began to fill his plate and eat. Arthur knew that the Maiden Melisa was surrounded by suitors but he felt confident that she fancied him above the others. At least she made him feel that way whenever they were together. He knew the tradition with women that bore the mark of Maiden to the Crown and realized it was her right to choose a spouse from any man in the kingdom. If it was in his power, he would have proposed to her long ago but since he couldn't, he was satisfied to wait until she felt the time was right. Melisa was studying and teaching mathematics at the academy and she had told him and all her friends she desired to finish her degree before choosing a spouse. Maiden Melisa of Archemeius was certainly a prize worth waiting for as far as Count Arthur was concerned. Arthur ate until he was full as the others chatted about the festival and the possibilities for change from the election of a new Great Father and various other subjects. The councilwomen and the other riders soon left to go down to the garden but Maiden Melisa and Councilman Trent waited for Count Arthur to finish dining. Councilman Trent was well over 50 and was a valuable mentor to all the royal family. He was one of the leading professors at the academy and was one of the most knowledgeable professors in both history and mathematics. "I heard the servant's account of Count Andrew's failed maneuver and it intrigues me." Councilman Trent said to Arthur once the others had left. "I think I will go up and discuss it with Count Andrew after breakfast tomorrow if he is capable and that's alright with you and I certainly don't mind escorting Maid Melisa." He smiled at Arthur. "Peter the medic is watching over him. You should check with him about the appropriate time tomorrow." Arthur replied washing his dinner down with another beer. "Excellent, I'll go speak to him now and then I think I will retire and leave the festival activities to the younger crowd." Councilman Trent chuckled as he stood. Maiden Melisa pouted playfully. "I thought I had successfully seduced an embrace on the dance floor from you Councilman Trent?" She sighed feigning disappointment and the councilman laughed leaning down to kiss her cheek. "You'll just have to make do with Count Arthur. I venture you favor his embrace on the dance floor over mine anyway." He winked at them and turned to leave. "I shall see you both tomorrow. My wife awaits my return home." He laughed walking away.

"So you were tempting Councilman Trent to dance with you." Arthur teased her as he finished his beer. "I feared you would stay at Mesina for the night and I would have no escort." Melisa replied. There was a tease of defiance in her voice as Arthur stood and took her hand. Arthur turned to his servant. "Go find my friends on the lawn and insure there is a glass of cherry wine waiting for both of us when we arrive." He commanded and his servant ran in front of them. "Did I not promise you I would return tonight?" Arthur smiled enjoying the banter. "You have made many promises. "Some you have kept and some you have not." Melisa replied curtly. She was very disappointed by the events that had dashed their plans for tomorrow and Arthur could tell by her demeanor as she took his arm. Melisa looked back at her servant. "Go back up to my room and bring me the red shawl that matches this dress and meet us on the lawn." She commanded and the girl turned to run back up the stairs.

Arthur stopped halfway down the stairs checking to insure they were alone. He jumped to the step below and gently pulled her into his embrace. "It is unfair for you to torment me over this. You need never doubt me on this Maiden Melisa of Archemeius. There is no man on the Island of the Seven Kings that loves you more than I." Arthur whispered and kissed her passionately as she melted into his arms. "You press me hard to make my announcement prematurely." Melisa whispered breathlessly and returned Arthur's kiss surrendering to him completely. "Please be patient with me as I am certain you will find my announcement to your liking." Melisa whispered again excitedly as they checked the staircase before sharing a third kiss with reckless abandon. They knew they would be severely chastised if they were caught in an embrace like this. They were both finding it harder and harder to avoid the passion that was growing between them. Melisa was certain Arthur had no understanding of how hot her passion burned for him. After all it was her who had lived at Castle Paternus and studied passion in the Hall of Maidens. It was her who had spent weeks with the eunuchs and the other maidens there exploring the art of erotic expression of physical love. It was her who had spent so much time learning how to raise passion to the highest level between a man and a woman prior to bearing a child with the Great Father to rule her city. She longed so desperately now to share all those secrets with Arthur. Sometimes the temptation was almost unbearable but she had to wait until she finished her degree at the Academy. Each kiss, each touch of his hand on her bare skin, each exotic embrace made her graduation in the fall seem so much further away. It was the sound of footsteps that pulled Arthur from his exotic trance and he took Melisa's trembling hand as they proceeded past the great fountain and onto the garden lawn. It was moments like those on the staircase that Arthur lived for when he saw Maiden Melisa. "I would gladly submit to whatever prison term a night with you would incur." Arthur whispered. "Shall we choose that course or be patient and share a thousand nights together." Melisa whispered squeezing his hand as they walked. "I leave that decision to you tonight Count Arthur for I have lost my desire to resist your advances." Melisa sighed heavily trying to regain her composure. "Regardless I will make my announcement of my intention to marry to the council tomorrow. I just pray the suitor I choose will postpone our honeymoon until after my graduation in the fall." Melisa said smiling up at Arthur. He stopped at the edge of the grass paralyzed and overwhelmed with excitement at Melisa's revelation. He knew it was a violation of custom and law for her to reveal her selection to anyone prior to making her declaration to the council. He wanted so badly to embrace her now but knew that would also be improper. "I am certain if you have chosen wisely your suitor will have no problem allowing his wife to finish her degree." Arthur smiled and squeezed her hand in his again. "Then Patience shall be the name I give his first daughter unless he spoils it by revealing to our friends that I have made my decision and my reputation is ruined." Melisa whispered nervously. "I know not what decision you speak of Maiden Melisa as I have been speaking hypothetically." Arthur laughed searching the crowd on the lawn for his servant.

The lawn was very crowded. Unlike the castle itself, all the citizens could enter the garden lawn and it appeared a vast number of them had chosen to do so. The short green grass of the massive garden was covered with people dancing to the spirited music emanating from the balcony above them. Arthur and Melisa kicked off their shoes, as was the custom, and went out and joined them. There were long tables under the trees that lined the garden and many of their friends sat and drank and danced barefoot on the grass. It was a fine warm night on the lawn and Arthur stayed with Melisa and his friends enjoying himself well into the early hours of the morning. He was quite intoxicated by the time he decided he needed to retire. It was imperative that he get a few hours sleep before he took Crimson back to Castle Sandista so he bid his friends goodnight at the table. "I should probably retire too." Melisa said excusing herself to their friends as she slipped her shoes back on. "Will you escort me to my quarters Count Arthur?" She asked taking his arm. "Be cautious Arthur." Count Richard called to them with a chuckle as they left. "Crimson shall not get the best of me!" Arthur replied brazenly. There was a little slur in his speech as he boasted to his riding skill. "I have no concern that you can handle Crimson." Count Richard chuckled drunkenly. "I worry you may stumble at Maid Melisa's door." He laughed heartily. Arthur stopped and turned slowly glaring at Count Richard. "Guard your tongue Count Richard. I already have one friend in the care of our medics." He replied angrily. "Ignore him. He is drunk." Melisa whispered urging Arthur to continue to the castle. Arthur held his ground glaring at Richard. Drunk or sober all his friends recognized what Count Richard had suggested was a tremendous insult to both of them. Intimacy prior to marriage was not only socially unacceptable it was illegal for members of the royal family. Count Richard was much younger than Arthur being on his first tour as a rider and was probably 17 or 18. "Your comment requires an immediate apology to Maid Melisa and to me." Arthur said moving closer to Count Richard who had stopped his drunken laughter just staring back at Arthur in confusion. He was unsure why Count Arthur had taken such offense at his joke but he was not confused as to Arthur's intentions as the distance between them closed. He folded his hands submissively at his side and bowed deeply toward Maid Melisa. "Please accept quickly my apology for my regretfully adolescent comment. I hold you in the highest regard and meant it only as jest knowing how absurd it would be to consider a lady of your standing would violate the law." Count Richard said nervously before he turned his gaze to Count Arthur and braced himself for the blow he was certain was coming. He wasn't going to raise his hand to Count Arthur knowing it would be futile and one blow from him would be preferable to several. "I do quickly accept your apology Count Richard!" Melisa shouted and Arthur stopped short of striking Count Richard which is what Melisa had hoped for. "Now, what say you to my friend Count Arthur?" Melisa said more calmly. Count Richard maintained his submissive pose turning his eyes to the ground away from Arthur's glare. "I know not what to say to my friend and my mentor as I am certain my youth prevents me from understanding completely the gravity of my offense to him but most assuredly my apology is sincere." Count Richard concluded nervously unsure of what would happen next. His posture before Arthur had attracted the attention of a nearby councilwoman who moved to them quickly. If the council got involved, Count Richard's comment would be investigated and at a minimum he would be punished for his wrongful insinuation. "What trouble is here?" The councilwomen asked moving between them. "Rise up and shake my hand Count Richard." Arthur commanded turning his eyes to the councilwomen and smiling. "It is of no consequence, merely a dispute between two riders over the advantages of youth and the liabilities of age." Arthur chuckled as he took Count Richard's hand. "There are no liabilities to experience young Count." The councilwomen laughed and Richard realized Count Arthur had helped him dodge a significant arrow as he laughed nervously with them. "We will talk about this more tomorrow when I return from Castle Sandista." Arthur said and Richard nodded watching the smile fade from Count Arthur's face before he let go of his hand. Count Richard sat back down at the table taking a long draw off his beer as he watched Count Arthur escort Maiden Melisa into the castle followed by their servants. The councilwoman went back to rejoin her friends several paces away. "You're lucky they call you friend." One of the other riders at the table said. "Your joke could have gotten you a beating from Count Arthur and then another one from the council or worse." He said seriously and Count Richard decided it was time for him to retire too.

CHAPTER 3

TO KEEP A SECRET

It was still very dark in Count Arthur's room when Jerome shook him. "The sun is rising on Sandista sir." He said as he offered Count Arthur the steaming mug of hot coffee he knew Arthur enjoyed in the mornings. Arthur sat up and threw his legs over the edge of the bed facing Jerome. "I fear the alcohol demon I fed last night has not released me yet." Arthur jested as he took the mug from Jerome. "I have the elixir from Peter the medic if your head hurts." Jerome replied pulling a vial from his pocket. "The pain has not arrived yet but I will take the elixir as I'm certain it will follow once my head clears." Arthur said and he chased the foul tasting elixir with his coffee. He set the coffee on the little table beside his bed and slipped on his house sandals as Jerome helped him into his robe. Jerome picked up the mug and followed Arthur down the hall to the privacy room. "How does our guest fair this morning? Have you checked in on Count Andrew yet?" Arthur asked as he relieved himself in the privacy room. "I just left him and he sleeps very soundly still. The potion Peter gave him last night worked quickly and he retired shortly after you left last night." Jerome replied. Arthur tried to shake the cobwebs from his head as he walked back to his room. "Make sure Peter is notified as soon as Count Andrew is awake. He is going to be in a lot of pain today." Arthur sighed and he pulled his riding leathers from the closet and handed Jerome the robe as he dressed. Once Jerome had helped him lace the vest up, Arthur sat down on the bed to pull on his boots and he noticed his spurs were different. "What are these?" He asked. "OH, those are Count Andrew's spurs. I thought Crimson might respond better if he felt something familiar at his side. Count Andrew said to roll them lightly rather than poke him with them when you want to bank." Jerome replied and Arthur chuckled shaking his head. "You are worth your weight in gold." Arthur complimented him. "I will have to come to you for a loan by the time my friend heals. You go prepared Crimson. I'm going to peek in at Count Andrew and I will be there shortly." Arthur said as he tied his hair back in the familiar tail behind his head. As Jerome left the room, Arthur leaned back on one arm and took another sip of the coffee. He would breakfast in Sandista before he took the carriage back to Archemeius. He smiled remembering the secret Maiden Melisa had revealed to him last night and felt excited knowing that in a few short hours she would make her declaration to the council. He was glad it would take place quickly so he didn't have to keep the secret for a long time. Still he wouldn't be able to say anything until somebody else told him about her declaration. He was glad he was going to Sandista early so he could avoid his friends and temptation. He took the torch off the wall and went to the room next door where he had left his friend. He cracked the large oak door and stuck the torch in the room and saw Count Andrew asleep on his back. He snored softly appearing to be sleeping very comfortably. Arthur withdrew the torch and proceeded up the stairs to the roof.

Jerome stood on the perch with Crimson tightening the last strap on his harness. The light from the fire and the torches illuminated the roof. The orange glow over the eastern mountains gave proof of the rising sun but there was still a chill in the air. Crimson whistled passively at Count Arthur as he closed the distance between them. "Yes you recognize me don't you Crimson." Arthur said confidently. "We're not going to have any problems getting you home are we?" He suggested hopefully climbing up beside Jerome on the perch. "Have you been up all night?" He asked Jerome concerned for him. "I split the watch with Lord William. I've had more sleep than you." Jerome replied with a chuckle. "Are you and William enough or should I add a third." Arthur asked as he mounted Crimson and clipped himself in. Between William and me and Peter the medic, you should not concern yourself with the care of your friend. Just make sure no other travesty falls under my charge for me to address. If you have an accident with Crimson know that I will charge you handsomely." Jerome taunted Count Arthur playfully. "Hopefully, I shall see you before the sun sets tonight." Arthur said as he rolled the reigns in his hands and urged Crimson toward the launch platform.

Arthur knew he should keep the commands simple and take the simplest route to Sandista. The direct route to Castle Sandista might be faster but it would require more maneuvers so Arthur planned to follow the coast. He had to admit to himself he was nervous as Crimson walked to the launch platform. He tightened his grip on the reigns and the harness leaning forward. He took a deep breath before he whistled and Crimson dove off the platform. An anxious moment filled Arthur's chest as Crimson fell much farther than he was used to before he began to pump his wings and climb skyward. Arthur hunkered down and clung to Crimson's harness as he let him soar all the way to the coast before he gave him a command. Gently he pulled on the left reigns and rolled the left spur against Crimson's side as Jerome had suggested. Crimson banked gracefully and turned due east as Arthur relaxed the pull on the reigns and flattened his feet. Even Emerald, his own dragon, wasn't as responsive as Crimson was. Arthur's confidence grew and he whistled giving Crimson the command to climb higher into the early morning sky. East of the mountains was a great wall that guarded the only entrance into the center of the island. It was no time at all before the great wall came into view and Arthur again pointed Crimson's head and directed him to follow the road on top of the wall. There was no one on the road yet. It was too early. "Can you roll for me Crimson?" Arthur said out loud as he gently dug the left spur into Crimson's side. The young dragon began to turn until they were upside down and Arthur continued the pressure with his left foot until he righted himself again. Arthur sat straight up on Crimson after they completed the roll enjoying the wind blowing over his face. On the horizon he could see the fires burning atop Castle Green Stone in the distance. Then suddenly a shadow fell over him and he turned his head to see the large white dragon so close to him he could hear it whistle. He was frozen with fear for a brief second before he banked hard with Crimson and dove to escape the ominous shadow but as he recovered and called for maximum speed from Crimson, the giant dragon circled him as if to demonstrate his superior speed and agility. It was unnerving to Arthur for he knew one blast from the mature dragon would surely mean certain death for him. As quickly as he had appeared, he suddenly whistled and banked away obviously content to chase Arthur from his domain and Arthur breathed a sigh of relief as he pulled back on Crimson's reigns. He wondered if it could possibly have been Arch Angel his first dragon. Maybe he had let him escape because he recognized him. He liked to think that was a possibility but there were lots of white dragons in the mountains and it was not probable. Arthur had released Arch Angel a long way from here and he rejected the idea and relaxed on Crimson to finish this leg of the trip.

Castle Green Stone is where the mountains opened to the sea and the forest was the only barrier to the valley of the Sons and Daughters of the Great Father. The engineers from Mesina had erected the great wall that followed the coast from the edge of the western mountains to the cliffs of the eastern mountains. It is made of solid oak and stone and Castle Green Stone is the only gate. The wall is 20 feet high and 20 feet deep supporting that road which runs east and west to the other two cities outside the mountains and connected to the northern highway at Green Stone castle. The highway north to Castle Gardinia from Castle Green Stone paralleled the Willow River which ran through the heart of the city of Green Stone onto the delta and out to the sea. Castle Green Stone was the most powerful city on the island with two gates. The south gate was in the great wall and had two iron doors that opened seaward. The highway ran over the top of the gate and two ramps gently sloped down on the north side into the city from the highway. The castle rose to a height of seven stories against the wall at the south end of the city and the ramps from the highway circled the castle sloping down under a great canopy until it met the highway that led north out of the city towards Castle Gardinia. Inside the solid iron gate, on the left and the right of the highway are the barracks on the first two floors separated by a stone archway over the highway. The entrance to the barracks faced inward to the highway and the elite guard lived and trained there. Two massive spiral staircases led to the second floor on either side of the highway on the north side of the castle and a grand balcony that overlooked the city. Both spiral staircases continued all the way to the seventh floor. The Kings court and throne room are in the center of the second floor facing the balcony with two grand halls on either side and the armory against the southern wall. On the third floor is where the kitchen and servants quarters are. The fourth floor is where the massive dining area and concert hall that opened to another balcony facing the city and the musicians and theater actors practiced and played for guests of the Royal Family. The music from the balcony could be heard across the entire city. The fifth and sixth floors had smaller balconies between the spiral staircases and the Royals quarters were there with large glass windows facing the city to the north and the forest to the south. The seventh floor or the roof is an observation deck where the large metal tubs held the hot and cold water for the castle and the servants to the castle kept fires burning there continuously. Water was brought to the roof from the river below on a series of buckets on a pulley at the northeast side of the roof. Queen Isabella ruled from Castle Green Stone and she and her husband Count Samuel of Castle Green Stone were present at the Festival of the Great Father at Paternus.

Arthur banked Crimson and circled the castle high above the walls to the city. As they turned back to the northeast, Arthur decided he wouldn't waste time following the coast. The sun was beginning to rise over the mountains on his right as they ascended over the forest. Arthur whistled giving Crimson the command to climb again and pointed the young dragons head in the general direction to Castle Sandista. Crimson was much more responsive than Emerald and much easier to fly. He was more than two years older than Emerald and Arthur was impressed at how much difference that maturity made. A mature dragon might live to forty. Like every other rider, Arthur could only speculate what an awesome team a rider on a mature dragon would make if he could just get past that barrier when the dragon matured and began to breathe fire. Crimson was cruising comfortably as they cleared the forest and the familiar mountains came into view. Crimson shook his head and turned to look at Arthur with one eye and whistled excitedly. Arthur got the distinct impression that Crimson recognized where they were going and gave Crimson his head. Without a command from Arthur, Crimson began to pump his wings and increase his speed. Arthur decided since he knew they were flying in generally the right direction to let Crimson's natural instincts take control and he hunkered down clinging to the harness. Crimson's speed was phenomenal and the mountains below them flashed by at an incredible rate. As they crossed the last peak and the ocean came into view, Crimson suddenly banked left and pumped his wings furiously. The incredible wind rushed by Arthur face and roared in his ears. Crimson was at least another measure faster than Emerald and Arthur found it very difficult to raise his head to check the horizon. It was definitely the most exhilarating experience he could remember on any dragon. As Castle Sandista came into view, Arthur knew he must not make the same mistake his friend Count Andrew had so at the proper distance he pulled back gently on both reigns. Crimson began to slow and spread his massive wings catching more and more air as the distance between them and the castle closed.

Now there are seven great cities below the mountain castle at Paternus. Three of these were on the coast outside the great mountains that circled the island of the Great Father. Archemeius, Green Stone and this city was Sandista; a powerful fishing community and home of the School of the Dragon Riders because that is where the expedition for the harvest of dragon eggs and bones begins each spring. Row after row of banana trees and mangos stretched out between the castle and the mountains to the west and coconut palms lined the road leading south to Castle Green Stone along the coast. A great boardwalk stretched far out into the shallow waters off the coast where children played and the young women sunned themselves during the day. Large stone blocks made up the 15 foot high wall that surrounded the whole city. Two huge iron doors stood open at the entrance to the city and a procession of carts and people on horseback filed in and out of the city from there. Here the towers had been completed and seven of the great cannons were manned by a single sentry and faced the open sea. Shops of all kinds surrounded the stone castle at the center of the city and the cobblestone streets were filled with merchants and citizens. Two mountain streams were diverted by the engineers from Mesina and fed into a large pool around the back of the castle where young men and women came to fill their buckets.

Castle Sandista's walls were stained with red dye and decorated with elaborate designs from sea shells. The large oak doors were closed signifying that the King was not in. On the inside, the great hall and the throne of the King occupied the entire first floor and two rows of stairs led to the second floor along the east and west walls. The second floor was the kitchen and rows of rooms that served as servants quarters on the west side and guest quarters on the east side facing the ocean with grand glass windows. The third floor was a common area with a great dining hall and concert hall where the city musicians practiced and performed for the royal family and their guests. The fifth floor was seven rooms for the Royal family quarters surrounded by an exquisite garden deck on the ocean side to the east. On the west side were the large metal tubs that held the hot and cold water supplied to the castle surrounded by stacks of lumber to feed the fires to heat the tubs. At least two young dragons were always on their perches ready to deliver a message for their Royal family and this is where Arthur pointed Crimson's head and whistled the command to land. A series of buckets on pulleys ran down the west side of the castle to bring water from the pools below to the tubs. Less than a mile north, small and large fishing boats were tethered to the larger dock where the fisherman of the villages tended their nets and brought their catch to the shore. Sandista is also the center for the Academy of the Air and Sea where the mysteries of the waters surrounding the island are uncovered.

King Jeffrey currently ruled the city in his 6th year and he and his wife, the Maiden Terea of Gardinia, were currently attending the festival. Their marriage, several years back, had been quite controversial as she had made her declaration to the council at Gardinia while then Prince Jeffrey was attending the Academy there. Prince Jeffrey had another year of study left at Sandista before he would have normally selected his bride and it was whispered that the Maiden Terea made her announcement to squash a romance between the prince and a girl from Sandista. As per law, Jeffrey could not refuse The Maiden Terea and it was believed he was forced into the marriage. However, that rumor slowly died as Prince Jeffrey and his wife, The Maiden Terea of Gardinia, began to have children shortly after they moved in together at Castle Sandista.

Crimson flailed his wings hovering over the perch before he lowered his back legs and found the solid platform. Arthur braced himself as Crimson fell forward catching himself with his front feet on the perch. Crimson immediately started to drink from the trough as Arthur unbuckled himself from the harness. Two servants ran up smiling broadly until they got close enough to see that it was not Count Andrew as they had assumed. The first servant's expression turned sour and he fell to his knees before Count Arthur. He was older maybe 35 and experienced enough to know that no good news would come from a messenger riding another man's dragon. "What evil message have you brought concerning my charge? Tell me quickly that he lives still." The servant pleaded. "I will answer you quickly. He recovers from superficial injuries from an accident. He rests at Archemeius in my bed and we expect full recovery in two to three weeks." Arthur reported. "OH, all praise to Orig." The servant sighed heavily returning to his feet. "If he is your charge you must be Lord Kenneth?" Arthur asked. "I am sir; pray tell me what horror has laid my charge in your hands for three weeks?" He asked as the other servant ran quickly down the stairs. "It was a high speed accident on Crimson that I am certain he would prefer to give you details about himself. Suffice for me to inform you his chest is badly bruised and may have fractures to his ribs so he must remain in my charge for a time. He requires only that you look to the care of Crimson as I assure you personally of his comfort while in my charge." Arthur promised him and took his hand to shake it. "You are Count Arthur of Archemeius. I am surprised we have not met before. Count Andrew speaks highly of you and often." Lord Kenneth said. "I have few occasions to visit your fine city since completion of my education at the Academy of Messengers but that does not diminish my admiration for its beauty or its citizens." Arthur said trying to demonstrate his respect. "What task can I perform for my charges dear friend?" Kenneth asked leading Count Arthur down the stairs. "Well it *was* my desire to breakfast and return to Archemeius quickly but in undertaking this task, I fear I have disappointed a dear friend back in Mesina that I had made plans with for today. I had to cancel those plans, breaking a promise to her and I believe only a significant gift will extinguish her anger with me." Arthur smiled. "Well breakfast I can handle with some certainty but buying a gift for a lady may prove more testing. I will be happy to escort you to any shop in the city if you have some inclination as to what you desire to purchase." Lord Kenneth replied as they walked down the stairs toward the kitchen. Abruptly, a young woman nearly knocked them all down running up the stairs and Arthur went for his dagger fearing she might be a diversion for thieves or even an assassin herself. "LADY KAREN!" Kenneth shouted. "Stifle your impetuousness. You disgrace your charge!" He continued pushing her against the wall while holding Arthur's dagger hand to prevent him from hurting her. She assumed a submissive posture against the wall and Arthur saw the tears streaming down the young woman's face. She was a gorgeous young woman with long auburn hair and Arthur was curious as to what travesty caused her tears. "You must allow me to speak with Count Arthur." She pleaded with Kenneth. "I most certainly will not! You, young lady, will go directly to your quarters and pray that Count Andrew does not here of *any* encounter between you and Count Arthur." He commanded and she looked to Arthur her eyes begging him. "Do not test me Lady Karen. Overstep your position and I assure you I will counsel Count Andrew to remove it from you." He commanded more forcefully. She dropped her eyes and moved quickly from their presence. "Please accept quickly my apology for that brash intrusion." Lord Kenneth sighed leading Arthur on to the dining hall. Arthur's curiosity was torture but he was hesitant to inquire of Lord Kenneth about the woman fearing his answer so he said nothing. Lord Kenneth had called her Lady Karen which was a formal title for servants. He had further identified her as Count Andrew's servant but what use did a male rider have for a female servant. He tried to put it out of his head all during breakfast by discussing gift possibilities for The Maiden Melisa with Lord Kenneth as they ate. "I must apologize Lord Kenneth but my curiosity burns about that young woman and I fear asking Count Andrew to quench that fire may have dire results beyond my comprehension of the circumstances. I feel it might be better if you define her position so I can use my best judgment to determine what course to take when conversing with Count Andrew." Arthur said and Lord Kenneth sighed heavily hesitant to respond. "She is an impetuous girl." Kenneth started. "She is a beautiful woman near my own age and you addressed her as Lady Karen. Is she Count Andrew's servant?" Arthur asked pointedly. "I have no need or desire to embarrass my dear friend." Arthur added. Lord Kenneth lowered his voice to a whisper. "While our customs are the same, the law pertaining to intimacy for the royal family is much different in Sandista. I have counseled Count Andrew just to marry her and be done with it but he is a stubborn man. I know not what agenda keeps him from matrimony and he confides more in her than me of late." Kenneth said dropping his head sadly. "Karen is his only concubine?" Arthur asked and Kenneth shook his head yes. "Does she refuse his marriage proposal?" Arthur whispered and Kenneth chuckled under his breath. "She lives for the hour or a hint of a suggestion that he might be leaning toward a proposal of like nature. I tire of her nuisance at pestering me to assist her in obtaining that proposal." Kenneth said still dejected in his demeanor. "So you find fault in her as a mate for Count Andrew?" Arthur asked. "On the contrary Count Arthur; Karen is a graduate of the Academy of Medical Arts at Red Oak and was the second medic to the crown. She is as smart as she is beautiful and Count Andrew only took her as his servant when she ran afoul of The King's wife, The Maiden Terea of Gardinia, who demanded the city council remove her from her position and they did. King Jeffrey allowed Count Andrew to take her as his second servant over the objection of his own wife." Lord Kenneth said shaking his head again. Arthur contemplated what Kenneth had revealed to him for a long while as he sipped coffee after his meal. He shifted in his chair uneasily. "I can make no sense of this puzzle. There is a piece missing and I fear Count Andrew has it in his pocket." Arthur said finally without a response from Kenneth. "Why did you refuse Karen an audience with me?" Arthur asked. "Because I know her intentions. She wants you to escort her to Count Andrew's side and we both know that is impossible given the difference in the law in Archemeius." Kenneth replied. A plan was formulating in Arthur's head and he began to smile at Kenneth. "I do not doubt your account of the circumstances so please do not take offense. There is a small chance I could return your charge to you not only healed from his mishap but properly wed to the Lady Karen if you will enter into a vow of secrecy with me." Arthur whispered across the table to him and Lord Kenneth's eyes brightened. "Name your desires sir and I will attempt to fulfill them." He replied. "You must allow Lady Karen an audience with me. I must know firsthand that her devotion to Count Andrew is real. Only tell her that I know of her circumstance and that I wish her to escort me in my pursuit of a gift for my friend in Archemeius. Counsel her not to press me to escort her to Mesina but only to answer honestly when I inquire of her relationship to Count Andrew." Arthur said. "I will decide my next course of action after I conclude my interview with her." Arthur added. "You risk much if you chose to escort her to Archemeius. The council there will certainly have her in chains at the first hint of their relationship and you too for your complicity." Lord Kenneth warned him. "It would not be uncommon that I return with a medic that has cared for him to relieve the burden on my own staff and I will not allow their cohabitation until Count Andrew makes legal the circumstances." Arthur replied and Kenneth took his feet. "You have no idea how I will pray for the success of your endeavors. I caution you to be firm with Lady Karen lest her impetuousness spoil your efforts." Kenneth said and he shook Arthur's hand and disappeared quickly through a doorway.

Lord Kenneth found Lady Karen's quarters and knocked at her door. She opened the door and bade Kenneth to enter. Her eyes burned red from her tears and she feared the worst of retributions was imminent from the senior servant. "As many times as you have broken customs and brazenly ignored my council, you still have learned little of the value of patience and your actions have always brought more discomfort to your situation." Kenneth said. He spoke harshly with her to drive home his point. "However, this time you have the slimmest of chances to obtain a positive consequence from your brass impetuousness if you will merely follow my council." Kenneth stated. "Has Count Arthur agreed to escort me to Archemeius and Count Andrew? My only desire is to be at his side and soothe his pain. If not, I will find my own way unescorted if necessary." Karen wept doubting her chances. "Listen to me Lady Karen." Kenneth whispered trying hard to show patience and convince her. "In Count Arthur lies your best opportunity to not merely obtain escort to Archemeius but fulfill your ultimate desire with Count Andrew but it is imperative that you heed my council completely." He pleaded with her. Karen knew Kenneth was her ally. She had all but resigned herself to being Count Andrew's concubine and was learning to accept her position. Her ultimate desire was to be his wife and she had not completely abandoned that dream but it had become increasingly improbable in her eyes. Kenneth's comment gave new fuel to that dream burning in her heart. "Do not tempt me to venture into a scheme with an unachievable goal. My heart cannot withstand much more disappointment." She begged Kenneth sadly. "I have chosen to confide in Count Arthur with regards to your circumstance with Count Andrew as he is a highly valued friend of his. You now have opportunity to secure him as your ally if you will only curb your tongue and open your heart to him." Kenneth whispered. Karen looked at him distastefully. "What do you hint at Lord Kenneth? Open my heart or my legs?" She protested. "I swear, your history of despair taints the very meaning of friendship. If you cannot quickly learn the true meaning of that word you will spoil this opportunity with Count Andrew's most valued friend. If his inquiries of you are of an intimate nature, be assured that it is his desire for Count Andrew's continued friendship and not yours that drives his questions. If you insult Count Arthur with an insinuation like that...., all will be lost." Kenneth said emphatically. "You truly believe Count Arthur is in pursuit of a proposal from Count Andrew to me?" Karen pleaded hopefully. "What I know is that he wishes you escort him to the square in pursuit of a gift for his romantic interest in Archemeius prior to his return. If you press him for escort to Mesina he will refuse. If he finds your devotion to Count Andrew worthy he will invite you to replace his own medic in charge of Count Andrew's care." Lord Kenneth replied crossing his arms over his chest. "I will obtain this audience with him for you if you can hold your tongue and present yourself in a manner that exalts and honors your charge Count Andrew." Kenneth concluded. Lady Karen went to the mirror and washed her face with a wet cloth and her excitement welled up inside her. "What gift does he desire for his mistress?" Karen asked. "Don't use that word." Kenneth warned her. "A mistress in Archemeius can be found only in their prison. Refer to her as his friend. As for the gift, he has no set inclination so it may take time. You should focus your inquiries to that end. I'm certain she is a lady of high standing so be cautious with your recommendations." Kenneth said as Karen ran a brush through her long hair. "I pledge to heed your council Lord Kenneth. Please make haste to present me to Count Arthur. Kenneth held out his arm for Karen to take. "Haste is a trait that you should leave here in this room." Kenneth said smiling at her as he opened the door and led her down the hallway.

Count Arthur looked up from his coffee as the two servants approached. He could certainly see why Count Andrew fancied Lady Karen. She was tall and uncommonly radiant. Her auburn hair hung in long waves to her waist reflecting the light magnificently and her gown fit snugly revealing a most voluptuous figure. He stood and faced them as they closed the distance between them. "My dear sir; as you requested, I present Count

Andrew's servant Lady Karen." Kenneth said as Karen bowed low before keeping her eyes at Count Arthur's feet. "It is my pleasure to meet the valued friend of my charge. Please accept quickly my apology for our first encounter as I was overcome with fear for the wellbeing of my charge." Karen said remorsefully. Count Arthur was impressed with the radical change in her demeanor and her current composure. "Please rise knowing I take no offense. I too was overcome with emotion upon discovering his travesty. Be assured that he rests comfortably and is in good hands now." Arthur said as she rose up before him. There was still a hint of redness in her eyes and Arthur knew she had just recently controlled her tears. "You must give my most heartfelt regards to my charge upon your return but Lord Kenneth revealed you have a task for me before you go." Lady Karen said as she looked into Count Arthur's smiling face for the first time. His eyes were reassuring to Karen. "It is true, if you are willing. I must purchase a gift for my friend The Maiden Melisa of Archemeius to quell her disfavor with me. I promised her a picnic today and had to break that promise to complete the task with Crimson." Arthur stated and Karen's eyes grew wide. "You are a suitor of The Maiden Melisa of Archemeius and chose to honor my charge and sacrifice the pleasure of her company?" Karen asked beginning to understand how deep the friendship between her charge and Count Arthur was. Arthur looked to Lord Kenneth with a glance that told him he could retire and held out his arm to Lady Karen. "You understand my desire to repair this wound upon my return to her and regain my preferred status in her eyes." Arthur chuckled as she took his arm. "Surely she does not hold your duty against you even at her disappointment for your absence?" Karen asked guiding him to the stairs that would take them to the square. "I am as confident in her eventual forgiveness as I am in the knowledge that a gift of significant stature will hasten its fruition." Count Arthur laughed.

The sun shone down brightly as Count Arthur and the Lady Karen walked out into the square. There was a gentle breeze blowing across the city from the ocean and the air was heavy. Karen asked and Arthur answered all her questions about Maiden Melisa to determine what kind of gift he should purchase. "I would prefer something unique to Sandista that she could not find in the shops of Archemeius on her own." Arthur said as they browsed one of the shops on the square. "I heard a rumor of something very unique at the tinker's store on the far end of the square if you care to investigate it with me?" Karen suggested. "I am not fond of long shopping tours but if you feel it is particularly unique I am willing."

Arthur replied and Karen waved to a carriage pulling Arthur to it. "We can shorten our tour with a ride in the carriage." Karen exclaimed as they climbed in. "Please take us to the tinkers store and then wait for us as we shall not be long." Karen instructed the driver before he urged his horse forward. The hoofs of the horse made quite a racket on the cobblestone street as they proceeded through the massive square. Shops of all sorts and sizes lined the street and the side streets and it seemed to stretch out forever. Some buildings were two story and some three story and Arthur wondered how they all stayed in business there were so many. Lady Karen was quite charming and obviously very intelligent. She was unlike any concubine he had ever met before. "It is not my intention to embarrass you or insult you Lady Karen but it is the absence of sufficient time to reveal the true nature of your relationship with my valued friend Count Andrew that forces me to ask you intimate questions. Please excuse my frankness but I must inquire. Is the physical relationship what you value most with regard to Count Andrew or is there more." Karen blushed bright red and she fought the urge to take offense to Arthur's question. She remembered the council Kenneth had given her and everything Count Arthur had said and done supported what Kenneth had warned her about. She had to have faith that his inquiries were not leading to a sordid request. "You speak frankly and so I will do likewise." Karen replied nervously. "Count Arthur and I had a normal courtship when I was 2nd Medic to the court. When I was falsely accused of medical malpractice and removed from my position without a trial, I would have had to move out of the castle. When Count Andrew was able to secure a position for me with the King's favor, I assumed that our courtship would continue in the customary fashion and Count Andrew would propose eventually. I waited patiently for some time devoted to Count Andrew and certain he was on the verge of proposing matrimony. Something sinister troubles Count Andrew about the future and as time passed it became evident to me that it bothered him so bad he could not commit to matrimony. I resisted his advances and seriously considered and threatened to terminate our courtship but my heart would not allow it." Karen's face burned red with embarrassment as she considered her words to reveal her intimate situation to Count Arthur. She felt the emotion begin to well up behind her eyes. "I assumed, wrongly as it turned out, that he would propose if I surrendered to him completely. Six full cycles of the moon have passed since that night and I am trying to learn to accept my position and my fate." Karen concluded and could no longer contain her emotion. In her youth she would never have considered being a man's concubine even a remote possibility. It was unfair and she was embarrassed and ashamed but she saw no recourse for her fate as she found it impossible to abandon Count Andrew. She began to weep uncontrollably and Arthur stretched his arm over her back and pulled her head to his shoulder. Arthur had no idea how Count Andrew felt about the Lady Karen because he had never spoken of her to Arthur but there was no denying her devotion to him was sincere and complete. It made him doubt the depth of his understanding of his friend Andrew. How could any man treat a woman this way regardless of their feelings for her? The Andrew he knew would send her away before allowing her to live with this shame if he didn't love her. It still didn't make sense to Arthur. "Has Count Andrew's blouse born these tears also?" Arthur asked. "I beg you cease crying as I am your ally in the pursuit of happiness for both you and Andrew." Arthur whispered purposely leaving off his title and speaking to her as a friend and informally. The carriage had stopped and the driver waited patiently with his back to them as he had seen Lady Karen's tears. "Dry your tears now Lady Karen and focus on the task of securing a gift with me for my friend. Let your demeanor brighten for I have a plan to shorten the days of your troubles that I'm certain you'll adore." He said lifting her chin to look directly into her eyes as he presented his handkerchief to her. They stepped from the carriage and Arthur motioned for her to go to the door of the shop. He turned to the driver and presented him a 5 mark gold piece. "I will wait for you as the lady requested." He smiled and Arthur moved close to him. "In addition sir, if by chance you gave ear to our conversation and I ever find that you have repeated it, it will not go well for you." Arthur said smiling at him. "A lesson a good driver learns early sir." The driver whispered smiling back at Arthur.

Arthur walked into the shop and looked for Karen who had already gone in. She waved to him from the back and he moved to join her. "This is the item I heard rumors of in the castle." She said handing Arthur his handkerchief. It was a large wooden box maybe 4 feet high with a metal face engraved with 12 numbers behind two glass doors. Two metal arrows were attached to the center of the face, one shorter than the other, pointing to the numbers. "It's a time piece." Karen said turning the box around. "Once a day, you have to take the sand from the lower bucket and return it to the upper bucket. As the sand falls though the mechanism, it turns the arrows on the front to reveal the correct time of day." Karen reported with a nervous smile on her face hoping for Arthur's approval. "That's ingenious. It's certainly unique." Arthur replied examining the box. "Unlike a sundial, it's accurate day or night." The shopkeeper said. Arthur inspected it very closely opening the door on the back to examine the workings. There was a very intricately arranged series of belts and pulleys and wheels spinning as the sand poured over a larger wheel kind of like he had seen in an hourglass and captured again in a bucket at the bottom. "The engineer that designed this is a genius." Arthur laughed. "Born right here in Sandista." The shopkeeper said proudly. "Do you have one prepared for shipment? My desire is to take it with me on a fast carriage to Archemeius." Arthur asked. "I do. It is very expensive sir. 200 mark gold." The shopkeeper said and Count Arthur chuckled. "My god man, I don't want to buy the whole shop I just desire this timepiece. I'll pay you 100." Arthur smiled and the shopkeeper did also. "You attest to the workmanship yourself. It would be an insult to the engineer for me to sell it for less than 175." He smiled. "It is fine craftsmanship but the value is in the eye of the buyer and I do not believe I could in good conscience pay more than 125. Arthur said with a determined look on his face. "I will lose my shirt and my shop at that price. 165 is the least I can let you have it for." The shopkeeper said folding his arms over his chest. Arthur scratched his head and looked at Karen. "I fear our shopping tour must continue for I cannot afford this timepiece." Arthur sighed and took her hand turning to leave. The shopkeeper watched them take a few steps to the door. "Ok…., 150 but if you tell anyone what price you paid I will deny it." He sighed heavily as Arthur wiped the grin from his face before turning back to the shopkeeper. "Alright sir, you are draining my purse but I will pay your price." Arthur said pulling open the belt at his waist. "I will tell my associates it was 200 if you write that amount on the receipt." Arthur smiled and the shopkeeper chuckled as he wrote it out. Arthur and the shopkeeper carried it out to the carriage and tied it down as Karen climbed into the open carriage. "Your skill extends beyond riding dragons." Karen giggled as the carriage got underway. "I was certain our shopping tour was extended when you took my hand." She said. "If he had let me get to the door, I would have paid 165." Arthur laughed and Karen did too.

"Kenneth warned me not to press you but I fear my excitement fuels my curiosity to the point of burning a hole in my chest with regard to your plan." Karen said gripping Arthur's arm tightly as she would an old friend. Arthur looked into her eyes and took a deep breath exhaling slowly and deliberately. "Can you swear to me your loyalty in a secret endeavor and promise to abide and honor my council regardless of circumstances as you may perceive them?" Arthur asked. "I do." Karen whispered excitedly.

"You answer too quickly Lady Karen and I fear you do not comprehend the gravity of our endeavor. The smallest hint of a mistake on your part or mine will certainly result in dire consequences for both of us." Arthur warned her sternly. "I promise to speak only the words you place in my mouth and to walk only the path you desire for me. I will throw myself on my own dagger before I put you or my charge in jeopardy." Karen whispered trying to demonstrate her conviction. Her enthusiasm made Arthur even the more nervous. Kenneth was right. For a woman her age, she seemed still very impetuous. "It is with some reservation that I now formally invite you Lady Karen to escort me to Archemeius." Arthur said and Karen threw her arms around Count Arthur and hugged him. Arthur pulled her arms from around his neck and forced them to her sides gripping her tightly. "This is precisely the conduct that will result in both of us ending up in chains." Arthur scolded her harshly. "Do you have no respect for tradition or custom?" Arthur asked heatedly. "We have no custom or tradition that keeps me from hugging a friend who is trying to make my dearest dream come true." Karen replied. "Understand this Lady Karen or I will be forced to withdraw my invitation. While I consider you my friend, I am not inviting my friend to escort me to Archemeius. You are a medic by profession and I am inviting Lady Karen, Count Andrew's Servant who has knowledge of his medical history and is skilled in the medical arts to relieve the burden on my staff while he recovers. Any physical contact between you and any member of the royal family is forbidden by custom and by law in Archemeius." Arthur said with conviction. "Convince me you understand that before I waste my time." He added. "I do. It won't happen again I promise you." Karen replied emphatically. She knew the laws were stricter in Archemeius and she would have to guard herself closely and maintain a more reserved demeanor if they were going to be successful.

The small carriage pulled up in front of the castle and Count Arthur stepped down to assist Lady Karen as she dismounted. Arthur was still nervous about his decision and upset by Lady Karen's outburst. He wondered if he was making a monumental mistake. "You have 30 minutes to gather up whatever professional tools you think you may need and pack a bag for a three week excursion." Arthur said still disturbed with her as she ran toward the castle. "Tell Lord Kenneth we are departing and both of you meet me at the fast carriage stables." Arthur shouted after her and she waved over her shoulder before she disappeared into the castle. Arthur felt frustrated as he climbed back into the carriage. "Take me to the fast carriage stables." He commanded and the driver turned and looked at him with a puzzled expression. "You know that's the stables right there at the foot of the ramp." The driver smiled and Arthur looked up still rubbing his head and chuckled. "So it is, pull over there so I can make arrangements and transfer my baggage." Arthur said laughing at himself as he climbed back down from the carriage. Securing the fast carriage took longer than he thought it would. Once they pulled the larger more roadworthy carriage out they had to round up and bridle the four horses that would pull it. Arthur pulled the driver of the fast carriage aside before he rounded up the horses. He pointed to the sky. "Do you know what that is driver?" Arthur asked him. "You refer to the sun sir?" The driver replied. "Yes we both see the sun now and I want to still be able to see the sun when I get to Archemeius so make your selection carefully." Arthur chuckled placing a 2 mark coin in his hand. "I am much more interested in speed than I am comfort for this trip." Arthur smiled and the driver nodded his understanding. The heavier carriage seated four comfortably and was covered. Arthur and the city driver loaded his crate onto rack behind the larger carriage and strapped it down. He was leaving much later than he had planned and he knew it would take 5 hours to get to Castle Green Stone and then another 4 hours to Castle Archemeius. He looked up at the sun that was already high over head. He was in a race with the sun that he knew he would lose if they didn't leave soon. He paid the city driver and he departed as Lord Kenneth and Lady Karen approached carrying two large bags. They put her bags in beside Arthur's crate and secured them as the driver finished hitching up the last horse. There was a high step to get into the carriage and Lady Karen just stared at Arthur after he opened the door. "There are no Royals that will help a servant into a carriage in Archemeius. It works the other way." Arthur said shaking his head and looking at Kenneth as Lady Karen awkwardly struggled to get into the carriage on her own. "Don't show leniency toward her Count Arthur. I fear a tragic outcome if you do." Kenneth said as Count Arthur joined her in the carriage and he closed the door behind them. "A beating at your hand would be preferable to prison and appreciated even by Count Andrew." He said looking directly at Lady Karen before the driver took up the reigns and they departed.

"Do you really beat your servants in Archemeius?" Karen asked pulling a second cushion underneath her as they began their journey. "None of my servants have ever given me cause to beat them but it is not out of the realm of possibility for me with any servant I encounter." Count Arthur warned her. She set a bag on the seat beside her. "There's water and food for the trip in the bag." She said smiling nervously at Arthur. He was an enigma to her. He could be so kind and caring and was certainly easy on the eyes but he could switch in an instant and be harsh and callus with his tone and demeanor. He certainly wasn't accustomed to public displays of affection of any kind. The driver waited until he cleared the gates to Castle Sandista before he cracked his whip and set the team into a full gallop. Arthur pulled a pipe from his belt and loaded it watching Lady Karen bounce uncomfortably each time they hit a bump in the road. Arthur stuck his head out the window after he lit his pipe. "Is that it driver? Is this as much as you can muster from your team?" He shouted up to the driver. "It's close to five hours to Green Stone. More speed risks a variety of injuries over that distance." The driver replied. "You are the expert. I defer to your judgment sir. But you also control the size of your bonus at Green Stone." Arthur concluded sitting back down on the bench. A long moment passed and the driver cracked his whip again and the carriage increased in speed considerably. Lady Karen grimaced bouncing on the bench more forcefully now and Arthur smiled handing her the last of the four cushions in the carriage. "I thought I would take a nap on the way to Archemeius. I guess I was wrong again." She chuckled sliding the last cushion underneath her. They talked at great length during the bumpy ride to Green Stone and Arthur drilled her about the expected conduct of a servant in Archemeius. She continued to impress Count Arthur with her quit wit and jovial demeanor. She was obviously very intelligent and she did respect the customs and traditions of the Sons and Daughters of the Great Father but the environment at Sandista had made her lackadaisical when it came to the fine points. She was a poignant example to Arthur of how the law guards against the erosion of a communities customs, traditions and moral values. Karen would say the citizens of Archemeius lived under a system that was too strict and oppressive but Arthur recognized that she would not be in the situation she was if she lived there. There were long periods of silence where they just rode and after one of them Arthur stuck his head out the window surveying the road ahead and recognized the great wall in the distance. "We will be at Green Stone soon." He announced to Karen pulling his head back in the carriage. "Oh thank God, are we going to dine there?" She asked and Arthur shook his head no. "We will change teams and drivers and proceed immediately to Archemeius." Arthur said. "Can you at least let me stretch my legs?" Karen pleaded with him bracing herself against the side of the carriage. "There will be a little time while we change teams. You can do it then." Arthur said sympathetically.

There are elevated stables beside both ramps to Green Stone so the fast carriages don't have to go down into the city. As they pulled into the stable area and stopped, Arthur bounded from the carriage and held out his arms to assist Karen and she was caught off guard. She placed her hands on his arms and he lowered her to the ground. "You confuse me Count Arthur. Your actions do not always follow your council." She said simply as a matter of fact. "Walk while you can. Time is short." He barked abrasively and she turned quickly to circle the carriage. Her legs were unsteady and her back ached. She put both hands in the middle of her back and pushed stretching the muscles there as she circled the carriage. Arthur went to help the drivers change out the teams. All four horses were heavily lathered and the first driver took them to walk the pen to cool down. "You did a fine job and appreciate your effort." Arthur said handing the driver a 5 mark gold coin as he walked his team. "A little over 4 hours and my team is uninjured; it was a fine trip." The driver replied and Arthur went to help the other driver hitch his team. Arthur watched Karen rubbing her legs trying to get the blood moving in them again and he wondered again what would keep Count Andrew from taking a woman such as her as his wife. "You have selected an excellent traveling companion." The second driver said noticing Arthur watching her. "She is a medic and the servant of a dear friend who is injured and recovers in my bed at Archemeius." Arthur replied and the driver chuckled. "I know not your friend but I am certain I would prefer her in my bed over him." He whispered jovially. Arthur chose not to take offense at the driver's harmless chat realizing Lady Karen's attractiveness was bound to illicit comments from men who saw her. "You should make haste to Archemeius so I do not fall victim to her charm and violate my friends trust." Arthur replied joking with the driver who was still admiring Karen. "I shall drive as fast or as slowly as you desire sir. I can fill the carriage with cushions if it fits your need." He suggested grinning at Arthur. "Extra cushions could make the ride to Archemeius very pleasurable." The driver whispered. "Make the cabin as comfortable as you can for the lady but speed is my pleasure. I have no desire for my dear friend's servant." Arthur said smiling convincingly at the driver who shook his head before he headed for the stable. "A wasted opportunity, if ever I saw one." He snickered as he departed and Arthur joined Lady Karen at the door to the cabin. "Has the feeling returned to your legs?" Arthur asked her and she giggled rubbing her behind. "It is not my legs that suffered the largest portion of trauma on that ride." She reported playfully and Arthur's face burned red but he chuckled at her comment. Karen noticed his mood had softened. "What offense did you take to my comment earlier?" She asked and Arthur sighed heavily. He hadn't taken offense with her at her comment but with himself. He was supposed to be preparing her for the strictest of conduct required for the law they would encounter at Archemeius and he had lapsed into leniency with her. "If a Royal offers you his hand, you may take it without offense. Just be conscious that any physical contact is a declaration of intimacy however slight. You should never extend your hand to a royal beyond your duties or your professional requirements." Arthur replied and Karen just smiled back at him. "This is why he is an enigma to me." Karen thought to herself because she realized he could have just explained that earlier rather than turn brash with her. Arthur noticed the driver climb into his seat and opened the door for Karen. He smiled and held up his arm to assist her into the cabin. "Oh my, I like this driver much better already." Karen giggled entering the carriage. Arthur surveyed the cabin as he closed the door behind him and every board was covered by at least two cushions and there were blankets folded on the seats. He stuck his head out the window and called to the drive. "We are aboard. Remember my desire is for speed." He shouted. "It wouldn't be my choice but I will press to satisfy your desire sir." The driver replied jovially as he cracked his whip and the carriage lunged forward. Karen recognized the insinuation in the driver's comment and grinned at Arthur. "He believes you fancy me." Karen snickered at Arthur jokingly and Arthur frowned at her. "Would you violate Count Andrew's trust to share intimacy with me?" He asked angrily and Karen recoiled utterly stunned by his question. "Be assured Count Arthur; that thought never entered my mind." She replied with as much indignation as she could muster. "Then do not jest in that arena for I find it equally offensive." Arthur commanded as he pulled out his pipe to light it again. Karen's anger was equal to Arthurs now and she vowed to herself not to speak to him again for the remainder of the trip. The bench was wide and she took all the cushions and arranged them three high on her side and grabbed the blanket. As she lay down on her bench she stretched the blanket over her and pulled it over her head without looking at Count Arthur. Arthur stuck his head out the window. "Don't let the sun go down on this ride." He yelled. "It shall not." The driver replied and cracked his whip again. Arthur thought of his friend Andrew as he watched the pouting figure under the blanket across from him bounce and he smiled. "My dear friend

Count Andrew has chosen well." He said but Karen retained her posture covered from head to toe under the blanket. Maybe it would serve their cause better if he let her remain irritated with him. She responded more like a servant in that mood and Arthur resigned himself to use that to his advantage. The rest of the ride to Archemeius was diverse of conversation and that was fine with Arthur but Karen wept softly under the blanket. She was fearful of what would happen in Archemeius and felt very alone. Her only ally was condescending and harsh and she wished so badly to have a confidante to share her thoughts with. She cursed her fate and the unfair circumstances she found herself trapped in. She found no solace in Count Arthur even though she knew he had her best interest at heart. She just wished the ride would be over so she could be by Andrew's side again and everything would be more bearable at least.

The ride smoothed out and Arthur lit his pipe again peering out the window. The highway from the great wall to Archemeius had been paved with an improved material that lends to a smoother ride as well as more speed. The mountains rose up into great cliffs on his right as they drew closer to oceans shore on his left. His thoughts turned to Maiden Melisa and joy and excitement filled his heart and his head remembering that she had presented herself to the council this morning and made her announcement. He hoped someone would make her declaration known to him early upon their arrival so he would not have to burn with that secret too long. The dense air and the familiar scent of the ocean filled Arthur's nostrils as he got closer to his home. Another hour passed before Arthur peered out the window and recognized the first buildings at the outskirts of Archemeius. "You can come out of your shell now little turtle. We approach Castle Archemeius." Arthur chuckled but Karen did not respond. He leaned forward and folded the blanket back off her head smiling at her. The smoother ride over the last part of their trip had lulled her into a deep sleep. It was easy for Arthur to understand why she found favor in Count Andrew's eyes. Her face was an angelic vision as she lay before him in blissful slumber. Arthur felt cruel shaking her shoulder and rousing her from her dream. "Wake up Lady Karen and right yourself as we approach Castle Archemeius." Arthur said casually. Karen opened her eyes and stared at him for a long moment wondering which Count Arthur was waking her. "Make yourself presentable Lady Karen for there will certainly be friends of mine present as we arrive." Arthur said. Karen said nothing as she sat up and straightened her gown pushing the blanket to the floor and reaching for her purse. Finding her brush, she ran it through her hair trying not to look at Count Arthur. "Is your head prepared to execute our deception? Take heed to how the other servants respond both to royals and each other." Arthur said trying to encourage her. "This is the same council Kenneth gave before we left." She replied. "It is a good one. They are not slaves but servants who are well paid and enjoy their lot and show respect to authority and position with dignity." Arthur said as the carriage slowed and came to a stop.

The door to the carriage flew open before Arthur could reach for it and Maiden Melisa filled the open door. Arthur could see the excitement in her face as their eyes met but the blood seemed to drain quickly from her cheeks as she surveyed the cabin. She looked at the multiple cushions scattered recklessly over the floor and benches. Her eyes moved to the ruffled blanket beside the gorgeous woman brushing her long brown hair sitting on what was obviously a makeshift bed. Arthur watched her face as the excitement in her eyes was quickly replaced by horror and pain as she slowly backed out of the cabin. "Stay until I call for you." Arthur said to Karen and he quickly followed Maid Melisa and caught her by the arm spinning her around to face him before she could run. A party of her friends and his surrounded them. "Unhand me Count Arthur." Melisa shouted glaring at him. "What evil does your mind accuse me of falsely?" Arthur asked still gripping her arm tightly. Melisa was suddenly aware all their friends were staring at them with their mouths open. "You think me a fool who cannot recognize a bed when she sees one." Melisa whispered fighting to free her arm from his hand. Arthur lowered his voice to avoid a scene and reveal his secret to Melisa. "Should I not make Count Andrew's **_betrothed_** as comfortable as possible as I escort her to him?" Arthur whispered taking care that only Maid Melisa heard him. Melisa quit fighting him wanting to believe his explanation but her jealousy still burned in her chest. "One or two extra cushions bring comfort to any rider. A cabin full of them attests to a very erotic journey." Melisa whispered still accusing him and unconvinced. "Your urgency to find me a scoundrel wounds me deeply given our faithful history and gives me cause for doubt." Arthur whispered remorsefully removing his hand from her arm. "Lady Karen is 2nd servant to Count Andrew and his medic. I pray you will keep the secret of her true relationship to Count Andrew and save us both from chains if there is any friendship left in your heart for me." Arthur whispered. Melisa looked into his eyes and her own emotions suddenly overwhelmed her knowing Arthur would never violate their trust. The pressure behind her own eyes burst through and she wept. As shocking as the scene in the cabin was, Melisa knew in her heart Arthur was not capable of betraying her in this manner. "You swear this to be true." Melisa pleaded. "I make vows with my friends. If our friendship is as deep as **I** assumed it to be, you would require no pledge in this moment but rely only on my declaration of undying love and devotion previously given in earnest." Arthur whispered pleading deep into her eyes as he took both her hands. "I will swear to **you** Arthur. I was so filled with fear at what seemed to be so obvious to me in the moment I saw the two of you in the cabin, that my faith was tested beyond reason. My mind is void of words to secure your forgiveness but my heart longs for it." Melisa wept uncontrollably now and Arthur wished he could embrace her but dared not to. They were already in a precarious position and Arthur still had to present Lady Karen to his friends and the court. "Please stifle your tears and I shall trade my forgiveness for yours. I should have considered your reaction and been more discreet in my arrival." Arthur whispered. "This scene puts my secret in jeopardy and I am fearful and require your assistance in its execution." He added still whispering as he handed Melisa his handkerchief. Melisa dried her face with his handkerchief and took a deep breath looking into Arthur's eyes. "You know normally I would have your back in any endeavor you chose to undertake but I fear I will not favor you unless you do me a favor first." Melisa whispered and smiled mischievously handing him back his handkerchief. Arthur's nervousness grew more real and his voice strained to whisper to her. "Why do you hesitate and toy with me now that I have revealed my fear to you." He said softly. "You are nervous because you know not what favor I require of you." Melisa said too loud for his comfort and he knew their friends had heard her. "Please what favor do you require?" Arthur asked whispering more urgently. Melisa grinned at him broadly. "I require a kiss from you immediately, for you are now my fiancé and your affection is my legal right as mine is yours." Melisa said boldly in a clear loud voice so all could hear. It took a long moment for her words to take shape and bring meaning to the change in their situation. Being engaged meant they were no longer inhibited by the laws of intimacy in any degree. Arthur pulled Melisa into his arms and kissed her passionately for the first time in front of his friends and they cheered and applauded excitedly gathering around them. Arthur felt a huge heavy spirit take flight from his heart and leave him as he shared his passion for Melisa publicly for the first time. As they reluctantly separated, all the men shook his hand and congratulated him and Arthur forgot about everything else getting wrapped up in the brief celebration. He couldn't let go of The

Maiden Melisa and keeping his left arm around her felt so natural as he shook hands and laughed with his friends. He had waited so long and he was truly excited that the day was finally here.

As he glanced back to the carriage and saw Lady Karen emerging, he suddenly remembered his other responsibilities. "Lady Karen; come join me with my friends." He shouted to her. Lady Karen walked nervously toward Count Arthur and the group. She had no idea what had just transpired and was most assuredly confused seeing Count Arthur embrace the tall blonde beauty that had burst into the cabin earlier. "I apologize Count Arthur but the cabin grows hot in the sun as the carriage no longer is moving." Karen said bowing before him. "Rise Lady Karen for it is I who should apologize for making you wait so long. My friends, I present to you Lady Karen of Sandista a highly skilled medic that has an intimate knowledge of Count Andrew's medical history. She has agreed to come and assist in the care and recovery of Count Andrew and give some relief to my staff. While our customs are similar between Archemeius and Sandista, our laws are very different and I implore you to have patience and watch over her during her stay in our city." Arthur said as each member of the party greeted her shaking her hand and trying to make her feel welcome. The young Count Richard, who had offended Melisa and Arthur the previous night, was the first to greet Lady Karen quickly. Nervously he approached Count Arthur and Maid Melisa as the rest of the group focused on Lady Karen. "I have had counsel today from many friends from Lord Jerome to Councilman Trent with regard to my adolescent blunder of last night. I present myself for your council at your leisure as you suggested last night." Count Richard said softly and humbly. Arthur smiled at Richard considering the mistakes he had made in his own youth when drinking. "I chose not to pursue this topic with you further to avoid repeating to you the wise council I am certain you have already heard from them. Suffice for me to warn you against speaking every thought that enters your head. In maturity you will learn, guarding your tongue is more difficult once you have drown it in wine and I too have made similar mistakes in my youth." Arthur chuckled to relieve Count Richard's discomfort. Count Richard *was* relieved and breathed a giant sigh bidding Count Arthur and Maid Melisa ado. He smiled to himself proud of his choice in timing to present himself to Count Arthur. He presumed the result would be favorable to him if Count Arthur's demeanor was joyous but he never expected Count Arthur to forgo his session with him entirely. His confidence was renewed as he departed the party having accomplished the task he had dreaded all day.

Arthur waved and Jerome came to his side. "I need for you to take charge of Lady Karen and find her adequate quarters close to Count Andrew. Guard against him hearing of her presence here until I meet with him. Help her with her bags and give her general council on the proper conduct of a servant in this castle. I will refrain from holding you responsible for any shortcomings she may experience with our law but your eye should be on her and your council in her ear if you see opportunity for error on her part." Arthur said quietly. "I understand completely sir." Jerome replied. "No…, you don't. Not completely Jerome but I will not put you in jeopardy with an explanation. Just be cautious with her and mindful and most certainly make no advances to her of a romantic nature or allow any other servant to entertain a like thought. Lastly, she must never be alone with Count Andrew." Arthur added and Jerome nodded. "My task is well defined even if the situation is unclear at present." Jerome said moving closer to Arthur. "You know you can confide in me without fear regardless of legal circumstance." Jerome whispered. "We shall avoid problems with legal circumstances by limiting the number of informed parties. You are a valued and trusted servant Jerome but I implore you to let me execute my plan in solitude for the time being." Arthur whispered back to him. "Give Lady Karen notice in front of me that she is to be my charge as it will make my task simpler." Jerome suggested and Arthur called her over. "Give heed to Jerome's council as you would mine for I have made you his charge. He will be a valued ally to you in assisting in Count Andrew's recovery as well as avoiding other problems. Show Jerome the crate and take it to the Maiden Melisa's quarters. I trust you will know how to set it in motion once it's set up." Arthur said smiling at her but she dropped her head looking at the ground. "I was hoping you had informed Jerome of my desire to go directly to my charge." Karen said sadly and Arthur reached out and gently lifted her chin with his hand. "Your pleasant demeanor is more preferable to us all. Remember your promise to me Lady Karen and I will escort you to Count Andrew's bed personally to inspect his injuries once you have finished my task. You and I will speak to him privately as I dine with him." Arthur said and her eyes brightened before she bowed and followed Jerome back to the carriage.

"What crate do you presume to store in my quarters and what nonsense do you propose that I will allow you to dine without me tonight." Melisa asked smiling up at Arthur from his side as they walked toward the castle.

"The crate is merely a small present I purchased in Sandista for you. Let them set it up while I quench my thirst at the bar and I will show it to you." Arthur said and he leaned down and kissed her again briefly as they walked. "And what of dinner; could I not be an ally in your quest and dine with you and Count Andrew?" Melisa whispered excitedly. "I am certain Count Andrew will reveal himself more fully in your absence and I have already shared with you more of this secret than I am comfortable with. It is not my desire to diminish your happiness but I must speak at length with Count Andrew in private." Arthur said pleading with her. "I have never been this happy to see you return from a trip. I wonder why that is." She giggled hugging Arthur. "We shall stroll under the moon in the garden after you dine with Count Andrew." Melisa suggested softly and passionately. "I fear I shall find focus on conversation with my friend difficult as I contemplate our rendezvous but I will make haste to join you." Arthur whispered softly and stole one more kiss in the hallway. Arthur was filled with nervous excitement. Maid Melisa had made her announcement in the council chambers per their custom and Arthur must accept in the dining hall. Usually, all the suitors would be waiting there until word came from the council as to The Maiden to the Crown's selection but since Count Arthur had been away on business, they had postponed until this hour. As they walked in, the entire crowd burst into cheers and applause greeting them. Arthur picked up Maiden Melisa and set her atop the first table and climbed up with her to stand and face the crowd there as it was the custom to do so. The table had purposely been left vacant awaiting their arrival. The hall got very quiet waiting for Count Arthur to speak. "I have heard the demand of The Maiden Melisa of Archemeius and it is my honor to submit to her desire and become her husband!" Arthur shouted and the crowd erupted with cheers and applause as the couple embraced and kissed atop the table.

"What day have you chosen?" One of the women in the crowd called to them and Arthur raised his hands above his head to quiet them again. It was the custom that the groom selected by a Maiden of the Crown would set the wedding day. By law he must accept but he could choose the length of their engagement. He could choose 7 days, 7 weeks, 7 cycles of the moon or 7 years if he chose to show his displeasure at his selection but he could not refuse. "Even though I am known as a man of abounding patience," Arthur began and many of the crowd chuckled, "The wedding between The Maiden Melisa of Archemeius and Count Arthur of Archemeius will be conducted in the Grand Hall in Castle Archemeius at this hour on the seventh DAY!" Arthur shouted and the crowd erupted into boisterous applause and cheering again as he kissed Maid Melisa passionately once again. After a brief period, Arthur stepped down off the table and assisted Maid Melisa into a chair at the table and many of their friends joined them to share a toast in celebration. Councilman Trent was the senior and did most of the speaking and told most of the jokes. They were expected to dine and drink for a while with their friends as it was the tradition. All four of Maid Melisa's servants were present and drinking with them equally but neither of Count Arthur's were present and Councilman Trent took notice. "What sort of man does not allow his faithful servants to celebrate his wedding announcement with him?" the councilman asked jovially. "A sorry sort I fear as I have tasked them heavily since the accident involving my dear friend Count Andrew. One is on task while the other sleeps." Arthur replied and Councilman Trent frowned at him showing his displeasure. "I would have gladly provided relief for your servants with my own so they could attend had you but ask." Councilman Trent responded. "And what hour…, nay what moment have I had to make such a request of you?" Arthur replied. "But I have taken steps to relieve their burden as well as the courts." Arthur added quickly. "Today I escorted a skilled medic from Sandista who has intimate knowledge of Count Andrew's medical history to assist in his recovery and relieve both my servants and the castle staff." Arthur concluded hoping for no further inquiry from the councilman. "An excellent decision and what of his servants, did they accompany you too?" The councilman asked. "I encouraged his first servant to remain at Sandista and see to Crimson for assuredly Count Andrew will be more concerned for him than his own recovery," Arthur joked and the party laughed, "but I did bring his second servant." He added quickly and stood up and took Maid Melisa's hand. "I beg your forgiveness and plead with you to dine and drink in our honor but the day has been long. It is my desire to dine with my injured friend and retire but I still must present the gift I purchased for my betrothed in Sandista in her quarters." Arthur said turning his glass up to finish it as servants began to fill their table with plates of hot food. "Certainly you jest. Why did you not present it to her here amongst your friends?" The councilman asked and Arthur chuckled. "You would have more pity on my servants and think my decision wise viewing the height and girth of my gift. Come with us and see what treasure I have secured." Arthur said encouraging the party to follow them. "My chair has grown too comfortable and the food is hot. I will view your gift at the Maiden Melisa's leisure tomorrow." The councilman replied as Arthur assumed he would. "I shall leave three of my servants to keep you company in my absence. Rest assured I will return shortly to dine and drink with you Councilman Trent." Melisa said bending to kiss his cheek before she took Arthur's arm and they disappeared into the hallway.

Jerome had never been inside The Maiden Melisa's quarters before. He had secured the assistance of another male servant in the yard to help him carry the crate to her room. It was extremely heavy and they both leaned against it outside her door panting from the strain of carrying it up the stairs to the fourth floor. Lady Karen was carrying her own bags to the sixth floor and Jerome had instructed her to wait for him in the hallway there. "If you have patience enough Lord Morton, I must show Lady Karen to her quarters and then we shall return to assemble this monstrosity in Maiden Melisa's room shortly." Jerome said breathing heavily. "I shall guard it until you return." Morton replied with a chuckle as he sat down beside the crate. Jerome exhaled heavily. "I shall hasten to return quickly. If you could remove it from the crate, it will save us time." He said walking to the stairs. Lady Karen was panting equally as hard sitting beside her bags as Jerome approached her on the sixth floor. He unlocked the second door passed the stairway and picked up one of her bags. "This will be your quarters during your stay. Leave your things inside the door and I will make adequate time for you to get settled after we assemble Count Arthur's gift." He said sitting her bag on the bed. Lady Karen surveyed the room quickly as she brought the other bag in. It was small but appeared very cozy with a great glass window facing the ocean and the city to the south that opened like a door to a narrow balcony. The bed was large for the room with small tables on each side against the west wall. A chair sat in front of a vanity against the east wall and there was a torch mounted on the north wall beside the door. "This is very nice. Where is my charges room?" Karen asked smiling at Jerome. He frowned at her fearing she might bolt from the room and run to Count Andrew's side. "Count Arthur will reveal that to you but it is close. Let us make haste to finish our task." Jerome said motioning to the stairway from her door. "The privacy room is the first door next to the stairs." He added closing her door. "Do I not get a key to my own room?" Karen asked. "You do not. There is a bolt inside while you occupy the room. You need not fear thieves on this floor or any other in Castle Archemeius. I maintain the key for emergency entrance should a guest fail to respond when called upon." Jerome replied as they hurried down the stairs. Lord Morton had removed the top and sides of the crate by the time they got back to him and Jerome opened the door to Maid Melisa room.

The three of them were stunned by the beauty of Maid Melisa's room. It was actually two rooms and an archway had been cut out between them where light cloth curtains hung separating her sitting room from her bed chambers. There was a giant rug made from the skin of a bear on the floor in the sitting room bracketed by couches with small tables on either side of them. Gorgeous multicolored curtains with gold fringe covered the glass window on the south wall that faced the city and the ocean. There was a low sitting chest of drawers on the east wall extending from the north wall to the south wall and it was covered by an assortment of figurines which were obviously gifts. "We could set it on that chest and she could see it from her bed chamber." Lady Karen suggested. "What is that thing?" Jerome asked puzzled by its shape and weight and Karen opened the back to reveal the mechanism to him. "It is a timepiece. Her servants will have to dump the sand in the bottom bucket back in the top once a day. We should do that now before we move it." Karen suggested pulling out the bottom bucket. As she filled the top bucket, the mechanism started to turn and she returned the bucket to its position once she emptied it and closed the door. "What time do you suppose it to be?" Karen asked opening the glass door on the front of the timepiece. "To my closest certainty, I would suppose it to be a little past the 7th hour as the sun has just retired." Jerome replied as she arranged the arrows on the face of the timepiece before closing the glass door. She went to the east wall and made a place for it on the low chest. "Set it here for us to examine." Karen suggested and Jerome and Michael lifted it onto the chest leaving room to get to the door in the back. Karen ran to the bed against the west wall in the other room through the archway. "I think it is the perfect spot to be viewed from all vantage points in her quarters. She will know the time of day before she rises." Karen said smiling as she sat on the bed. "I will remove the crate and take my leave of you if your task is complete." Lord Morton said. "That is truly a magnificent gift." He added as he stacked the parts of the crate to remove them. "I appreciate your assistance as I am certain I could not have completed this task without it." Jerome said smiling at Morton. "What say you to dinner? I think you owe me that much." Morton suggested with a grin. "I will do you one better. "You will join me at Count Arthur's announcement feast once I am relieved of my duties." Jerome replied. "What hour will that be?" Morton asked. "Shortly I presume. Look for me in the dining hall." Jerome replied as Morton departed with his arms full of the parts to the crate.

Lord Morton met Count Arthur and Maid Melisa followed by her servant as he went down the stairs. He knew better than to reveal the nature of Count Arthur's gift. "Are they prepared for us Lord Morton?" Arthur asked recognizing the crate. "They are and may I say, I have never seen a more magnificent gift." Morton replied grinning at Maid Melisa. "My curiosity burns. What is this thing that inspires such admiration?" Melisa giggled excitedly. "Did they cover it for a proper reveal?" Arthur asked him. "I fear not. You shall see it upon entering the room." Morton replied and Arthur pulled out his handkerchief. "Oh that will not do. I will see the surprise in your eyes with a proper reveal." Arthur chuckled and tied the handkerchief over Melisa's eyes. Lady Erin was a mere 16 years and had just become Maid Melisa's servant. On Count Arthur's suggestion, she took Melisa's other arm and they led her into the room. As they entered, Lady Karen and Lord Jerome stood on either side of the timepiece wiping it down with lightly oiled rags to make the wood shine. "Oh my God, that is truly magnificent." Lady Erin gasped as they entered. "Are you certain Lady Erin? You don't think it too gaudy?" Arthur asked teasing Melisa. "Certainly not sir, it matches the other furniture perfectly." Erin replied and Melisa reached for the blindfold but Arthur stopped her playfully. "What say you Lord Jerome? Should I present or venture on a new shopping tour?" Arthur chuckled. "I will take it if she finds offense with it." Jerome replied. "I beg you cease my torture and let me see it." Melisa pleaded giggling and Arthur moved behind her and removed the handkerchief slowly. "It is a timepiece. Certainly the first one in Archemeius and probably the first one in the kingdom." Arthur whispered. Melisa was completely stunned by not only it's beauty but by the prestige Arthur had bestowed upon her with such a magnificent gift. "This should be displayed in the great hall or the council chambers. It is far too eloquent for my chambers." She gasped admiring it. "I'm certain one will find its way to each of those rooms and more in short order but this one is for my fiancé." Arthur said wrapping his arms around her from the back as she stood mesmerized by the timepiece. Jerome pulled Lady Erin to show her and describe to her the requirements of the timepiece as Maid Melisa stood paralyzed for a long moment just admiring her gift. She turned in Arthur's arms and looked into his dark brown eyes. "I find no words adequate to express my appreciation for such a gift." She whispered softly. "Then pray give me a kiss for it too exceeds the limitation of mere words when passing from your lips to mine." Arthur said breathlessly. He kissed her passionately and Melisa seemed to melt against him. He inhaled the sweet scent of her perfume into his nostrils and his legs became weak feeling her tender body press full against him. Jerome cleared his throat and began to escort the two other servants from Maid Melisa's quarters. "Do not flee from my presence Lord Jerome for neither my tasks nor yours are complete as of yet." Arthur said reluctantly pulling his mind from the erotic trance that threatened to engulf him. "I must dine with Count Andrew and spend my hour with him. "If it is well with Maid Melisa, I desire that you and Lady Erin escort Lady Karen to the kitchen and retrieve a plate to present to each of us in Count Andrew's room. We three shall dine in Count Andrew's room and discuss his recovery." Arthur said before pulling Jerome into Melisa's bed chambers away from the others. "Guard against any encounter with the council especially Councilman Trent. I will have council with Count Andrew before you return in an effort to shorten our deception. Do not share our secret with Lady Erin and give me time, maybe half the hour, to make adequate conversation with Count Andrew before you return. Once you have presented the meal, you and Lady Erin may retire." Arthur whispered and sighed heavily showing his concern. "I am your advocate." Jerome whispered and he took the other two servants and departed. "Please do not tempt me further but go quickly to show favor to Councilman Trent and dine with him. All will be revealed shortly if my conversation with Count Andrew goes well. I will not tarry to meet you in the garden after dinner." Arthur said kissing Melisa quickly before hurrying to Count Andrew's room.

Lord William rose to his feet as Arthur entered the room. "He sleeps like a dead man but Peter says that is what he needs." William reported as Arthur walked to his friend's bedside. "He was in a lot of pain today and I was contemplating waking him for dinner soon." William added and Arthur placed his hand on William's shoulder. "You have done more than your share. Go now and partake of my feast in the dining hall. Lord Jerome returns with a meal I shall share with Count Andrew. Speak with him as to the time for you to return after we dine." Arthur said softly and William nodded before he left. Arthur pulled the chair up close to the bed before he took his friends hand. He was uncertain where to touch him to avoid causing him pain. Count Andrew, awaken now for I have come to dine with you!" Arthur said in a loud voice as he squeezed his hand. Andrew's eyes flashed open and he grimaced before he focused on Arthur and smiled. "Thank you. I was having the most horrific dream. The fattest, ugliest woman you could imagine was sitting on my chest preparing to have her way with me." Andrew chuckled and then grimaced from the pain in his chest. "It's nice to see you retain your sense of humor." Arthur replied smiling at him. Andrew pushed at the bed with both hands and Arthur could see the struggle of intense pain as he tried to sit up. "Help me right myself so I can at least feed myself if we are to dine." Andrew pleaded and Arthur stood and lifted under Andrew's armpits until he was sitting. "Your pain diminishes slowly." Arthur acknowledged. "Yes but it does diminish. Peter's potions keep the pain subdued. You have brought no food." Andrew said surveying the room. "My servants come quickly with a feast but I wanted to take council with you prior to dining." Arthur said seriously. "Council...., what formal conversation is required between us?" Andrew said with a softer chuckle to avoid the pain. "There was no serious problem with Crimson? I heard you took him back to Sandista at first light." Andrew said feeling more comfortable sitting upright. "There is no cause for worry with regard to Crimson. He is in good hands with Lord Kenneth I am sure." Arthur replied. "I had deep council with Lord Kenneth and he revealed your secret regarding your second servant Lady Karen after a troublesome encounter I had with her upon revelation of your accident. I have heard her account of your long relationship with her and it wounds me that you have never so much as revealed her name to me." Arthur said almost in a whisper. Arthur could tell the pain in Count Andrew's face was not emanating from his bruised chest. "Do you love this woman Count Andrew because her confession to me revealed her devotion to you was complete and without deception?" Arthur said revealing his deep concern. He could tell Count Andrew was hesitant to respond to his inquiries. "Regardless of your feelings for her, your conduct as related to me regarding this affair, does not reflect the nature of the man I call my dearest friend." Arthur added pleading with Andrew. "The man I know would terminate the affair or marry her but would never draw out this circumstance that is so obviously painful to all concerned who have a heart for justice." Arthur suggested defiantly. "You **are** my dearest friend but you do not know my circumstances completely." Andrew confessed. "I do love Lady Karen deeply but I cannot in good conscience marry her." Andrew added with extreme sadness. "Shall I make her a wife and a widow in the same year?" Andrew whispered remorsefully. "What evil lurks in your future that surpasses her shame in the current circumstance and makes you so certain of your death?" Arthur asked seeing that Andrew was sincere in his belief of imminent danger for him. Andrew stared deeply into

Arthur's eyes and his tremendous struggle for words was very evident to Arthur. "I love you as a brother and it is for this reason I beg you not to press me further lest I reveal my secret and place you also in mortal jeopardy." Andrew replied his demeanor tortured to the brink of tears. Arthur fell to one knee at Andrew's side clutching his hand. "What trial have I avoided to place the value of my life above yours? If our friendship is as you say, take me as your ally and we shall find remedy to this situation together." Arthur begged him fervently. "I see in your eyes that you will not relent regardless of how passionately I plead with you. Rise up before we are discovered and required to make explanation for your position." Andrew said nervously and Arthur returned to the chair and waited for Andrew's reply. "First let me reveal the dire nature of my secret so that you may choose wisely whether to involve yourself further as my ally or not." Andrew sighed heavily hoping to deter his friend from joining him. "I already have a select few allies across the kingdom that keep this secret and risk their freedom as well as their fortunes for this endeavor. My next task draws near and no man has ever survived who has attempted it. My chance for success is small and if we are discovered we will all most certainly be thrown into chains for life. Any dreams you have of a life with The Maiden Melisa will most assuredly be crushed permanently if you are ally to my cause. My council to you and my sincere desire is that you cease your inquiries, forget this conversation and leave me to my fate in solitude." Andrew concluded his face contorted in the agony of his physical pain and concern for his friend. Arthur was unnerved by Count Andrew's confession. "Let us take pause as I reflect and contemplate." Arthur said pulling his pipe from his belt and sitting back to light it in his chair. Arthur had his suspicions as to the nature of Arthur's secret task. He knew of only one task that involved messengers that no man had attempted and survived. Crimson neared maturity and the date of his release. Arthur tried to remain calm as he contemplated Count Andrew's revelation. Surely Count Andrew's secret scheme could not be what he surmised it to be. "I know you Andrew. You must have some assurance that you will succeed or you would not attempt it." Arthur said longing for more information. "My allies are well educated men and our plan is years in the making and complicated but there are many opportunities for failure." Andrew replied reservedly and Arthur searched his own mind for another explanation but he was almost certain he knew what Count Andrew and his allies were planning. Arthur knew also that Count Andrew was not a fool or inclined to impetuous excursions into frivolous adventures. He was curious as to what knowledge he possessed that made him believe he could be successful. The danger and the threat of imprisonment weighed heavily on Arthur's mind. Long ago, it had been written into the law that the term of imprisonment would be life for anyone who even attempted to formulate a plan to ride a dragon after it had matured. So many riders had been lost that it was deemed an impossibility and was banned by law to stem the loss of lives. Even if Count Andrew was successful it would take a decree from the Great Father and the supreme council to save them from imprisonment for life. "You're not going to reveal your allies to me unless I join you are you?" Arthur asked and Count Andrew shook his head no. "I implore you to stifle your curiosity and leave this to us as your involvement will not increase our chance of success and you would risk entirely too much." Andrew replied his voice pleading with Arthur. "This is truly a perilous decision and I will belay my involvement and contemplate my verdict with more thought over time but I desire to return to the original issue." Arthur said puffing on his pipe and handing it to Count Andrew who took it from him feeling somewhat relieved. "I fear your involvement in this secret endeavor has clouded your judgment in regards to Lady Karen. If you fail, will she grieve less as your concubine at your death? Whose support will she have?" Arthur reasoned with him. "I have made uncommon mention of her in my will." Andrew said nervously. "And what will the community say of her after you are gone. Do you hear yourself Count Andrew but have no concern. What group will abide with a wealthy whore?" Arthur said indignantly. "Guard your tongue when you speak of her for I shall not be in this bed for long." Andrew replied angrily. "The title is not one I choose for her. It is a name you doom her to for the rest of her life if you allow the situation to continue un-remedied." Arthur suggested with less animosity. "I have spoken with her in length and find her worthy of much better than you present to her for a future whether you live or die." Arthur said more softly. "I see no recourse save you marry her immediately." Arthur said smiling at his friend and Andrew took a long puff off of the pipe. There was a knock at the door and Arthur stood. "Give us an additional moment Lord Jerome." He said in a loud voice. "This is good council with regard to Lady Karen." Andrew replied shaking his head. Count Andrew had considered all these things and more but hearing his dear friend articulate them out loud, set his course in plain view. "Rest assured that I will remedy our situation as soon as I am able to return to Sandista." Andrew said with a smile handing the pipe back to Count Arthur. "I have my own secret to reveal to you my friend as I have made it my mission to increase your happiness and that of my new friend." Arthur said grinning at him. "Jerome, bring in our dinner!" He said in a loud voice. "Do not speak in haste at my surprise for Maiden Melisa's servant is not party to it." Arthur whispered to Count Andrew.

Lady Karen could barely contain herself as she waited with Lord Kenneth and Lady Erin outside the door. Her hands were full balancing her own plate of food in one hand and the cup and pitcher of wine in the other. When they heard Count Arthur invite them in, she followed both of them as Lord Jerome had suggested. There was no denying the surprise and joy on Count Andrew's face as their eyes met. Lord Jerome had counseled her against doing anything that would reveal the situation to Lady Erin so she waited silently as Lady Erin presented her plate to Count Andrew and then the cup. Jerome gave his plate to Count Arthur who sat down immediately and then he moved a chair closer to the bed and motioned for her to sit down. Lady Karen set her plate on the table beside the bed and began to pour the wine. "I have completed my duties for the day and desire to retire sir." Jerome said to Count Arthur. "Then do so with my blessing and my appreciation Jerome and escort Lady Erin back to her charge. Count Andrew and I will discuss his recovery with his medic over dinner and I suspect Lord William will return in an hour or so. If you are still in the dining hall after I have dined, I will share good tidings with you over a beer but do not think it a requirement and make plans that serve your own desires." Arthur said smiling at Jerome as Lady Karen filled his glass. "I will be most anxious to share drink with you. Look for me when you return to the dining hall." Jerome replied before he escorted Lady Erin from the room.

Lady Karen was trembling from the struggle to contain her emotion and looked to Count Arthur unsure of her next step. "Why do you hesitate? Am I not your friend an ally in this deception? Greet your charge with a kiss if that is your desire." Count Arthur laughed loudly feeling relieved his plan was coming to fruition and they had been successful so far. Karen sat quickly on the bed beside Count Andrew cautious not to upset his plate. "Shall I be so bold as to succumb to my desire for you in front of your dear friend?" Karen whispered softly and seductively drawing her face closer to Andrews. "Cease torturing me Lady Karen for you shall know shortly what a dear friend he is." Andrew whispered pulling her lips to his and kissing her passionately. Arthur giggled watching them as he ate his meal. "If your desire is for more than a kiss I can retire but I fear you will find his wound a barrier to much more than a kiss." Arthur chuckled drinking his wine. Lady Karen giggled at his comment until she noticed the grimace on Count Andrew's face. "Take heed to avoid my chest for it is very sensitive to even as soft and desirable a touch as yours." Andrew said softly trying to smile at her. She untied the nightshirt that covered him and pushed it aside gasping in shock as she viewed the dark purple and red color that dominated his chest. "What evil has befallen you that results in such a wound." Lady Karen asked grimacing at the horrific sight. "My own stupidity I fear." Count Andrew replied. "I had Crimson at top speed and I gave too much resign to his nature upon landing and no concern to the consequences of relinquishing control to him and this is the price I paid. Crimson had no problem landing at that speed but I was crushed against his back when he stopped so abruptly." Andrew reported. "What council have you had with Lord Peter the medic here concerning this injury?" Lady Karen asked examining his ribs closely. "He keeps the pain subdued with this potion and has declared the wound superficial but warns me the ribs may be broken and require a long recovery exceeding three weeks. He warns me to remain immobile and not attempt to stand or leave the bed for seven days. He waits for the harsh color to diminish to make that determination about my ribs." Andrew replied revealing his fear of extended treatment. "Show me what range of motion you have in your arms without pain." Lady Karen demanded sitting upright beside him. Count Andrew raised his arms over his head and grimaced as he touched them together. Lady Karen reached up and pushed his arms back to his side smiling confidently. "I agree with all Lord Peter's recommendations but there is no fracture or break in your ribs. You would not be able to raise you arms without a fracture revealing its presence with severe pain." Lady Karen said confidently and she reached to touch the purple skin of his chest before sniffing her fingers. "Why is there no ointment on you wound?" She questioned and Andrew looked puzzled. "Lord Peter said there was an ointment that he would apply on the third day." Andrew replied and Karen frowned at him. "He wants only to avoid your wrath as it will be painful to apply but he wastes three days of its benefit to you and prolongs your recovery. I will secure this ointment and apply it after dinner." Karen said and leaned forward to kiss Andrew again briefly as he frowned. She went back to her chair and began to eat looking up at Count Andrew who was contemplating how much pain the application of the ointment was going to cause him. "Eat quickly so I will not have cause to delay my task." Karen said rushing through her own meal and Andrew looked to Arthur as he began to eat. "I thought you said you brought her here to relieve my pain." Andrew chuckled and Arthur did too. "I brought her here to aide in your recovery. I surmise she has her own professional opinion with regard to accomplishing that task." Arthur laughed. Lady Karen finished her plate first and stood and kissed Andrew quickly. "I go to retrieve the ointment from my bag in my room and will return shortly." She said smiling at Count Andrew before she turned and departed the room. Count Arthur looked at Count Andrew and threw up his hands. "You hesitate still!" Arthur said impatiently. "My mind fails to provide adequate words for this task." Andrew replied dejectedly and Arthur laughed. "It requires but two. MARRY ME! And she will respond with one I am certain. YES." Arthur laughed heartily. "Leave the words to me Arthur!" Andrew responded curtly. "Well make haste, I weary of waiting to bear witness to her joy and yours." Arthur replied before Lady Karen came back into the room.

"Before you begin this torture with the ointment, I desire to speak with you to make certain you understand our situation." Count Andrew said softly patting the bed signaling Lady Karen to sit beside him. Lady Karen did not like his demeanor or the expression on his face. "Archemeius is not the liberal forward thinking city that Sandista is. Count Arthur put himself and all his friends at great risk bringing you here." Andrew said nervously and Lady Karen became nervous fearing he was about to tell her she could not stay. "I have tried to express my gratitude to Count Arthur and I am aware of the difference in our laws. I swear I will do nothing to put your friend in jeopardy." She pleaded taking Count Andrew's hand. "I am certain you would do nothing purposefully to reveal this deception but I am equally certain the gossip about us will begin and will grow the longer you stay." Andrew said sadly and Lady Karen bowed her head certain of what Count Andrew would say next. "Hand me my belt." Andrew said pointing to the hanging stand that held his clothes. Lady Karen reluctantly retrieved the belt and handed it to Count Andrew. "I beg you. Do not send me to Sandista to wait your recovery for I have no confidant or friend there." Karen said feeling the pressure build behind her eyes. Count Andrew placed his entire money pouch in her hands. "Then you should hasten to secure a confidant here in Archemeius that will agree to be your bridesmaid and witness to our marriage." Andrew said smiling at Lady Karen as he lifted her chin. "As my wife we will have no gossip…, if only you will accept my proposal." He whispered softly. "What trick is this that you play with my heart after all these years?" Karen replied not believing she was hearing him correctly. "I pray you will not torment me with a jest regarding this topic for my soul cannot bear it." She whimpered tearfully. "It was my council with Count Arthur that brought our circumstance to full understanding in my mind. I regret greatly the time that has passed since first I should have asked you and beg your forgiveness. I assure you…., my proposal is sincere." Andrew said and Karen sat stunned and frozen at the realization of her greatest desire. She looked back at Count Arthur to verify Count Andrew's sincerity. "Why do you delay in your answering him? Is this not why I escorted you here?" Arthur smiled at her and she turned her eyes back to Count Andrew. "Idos save me, my joy is complete. I will be your wife Count Andrew." She whispered and Andrew pulled her lips to his kissing them passionately through the flood of her tears. Arthur stood sharing their joy and waited for them to break their embrace. It was a long moment and he began to feel awkward and chuckled when they finally parted. "As is our custom it is my desire to be first to kiss my dear friends betrothed and congratulate you both." He smiled and Lady Karen's excitement overwhelmed her. She stood and threw her arms around Count Arthur's neck. "I pray you will not take offense and share this intimacy with me for it is you that makes possible the fulfillment of my most ultimate desire." Karen whispered kissing him full on the lips with intense enthusiasm. Count Arthur was caught by surprise and momentarily savored her passionate kiss before embarrassment began to fill his face. As she pulled her lips from Arthur's; Count Andrew viewed his friend's reddened face and laughed out loud. "I fear my dear friend is not accustomed to such a brash display of gratitude. You better stifle your enthusiasm lest he faint." Count Andrew chuckled and Lady Karen giggled seeing Arthur's embarrassment but held tight to his side. "Certainly Count Arthur knows the true meaning of my sweet kiss and has accepted it as my friend as payment without insult." Lady Karen giggled hugging him playfully and Arthur relaxed chuckling with them. "Neither you nor I know what price I would pay should **my** betrothed witness such a kiss between us. We already tested her patience with the scene at the carriage. I fear one shall have to last the remainder of our friendship but I shall remember it." Count Arthur teased his friend Andrew who snickered at him. "Return to my side woman lest this scoundrel continue to pursue you." Andrew laughed and then paused catching the words of his friend. "**Your** betrothed, did Maid Melisa make her announcement?" Andrew asked as Lady Karen returned to his side. "She did and I accepted less than an hour ago." Arthur replied and Andrew was stunned. "Why, in heavens name, do you tarry with me. Join your betrothed and your friends at your feast immediately. I demand it." Count Andrew said emphatically. "I await Lord William's return and I shall." Arthur replied. "I have no need of Lord William. Depart…., Make haste to your betrothed." Andrew said. "I cannot. Shall we stumble this close to our goal and violate the law. You know I cannot leave her unaccompanied with you until we make legal your circumstance." Arthur said regretfully and Count Andrew took Lady Karen's hand. "My body and soul burn to embrace you intimately and you know I cannot abide this trouble on my dear friend and his staff. He is right. Make haste tomorrow as the sun rises. Secure Lady Erin as your confidant and bridesmaid or whomever you choose and shop for whatever you desire to wear for you and her. We are not under restriction of law as Count Arthur and the Maiden Melisa are with regard to the length of our engagement. Invite who you will but I desire that we marry before the sun sets tomorrow. Count Arthur can secure someone from the council to wed us. Councilman Trent has authority to act in matters such as this." Andrew concluded and kissed Lady Karen again. "I fear Councilman Trent may take offense at our deception to this point. I had further plans to this end." Count Arthur warned but Andrew shook his head no. "He will not. You would be surprised what secrets Councilman Trent and I have shared previous. Seek audience with him early tomorrow for me and I will speak of it with him." Andrew said looking at Arthur sternly. "We may have other matters to discuss with him if I know your heart and your intentions and judge your mind correctly." Count Andrew said and Arthur could see the definitive change in his demeanor and understood. They talked more casually and Lady Karen applied the ointment to Count Andrew's chest as they waited for Lord William. The pain during application was tremendous and Count Andrew struggled through it resisting the temptation to cry out as Lady Karen massaged the ointment in as tenderly as she could. He begged her for the potion Lord Peter had left and she gave him a double dose which he chased with wine. By the time Lord William arrived, Count Andrew was ready to retire. Count Arthur turned Lord William's back to the bed to converse with him as Lady Karen kissed Andrew goodnight. "I am certain he will be asleep soon. I have expressed my appreciation to Lord Jerome and desire to share the same with you Lord William. I am aware of the time and energy this task has demanded and I shall reimburse you handsomely for your extraordinary efforts." Arthur said sincerely. "I assumed you would do so but know that I would serve you with equal devotion without concern for coin." William replied smiling at Count Arthur. He turned to take a seat beside Count Andrew's bed as Count

Arthur escorted Lady Karen from the room. Arthur smiled considering Lord William's comment because he knew it wasn't quite true. Unlike Lord Jerome, Lord William weighed the value of each task in coins and Count Arthur was mindful of that difference. It did not trouble him that Lord William was ambitious but he did trust Lord Jerome more highly because of his priorities and his loyalty. They were both very good servants and it would be imperative that he reward them equally and well.

Arthur could see the excitement on Lady Karen's face and he could tell she was by no means ready to retire as they walked to her room. She spoke rapidly stringing her thoughts together quickly. "Does Count Andrew have more friends that could stand up with him tomorrow beside you I mean obviously? I wouldn't presume that Maid Melisa would attend unless you think it suitable for me to invite her but she has four servants and I'm certain they would be excited to assist me…." Count Arthur raised his hands as if to surrender laughing. "Count Andrew has many acquaintances and friends so if you give Lord Jerome the number you require he will make invitation of the men. If you promise to contain yourself, I will escort you now and present you to the Maiden Melisa who will introduce her staff to you beyond Lady Erin whom you have already met." Arthur grinned at her enthusiasm. "I feared my task was not complete when you said yes and I will assist you as your friend until your vows are fulfilled." Arthur chuckled and Lady Karen moved to hug him again but Arthur caught her hands. "I pray you not to revisit that sweet kiss however innocent you perceive it to be as my support requires you to maintain a reserved demeanor." Arthur said sternly. "It is innocent but I will abstain from tempting you since you find my kiss so repulsive." Karen pouted playfully teasing Count Arthur. "You are puzzlement to me Lady Karen. Is our bond of friendship to be an honorable one?" He asked. "I assure you I desire nothing less." Karen replied surprised by his question. "Then try desperately to understand my meaning when I reply that I by no means find your kiss repulsive but revisiting it would not lead us on an honorable path in our relationship." Arthur sighed nervously but with conviction. Lady Karen found his statement oddly flattering and a little confusing. "Fear not Count Arthur. My affection to you is as an intimate friend and it is not my intension to seduce you beyond an honorable friendship. I implore your patience with me for I have had few friends, male or female, over the past few years save Count Andrew. Teach me what it means to be an honorable friend to the dearest friend of my fiancé." Karen whispered softly and sincerely. She stood in front of him with her hands behind her back. Arthur considered her past and the trials she surely had faced having been removed from her position and forced to become Count Andrew's concubine. He felt a soft spot in his heart for her knowing how she must have been treated by the other members of the court. He took her hand and walked to the stairs. "I shall strive to be your most intimate friend save Count Andrew if you will be but mindful of my concerns about public perception." Arthur said smiling at her compassionately as they walked down the stairs. Lady Karen stopped just prior to exiting the stairs at the dining room. "Give me your handkerchief so I can show my concern for public perception is equal to yours." Karen whispered and he handed it to her before she wiped his mouth. "The color of my lips is on yours and Maid Melisa would surely notice if no one else." She smiled handing him back the handkerchief. Count Arthur blushed and wiped his mouth again to make certain it was completely clean before proceeding to the table.

The Maiden Melisa sat conversing with Councilman Trent and both were feeling very relaxed and giddy as they drank with the rest of the party at the table. She had danced several turns on the dance floor with her father figure, Councilman Trent as well as some of the other male friends like Count Richard. Her eyes were a little glassy as they met Count Arthur's when he joined them. "There is my fiancé!" She said standing to greet him with a kiss. "I have danced with everyone else and now you must indulge me." She said tugging at his arm. "I will." Arthur laughed resisting her. "But first let me greet my friend Councilman Trent while you introduce our new friend to all your servants." He said and move to whisper in her ear. "I was successful in my task and she has need of bridesmaids for tomorrow night." He whispered and Melisa leaned back staring at Arthur with wide eyes pleasantly surprised before running to gather all her servants to her. "Who is your new friend? She is quite charming." Councilman Trent asked slurring his speech slightly and admiring Lady Karen. "I will make introduction in time but first tell me why you have come to my feast absent of your own wife." Count Arthur said filling a glass with beer. "I did no such thing. She is in the capable hands of your servant Jerome on the dance floor." He replied turning to point to them. "Now make haste to introduce me before they finish their dance and I am forced to conduct myself as a proper husband." Councilman Trent laughed heartily. "Give me your ear and I shall tell you my secret concerning her first." Arthur whispered and Councilman Trent's eyes reflected his curiosity as he leaned forward. That fine beautiful woman is Lady Karen. She is Count Andrew's fiancé and a medic of substantial skill." Arthur stated and Councilman

Trent sat back looking disappointed. "What bland sort of secret is that?" He chastised Count Arthur frowning. "Oh that's not the secret. You must first become my ally if I am to reveal my secret to you." Arthur laughed and Councilman Trent looked at him intrigued. "Is it a scheme that falls short of legal boundaries?" He whispered. "Of course it does. What need would I have for secrecy if it was not?" Arthur laughed and he leaned forward again. "Count me as ally and tell me your secret." He whispered. "Count Andrew wishes to have audience with you concerning her after 1st light tomorrow. His desire is that you perform the wedding ceremony." Arthur whispered. "He only made his proposal to her less than an hour ago. I had to sneak her past a prominent Councilman so he could do so." Arthur concluded and sat back watching Councilman Trent digest his message. His eyes finally lit up into a smile and he laughed. "You mean me!" He laughed heartily again. "You deceived me earlier saying you brought his second servant with the medic." He snickered. "I did not lie for she is both a medic and his second servant." Arthur replied and went on to explain their complete circumstance and history to the councilman. "That is a juicy secret and requires a remedy. I will meet with Count Andrew for breakfast and provide him a remedy." Councilman Trent replied smiling. "Now make the introduction quickly." He added. "I pray you do not be offended by her. She is affectionate to a fault with her allies sometimes." Arthur smiled. "I should be so lucky." Councilman Trent laughed as Arthur waved to beckon her to them.

Lady Karen looked up from her conversation with Maiden Melisa and her servants and saw Count Arthur signaling her. He was seated with a very distinguished looking gentleman who smiled at her warmly. "Are there any ugly men in Archemeius?" She giggled smiling back at the gentleman. "Yes but they are deceiving because they are ugly on the inside." Lady Erin joked and they all laughed before Karen excused herself and walked to Count Arthur. Councilman Trent reached and pulled another chair between himself and Count Arthur motioning for her to sit. "I have made another ally in our quest to fulfill your ultimate desire. Councilman Trent I present to you Count Andrew's betrothed Lady Karen." Arthur said quietly and Councilman Trent kissed her hand. Karen felt the nervousness rise inside her. This was the very man she had been warned to avoid by Lord Jerome. What she said to him could bring all her dreams crashing around her shoulders. "I am not surprised Count Andrew hides you in Sandista and keeps you a secret from us all." Councilman Trent sighed heavily. Count Arthur told me of your deception to this point and I was intrigued." He added. "I beg your forgiveness for my friend Count Arthur and myself but our desire was to avoid violating any law in Archemeius." Karen replied. "Rest assured you are forgiven and fear no reprisal from the law as I am your ally and will be your eternal advocate. I shall secure the garden terrace for your ceremony tomorrow night." Councilman Trent responded smiling at her. Lady Karen's nervousness dissipated slowly looking into his eyes replaced by overwhelming excitement and she searched Count Arthur for her proper response. "I assure you Councilman Trent will not take offense at whatever level of affection you deem fit to show him." Arthur chuckled and Karen leaned forward and pressed her lips to Councilman Trent's delivering a short but sweet kiss to the elder statesman. A pang of fire rushed through Arthur's and he froze with panic and quickly surveyed the room to see who else witnessed their kiss. He reached and jerked her arm staring astonished into her eyes. "My apologies Councilman Trent, I warned you she was affectionate to a fault at times." Arthur said quickly still staring at Lady Karen in disbelief. Karen sensed Count Arthur's panic but said nothing fearful of stirring his wrath and further escalating the situation. "I see no reason for your apology Count Arthur. How could I take offense at such a charming innocent demonstration of gratitude? You flatter an aging statesman adding sweet pleasure to friendship I hope will last a lifetime." Councilman Trent replied. "What gentle words you share with me. I too long to nourish an intimate friendship with you that will last a lifetime." Karen said as Count Arthur pulled her to her feet and escorted her back to Maid Melisa. Arthur stopped halfway and spun her to face him gripping one arm. "What possessed you to kiss him in that manner?" Arthur whispered angrily. "Was it not an innocent kiss no more than I shared with you and did you not encourage me saying he would not take offense and he did not?" Karen replied thoroughly confused. "I did not imagine you would press your lips to his after mere moments of acquaintance having just met him. Do you have no perception of proper behavior between friends?" Arthur snapped at her and Karen's eyes filled with water. "I do not…, I looked to you…., and your eyes and words indicated a kiss was proper and as it seemed pleasurable to me I delivered a sweet innocent kiss which he accepted and took no offense to." Karen whimpered full of self doubt. Arthur sighed heavily shaking his head. "I tire of trying to make explanation with you. Seek companionship with your bridesmaids and kiss no one else save Count Andrew come running down the stairs and tempt you." Arthur said pointing her toward Melisa's servants but she turned back to him. "I fear my naivety taints our friendship and you will find favor with me no more. Why is your anger so intense if jealousy has no part in it?" Karen asked wiping the tear from her eye. "Truly Lady Karen…, a <u>child</u> raised in Archemeius would understand a kiss was not appropriate. I find it difficult, even knowing your history, and the fact you were raised in Sandista, you could not reason thusly." Arthur said feeling frustrated because he **had** felt the pang of jealousy but he would not share that with Karen. She bit her lip before responding to him. "So now you think I feign naivety to work some deception? To what end would I play this game and risk achieving my ultimate pleasure which is to be Count Andrew's wife." Karen pleaded with him. Arthur rubbed his forehead wishing to end this conversation. "I regret my anger. I beg you accept my apology quickly. I know your intentions are innocent and honorable and I am clumsy in these matters. I shall not turn you away by no means but seek counsel with Maid Melisa or her servants in this matter for you have misinterpreted my council at no fault of your own and I am at a loss for remedy." Arthur sighed looking sympathetically into her eyes. "So a kiss as we part company to demonstrate our continued friendship is not proper even though I desire it?" Lady Karen asked sincerely and Arthur shook his head and chuckled softly. "No Lady Karen it is not….., even though I desire it also." Count Arthur admitted. "See…, I can learn if you are patient with me and speak softly." Karen smiled and turned to go join the other women at the table and Arthur returned to join Councilman Trent whose wife Camille now leaned heavily on his arm. She was obviously exhausted from dancing with Lord Jerome who sat on her other side.

Camille is a handsome woman of equal age to her husband. She was not a Royal but took pride in her chosen profession as mother to Councilman Trent's children. She and Councilman Trent had been married a long time and they had 6 children but you would never suspect it to see Camille. Jerome flirted with her mercilessly and playfully to the amusement of their party as everyone knew she was completely devoted to the Councilman and her family. Councilman Trent often referred to Jerome jokingly as her "boyfriend" because Jerome would do all those things with her he detested like dancing. Count Arthur could tell the three of them were well intoxicated as he joined them. "I am angry with your boyfriend." Trent said sipping his beer as Arthur sat down. "If you would but dance with me, you would have no occasion to be jealous of Lord Jerome." Camille laughed messing up the councilman's hair with her hand playfully. "I have no inclination to jealousy with your dance partner inviting him eagerly to perform that task for me. It is rather his party to the deception Count

Arthur has revealed to me that stirs my anger toward him as he has played me the fool once again." Trent said feigning pain in his chest playfully as the party chuckled at him. "I had no part in deceiving you." Jerome replied rebuking him with his denial. "Did you not tell me Count Arthur returned with a medic and Count Andrew's second servant enticing me to assume there were three in his party? Now being sourly wounded by this deceit, I must perform their wedding tomorrow night." Trent chastised Jerome humorously and Jerome's eyes grew big looking to Count Arthur. "So Count Andrew made proposal to Lady Karen?" Jerome asked exceedingly surprised. "Ohhh.., who appears more foolish in this deception now?" Trent laughed. "You knew not that this was the end to which Count Arthur ran his secret game. My honor is redeemed and my anger with you extinguished." Trent laughed heartily. "Lady Karen is putting her wedding party together as we speak. I presume she will have four bridesmaids for which we require four of Count Andrew's friends to escort them as groomsmen." Arthur said. "I will stand with Count Andrew as will Lord William and Count Richard who is close friend and ally to him." Jerome replied scratching his head. "We need but a fourth." He added contemplating. "What of Lord Kenneth of Sandista his servant. I know he and Count Andrew grew and trained together being lifelong friends. If he leaves early he will arrive in time." Arthur suggested. "Jerome…, find Count Richard and tell him he has my permission to fly to Sandista at his earliest convenience to invite Lord Kenneth." Arthur said as he opened his belt and pulled out several coins. "As I do not know Lord Kenneth's finances, give him this to purchase a fast carriage." Arthur said handing Jerome the coins as he departed and Camille frowned at him.

"I hope you have a replacement in mind for my dance partner." Camille pouted playfully at Arthur. "I shall make an effort to satisfy you in his absence but I'm certain he will not tarry to return to you Camille." Arthur smiled. "Take care to embrace no one on the dance floor before me." A familiar voice sounded behind Arthur and he turned to see Maid Melisa hovering over him on unsteady legs. Arthur stood to embrace her but she quickly took the chair next to Councilman Trent. "If you do I shall seduce Councilman Trent to embrace me on the dance floor and tease you with my affection for him." Melisa giggled flirting with the councilman playfully. "That scenario suits me." Camille laughed. "It is preferable to being left without a dance partner should you choose to dance with your fiancé." She added and they all chuckled save Trent who stood and took Camille's hand. "You press me hard and unfairly. Come dance with your husband." Trent said smiling at her. Camille had a stunned smile of disbelief as she rose and followed the councilman to the dance floor. "What possess you to so suddenly become my dance partner?" Camille asked as she was pleasantly surprised. Trent pulled her tight against him as they moved to the gentle music of the orchestra. "I am possessed, my wife, to whisper in your ear those words I fear I utter far too infrequently and do not wish to share with even my dearest friends but you alone. There are many gorgeous young women here. I pray you never forget I find your charms more irresistible than any Lady or Maiden I have had acquaintance with in my life." Trent whispered and kissed her neck passionately. "I am overwhelmed by your affection so early as the night is still young." Camille sighed. "Do you press me to retire early and retreat to the privacy of our bedchambers, for you know I will surrender to you at any hour?" Camille whispered in his ear. "I do not…., for I know what pleasure you derive from the innocent embrace you share with your other dance partners and my desire is for you to have your fill of dancing but I will make confession to you." Trent whispered softly. "I received a sweet innocent kiss from a most precious young lady earlier and I would make it known to you for two reasons. Firstly to reassure you should some ugly rumor take seed from it and grow to burn your ear but more importantly because of what I felt receiving it. There was no thought of seduction in her heart but only a sincere desire to share affection in gratitude with a friend. It made me mindful of how infrequently I demonstrate my affection and devotion to you with an innocent embrace or kiss of like nature. We kiss always to drive passion to its erotic conclusion. You deserve also that sweet innocent kiss that reveals I am proud and appreciative to be called your husband." Trent smiled and kissed Camille's lips tenderly. "You are my sweet hero. You have no idea how this tender message fuels my desire for you even more. "If it is pleasing to you, let us return to our friends for I have had my fill of dancing and my mind and my body now yearn to pursue other endeavors with you in privacy." Camille whispered breathlessly in Trent's ear.

The table was full again as Lord Jerome had returned with Count Richard. All of the servants of Maiden Melisa and Count Arthur save Lord William were there when Councilman Trent and Camille returned to the table. Lady Karen was at the center of the group conversing and laughing as if they had been friends forever. "King Thomas will return tomorrow. I imagine all the royals will be back in their home cities tomorrow sometime." Lady Erin said. "Do you think he and his wife will make their presence known at my ceremony?" Lady Karen asked. "I'm certain of it for his wife is Councilwoman Marion and she is most fond of weddings." Councilman Trent replied. Maid Melisa leaned back against Count Arthur as the orchestra began a new musical piece. "If this serenade is pleasing to you I would press you to embrace me on the dance floor now." Melisa said. "Do you have legs for it?" Arthur chuckled seeing she was well oiled by the wine. "I fear not but you shall surely catch me if I fall." Melisa giggled jumping to her feet and pulling at Arthur's arm. The serenade was quick and Melisa felt revived and excited as the air rushed over her face and her hair swirled around her head spinning around the dance floor with Count Arthur. "Your step is light and sure for the amount of wine you have consumed." Arthur said impressed by her agility on the floor as he chuckled. "I feel superbly embraced by the wine and my dance partner." Melisa laughed as he twirled her around on the floor again. Arthur enjoyed dancing with Melisa too but he was certain the one serenade would do her in and when it did not he was surprised. Melisa kept Arthur on the dance floor a long time but as the third serenade concluded Arthur pleaded with her and they returned to the table. "We have been awaiting your return." Lady Karen said excitedly and Arthur noticed she was also succumbing to the wine. "Count Richard presses me for a kiss from the bride to be but in the absence of the groom or his best man it would not be proper. I would grant him this kiss now since you are my fiancé's best man as long as you are willing." Lady Karen smiled excitedly as Count Richard beamed anticipating Count Arthurs' approval. Arthur was troubled briefly by the protective feeling he had for Lady Karen but he knew the tradition and smiled at Count Richard. "Be aware that my eyes are on you in the absence of Count Andrew and make no mistake…, I will hold you to the same standard as he." Arthur laughed. Now the kiss is supposed to represent the bride's last embrace of frivolity before she married so it was expected to be passionate but playful. It was usually one of the many games that were played during the dinner and celebration the night prior to the wedding so Arthur could find no fault in it. Count Richard pulled her head to his shoulder and made a dramatic production of brushing her hair from her face and positioning her just right before he wet his lips and pressed them to Lady Karen's. Count Richard kissed her passionately embracing her back and Arthur could see him explore the curve of her side with his hand. Lady Karen responded with equal passion returning his kiss and his embrace. Arthur was on the verge of articulating a protest when Count Richard abruptly and dramatically released her. He could not avoid the expression on Lady Karen's face as she was momentarily transfixed on

Count Richard's eyes after he removed his lips from hers for a brief matter of seconds. She took longer to recover from the kiss than Count Richard who laughed and accepted the jovial ribbing and jesting of the rest of the party. Then suddenly Lady Karen snapped back to reality and began to laugh with the party. "Count Richard has played this game before!" Maid Melisa laughed. "I see why so many young girls show him favor as I would press for another was I not faithfully betrothed." Lady Karen giggled taking another sip from her wine. "Is this the end of those that call my fiancé friend and wish to congratulate me thusly?" Lady Karen laughed looking around the room. "I shall not tire of this game quickly if Count Richard's skill is shared by more of his friends." She added and the party laughed hysterically. "What say you Count Arthur? Will you bear witness as I indulge Lady Karen and share intimate congratulation with her?" Lord Jerome laughed moving to Lady Karen's side. "Be of like mind as Count Richard for my eye is on you also." Arthur replied in the spirit of the celebration and Jerome pulled her to her feet to embrace and kiss her playfully but with equal dramatic passion as Count Richard had. The party roared with laughter and jesting as they broke their embrace and Lord Jerome allowed her to return to her chair. Lady Karen fanned her face giggling with Lady Erin. "All my fiancés friends are equally skilled at this game." She laughed. "I fear we must call an end to this game of frivolity as I have promised my betrothed a walk under the moonlight." Arthur said as he stood and held out his hand to Maid Melisa. "Lady Erin, I pray you will insure Lady Karen returns to her quarters ALONE once she has had her fill of dancing and celebrating." Arthur laughed. Lady Ann was one of Maid Melisa's other servants and she stood as Maid Melisa took Count Arthur's hand knowing custom required she have a companion. "Shall I escort you also?" She whispered to Maid Melisa. "At a distance." Melisa replied smiling at Lady Ann.

They walked in silence out to the garden as Lady Ann trailed several steps behind them. "The moon is as full as my heart." Melisa said as they stepped onto the short grass that surrounded a fountain. "Your demeanor has been varied and a puzzlement to me. Are you satisfied with our course and the events of the day?" Melisa asked softly. "I am exceedingly relieved having struggled though the tasks of this long day to get to this hour with you in the garden." Arthur replied and stopped under a large willow tree and kissed her. The air was thick and the smell of the roses in the garden teased their senses on the soft breeze that blew in from the ocean. Melisa melted against Arthur feeling intoxicated by his kiss as well as the wine.

"Everyone looks to you Arthur because you never hesitate to share your time and energy with your friends. I fear you are pressed to exhaustion with your love for them." Melisa said as they sat down at the edge of one of the pools on the short stone wall that retained the water. She kicked off her shoes and swung her legs over the barrier to dip her feet in the cool water pulling her gown above her knees. Arthur sat with his back to the pool and leaned back cupping the water in one hand and pouring it over her exposed knee. Melisa leaned against his shoulder enjoying the sensation as Arthur dispensed the cool water over her legs again and again. Arthur watched the gentle flow of the water as it streamed over her knee and followed the curve of her calf back into the pool. "How I long to embrace these gentle limbs." Arthur whispered as she kissed his neck. "Why do you hesitate? Do you not perceive that I entice you with them and long desperately to the same end?" Melisa whispered breathlessly. Arthur dipped his hand again in the cool water and began to spread it over her calves washing gently both her legs up even beyond her knees and onto her thighs as she kissed his neck not resisting him. He looked over her shoulder at Lady Ann standing several paces from them with her back to them now. "What magic do you spin that this cool water fuels such fire in me?" Melisa whispered her breath becoming more labored at his throat. "Do you cast a spell on the water or on me?" She added moving ever so slightly pulling the gown up to reveal more of her legs to his caress. Arthur poured the water upon her legs gently smoothing his wet embrace even higher exploring the tender skin with his trembling fingers. "Your Lady pays no mind to us. I fear taking undue advantage of your intoxicated demeanor." Arthur whispered gazing at Lady Ann again who still had her back to them. "And I fear you will not." Melissa sighed softly. "Which of our friends would show us rebuke finding you in my bed chambers tonight?" Melisa whispered brazenly her breath heavy in his ear as her hand covered his. "I encourage you. Seek the flower of my passion and see how it weeps for your intimate embrace." Melisa sighed kissing his neck as she guided his hand. Arthur gave control of his hand to her and began to explore the sweet spot she led him to and his own passion brought weakness to his knees. Melisa moaned pleasurably responding to his soft intimate caress. "What would you ask of me for my passion exceeds reason caressing your sweet flower this way?" Arthur whispered as his whole body now trembled and ached for her. Melisa pulled his hand back up and held it to her breast with both hands and kissed it. "Shall we remain and tease at affection or will you give me but a moment alone in my quarters to dismiss my Lady Ann. Come slowly to my quarters but do not tarry too long. If the door be unlocked enter and lock it behind you and if it is locked retreat for a while for she is still with me." Melisa panted breathlessly excited staring into Arthur's eyes. "Go quickly and beg Lady Ann to retire and I will follow in due course." Arthur replied kissing her briefly but passionately before she gathered her shoes and ran to Lady Ann's side. Count Arthur waited beside the pool watching them disappear back into the castle before he rose and walked slowly in the same direction. He was unsure of the wisdom of the path they were choosing but his desire for her was too great. He was fearful they would be discovered and bring shame to them both but he would guard to insure no one saw him following a safe distance behind.

Count Arthur felt like a thief, hiding in the shadows of the staircase below the third floor. He was praying Lady Ann would retire to her quarters after leaving The Maiden Melisa's room. If not, he would have to pretend he was on route to his own quarters on the sixth floor. He heard the light footsteps above him and watched as she disappeared into her own room before quietly climbing the stairs to the fourth floor. His heart was racing as he moved quickly to Melisa's door and opened it slipping in quickly and locking it behind him. He exhaled deeply a sigh of relief that he was certain no one had seen him. It would be just as treacherous sneaking out. The room was completely dark save the light from the full moon shining in through the window in Melisa's bed chamber and illuminated very little in her parlor. He could hear the familiar rush of water into a tub coming from her bed chamber. "Melisa!" He whispered. "I am here Count Arthur." Melisa whispered back from the bed chamber. "What game do you play? Light a candle lest I fall for I scarcely see the doorway." Arthur giggled. "The moon fills my bedchamber and it's all we require for our romantic interlude. Find your way to my side and see if you find it as appealing as I do." She whispered and Arthur pushed the curtains aside stepping through the archway into her bedchamber. The pale light of the moon did fill her bedchamber. Her bath was directly in front of the window and Melisa was leaning over it. She wore a lighter gown now much thinner and the light of the moon shown through it and revealed the curves of her form completely to Arthur. "You are like a vision to me in the moonlight and nothing is hidden from my eyes in your nightgown. Shall I draw near or watch you bath from afar and drink in your beauty with my eyes for a time." Arthur whispered leaning against her bedpost. "The bath is for you Count Arthur. I would prefer you not taint the scent of my bedcovers with that of your dragon but allow me only to breathe in that aroma of our passion together when I awake in the morning and have only my pillow to embrace." Melisa whispered turning to reveal two glasses of wine. Arthur stepped closer and took the glass from her sipping it still admiring the inviting curves revealed by the moonlight. "Be quick to undress and I will treat you with a gentle sponge and strive diligently to remove the smell of your dragon from every curve of your frame." Melisa smiled seductively and Arthur placed his glass on a small table beside the bath and sat on the edge of the tub to remove his boots. He dipped his hand in the tub to gage the temperature of the water before her removed his shirt. "If it is not pleasing to you I can raise the temperature." Melisa said pouring a small amount of scented oil into the bath. "To reveal myself to you in cold water could be an embarrassment to me. It is fine." Arthur chuckled and Melisa blushed and giggled. "What fragrance is this that you seek to bath me in?" Arthur asked as he turned his back to her to remove his britches. "It is a manly scent that I find pleasing. Why do you lengthen my curiosity and turn away from me at the moment of your revealing to me?" Melisa giggled teasing him. You can cover yourself with a towel being shy but I will have full viewing of you before the bath is complete." She laughed softly still teasing him. "I am shy." Arthur chuckled picking up the small towel and covering himself as he stepped into the bath. The water was very warm and Arthur felt at a disadvantage. "I am aware of your training as Maiden to the Crown and your experience with the eunuchs. I fear you may find me less appealing in my comparison with them." Arthur replied honestly sitting on the towel to secure it in place before he picked up the wine glass again. Melisa knelt down behind him taking a cup and pouring the water over his head and his hair. She said nothing for a moment, contemplating what he had said. "Does my time at Castle Paternus taint your desire for me? Would you not prefer a virgin as most men?" Melisa asked and Arthur tilted his head to look in her eyes. He knew she had heard crass men violate custom and tradition and insult her by insinuating that her training in the romantic arts made her somehow less appealing as a bride. It was a ridiculous position for what man would prefer uneducated over educated. Most men agreed that Maidens of the Crown were by far the most desirable women in the kingdom. "That sentiment is uttered by men who know in their hearts they have no chance to wed a Maiden to the Crown. I have no regrets at not being your first Melisa. I desire only to be your last." Arthur whispered and Melisa kissed him. She poured the scented liquid soap on his head and worked it into lather before rinsing it out. Then she took the large soft sponge and began to wash him.

Arthur closed his eyes and relaxed enjoying the sensation of the sponge against his skin. Melisa knew Arthur was a strong man but she never considered how finely sculptured his muscles looked to her now in the pale light of the moon. She washed his arms and neck and torso down to the towel before she moved to the side of the tub and washed his feet and his legs back up to the towel. "I will have this towel now Arthur so I can complete my task." Melisa whispered and Arthur opened his eyes. "Quench your curiosity and remove the towel if you must. I pray you not share your disappointment with me." Arthur whispered and Melisa slowly pulled the towel away. Even with all the wine she had drunk, Melisa felt her face burn red and she could not pull her eyes from Arthur's eyes. She began to wash him first with the sponge and then dropping it to explore him with a trembling hand. "I know not what cause you have to fear comparison with any man." Melisa panted her heart pounding in her breast as she leaned forward and pressed her lips to his. "I beg you dry off quickly and join me in my bed for my desire for you consumes me." Melisa gasped breathlessly as she rose and turned stepping quickly to the bed as she pulled the nightgown over her head and climbed into it pulling the bedcovers over her bare frame. She watched Arthur rise from the tub and find a large towel to begin patting against his skin. His massive muscles rippled in the moonlight as he dried his long brown hair and Melisa wondered if the wine made his naked form seem so powerful and enticing to her now. "My hair will not dry this quickly. We should have belayed the washing of it." Arthur said frustrated as he shook his head and attacked it with the towel. "Give no further concern for your hair. I will suffer the dampness of your hair. Come let it fall across my breasts as you lay with me. It will be my head on the pillow and my passion will dry your hair." Melisa whispered holding up the bedcovers beckoning and enticing him. Arthur dropped the towel and moved to her on the bed and she spread out below him and pulled the bedcovers over them. "Your skin feels so hot." Arthur whispered pulling her body against his as his hands explored her curves in a way he had only dreamed of before now. He kissed her neck and Melisa breathed softly into his ear. "I have waited too long for your intimate embrace and my fire burns deep inside me for you. I pray you search it out quickly and extinguish it lest I be consumed." Melisa whispered breathing more urgently into his ear. Arthur pressed his lips to hers and pushed forward and they became entangled in an erotic embrace. The moonlight sparkled in Melisa's eyes as Arthur made love to her slowly and deliberately. Melisa surrendered to him completely and let her body respond naturally to his power. Unimagined pleasure began to surge through Melisa's veins. She searched deep into Arthur's eyes to understand this feeling of physical passion she had never experienced or expected. It grew inside her like an erotic balloon as their passion rose together and their blissful union gained momentum until the balloon burst in zealous explosions of waves of ecstasy and emotion. It was beyond what Melisa had experienced previously or expected. They lay together for a long while after their passion had subsided in silence and Arthur continued to caress and kiss her softly unable to find words to express his extreme joy. Their bond was complete at last and Arthur desired only to remain and embrace her until sleep overcame them both but he knew he could not be discovered in Melisa's quarters. Melisa pulled his hand to her bare breast. "Do you feel my heart beating now for you Arthur?" Melisa whispered. "I fear it shall never beat the same after the experience of this night." She sighed kissing his neck. "You see the moon filling your bedchamber with its light. If it be in my power, I would stop the moon in its journey and live eternally in this sweet embrace." Arthur whispered and kissed her tenderly. "The future promises a thousand nights such as this and I will not tempt you to tarry save you make an intimate vow with me now." Melisa whispered fixing her eyes on his. "I could not deny you prior to this night. I surely will make certain any request from you now." Arthur replied. "Then I beg you; make this your promise. Whether it be moonlight or sunlight that bathes our souls you will not delay in granting me a rendezvous to revisit this pleasure with you quickly as my desire for you shall be tenfold having memory of this night." Melisa concluded pressing her bare frame against his softly and kissing him passionately. Arthur felt his passion for her rising up from inside him again and was certain he should make his retreat quickly. "I will gladly make this vow to you but you must allow me a hasty though reluctant escape as my desire for you swells inside me and I fear the moment draws close that I will be unable and unwilling to depart from this sweet intimate embrace." Arthur sighed heavily avoiding her lips again because of his fear. "I will not." Melisa giggled in his ear caressing him seductively. "I confess to you now that I have tricked you and belayed your departure with this sweet conversation to this end. I have secretly awaited the return of your passion. The moon has sufficient journey yet to complete that you shall find time to satisfy my lust for you and still retreat to your quarters before the sun can make its discovery of you." Melisa whispered moving over Arthur and trapping him against her pillow. Arthur did not resist her but only smiled and surrendered to her passionate assault. He made love to Melisa a second time and their time entangled in the intimate embrace was increased but the result of their passion was equal in intensity at its conclusion to the erotic explosion they experienced the first time. Now Melisa knew to a certainty that it was her deep love for Arthur that made their experience together so completely dwarf her other romantic encounters at Castle Paternus.

Arthur stared out at the diminishing moon searching for the first glimmer of the sun's rays that he was certain were soon to come. He looked back at Melisa, nervously now, her head resting on his arm in gentle slumber. Slowly, he pulled himself from the bed allowing her head to fall gently to the pillow. He was relieved she did not awaken and dressed quickly carrying his boots to the door. He unlocked it and opened it cautiously peering into the hallway. It was empty but he was aware that there were servants awake at all hours to maintain the watch. He regretted his inability to relock her door from the outside. He ran to the stairway and strained to hear any sound that might reveal anyone who might discover him. He made his way quietly up to the sixth floor and breathed a sigh of relief seeing it too was empty. He heard footsteps coming up the stairs behind him and made a mad dash for his quarters slipping inside and closing the door behind him. Again he exhaled deeply and dramatically as he undressed and found his nightshirt before falling face first onto his bed.

Arthur awoke finding Jerome's hand on his shoulder. "Awaken Count Arthur for the sun is high." Jerome said and Arthur rolled opening his eyes. "I knocked and when you did not answer I tried the door and it was unlocked. Is it your desire to sleep the day away?" Jerome smiled. "I do not sleep well. I am exhausted by the events of yesterday and too much wine. I pray you suffer me sleep until the noon meal and awaken me at that fine hour." Arthur pleaded before rolling back to bury his face in his pillow. "As you wish; Lady Karen awaits my return to present her to Count Andrew with his breakfast. They will be disappointed you will not join them." Jerome said. "Make my apologies and leave me to sound slumber." Arthur pleaded again his face still buried in his pillow. Jerome backed out the door closing it before turning to face Lady Karen and Lady Erin. "He is not well and desires to sleep until midday." Jerome said and Lady Karen looked sorely disappointed. "I beg you allow me to make personal my plea for his company at breakfast with us for I wish to demonstrate my friendship to him? I have brought his breakfast also." Lady Karen replied. "I fear you would better demonstrate your friendship by suffering his absence this morning. Do you have no pity on him having exhausted himself in the execution of tasks meant only to increase your happiness over the entirety of yesterday? You being the source of his exhaustion; cease tormenting him now for a time and give him slumber." Jerome said insistently. Karen let her shoulders fall and turned to Lady Erin. "It appears we shall have no need for your plate. Please accept quickly my apology for your troubles so early Lady Erin." Karen said dejectedly. "It is of no consequence. I will leave you to breakfast with your fiancé." Lady Erin said turning to walk away. Councilman Trent exited the staircase and seeing Lady Erin carrying the plate stopped her. "What is this? Is someone ill that they refuse breakfast from our fine kitchen? Councilman Trent asked. "Count Arthur chooses slumber over dining with Count Andrew and his betrothed." Erin replied. "His loss is my gain and fits my desire nicely for my intent was to breakfast with Count Andrew. I will relieve you of this plate save you have no other plans for it." Trent said smiling at Lady Erin and she handed him the plate and bowed before continuing down the stairs.

A PLAN FOR CRIMSON

Count Andrew sat upright in his bed reading from the scroll of the events of yesterday. It was only the second day since his accident but Andrew's patience at being forced to remain in bed was wearing thin. His pain was still severe and he knew it was important to follow Lord Peter's advice but he grew tired of the bed. The door opened to his room and Andrew looked up rolling the scroll back up and setting it on the table as his friends entered. Lady Karen smiled at him excitedly and set the plate of hot food in his lap and kissed him. "You seem in good spirits this morning." Councilman Trent said waiting for Jerome to move a chair for him closer to the bed. "A demonstration of how looks can be deceiving." Andrew replied smiling reservedly. "This mattress feels more like a bed of stone with each passing day." He added with a chuckle. "Where is Count Arthur? I assumed he would be partner to this party." Andrew asked. "Count Arthur sends his apologies but the events of yesterday have left him exhausted and begged me to suffer him sleep until midday." Jerome reported as he filled Count Andrew's cup with coffee from a pitcher. Arthur was puzzled. He had been certain, knowing Arthur's mind and heart that his curiosity would bring him into allegiance with his secret venture and he wanted to share council on the matter with him and Councilman Trent. He wondered if his absence now meant Arthur was choosing to abstain from involvement. "Are you certain it is fatigue that keeps Count Arthur from breakfasting with us?" Andrew asked solemnly and Jerome chuckled. "I assure you. Count Arthur sleeps as a dead man." He laughed jovially.

"He avoided his bedchamber drinking and dancing until late last night. I know not what hour he retired but I am certain it was very late and he suffers the consequence now." Jerome smiled and they all chuckled. "I'm certain he will recover in sufficient time to take the noon meal with you." Jerome added. "Let us turn our attention to your wedding." Councilman Trent said. "My wife is overjoyed at her invitation and makes plans with the chief gardener at this very hour." Trent reported between healthy bites of sausage and eggs from his plate. "Maid Melisa's servants await me for a rendezvous with a dressmaker in the square." Lady Karen said excitedly as she too ate quickly. "What color shall our theme be?" She asked Andrew who smiled broadly. "Red, as an explosion, for our decision is sudden and will change our circumstances quickly and dramatically." Arthur chuckled as he peeled a bright yellow banana to consume. "Red it shall be." She replied and washed the last of her breakfast down with the coffee before she rose. "I pray you forgive my haste but I have many tasks to perform in preparation for tonight. Lord Peter has agreed to apply the ointment soon after your breakfast." Lady Karen said enthusiastically before she leaned over Andrew and kissed him. "Lord Peter?" Andrew protested. "And when shall you return to tend my wound?" Andrew asked dejected. "I shall not." Karen laughed. "When next you see me you shall make your proposal publicly in the garden and I shall answer you with a pleasing response." She giggled as she departed the room quickly.

"These women will turn this ceremony into a grand event quickly that I fear exceeds my coin pouch." Count Andrew sighed feigning contempt jovially. "The garden is my gift to you but I fear you are right seeing her depart to purchase a dress for herself and all four of Maid Melisa's servants." Trent chuckled and Andrew's eyes grew large in surprise. "Four? What choice of friends do I have here to escort four bridesmaids?" Andrew gasped looking to Jerome. "Fear not. Count Richard flew at first light to invite Lord Kenneth whom I am certain will arrive by fast carriage in time and Lord William and I will finish the party." Jerome replied and Andrew retrieved a pen and paper from the nightstand after setting his empty plate on it. As he wrote a letter quickly he looked to Jerome. "My God, I assumed she shopped for two dresses not five!" Andrew sighed. "Make haste to catch up to Lady Karen. I know not what sum of coin is in my pouch that I gave her previously. As you are surely known by the banker, discover what cost will cover whatever she desires for this event and present her and this promissory note to him to obtain the balance." Andrew said handing Jerome the letter. Jerome turned to leave and Andrew stopped him. "I would not suffer you follow these women aimlessly as they shop but instead give her an appointed time sufficient for her to complete her task and meet with you at the bank. Once she knows the cost, you can secure the balance so she can return and make final payment at the store. Please remind her I am not King of Sandista but merely a poor dragon rider." Andrew concluded with a heavy sigh and Jerome chuckled departing from them.

Councilman Trent moved his chair even closer to Count Andrew after Jerome left the room. "I perceive a double purpose at you tasking of Lord Jerome. Do you seek private council with me now?" Trent asked and Andrew took his pipe from the nightstand to light it. There was a grimace on his face as the pain of his wound still troubled him. "You are correct dear friend." Andrew replied. "I suspect further that you have secured Count Arthur as our ally fearing you will not heal in sufficient time to perform your part in our task." Trent whispered. "You are neither entirely accurate nor are you entirely wrong. I will still perform my task but I did give hint to Count Arthur not revealing our secret entirely." Andrew replied and Trent's expression turned sour. "God man! To what end would you involve him so if not as your replacement in the task?" Trent asked nervously. "You have shown faith in me and my judgment. I beg you trust me and him also if he chooses to join us. He may yet decline but I perceive his curiosity as to the nature of my secret will draw him to us." Andrew whispered. "This is unwise. We have avoided discovery to this point by limiting the number of our allies in this secret. His inclusion will not increase our chance of success." Trent said unflinchingly. "I assure you it will, both on the ground and in front of high council when he bears witness to the righteousness of our success!" Andrew whispered insistently. Councilman Trent folded his arms over his chest glaring at Andrew. "Count Arthur will not betray us. You know him as well as I. I beg you take council with us at midday and consider it?" Count Andrew pleaded. Councilman Trent gritted his teeth and leaned closer still to Andrew. "It would appear I have no choice as you have set my course for me. I warn you desperately Count Andrew. Add no other allies to our cause save Arthur. You place the cause and all our very lives in jeopardy in doing so." Councilman Trent said angrily as he stood and departed the room.

Arthur rolled in his bed uncomfortably. The sun shined brightly through his window and it was hot in his room. He was sweating profusely as he sat up and swung his legs off the bed. He still felt tired but the smell of Maid Melisa's perfume filled his nostrils and he realized it covered him as he remembered last night with her. He stripped off the wet nightshirt and moved to his tub setting the plug and turning the valve to run cold water into it as he climbed in. He argued with himself over the wisdom of his choice to make that secret rendezvous with her as he washed her scent from his body with the cool water. It was refreshing and he realized how hungry he was as he pulled the plug and exited the tub to dry and get dressed. He vowed to find time to cut his long brown hair today as he ran his brush through it. It was on his shoulders already and he had procrastinated long enough. "I see you return to the land of the living." A familiar voice sounded behind him and he turned to see Jerome holding a plate at his door. "I could sleep no more. This room grows too hot at midday." Arthur said wearily. "I pray you took pity on me and there is coffee in that pitcher." Arthur sighed waving him in as he sat down in a chair. "Your prayer is answered." Jerome chuckled handing him a cup before filling it from the pitcher. "I beg you not to get comfortable for you have a fervent request from Count Andrew to join him and Councilman Trent to dine in his room." Jerome advised him still holding the plate. Arthur was concerned as he remembered the private conversation he and Count Andrew had yesterday. Is it possible Councilman Trent was one of his allies? "What do you know of the nature of this fervent request?" Arthur asked and Jerome shrugged his shoulders. "Nothing; I assume it stems from their conversation of the wedding they discussed at breakfast." Jerome replied. "Councilman Trent has been his guest all morning?" Arthur asked with surprise. "No he left after breakfast and I saw him with his wife in the garden but he has returned and they await you eagerly in Count Andrew's room. Arthur stood and took the plate from Jerome as headed for Count Andrew's room. "Take this hour to yourself for I will take council with them privately." Arthur said as Jerome opened the door for him before he departed.

"I feared that you were ill when you failed to join us for breakfast." Andrew said as Arthur locked the door and moved toward a chair. "My apologies to you both but I did not sleep well last night. The events of the day followed by too much wine and dance gave deterrence to slumber but I am revived now." Arthur replied smiling as he sat down. Councilman Trent looked very troubled and had not touched his meal. He stared at Arthur nervously waiting for him to speak. "I have never known you to contemplate a meal so long. Have you lost your appetite Councilman?" Arthur asked casually. "I do not have stomach for food at present." Trent replied. "You must have been fairly certain of my response to invite your ally to hear it." Arthur said looking to Andrew. He did not know for certain so he tested Andrew. "I could see your answer in your eyes as we parted company." Andrew replied with equal reserve and Arthur smiled at him setting the full plate on the floor before looking to Councilman Trent. "I am very hungry but I will not eat until I have convinced you that you need have no fear of my betrayal of you or your cause." Arthur said sincerely. "What cause do you assume I undertake with Count Andrew?" Trent asked nervously because Andrew had told him he did not reveal the secret to Arthur. "I suspect that Count Andrew has an alternate plan to releasing Crimson on his appointed day and you and he and others have developed a plan that shows promise of success. I know you must have some degree of certainty because I know Count Andrew is no fool and would not attempt it without surety." Arthur said confidently. "I fear discovery far beyond my fear of failure." Trent said emphatically. "The combined efforts of my allies over the last several years, makes this attempt much different as you shall see should you ally with us and we reveal the secret completely." Trent said enthusiastically. "What assurance can I give you that will extinguish your doubt and return your appetite for I truly desire to become ally to this cause without reservation." Arthur said eagerly. Councilman Trent looked to Count Andrew. "What role will he play?" Trent asked. "Give him full knowledge of our plan and let him chose what role to play." Andrew suggested and Trent took the first bite of his meal and smiled.

"These are our allies; I, Count Andrew, Countess Rebecca of Gardinia who is Headmaster for the School of the Dragon Riders, Chancellor Winston from the Academy of Medical Arts and now you. We have an encampment north of Willow Lake at the foot of the mountains deep in the forest. You would not find it save one of us show you its location. We have never taken a carriage or cart but journey there by single horse by ground. The forest is so thick, the smoke from our fires dissipates before it reaches the sky and the light from them cannot be seen from the air or the ground even after dark. Count Andrew will take you to it once he recovers. My part has been primarily research. We've always known a dragon does not develop the glands that produce fire until puberty. Only then do the protective scales form on each side of his mouth. There are two separate glands, one on the right and one on the left. They produce two separate liquids and when the dragon discharges them and they combine in front of him they combust and burn so he appears to breathe fire. For the first week after they form they are tender like a babies teeth and each time he expels the fluids that combust and burn in front of his face it is extremely painful and unnerving to the young dragon. This is what I have discovered. This is why a pubescent dragon shoots fire with reckless abandon at everything during that first week. He's in severe pain as he learns to adapt to his new skills. After the first week the glands become callused and the pain dissipates. If a rider could survive that pubescent week, he could continue to ride the dragon in maturity. This is where Countess Rebecca and Chancellor Winston come in to play their part. Chancellor Winston is a senior medical instructor at the Academy of Medical Arts in Red Oak. A Dragon's scales are highly resistant to fire but as Countess Rebecca found they are not just dead scales. Dead dragon scales will burn. The dragon's blood keeps them healthy. Countess Rebecca and Chancellor Winston working together have designed a new vest and britches made of living dragon scale. Their first suit had a pouch that supplied dragon blood to the scales but it failed because the blood dried up after a time. Chancellor Winston developed a needle and syringe that drains blood from the dragon into the suit and then back to the dragon again. He inserts the two needles under the scales on the dragon's neck. When coupled with the gloves, boots and helmet, a dragon can no more burn his rider than he can himself." Councilman Trent concluded and sat back in his chair. "You must see this armor to believe it." Andrew added excitedly. "When I put this armor on and attach the tubes to Crimson, I can feel his blood flowing all around me as if I am truly a part of him." Andrew said enthusiastically. Arthur could see the emotion in Andrew's face. "You said the suit needs blood to survive. How does it live now?" Arthur asked. "Ingenious architecture and design. The scales require very little blood. Countess Rebecca constructed a closet which contains a pouch and a pump that keep blood flowing through the suit. She takes a dragon there every week to refresh the pouch with new blood." Trent replied. "We have constructed an iron pen to restrain Crimson while we make or attempt. I am hopeful it will not take a full week to find success." Andrew said confidently. "The suit is resistant to fire but you are not Count Andrew. How much heat can you stand? How do you propose to mount Crimson if he is determined to burn you?" Arthur asked. "It is true. If he is persistent in his attack, Crimson will burn me. The cage is designed so I will approach him from the rear and gain control of his head early. I will have to be cautious and mindful of his intent." Andrew replied. "I will be your second and assist you on the ground. No one knows the mind and heart of a dragon better than you and I." Arthur said excited by the prospect. "That is Countess Rebecca's position. You forget she has more experience than you or I and has been ally to this cause from conception." Andrew replied showing respect to Countess Rebecca. "Then I shall be her servant and servant to all of the party also for I will contribute to your success and insure your safety or follow you into chains as fate will dictate." Arthur stated and shook Councilman Trent's hand and then Count Andrews. "King Thomas is back in the castle and is accepting audiences at his throne. I will greet him and share news of his time at Castle Paternus." Councilman Trent said and he departed.

CHAPTER 5

VISITORS BEFORE THE WEDDING

Countess Regina stared at her image in the mirror as she brushed her long brown hair. Lady Sharon had been assigned to her as her servant by the city council at Red Oak. She was two years older than Regina but had been thrilled by her selection and knew it was a great honor and presented great opportunities to her. Servants were all well paid by the council and it was a much sought after title. It was a time consuming occupation but she found nothing that difficult about it. She had to be up before Countess Regina to wake her at first light and be available to perform whatever task for her during the day but Countess Regina usually allowed her to retire shortly before dinner. She had a room in the servant's quarters that she shared with three other girls but she spent a lot of her time at her home in town with her family. "Do you have a boyfriend Lady Sharon?" Regina asked casually. "I have friends who are boys but share no romantic interest with any of them at present but I have shared a romantic relationship with a young man previously." Sharon admitted smiling at Regina. "Do you have a suitor?" Sharon asked. "I do." Regina replied looking frustrated. "And it is puzzlement to me for I am uncertain how to react to him." Regina admitted. "His attentiveness to me when we are together creates awkwardness in me and I feel uncomfortable. I feel unnaturally aware of everyone else's perception of us when we are in a group." Regina said still standing in front of the mirror but watching Lady Sharon in it now. "Who is this boy? Does he live here at the castle?" Sharon asked and Regina giggled. "It would irritate him to hear himself referred to as boy even though he is the same age as you are. He is Count Cameron of Mesina. I dined with him after the ceremony at Castle Mesina and I became aware of his affection toward me." Regina sighed heavily and moved to sit next to Lady Sharon on the bed. "Do you think me too young to have a suitor because my father does?" Regina asked looking confused and Lady Sharon smiled. "Your father will think you too young at 27. I perceive that it would suit your purpose if I said yes but I cannot make that judgment of you. Make account of your dinner with him to me." Sharon asked her. "It was a servant at the castle, Lady Marian that first brought it to my attention that he fancied me. When he begged me stay and dine with him I did so mainly because I was hungry but curiosity at the change in our relationship also bade me stay. I fancy Count Cameron. He is handsome and strong and everything else you would think desirable in a suitor but now that his affection has been revealed to me, I feel awkward in his presence. His demeanor reveals his awkwardness also. He spoke of the beauty of the garden in Mesina and begged me walk with him after we dined but that was torture. It was dark. There was nothing to see. We just kept walking and spoke sparingly holding hands which became clammy and damp. He made no advance beyond holding my hand. It was not pleasurable for either of us and I took my leave and returned to Red Oak shortly after its completion." Regina said frustrated and Sharon leaned closer. "Would you shy from his kiss?" Sharon smiled whispering and Regina blushed. "I have curiosity to that end should he be so bold and would have suffered him a kiss to satisfy it but he made no advance." Regina whispered showing her frustration again. "I would counsel you to be patient with Count Cameron and also with yourself. Your awkwardness is not unnatural nor his though it feel so painfully I know. Make sport of it, be playful to the point of silliness and lighten the moment of your awkwardness. Treat him as friend patiently expecting nothing and he will make his advance in his own time." Sharon said confidently.

"I am glad the council selected you as my servant. It pleases me to have a confidant." Regina said rising off the bed. "I desire to go visit my parents after midday meal. You can go with me into the city and make your way to your own home if you wish or meet my family." Regina suggested and Sharon's eyes brightened. "It will be nice to see how my mother fairs." Sharon replied as they walked to the dining hall.

In the hallway outside Regina's quarters, Count Terrance laced his vest quickly heading for the stairs. "Did you hear? There's a ship in the harbor at Sandista." Count Terrance said anxiously. "There are many ships in Sandista's harbor." Regina replied with a snicker. "Not like this one. It doesn't belong to any of the Son's of the Great Father." Count Terrance reported and Regina froze in her place to hear more. "It's huge bearing 10 cannons and 10 long boats. Count Samuel brought us news from Green Stone and I have been dispatched to Mesina. Enjoy your day off Count Regina for I fear tomorrow shall be a busy day for messengers." Count Terrance called to her as he disappeared on the stairs. The dining hall was unusually filled with people as Countess Regina took a seat at one of the tables. The smell of roasted beef filled the hall. Count Charles pulled out a chair and sat down beside her. Count Charles was an experienced rider being in his mid twenties. "Did you hear about the ship?" He asked excitedly. "Yes I did. I wonder where it came from." Regina replied as Lady Sharon brought her a plate and a glass of fruit juice. "No one knows yet. It just sits out there having dropped its sails. I imagine the council at Sandista will send an envoy to greet them and determine their purpose." He said sipping from his glass. "Oh there is other news from Archemeius that might interest you. Our friend Count Andrew is getting married tonight." Charles said grinning broadly and Regina was surprised. "Tonight? This is the first I heard. I thought he was recovering from an injury in Archemeius?" Regina asked and she took two apples from the table and stuffed them into her pockets. "I guess his accident made him mindful of his future and he decided to change his situation quickly." Charles chuckled. "Regardless, he marries a girl from Sandista named Karen in the garden at Archemeius at sunset. Do you know her?" Charles asked. "I do not. I wonder if I could find cause to deliver a message to Archemeius and witness their ceremony." Regina asked. "I'm certain with the news of the ship in harbor at Sandista there will be a vast number of messages to deliver." Charles speculated. "After the midday meal, I deliver a message to Mesina and it requires me to wait for a response." He added and Regina had a thought. "If by chance you see Count Cameron, inform him of my intention to witness Count Andrew's wedding and encourage him to join me there if he can." Regina suggested and Charles smiled. "I was not aware you fancied Count Cameron or him you." Charles said teasing her and she stood having finished her meal. "There is much you do not know about me Count Charles. I go to visit my family as it is my day off." She said impetuously and departed as Lady Sharon followed her.

The sun was shining brightly as they stepped from the castle. Two story wooden buildings lined the main street in the city that began just after the edge of the castle garden. Regina turned to Lady Sharon as they stepped onto the first street after the garden wall. "What street is your parent's house on?" She asked Lady Sharon. "16th street, just inside the city walls." Sharon replied. "My parents live on 12th street. Shall we walk or take a carriage?" Regina asked cheerfully. "I would prefer to walk. It is such a fine day." Sharon replied and they took off together. "If you are going to attend your friend's wedding, you should take them a gift." Sharon suggested as they passed through the market square. "I have no idea what a proper wedding gift would be." Regina said as they wandered through one of the stores. "Come Countess Regina, what think you of these?" Lady Sharon asked holding up two gold chains. Each chain supported a medallion shaped as half of a heart. When you put the medallions together, they matched perfectly forming a heart. "I can etch the name of you lover on one and yours on the other Countess." The shopkeeper said and Regina blushed. "Andrew and Karen, it is a wedding gift for my friends." Regina sighed and Lady Sharon giggled. "Maybe you should buy two sets." She laughed and Regina poked her playfully chastising her. They waited patiently for the shopkeeper to engrave them before departing. The deeper they walked into the city, the more the buildings changed until they resembled cabins. The cabins were not as big and each lot had a yard with trees and flower gardens or vegetable gardens. Some of them had little fences around them or hedges but they were all very well kept. Everywhere you looked the colors of brown and green dominated the city. A creek, that used to be the sewer before the engineers from Mesina built the new one under the road, ran alongside Main Street. At 10th Street there was a park with a fountain and another well. Several children played under the trees as their mothers sat at wooden tables eagerly chatting. It wasn't that long ago that Regina's mother used to bring her and her two younger brothers here to play and have lunch on sunny days like this one. The breeze coming from the south was blowing through the trees and they gently swayed casting their shadows over the park and the tables where the women sat. A great swan barked a warning to one of the children who got too close at the fountain and Regina could hear their laughter. A carriage rattled past them as they approached 12th Street. "My house is the fourth house on the north side west from her." Regina informed her servant. "You should enjoy the rest of the day with your family but someday soon I would suffer you to accompany me home and meet my family." Regina said with a broad grin. Lady Sharon was surprised and elated by Countess Regina's statement both at the invitation and the news of being relieved of her duties so early. "Make known to me the date and I shall inform my family and plan a grand midday picnic for both our families in the 10th Street Park if that is to your liking." Lady Sharon suggested. "I will discuss the same with my mother and relay a date to you tomorrow." Regina smiled and Lady Sharon bowed before continuing down Main Street quickly.

As Regina drew closer to her parent's home, she could see her brothers playing in the front yard under the large redwood tree. Vincent was 12 and Solomon was 10. When they saw her, they stopped what they were doing and screamed her name excitedly running to greet her. She hugged them both and pulled the apples from her pocket and gave them each one. They bracketed her as made her way up the walkway to the front door between the flower beds filled with multicolored carnations. Her parent's house was a two story redwood cabin with a fine porch. As she opened the door, the smell of chocolate filled the house and she knew her mother was baking something good. "I don't know why you can't bring Waterbird when you come home." Solomon pouted biting into his apple and Regina giggled. "You know dragons aren't allowed in the city. He would eat all Moms' flowers." She laughed rubbing his head playfully. Regina was hoping her father would be home too as this was the seventh day. He was a woodsman by trade and a skilled hunter. She feared he might be out with his friends on a hunt. She was pleased to find him sitting at the kitchen table with her mother when she entered the kitchen. There was a long staff made of metal and wood that he was cleaning on the table. When they saw Regina, they both smiled warmly and stood to embrace her. "I knew you would be visiting us today. I made your favorite cookies." Her mother beamed kissing her cheek. "How fairs my champion." Her dad said proudly embracing her with both arms. "Much better than I deserve." Regina smiled taking one of her mother's cookies. "What is this staff that you have on my mother's table?" Regina asked inspecting it from a distance. Her father picked it up and held it to his shoulder pointing it out the open back door. "It's called a shoulder cracker and I purchased it at some expense from a tradesman from Green Stone. It will replace the long bow someday." Her father said handing it to her. She pulled it to her shoulder as he had done. "It's very heavy." Regina said lowering it and looking closer at the mechanism that made up the trigger and hammer that had a piece of flint rock attached to it. Her father picked up one of two pouches on the table and opened it producing a small metal ball for her to examine. "It's like a cannon for your shoulder." He beamed showing her the other pouch that was filled with a dark black powder. "You put a measure of this powder in the tube followed by a patch of linen and then pack it tight with the ball on top.

Then you add a small amount of powder here and pull this hammer back. When you release the hammer with this trigger, the flint strikes this plate and ignites the powder. When it explodes it makes a loud crack and sends the ball hurling out the tube with tremendous energy. I am far more accurate with the long bow but I will master it in due time." Her father said and he hung it on the wall behind the table. "Will you teach me the cracker as you did the long bow?" Regina asked enthusiastically. "If you can find time for your father, he will find time for you but your visits become less frequent as your duties increase at the castle." He said turning his head sideways to look at her suspiciously. "Or does your young suitor consume time better spent with your family?" He added frowning at her and Regina frowned back at him. "You rush to call him my suitor as I consider him but a friend. Count Cameron lives and works in Mesina and I have not set eyes on him since last I saw you." Regina replied hugging her father before she grinned at him mischievously. "Do you press me to give attention to Count Cameron's pursuit of me now?" She giggled and her father stiffened. "Hardly, for you know my mind on the topic. You are far too young to entertain suitors and would fair better with your focus on your duties and your family." He said with conviction as Regina smiled. "And remind me again, at what age did you take my mother to be your wife?" Regina said teasing him and her father's face turned red. "We have had words previously on this matter. Our circumstance and goals were far different than those that present themselves to you." He said fighting to present a calm demeanor. "I pray you meet your potential before you meet your husband." He added more calmly. "Have no fear father for I am still your virgin daughter and my desires for my future differ little from yours." Regina said still grinning as she kissed his cheek. Now Regina's mother's face was crimson as she turned to scowl at her daughter. "Regina! Do not speak so crass to your father or in the presence of your brothers." She chastised her. Sometimes Regina forgot that there were words or phrases or topics that were ok around the other riders that did not set so well with her family. Her father stood and walked to the back door. "Shall we inspect your mother's garden and you can tell me more of your duties at the castle." He suggested but Regina knew he was most concerned with her suggestion that she may be contemplating taking a suitor. His demeanor always bordered on anger when he talked to her about boys and it made Regina uncomfortable. She had a strong bond with her father and didn't like to see him mad or disappointed in her.

"I do not want to take a hard line with you Regina for I have seen those become barriers between my friends and their children." He began. "You have a lifetime of experiences and opportunities in front of you." He smiled looking deep into her eyes. "Your father worries because he knows how infatuation can overwhelm all other aspirations and become the primary focus for a young man or a young woman." He stated. "I have not taken a suitor father." Regina sighed knowing she couldn't avoid his concern. "But Cameron is a messenger same as me. His goals and dreams are like mine. If I did take a suitor would a man of his circumstances find favor in your eyes?" She asked and her father smiled painfully. "The fact that you consider it now at 16 gives me cause for concern. Could you not postpone this experience for but a few years until you can see your future more clearly?" He suggested. "You avoid my question father and I am almost 17." Regina replied. "I will be satisfied that your suitor be game fully employed and show respect for our values but I would prefer you wait a couple more years. Why must you be in such a hurry for every experience in life?" Her father replied and Regina could see the frustration in his face. She took his hand in hers as they walked through the flowers in his back yard. "Did you think the boys would avoid making advances to me until **you** were prepared?" Regina giggled bashfully. "I am the only female messenger save Countess Rebecca who is Head Master at the academy." She said and her father frowned at her. "Yes and she is still single. Maybe you should take council with her and follow her path." He suggested with a grin as they began to walk back to the house. "You know your mother and I are very proud of you and trust your judgment." He sighed and kissed her forehead as he hugged her. "I am not in a hurry father but when you constantly return to this topic with me, I sometimes think I should just take a suitor and put this conversation behind us." Regina said playfully but her father just frowned again as they entered the house. Many of the things her father said to her either did not make sense or seemed to be out dated to her but she knew he loved her and had her best interests at heart. Now Regina loved her time with her family and returned to them often. She stayed several hours this day visiting with her parents and playing games with her brothers. They were disappointed when she told them of her intention to try and attend Count Andrew's wedding in Archemeius as they hoped she would dine with them. Her mother suggested the next seventh day for the picnic with Lady Sharon's family and Regina reluctantly kissed them goodbye before she headed back to the castle on foot.

As Countess Regina approached the castle, she saw a vast number of carriages at the entrance preparing a caravan of some sort. "What is the meaning of the caravan?" Countess Regina asked one of the men that served as a guard at the gate. At first he thought to dismiss her as a curious child until he saw the emblem of the messengers on her vest and her tattoo of the dragon on her arm. "The Supreme Council has instructed each city to deploy 50 archers and 5 cannon to Sandista. It's for a show of force for the visitors from the boat in the harbor." He replied. "Have they come ashore already?" Regina asked surprised for she had heard they were only recently discovered some distance out at sea. "No but the Great Father wants them to witness that we are well defended when they do come ashore. He is building a military encampment between Sandista and the port." The guard replied as a familiar whistle sounded high over head. Regina looked up and caught a glimpse of the red and black dragon soaring northwest from the castle and she surmised it was Count Charles taking a message to Sandista. She hurried into the castle and bounded up the stairs to the office of messengers. The door was open and the scribes were all very busy copying manuscripts and one of them brushed past her in a hurry toward the council chambers. There were several bundles of scrolls on Lord Mitchell's desk and he looked up and smiled when Regina approached. "I thought this to be your day of rest. I did not expect to see you today." He said. "Do all these bundles need to be delivered?" Regina asked surveying them. "They will be eventually but nothing here is pressing. I just sent our response to the Great Father's instructions to Sandista with Count Charles. These other bundles can go at first light to the other cities." Mitchell replied. "If there be a bundle for Archemeius, I would take it for you now and bring back their bundle for us at first light? Count Andrew's wedding is at sunset and I would attend it there if you have need of me." Regina suggested and Lord Mitchell smiled. "The scribes have one more scroll to add to their bundle. Prepare Waterbird and I will have them present your bundle at the perch." Lord Mitchell said and Regina began to braid her hair thanking him before she departed. She climbed the stairs to the roof and found the servant there. "Make haste to harness Waterbird for I fly to Archemeius as soon as he is prepared." Regina commanded and the servant ran to the cages as Regina finished her braid. Regina walked to the edge of the roof and looked over in time to see the caravan departing the gates. There were 10 fast carriages and 5 of them pulled cannons raising a cloud of dust as the drivers cracked their whips urging them into a fast trot. One of the scribes ran up to her and handed her a bundle of scrolls and the servant came from the pen leading Waterbird in front of the launching platform. He whistled excitedly as Regina inspected the harness and buckled the bundle into it before mounting him. Waterbird was excited and stepped closer to the platform as Regina hooked herself in. "Wait for me!" Regina barked pulling his head back before finishing the clips that secured her to the harness and Waterbird whistled a protest. "Ok, now we can go." Regina whispered wrapping the reigns tight in her hands and urging him forward. Regina gave a brisk whistle and Waterbird dove from the platform spreading his wings. She was growing accustomed to the feeling of exhilaration as the ground rushed up at them. A violent pump from his wings, and they began to accelerate and climb above the trees. Regina felt the sun on her back as the rush of air blew against her face and she checked the horizon. She turned Waterbird's head to the southeast and the mountain pass and whistled for more altitude. This was a perfect day to fly. It would take Regina less than an hour to get to Castle Archemeius and she relaxed sitting upright on Waterbird to enjoy the flight. Flying at altitude was not to Waterbird's liking at all. He preferred to soar just above the treetops and every time Regina would bring him high in the sky he would dive back down just above the trees. Regina finally gave up satisfied to keep him on course for the castle. She knew it was imperative when they flew to remind and practice all maneuvers so she dug her spurs into Waterbird's left side and urged him through a complete roll hugging tightly to his back and the harness. It **was** exhilarating and Waterbird whistled his approval once they completed the roll. The mountain pass came into view quickly and Regina sat back up as Waterbird banked and turned through the pass. The suddenly, a shadow fell over them and Regina turned her head to look up. Fear gripped her frame quickly and totally as the wings of a mature dragon stretched over them. His brilliant Orange head was but mere feet from Regina's head and she heard his ominous whistle. It was the first time Regina had encountered another dragon in the mountains and she was terrified. She hunkered down on Waterbird and called for maximum speed as the school had taught her. Waterbird pumped his wings ferociously and the wind against Regina's face began to roar past her ears. The shadow disappeared over them but Regina was horrified to see the larger mature dragon do a roll around them as if taunting them and demonstrating his superior speed. She felt helpless seeing the sun reflect bright orange off the mature dragon's back below them before it rolled back over them and the shadow enveloped them again. As Waterbird pumped his wings furiously to escape, suddenly just as quickly as it had appeared, the mature dragon banked away and dove back down into the valley. Regina pulled back on the reigns slowing

Waterbird back to cruising speed and searched all around them frantically for the mature dragon. She breathed a heavy sigh of relief not finding him. "That's why I want to fly at altitude." Regina shouted at Waterbird and he turned his head whistling as if he agreed. Regina was still shaking realizing the larger dragon could have torn them to pieces with his superior size and speed and was thankful it had been satisfied just to chase them away. She checked the horizon and turned Waterbird's head straight south to clear the mountains as soon as she could. She would follow the coast the rest of the way to Archemeius to avoid another encounter like that. As the white sand of the beach and the blue green ocean came into view, Regina relaxed again on Waterbird turning his head eastward. A short time later, the first buildings of Archemeius City came into view and Regina pulled the reigns turning Waterbird's head to the castle. Waterbird spread his wings wide as they slowed and Regina gave the double whistle command to land. The powerful young dragon soared to the perch and hovered briefly before lowering his back legs onto the perch. Regina clung tightly to the harness as Waterbird fell forward extending his front feet to catch himself on the perch. Immediately, Waterbird began to drink from the trough as Regina unbuckled herself from the harness and dismounted. Her hands trembled still shaken by her encounter with wild dragon. "She would have to be more cautious in the future." She thought to herself as she retrieved the bundle of scrolls from the harness. A servant stood watching her from the bottom of the perch. "You can put him away and feed him for I will not return to Red Oak until tomorrow." Regina commanded smiling at the servant. She handed him the reigns and walked briskly toward the staircase before remembering. "Has Count Cameron of Mesina arrived yet?" She asked the servant. "No Countess. I don't believe he has." The servant responded. "Please inform him I am here when he arrives. I will look for him in the dining hall." Regina said turning back to the staircase. As she made her way to the office of messengers, she undid the braid in her hair and shook it out. The door to the office was open and Regina handed the bundle to the servant there. "These are from Castle Red Oak. I will return at first light to retrieve anything you have for us." Regina said still fussing with her hair. "Very good countess, I will have a bundle for you I am sure. Would you like a brush?" He said smiling and waved at a female servant. The young girl came over and handed Regina a brush from her bag. "I guess I should start carrying one in my pouch." Regina giggled taking the brush from her and working it through her hair. "Has your caravan left for Sandista yet?" She asked casually. "We sent 50 Crackers instead of long bowmen. Do you know what those are?" The servant asked proudly. "Yes I do. My father just purchased one of those. Castle Mesina's contribution to the encampment will be most impressive." Regina replied admiringly as she handed the young girl back her brush. "I pray our visitor's intentions are peaceful and we won't have need for them." Regina said with a smile as she turned walking to the stairs.

Regina was looking forward to a cool glass of the cherry wine as she made her way to the second floor. Count Arthur met her in the stairway escorted by Lord Jerome and Lady Erin. He smiled broadly looking surprised. "Countess Regina, what brings you to Archemeius? Are you working?" Arthur said extending his hand to her. Regina shook hands greeting him. "I have finished my tasks for today and desire to attend Count Andrew's wedding. I brought them a gift." Regina replied proudly digging in her bag to retrieve it. Arthur took her arm giving the servants a look to give them privacy before leading her away from them several paces. Count Arthur knew she was young and naïve but he chose not to tease her in this moment feeling sorry for her. "I'm certain Count Andrew will be honored that you choose to attend his wedding and I, as your friend, would not have you embarrassed. Is it your intent to wear your uniform to his ceremony?" Arthur whispered. "I am not *in* the ceremony but desire only to watch and make my presentation." Regina smiled nervously. "That would be fine for a servant but you are Countess Regina of Red Oak. Did you not take counsel with your servant about proper attire for a wedding? This is why the council pays for your servant. She should be here with you." Arthur asked sympathetically and Regina dropped her head. "I did not." She admitted and Arthur chuckled softly. "There are many points for consideration with regard to attire at a wedding. There theme is red." Arthur informed her and Regina felt her face turn hot realizing the gravity of her mistake. "What can be done now? I have no time to return to Red Oak for a proper gown." Regina sighed. "Will you suffer my assistance in this matter as your friend and take no offense." Arthur whispered and waved the servants back over. "There are two hours before the ceremony and you can pay me back later." Arthur whispered before turning to Lady Erin. "Countess Regina was misinformed with regard to the color scheme and her gown is all wrong." Arthur said pulling several coins from his belt. "I perceive you revel in shopping. Could I convince you easily to escort Countess Regina to a dress shop for a proper red dress?" Arthur asked and Lady Erin's eyes brightened. "I would be overjoyed at the task." Lady Erin replied bowing before Countess Regina. "Make haste Lady Erin and return quickly for I know you have other responsibilities and the shops will close shortly." Arthur smiled as Lady Erin led Regina down the stairs.

"I feel so foolish sometimes at the mistakes I make when formal engagements arrive." Countess Regina said as they turned the corner in the square and entered the dress shop. "Take no mind of it. I saw this dress only this morning when shopping for my own and was sorely tempted to buy it also. It will be perfect for the ceremony and you." Lady Erin replied pulling her to the back of the shop. "If you find this gown to your liking, we can dress and prepare you here and I will keep your uniform in my room until you depart. I still have to go there to change into my gown as I *am* in the ceremony." Lady Erin said proudly as she pulled a beautiful red velvet dress from a hanger and held it up to Countess Regina sizing it up. "Congratulations." Regina replied. "I think this will fit you. Try it on." She suggested ushering Regina toward the fitting room. Regina closed the curtain and stripped out of her uniform quickly to slip on the gown. She was determined to wear it if it fit not wanting to waste any more of Lady Erin's time than she had to. She was praying and banking on Lady Erin's judgment being better than hers with regard to the attire. "Try these on. They match the dress." Lady Erin said and slipped a pair of red velvet shoes under the curtain. The gown had long white leather laces in the front from her naval to her breasts and in the back from below her waist to midpoint on her shoulder blades. She got the lacing done in the front but couldn't get the back. "Lady Erin will you help me with the back of this gown." Regina asked and Erin came through the curtain and giggled when she saw her. "It's not supposed to be laced that tightly in the front. Turn around and let me adjust it for you." Erin giggled and Regina turned her back to the mirror. Again she felt uncomfortable wearing a gown that lifted her breasts the way it did but she was not prepared for her image in the mirror when Lady Erin completed the adjustment on the straps. As she viewed the dress on herself, she had to admit it was gorgeous but this didn't look like her. How could a gown that felt so comfortable look so uncomfortable to her in the mirror. The white lace work seemed to start at her back and go over her shoulders. It crisscrossed over her front creating a deep plunge below her naval where Lady Erin tied it. Her breast clung to the fabric inside the dress but she felt too much of them were exposed by the plunging neckline. She had admired other, more mature, women in dresses like this but she never imagined herself in one. "Lady Erin I have never made purchase of a dress like this or any other formal attire. You are much my senior in age and experience. I am depending on your judgment entirely. Are you certain my friends will not view me as a harlot in this gown?" Regina asked sincerely nervous. "You are the queen of hearts in that dress. I could not imagine a more eloquent gown to compliment your figure with more dignity." Lady Erin said admiring the dress as she adjusted the white lacework. "Every eye will be on you." She whispered. "And I am certain I will feel them." Regina replied with uncertainty trying to pull the plunging neckline together. Now the last piece of the dress was a red transparent shawl that Lady Erin draped over her shoulders and tied below her chin. It covered all her bare skin from her shoulders to her hips but hid nothing. "You need only a little red powder for your cheeks to make it perfect." Lady Erin said as Regina put on the shoes. She was growing more comfortable with gown as they talked. "I wonder what Count Cameron will think of this dress." Regina giggled turning in the mirror. "Count Cameron is your suitor?" Erin gasped. "No…., but I would entertain a proposal of like nature if he were so bold and I think he gathers courage to do so." Regina giggled and Erin did too. "I would wager, he will be in a long line of men and boys with various proposals tonight." Lady Erin laughed heartily as she finished her adjustment of the laces. Countess Regina was ready to purchase the dress and get to the ceremony now remembering Lady Sharon's council and thinking it the perfect accent to present herself to Count Cameron. "Are you certain I do not present too seductive a demeanor in this gown?" She asked Lady Erin one final time hoping she would be honest. "Having seen you in the gown, I am only sorry I did not purchase it for myself." She replied and they walked to the shopkeeper and made payment for it before heading back to the castle and Lady Erin's room. Together they finished preparing and Lady Erin applied the red rouge to her cheeks. "We should go quickly to the dining hall. I cannot wait to see Count Arthur's face when we reveal to him our selection his loan to you has purchased." Lady Erin smiled proudly. "It is Count Cameron's expression that I am curious to see." Regina admitted giggling as they departed.

Count Cameron pulled back hard on Lightning's reigns and whistled twice pointing his head at the perch atop Castle Archemeius. He braced hard against Lightning's back as the young dragon hovered before lowering his back legs and then falling forward. "That's my boy. Nice landing Lightning." He said slapping the dragon's neck before he unbuckled. Lightning shook his head and whistled before he began to drink. Cameron unbuckled his bag and the pulled the bundle of scrolls from the pouch attached to Lightning's harness. "We're spending the night." He told the servant that took his dragon's reigns and he walked to the stairs. "Is the first room open? I need to change." Cameron asked. "No that's Lady Karen's room. You'll have to go to the third door." The servant replied and Cameron chuckled. "I certainly don't want to walk in on the bride. Thank you sir." He laughed and headed toward the stairs. "Countess Regina bade me inform you she awaits you in the dining hall." The servant shouted to him as he departed the roof and Cameron smiled. He had been excited to hear of her invitation to be her escort at the wedding but now he grew nervous knowing she waited for him. He opened the door to the room and set his bag and the bundle of scrolls on the bed after he locked the door. He thought to himself how great it was that Arthur had been given control of all the rooms on the sixth floor and wished he could do that at Mesina. He disrobed quickly and pulled the formal suit from his bag and laid it out. Finding out the color scheme for Andrew's wedding had been difficult but he had finally managed to get it from another rider earlier. He pulled the canister of body powder out of the bag and doused himself thoroughly before he began to dress. As he pulled his boots back on, he wondered what it meant that Regina had left a message for him. Folding his uniform neatly, he placed it in the bag replacing the gifts he had bought for Count Andrew and the one he had selected for Countess Regina and picked it up. He picked up also the bundle of scrolls with the other hand and walked quickly toward the fourth floor and the office of messengers. "These are from Mesina. I will take whatever you have for us when I return at first light." Cameron said. "You and Countess Regina have duplicate tasks." The servant said. "Oh so she *is* here." Cameron said. "Yes, she said she would look for you in the dining hall." He replied. "Thank you sir, can I leave my bag here for a time." Cameron asked and the servant nodded yes pointing to a closet in the room.

Cameron walked straight to the bar when he got to the dining hall and ordered a beer. The place was extremely crowded. He turned his back to the bar, once he got his beer, and surveyed the tables. The wedding ceremony wouldn't start for another hour so he didn't expect to see Count Arthur or Count Andrew as they were probably engaged getting ready. He surmised the hall was so full because it was dinner time and people were probably still discussing the visitors. There was one table that was particularly crowded and most of them were in formal attire. He recognized two councilwomen and Count Richard and assumed they were attending Count Andrew's wedding so he started that direction. Count Richard was flirting with a gorgeous looking woman who had her back to him. There were several men around her but Count Richard had her attention and

Count Cameron wondered who the woman in the red velvet dress was. As Cameron approached her from behind Count Richard saw him and looked surprised. "Shouldn't you be working Count Richard?" Cameron teased him chuckling loudly and the young woman turned to him hearing his voice. Cameron felt all the blood drain from his face and nearly dropped his beer as he stared at Countess Regina. "I guess you're right, if you will excuse me I should go find Count Andrew." Count Richard said and departed quickly. "Count Cameron…, I wasn't sure you would come." Regina said stepping closer to him to take his arm. Cameron didn't speak. He couldn't take his eyes off of her. She was stunning in that dress and Cameron just felt stunned. "I should tell you what happened to me flying from Red Oak." Regina said smiling because she could tell he liked her dress. "Count Cameron? Do you want to hear my story?" Regina asked again. Cameron was suddenly and awkwardly aware that everyone standing around them was staring at them more particularly at Countess Regina. "I'd rather hear where you got that dress." He finally whispered. The simple single pearl necklace he had purchased for her seemed far too simple for him to offer it to her to wear with this dress. "Do you like it?" Regina asked excitedly. "I'm not sure. I've never seen you in a dress like that before." Cameron said nervously leading her away from the table. Regina felt oddly uncomfortable holding his arm and let go. "It must have cost you a fortune." Cameron said sipping his beer. There was something about the way he spoke that sounded accusing and disrespectful and Regina didn't like it. "A friend picked it out and bought it for me." She replied watching his eyes. "Is this friend of yours a man?" Cameron asked and his face turned red. "The friend that paid for this dress is a man, yes." She replied. "So you do have a suitor." Cameron said gritting his teeth to mask his disappointment. "No one has made that proposal to me and now I am not sure that I would accept it from anyone." Regina replied obstinately turning her eyes from him. "This is not a dress that a father buys for his daughter. By accepting his gift you give him permission to pursue you." Cameron said angrily taking her arm back but Regina pulled away. "I sincerely doubt that." She replied curtly. "You are terminally naïve Countess Regina." Cameron whispered angrily. Regina's eyes filled with water but she fought the emotion. "I *am* naïve." She replied and turned back to glare at him. "You wound me Count Cameron so now I shall attempt to wound you and I pray it hurts you as you have hurt me. I came to Archemeius without a dress not knowing formal attire was expected. My friend Count Arthur, who is fiancé to the Maiden Melisa of Archemeius, remedied my circumstance by having one of her servants escort me to a dress shop where I made purchase of this gown with his loan in full mind that you would lay eyes on me and find it pleasing. I beg you forgive me for my poor judgment." Regina whispered angrily as she departed quickly toward the stairs. Cameron watched her disappear into the stairway stunned for the second time. "You are a complete ass!" He said to himself and he sat down his beer and ran after her.

As he ran up the stairs, he encountered all of the women in the wedding party coming down the stairs. "Count Cameron…, you're going the wrong way. If you are here for Count Andrew's wedding it's in the garden." Maid Melisa laughed. "I am…, but I must catch my escort and fall on my dagger to appease her anger at my stupidity." Cameron said moving past them hastily. "If you are referring to Countess Regina, she is probably headed to my room which is the 3rd door on the 3rd floor." Lady Erin giggled and Cameron ran to the door and tried it but it was locked. "Are you in there Countess Regina?" Cameron said nervously. "Be gone Count Cameron, I have had my fill of you for today and this week." Regina cried and Cameron leaned heavily against the door and remained silent for a long while. "Leave this door between us then for I will find it easier to say what's in my heart. I brought you a gift from Mesina that I was hoping could say what my lips and my mind continually and painfully fail to reveal from my heart when I look in your eyes. I know little of how to be a suitor and less of how to speak to a beautiful woman whom I once called my dear friend. I can't find the words worthy of my apology now. You look gorgeous beyond words in that dress. My gift pales in comparison to it. To hear that you showed another man favor by accepting it as a gift was unbearable to me. Can you not see how my jealousy has made me a fool? My desire was not to become one of your suitors but your **only** suitor for I cannot tolerate those women that pit one man against another as a sport and I would never pursue another save you. This night I came here to make that proposal to you trying desperately all day to convince myself that I was worthy to do so. I pray you someday forgive me as we both realize now….., that I am not." Count Cameron concluded and turned slowly and sorrowfully walking to the stairs. As he got back to the dining hall he could see that everyone had moved out to the garden and the wedding ceremony was about to begin. He remained in the darkness of the stairway not wanting to reveal his pain even to the bartender who remained at his post. He heard a small quiet voice behind him. "Cameron…, shall we prolong this day of foolishness and injury or shall I accept your apology as well as your proposal for it is as sweet music to my ears." Regina whispered and Cameron turned to her. She was a vision standing on the stairs above him in the dimly lit stairwell. "Would I be foolish to think of kissing you at this moment?" Cameron whispered enthusiastically. "You would be foolish to hesitate." Regina replied and Cameron pressed his lips to hers. Regina's curiosity and the intense emotion she felt drove her to allow Cameron this kiss and she was pleasantly surprised. His lips were soft and tender as they spread their magic through her senses. This, being her first kiss, did not feel at all as awkward as she had assumed it would be but Cameron pulled his lips away just as Regina began to surrender. "I fear we should not linger here but join the ceremony in the garden." Cameron whispered urgently fearing discovery. "Share with me one more sweet kiss and heal my wound completely suffered at your words and then we shall go." Regina pleaded and Cameron smiled before kissing her passionately again. As they parted lips again Regina exhaled softly and smiled at Cameron. He took her hand and they walked together toward the garden. Regina watched Cameron carefully wondering if he felt the same way she did when they kissed. "Have you kissed a lot of girls Cameron?" She asked softly. "A few, not many really, why do you ask me this?" Cameron asked feeling awkward again. "Is your kiss sweet to me because you are skilled and well practiced or is there some other reason." Regina giggled and Cameron smiled stopping short of the garden and the people at the ceremony. "I am neither skilled nor well practiced. If it pleases you we will investigate at every opportunity to discover the reason." Cameron suggested grinning at Regina who broke out in a wide smile. "I agree." She replied and they joined the other people in the garden.

Count Andrew sat in the chair that Count Arthur and the rest of the men in the wedding party had carried him down in with Councilman Trent standing behind him in a white and silver ceremonial robe. Count Arthur stood on his right and Count Richard on his left dressed in the formal dark red uniforms of the messengers of Archemeius. Count Andrew and the other men in the party wore the red ceremonial robes. They all stood on the gazebo in the center of the garden watching the wedding tent where Lady Karen and her party prepared to make the ceremonial procession and join them. The pain in his chest was subsiding but Count Andrew still found it impossible to stand for any more than a few minutes. Lord Peter the medic was close and he would have preferred Count Andrew remained in bed but Andrew was not going to deny Lady Karen the ceremony. King Thomas was on his balcony with his wife Councilwoman Marion and raised his hands to quiet the crowd in the garden. Count Arthur and the other men in the party moved quickly to the entrance to the tent.

"We the citizens of Archemeius gather today to bear witness to the proposal of Count Andrew of Sandista to his chosen bride from the daughters of the Great Father. As King of Archemeius and servant of the peoples will, I give authority to Councilman Trent to conduct the procedures of this union and call forth the bride." King Thomas shouted and Councilman Trent bowed deeply in the direction of the King before raising his hands in the direction of the tent. "In the presence of these witnesses, I summon Lady Karen of Sandista the daughter of Lord Jamaal and Lady Renee." Councilman Trent shouted and the orchestra on the balcony began the processional serenade. One by one the women of the party exited the tent in fine red gowns and were escorted to the foot of the gazebo by the men in the party. Maiden Melisa's servants were first and she followed taking Count Arthur's arm. As each lady exited the tent, the orchestra added more instruments and the serenade increased in intensity until finally Lady Karen came forth without an escort to make the procession. Count Andrew chose this moment to rise to his feet and Councilman Trent moved the chair to one side.

Count Andrew's heart was pounding in his chest painfully and he was unsure whether it was his wound or the extreme emotion he felt watching Lady Karen make the journey to his side on the gazebo. The long red velvet dress trailed behind her and the hood and the veil covered her head. It was still warm in the garden and Lady Karen had to lift the front of the dress to avoid stepping on it. The procession represented her last unescorted journey and was very traditional to all the Sons and Daughters of the Great Father. The meaning was not lost on her or Count Andrew as she took her place facing him and the serenade from the orchestra concluded. Councilman Trent reached and folded back the hood and removed the veil. Lady Karen was even more radiant and beautiful than Andrew had ever seen her. "Is this the Daughter of the Great Father to which you desire to make a proposal?" Councilman Trent asked. "It is." Andrew replied and Trent turned to Karen. "Do you desire to hear his proposal?" He asked. "I do." Karen replied. "Is there present those who will bear witness to this proposal?" Trent asked looking to Arthur and the whole wedding party replied in unison. "We will." Andrew took Karen's hands in his. "What proposal do you make in the presence of these witnesses?" Councilman Trent asked. "I propose that Lady Karen suffer me, Count Andrew to serve her as her husband and that she serve me as wife until death overcomes us."

Andrew said boldly. Lady Karen's eyes filled with water hearing finally the words she had prayed for so long. "And what be your response to Count Andrew's proposal?" Trent asked looking to Lady Karen. "I accept Count Andrew's proposal without reservation and bind my fate in his hands until death overcomes us." Karen replied and bit her lip fixing her gaze on Andrew's eyes. "I present Count Andrew of Sandista having made his proposal and Lady Karen of Sandista having accepted the same proposal and declare them legally ordained in marriage until death overcomes them." Councilman Trent announced and Karen and Andrew kissed as the orchestra began again and the crowd roared to their feet breaking the silence in the garden.

"I made it." Count Andrew whispered painfully and Lady Karen could see the torment in his eyes. Lord Peter hurried to Count Andrew's side presenting the chair to him and he sat quickly. "For heaven's sake Count Andrew, will you now finally heed my council and return to your bed?" Lord Peter pleaded with him. "I will not! I will share wine and celebration in the dining hall and this chair shall provide me sufficient comfort next to my wife." Andrew replied smiling through his discomfort at her. Karen knelt down beside him showing sincere concern. "Are you certain my husband for I shall find it sufficient to retire with you and make an end to your suffering?" Karen whispered. "I fear I will not embrace you on the dance floor this night but it is my desire to witness your enjoyment of that embrace with all our new friends until you have had your fill of it as is our custom. Do not deny me the pleasure of this celebration having suffered through the ceremony for your pleasure." Andrew laughed teasing her and he looked to Count Arthur. "Join with your servants and provide me transport to the dining hall with haste if you be my friend and desire a turn on the dance floor with my wife." Andrew laughed and Arthur returned his smile with an impetuous grin as he knelt down to grab his chair. "I will call you friend…, but for a chance to embrace your wife on the dance floor, I would carry you back to Sandista." Arthur teased him as the four of them lifted him and headed for the dining hall. The first table in the dining hall was always the honored table and it was already covered with gifts for the new couple as they entered and sat Count Andrew at the head of it. As was customary, each guest set his gift on the table and there was no hint as to who presented it to them with one exception. The present from the King and his family, should you receive one, had his seal on it and it was customary to reveal it first. Councilman Trent pointed it out to Andrew once he was positioned. It was a scroll and the crowd in the hall grew silent again curious to its meaning as Andrew unrolled it. Count Andrew clutched it to his chest as his eyes filled with water and his face with emotion. He looked stunned at Lady Karen and presented the scroll for her to inspect. "It is a deed for a section of land facing the ocean. He invites us to citizenship in Archemeius." Andrew cried and the crowd erupted into applause showing their approval.

Countess Regina quickly set her gift on the table while the new couple was distracted and Count Cameron did the same. He had scarcely released her hand during the entire ceremony and he was not about to now seeing how the other men admired her. "What words did you share with Count Richard for he avoids me and turns his eyes from me suspiciously?" Cameron asked her. "Give no thought to Count Richard. His sweet words are familiar to me as the same words he has for many young girls." Regina replied. "He tempts you like a fox lurking a few paces from a birds nest waiting for opportunity." Cameron whispered. "He tempts many knowing but a few will surrender to his charms and this is satisfying to him." Regina replied smiling at Cameron and pulling him toward Count Andrew. "His demeanor is displeasing to me and I will have words with him." Count Cameron said. "I pray you will not." Countess Regina said stopping to glare at Cameron. "Do you forget so quick what pain your jealousy causes us both? If you show interest to his intentions, does it not demonstrate your lack of faith with me and my promise to you?" Countess Regina said sincerely. "I beg you ignore Count Richard and show faith that I will do the same." She pleaded and Cameron looked at her confused but smiled. "You do not desire a protector?" He asked and Regina grinned. "A protector yes, but from real adversaries not imagined or contrived."isHis

Regina smiled and pulled his hand leading him to Count Andrew again.

Count Andrew looked up as Count Cameron and Countess Regina approached and his smile broadened into a grin covering his face. "My goodness Countess Regina, do I grow old so quickly or have you transformed from a boney young girl to a beautiful woman overnight?" Andrew gasped appreciatively. "I belayed my transformation until you were wed knowing I would never find favor in your eyes and hear that sweet proposal from you." Regina replied sarcastically and playfully and all who heard her laughed knowing how Andrew and Regina teased each other mercilessly. Andrew smiled seeing she had bested him again and shook his head. Count Cameron stuck out his hand to Count Andrew. "We came to congratulate you and Lady Karen." Cameron said and Andrew shook it. "I pray you recover quickly from your misfortune." Cameron added referring to Andrew's injury. "I fear my body will heal before my pride does." Andrew sighed regretfully. "But let's have a different topic more favorable to me and you. Have either of you been given word of your task tomorrow?" Andrew asked smiling again and Cameron and Regina looked puzzled. "I promised merely to return a bundle on my return flight as Count Cameron has." Regina replied and Andrew shook his head and his hand dismissing it. "Someone else will do that. You and Cameron have been selected by the Great Father to join Count Arthur and four other riders to execute a fly over of our visitors tomorrow at midday. You are going to fly a ten man formation and execute a four point formation roll over their ship and then circle it seven times before landing at Sandista. We want them all to get a good look at you. The Great Father has planned it himself as the centerpiece for his demonstration of power to them in hopes to stifle any thoughts of war or conquest they may currently embrace." Andrew concluded and Regina felt uneasiness in her stomach. Andrew recognized the excitement on Count Cameron's face as well as the reserve in Countess Regina. "Do you have concerns Countess Regina?" He asked. "We have little training for battle." Count Cameron suggested. "They don't know that and this is but a demonstration." Andrew replied. "I fear only that I am not worthy to follow Count Arthur in such an honorable and historic task." Regina admitted and Andrew laughed. "If that gives you pause, I hesitate to make known to you this detail for fear you may faint but you will not follow Count Arthur." Andrew said grinning at Regina who now felt nervous **and** confused. "Do not tease me in this manner Count Andrew. This goes beyond what tricks you have played with me thus far." Regina replied and Andrew grinned. "As Waterbird is the youngest dragon; the rest of them, in their maturity, will respond better if you are on point. Count Arthur…, will follow you and you shall depart from here at first light." He smiled and Countess Regina leaned against Count Cameron heavily fearing Count Andrew had predicted correctly and she was about to faint. Count Arthur stood and offered his chair and Cameron guided Regina into it. She stared at Count Andrew in disbelief as he laughed. "I suggest more food and less wine for this one for the duration of the celebration." Andrew laughed heartily. "I have flown formation flight but a handful of times and never on point." Regina protested. "Do you experience problems getting Waterbird to roll to the four points?" Arthur asked and Regina shook her head no. Arthur filled his lungs with air expanding his chest. "Then fear not Countess Regina and execute this task confidently and boldly. The formation behind you will be manned by the kingdom's most experienced riders mounted on the most mature dragons and they will respond to you naturally at all four points. You need only have patience and turn slowly." Arthur said with conviction trying to inspire confidence in Countess Regina. Regina took another sip of her wine feeling no better and smiled at Arthur. "Join us for dinner but I beg you return my seat beside Maid Melisa if the blood has returned to your legs." Arthur chuckled and Regina felt embarrassed as she took Count Cameron's hand and stood. Cameron led her to a chair on the far side of Lady Karen. She sipped her wine and watched as the bride and groom opened their presents but said little. Cameron squeezed her hand as the kitchen servants cleared away the opened presents and began to lay food on the table. As they ate, the conversation was primarily about their task for tomorrow. A four point roll was pretty simple to execute and Regina's mind was filled with visions of what it would look like from all angles as she ate.

After dinner, a small group of musicians began to play in the great hall and the party migrated to that room. "I long to share an embrace with you on the dance floor." Cameron smiled at Regina. "One or two would be pleasing to me also but I desire to retire early and present a clear mind and well rested demeanor for our task tomorrow." Regina replied and they moved to the center of the floor. The serenade of the musicians was slow and soothing but Regina's mind was still filled with concerns for their task. Regina laid her head on Cameron's shoulder as he turned her gracefully on the dance floor. "I fear I find no place for my hand that does not find the warm softness of bare skin on your back in this dress. I mean no offense." Cameron whispered and Regina's thoughts of tomorrow's task dissipated as she became aware of Cameron's caress just below her shoulder blade. "I pray you do not assume I give you improper liberty but I find your embrace pleasing and by no means take offense." Regina whispered smiling and she felt his soft caress move lower just above her hip. The sensation was enticing to her and she hesitated in her thoughts because it was a pleasurable caress. "Cameron, do not tempt me to embarrass you in the midst of our friends. Return your hand to my back where it was." She whispered urgently and he did so. "The temptation is yours for I find you irresistible in this dress." He replied with a sigh. "Find control in your public displays or find a new partner to embrace you on this floor." Regina whispered smiling to herself. Cameron turned her on the floor several more times before saying anything else and then he lifted her chin to look in her eyes. "Are you aware of how the softness of your skin tempts me or does it elude your understanding?" Cameron asked honestly searching her eyes. "I perceive your question is sincere." Regina replied. I will ask you a question in modesty. See if you find my answer in its meaning. "Are you aware of how your caress tempts me or does it elude your understanding?" Regina whispered repeating the phrase back to Cameron and blushed laying her head back against his shoulder. Again they made several turns before Cameron spoke. "I will make a confession if it pleases you. You inquired of me earlier with regard to how many girls I have shared a romantic kiss. I confess to you now, each caress we share is new to me and my desire for the next caress is fueled by the newness of it fervently. I fear my haste will incur your wrath and you will rebuke me but I fear your surrender equally." Cameron whispered and frowned thinking he had not expressed himself adequately. It surprised Regina to hear his admission but she knew he was sincere. "This is truly a sweet confession. The words are like warm honey that melts my heart. I pray our friendship will grow as well as our romance for my desire for you is so much more than physical and I perceive yours is too. If you have faith that my desire is for you only...., I will also. Shall we throw caution aside and rush to fulfill that desire awkwardly or slowly and patiently savoring each new caress completely on the journey?" Regina whispered softly and kissed his neck quickly surprising Count Cameron. He searched the dance floor to see if anyone had witnessed it nervously as Regina returned her head to his shoulder. "It was Count Richard's gaze that caught his eye and he stared at them with a stunned expression on his face. "Your boldness in that affection to me was not missed by Count Richard." Cameron reported and Regina giggled. "Well maybe he will cease his pursuit of me and quell your animosity toward him in doing so." Regina suggested playfully. "Would you demonstrate your faith in my devotion to you before I retire?" Regina asked grinning at Cameron. "I don't like this grin. What proposal have you?" Cameron asked suspiciously. "I desire to share an embrace with Count Richard on the dance floor and secure him as friend to us both by bringing his romantic pursuit of me to an end." Regina suggested and Cameron glared at her showing his disapproval. "I would have you escort me to my quarters at its conclusion and share another sweet kiss before I retire." Regina smiled suggestively. The idea was far too tempting to Cameron and he smiled. "It should not take many turns on the floor to present your position to him. I will wait at the table for your return." Cameron replied backing away several paces before he turned to the table.

126

Countess Regina walked directly to Count Richard through the crowd and he smiled at her when he saw her approaching. He was leaning against a table conversing with a small group and there were two young women fawning over him. He stood up as she drew near realizing her eyes were fixed on him for some intention. "Has Count Cameron released his spell over you for a time that the rest of us may enjoy your company?" He laughed and the young women giggled at his jest. "Count Cameron's spell is unending but I have need of a new partner to embrace on the dance floor." Regina replied grinning broadly. "Do you encourage me to accept this task?" Richard said teasing her. "If you are otherwise occupied, I can find another." She replied turning her back to him casually to survey the hall. "No I will gladly surrender this time to embrace you on the dance floor or anywhere else you choose." Richard whispered quickly moving to her side and placing his hand on her back to guide her to the center of the dance floor. She turned to him and they began to sway to the serenade from the small orchestra. Count Richard's hand felt equally warm and comfortable on her bare back and he was much more subtle and skilled at dancing than Cameron. "I'm certain Count Cameron and every other man has told you what a beautiful dress you have." Richard said with a grin. "You flatter me Count Richard." Regina replied. "No the dress flatters you but it is what it reveals that intrigues me." Richard whispered softly in her ear as his hand pressed firmly against her back pulling her to him as they began to turn on the floor. Richard was certainly a skilled dancer. Regina thought to herself as she leaned back from him slightly. "I sought you out Count Richard, to secure your friendship for me and Count Cameron." Regina said. "What cause do I give that you would doubt our friendship? You tease me Regina for you know my desire is to be more than friend to you." Richard replied softly. His voice was soothing and enticing as was his embrace on the dance floor. Regina was confused by how comfortable she felt in his arms and leaned back to look in his eyes and refocus. "I have named Count Cameron as my suitor but it is my desire that we all remain friends." Regina whispered in his ear as if it were a secret. "A woman can have more than one suitor. Do you entice me to seek that position with you also?" Richard whispered suggestively and Regina blushed bright red. "I certainly do not. Count Cameron is my only choice and I his." Regina replied surprised by Richard's assumption. "Are you an honorable man Count Richard? Would you play the part of thief to a friend's treasure?" Regina asked and Richard chuckled and grinned. "There are some treasures so precious and desirable to coax a thief from the most honorable of men."

Richard whispered pulling her again gently against his frame as they turned on the floor. For the first time, Regina understood the power of Richard's charm and she felt guilty at how he seduced this feeling in her. "Shall I tell you now why you sought me out?" he whispered and his hand began to caress her back ever so slightly. You perceive the difference between Cameron and me. Have you yet shared a passionate kiss with him?" Richard whispered and Regina blushed. "We have." Regina admitted reluctantly enticed to hear what Richard would say next. "His kiss is sweet upon your lips and stirs inside you a magic you don't understand and I warn you neither does he. The romantic encounter is not new to me and I know precisely the source of your pleasure and will seek it out skillfully without awkwardness as Cameron does." Richard whispered softly directly into her ear. "Romantic moments are far more exciting and pleasurable when stolen." He continued and Regina was confused as to why Richard's words seemed so powerful and she leaned back and looked into his eyes again. "I will not seek public pronouncement as your suitor as Count Cameron has but you and I will know the full measure of passion I am certain of it now." Richard whispered as he stopped turning her on the dance floor and Regina realized they were back by his table. "You need only give me a sign and I will make haste to secure a rendezvous and satisfy your curiosity completely." Richard whispered lifting her hand to his lips and kissing it softly. Regina pulled her hand back to her side quickly. She knew her face was still beet red and she felt breathless from their embrace on the dance floor. Her present condition confused and angered her. "Count Richard, I assure you there will be no *sign* between you and me." She said before she turned and walked quickly away leaving Count Richard smiling at her.

"Well.., did you get the results you sought in your dance with our friend Count Richard?" Count Cameron asked. "Count Richard is neither your friend nor mine." Regina replied picking up a glass of wine and drinking from it. "It is my desire that you avoid him as will I." Regina said curtly. "Did he insult you Countess Regina?" Cameron asked with a chuckle. "No, it was not an insult per say, but I find his concept of friendship repulsive. If you and Count Richard were dear friends I would have reason to be wary of **you**. I will not repeat his counsel with me for I find it distasteful to consider even the thought. You were right to distrust him." Regina concluded taking another sip of wine as if trying to wash a bad taste from her mouth. "He proposed you meet with him secretly." Cameron said knowingly and Regina blushed red and stared at

Cameron stunned. "Is this acceptable to all men?" Regina gasped. "No but it is widely known to be Count Richard's preference. Some men can demonstrate great honor in one arena of life and fail miserably in another. Count Richard considers his romantic prowess a badge of honor. I do not. I am pleased you are not company to those women that would fall prey to a fox like Count Richard. Knowing Count Richard's intentions, you may find him humorous as we do." Count Cameron concluded still chuckling. "All his friends know this about him?" Regina asked and Cameron came close and whispered. "The talk of Count Richard is you can trust him with your life but not your wife." Cameron laughed and Regina did too but uncomfortably as she looked back to the dance floor. Count Richard had already found another partner and was dancing again. "Do we have something stronger than wine." Regina asked turning her eyes back to Cameron. He smiled pushing his glass to her. "See if this is to your liking and I will get you one." He whispered and squeezed her hand under the table as she lifted it to her lips.

Now many of the party and guest had left when Countess Regina turned to Count Cameron but it was still early. The drink Cameron bought her had the effect she had hoped for. She enjoyed it so much she had bought another for herself in Cameron's absence and she felt more than comfortable now. "I hope there are quarters left for me to retire to. I did not think to secure them and the ceremony has had many guests." Regina giggled. "One drink and your eyes are closing." Cameron chuckled. "You are not a drinker." He teased her. "I had two." Regina protested and pouted. "Besides, I have your promise to escort me to find quarters. Do I not?" Regina smiled innocently at Cameron but she did feel awkward as she rose. "I better seek now the servant Lady Erin and secure them quickly." She giggled taking Cameron's arm. "She has charge over all the servants rooms." Regina added. "I would not refuse you if you pleaded righteously to share my quarters. Do you snore?" Cameron chuckled and Regina punched his arm. "I would give up all claims to virtue being found in your quarters at first light. Escort me now to Lady Erin." She giggled and squeezed Count Cameron's arm as they walked to the stairs. Countess Regina knocked on the door to Lady Erin's quarters. "Lady Erin, have you retired?" She asked and heard a scuffle and several giggles from the other side of the door before Lady Erin opened it and stuck out her head still laughing. Her hair was in disarray and she smiled as if she guarded a secret. "My apologies but I need my things and I must inquire what room is available for me. Lady Erin let the door open just a bit more and giggled.

She was in her nightshirt and intoxicated blocking Regina's view into her room. "Your things..., Oh yes, wait here and I'll get them." She giggled slurring her speech and closed the door on them abruptly. There were more giggles before the door opened slightly again and Lady Erin handed Regina her bag. "There is an empty room at the end of this hallway on the left." Lady Erin said with an inebriated smile. "Show them in. They will not betray us!" Countess Regina recognized Count Richard's voice and pushed on the door. Lady Erin fell backwards laughing as Regina stepped into the room. Count Richard smiled at them sitting on the floor with the other three servant girls and another man she didn't recognize. "Would you like to join us in our drinking game?" Count Richard chuckled holding a pair of dice in one hand and a cup in the other. "Count Richard, we have a serious task to undertake at first light." Cameron said showing his disapproval. Count Richard seemed to straighten a little and put his arm around one of the giggling servant girls looking up at Cameron disdainfully. "Sir I will awaken before you from a much more pleasurable and satisfying sleep I am certain." He replied breaking out into a grin as the girls giggled and then he looked at Regina. "Or maybe not." He laughed and the group joined him in drunken laughter. Count Cameron backed out the door pulling Countess Regina with him and Lady Erin closed it winking at Regina. Regina tried unsuccessfully to imagine what possessed the servants to invite Count Richard to their room.

They stopped at the door Lady Erin had suggested and Cameron opened it looking inside before Regina moved past him to set her bag beside the bed. She pulled the tie under her neck that held the transparent shawl and it fell on the floor. Now Cameron was stunned waiting patiently at the door hoping to steal a kiss before departing for his own room. She moved back to him and pulled him inside the door and shut it before turning to him. "Cameron; am I merely a naïve child or does virtue in a woman have no value to men?" Regina asked him honestly and Cameron felt overwhelmed by the intimate question. "You pull me in this room and close the door to ask me this knowing how tempting you are to me?" Cameron replied painfully and took her in his arms. Your virtue is as gold to me more precious than you can imagine. I pray the debauchery we witnessed has not softened your resolve to remain virtuous until you wed?" Cameron asked nervously. Regina laid her arms on his pulling them around her waist as she looked into his eyes. "I assure you it has not." She replied frowning at him. "Is this love I feel for you Cameron? I see my value and the value of my virtue also in your eyes and I do not fear privacy with you certain you will not tempt me beyond the limits of my virtue." Regina whispered and Cameron relaxed searching her eyes. "I have been taught, the hard path leads to great riches and the easy path to disappointment." Cameron said looking at the bed and grinning. "The easy path is but a step away. Why is that path so tempting?" Cameron grimaced and chuckled nervously. "I closed the door because I promised you a sweet kiss and I will not share it with those servants or that scoundrel as we pursue understanding of this feeling between us." Regina giggled turning her head inviting him to kiss her again. Cameron leaned against the door before pressing his lips over hers and Regina melted against him. His hands caressed her softly working their way between the laces of the dress to explore her back completely and Regina did not stop him. He pushed his hands downward onto her bare hips and the soft skin covering the muscles there before caressing the curve of her bottom and up to her back again and all the while Regina made no move to stop him. As they kissed passionately, Cameron stroked the full length of her back between the laces of the velvet of her dress exploring each sensual curve he found and their passion rose quickly. Regina pulled her lips from his breathing heavily. "I am unsure where your most powerful magic resides. Is it in your lips or in your hands Count Cameron? I fear I shall never tire of your kiss or your caress." Regina sighed and returned her lips to his tugging to pull Cameron's shirt from his britches. "What boundary do we have?" Cameron gasped. Her skin felt deadly hot to his touch and his head began to swim in pleasurable confusion as her aggressive demeanor overwhelmed him. "Shall I enjoy your caress against my bare skin and deny you the same?" Regina giggled as she began to explore the massive muscles on Cameron's back under his shirt. "Are my hands magic to your skin as yours are to mine." Regina gasped kissing his neck. "Why do you not speak Cameron?" She whispered. The experience was more intense than Cameron had envisioned. "I cannot bear it." Cameron sighed kneading the muscles under her soft skin. His mind urged him to cease his erotic embrace but his hands would not obey. "Cannot bear what?" Regina whispered urgently. "I have no words worthy of this temptation." He sighed heavily returning his hands to caress what he knew should be forbidden to his touch. "I do love this dress." Cameron chuckled nervously again massaging her firmly while kissing her neck. Regina made an effort to push Cameron's shirt over his head but he resisted. He forced his hands to obey and moved them to her back again. "I beg you tempt me no further for if you remove my shirt I will press to remove your dress." Cameron whispered gasping for air in short breaths. "Do you propose an end to this sweet kiss?" Regina panted kissing his neck. Cameron resumed the soft strokes of the length of her back as far as he could reach enjoying also her lips on his neck. "Is your desire less than mine? In this moment I have control and can stop to retreat to my own quarters. If you place your dress in my hand, will you resist me when I urge you to the bed?" Cameron whispered breathlessly. Now Regina was consumed with desire and curiosity. "I find no boundary as of yet. Seeking comfort on the bed as we caress is acceptable to me now." Regina breathed into his ear writhing against him comfortably. "But my mind does struggle with this growing obsession to find a boundary." She admitted breathlessly. Cameron reluctantly pulled his hands to her shoulders. "Then yes, I beg you kiss me goodnight and let me escape to my bedchamber and to my sweet dream to wake with my self-respect at guarding your virtue." Cameron concluded and Regina kissed him passionately. "How lucky am I to have found you Cameron. Shall I tell you now that I love you? You are my protector even from my own desire for I fear I would not have resisted you and we would have found sorrow in it tomorrow." Regina whispered before kissing him again. "This shall be our boundary for a time if you find this sweet caress as pleasing as I." Regina sighed and Cameron was trembling as he created space between them reluctantly. "You shall know by my expression and my smile that it fills my thoughts when next our eyes meet and we both shall blush at the memory of it." Cameron whispered and kissed her quickly before he departed to his room.

Countess Regina leaned against the door to her room for a long moment savoring the memory of Count Cameron's kiss after she locked the door. The fire he had stirred inside her still glowed warm under her skin as she pulled the bedcovers back and removed the red velvet dress. She had no desire for the nightshirt and dove into the bed wrapping the covers around her to replace Cameron's embrace. Her head was filled with Cameron's eyes and his lips and his hands and their erotic experience. Cameron was so perfect for her, she thought. She trusted him completely and wondered if that was what love was. It was the first time she had allowed herself to explore intimacy with any boy. She had never even wanted to with anyone before and her curiosity now was powerful beyond her own understanding. Her emotions and reasoning got so confused when he kissed her. It was exciting and frightening at the same time. Her father's words echoed in her ears as she tried to make sense of it now and they suddenly made sense to her. "Passion will imprison good logic and consume any desire for restraint in its fire." He had told her. "It should be avoided until after all the other

reasons for selecting a husband are met and saved for the marriage night."
She knew now why her father had told her this. The memory of Cameron's
caress lingered on her body and in her head until slumber overcame her.

C H A P T E R 6

✳

NEGOTIATIONS

ount Arthur woke to Lord Jerome's knock at his door and he stretched sleepily for the ceiling in his room. "I have brought coffee and a dozen cups to the perch on the roof for all the riders." Jerome reported from outside the door. "Make certain all the riders have been awakened and I will be there shortly." Arthur replied swinging his legs from the bed and lifting the nightshirt over his head. He splashed water from the bowl beside his tub on his face before quickly pulling on his leathers and his boot. The faintest rays of sun barely illuminated the night sky over the mountains outside his window. As he watched, two dragons appeared flying in formation and circled past his window to land on the roof. He recognized the flash of red from Crimson's scales and hurried to finish dressing and to see who rode him. The seventh floor was crowded with riders and dragons as Arthur stepped from the stairway. Count Andrew was in a chair beside the coffee surrounded by several of the riders. Arthur was pleasantly surprised to see Countess Rebecca of Gardinia the headmaster of the dragon rider's school unbuckle herself from Crimson and join Count Andrew. Now Countess Rebecca was a short woman built sturdy and handsome. Everyone recognized her superior skills as a rider and her experience was unmatched in the kingdom. Even so she was very fair to look at and one could forget she was the epitome of a dragon rider when she let her long blonde hair down. She was an enigma to all the men having averted or discouraged any romantic involvement in favor of her career. "If I have assumed improperly, I will beg you accept quickly my apology for selecting Crimson for my mount and will seek another from Count Arthur." Countess Rebecca said and Andrew shook his head no. "Crimson is the logical choice being the eldest dragon. You honor me by your selection." Andrew replied. Countess Rebecca took survey of the riders counting heads as she pulled Countess Regina to her side and smiled at her. "We are missing one. Let us drink coffee as we await the final rider." Rebecca smiled. "It is Count Richard and he is on his way to the perch as we speak." Lord Jerome reported. "It is fine…, we have sufficient time." Rebecca said putting her arm around Countess Regina's shoulder. "Are you nervous young Countess?" Rebecca asked sipping her coffee. Regina was particularly awed and respectful of Countess Rebecca. She had shown Regina no favor when she was attending the academy and Regina knew she was the inspiration for her confidence now. "I am excited but I am not fearful." Regina replied trying to demonstrate her confidence to her mentor. "You have no cause to be fearful for your part in this task is actually the simplest of the group." Rebecca said softly. "If a mistake occurs, take care not to panic but focus correcting it quickly. No one will be aware of a mistake save us that follow you. Make your maneuvers very slowly and deliberately watching you wingmen to insure they have completed the maneuver before you attempt the next one. A four point roll takes a long time with a formation this size. Patience on your part will serve us all well." Rebecca smiled warmly and Count Richard came out from the stairway and greeted everyone on his way to the coffee. "Am I late and owe apologies?" Count Richard said and Rebecca laughed. "No Count Richard. You are simply not as early as the rest." She laughed. "We will wait until the sun presents itself fully." She added shaking his hand.

"I will give details to our task if you will all give me your ear." Countess Rebecca said loudly and all the riders took one knee and Countess Rebecca giggled. "It's as if I were back in class with all my favorite pupils." Rebecca smiled pacing in front of them. "This is a simple task. Countess Regina will take to the air and circle the city until we all have joined her in wedge formation. I shall be the last. She will head straight south from here to the shore maintaining an altitude of 200 feet and we will follow in that same formation. Give your mount his head and he will respond to Countess Regina and Waterbird. At the shoreline she will turn east and follow the coast and dropping altitude to 100 feet. Then we will practice the four point roll one time. Look to me Countess Regina and wait for my signal after each point. If successful we shall continue in formation to Green Stone. If not we will practice until we get it right. At Green Stone we land

and rest our mounts for 30 minutes. I want cool calm dragons landing at Sandista upon completion of this task. We will leave Greenstone in the same manner as we do here as Countess Regina circles the city. She will head east following the shore and we will have one final practice of the four point roll before turning north and following the coast to our guests. The ship is 30 feet high so you must maintain 100 feet altitude during the roll Countess Regina. You will begin the roll on my signal so keep an eye to me as we approach the ship. As soon as we complete the roll, I want you to bank right and begin the seven circles of the ship. I want us right down against the water as we pass the ship and take altitude enough to bank and turn in formation before going back on the deck. Seven times and then we land at Sandista. The final pass we will do at maximum speed." Countess Rebecca concluded and took a knee in front of all the riders. "You are the elite of the order of messengers from the Island of the Great Father. I challenge you now. Fly with me and deliver a message to our visitors they will relate to their children's children for decades to come. Make this our message. That this island belongs to the Sons and Daughters of the Great Father NOW and FOREVER!" Countess Rebecca shouted enthusiastically and the riders all cheered. "NOW and FOREVER!" Countess Rebecca stood and embraced them all in turn. "Mount up Countess Regina and let us depart." Countess Rebecca commanded and Regina ran to Waterbird taking the reigns from Lord Jerome.

Countess Regina could feel Emerald's breath on her back he was so close as she moved Waterbird into position on the platform. Count Arthur was keeping tight to her rear as they prepared to launch. Regina doubled the reigns in her hand and looked back at Arthur just before she leaned against Waterbird and whistled. The wind began to rush violently past her ears as Waterbird pumped his wings and they turned skyward. Regina whistled again urging Waterbird higher above the trees and looked back. A steady stream of dragons departed from both launch platforms and were speeding to catch her. She heard the triple whistle and saw Arthur and Emerald were already in their positions as Cameron and Lightning joined them. She banked left and before she had completed her circle of the city all 10 dragons flew close quarter behind her. Regina turned Waterbird due south and whistled again for more altitude. Her heart was pounding. She knew this was going to be her only challenge on the task. Waterbird was more inclined to fly just above the treetops and Regina would have to be persistent to keep him at 100 feet. Regina looked over her shoulder at Countess Rebecca and the sight was tremendously exhilarating. When

Waterbird glided with his wings spread wide, so did the other nine and when he pumped his massive wings, it was if by instinct the other nine pumped their wings in perfect sync. Regina watched the group behind her transfixed by the spectacle before she realized Countess Rebecca signaled her for more altitude. She had let Waterbird glide back to the treetops. Lowering her head she whistled and Waterbird pumped his wings and climbed. "Now stay here." Regina shouted frustrated knowing he would return to the treetops if she was not diligent. At the shoreline, Regina dug her left spur into Waterbird's side and banked and turned eastward. She watched with one eye to the horizon and the other on the formation as they turned as a single unit. Regina checked her altitude before looking back for Countess Rebecca. Her hand circled in front of her and Regina took a deep breath. "Make me proud Waterbird." She whispered easing her left spur against his side. Slowly he began to roll and Regina held it there until they got to the first point and released the pressure. She glanced over her shoulder to see Countess Rebecca wave once she finished the first point and curled the spur back into Waterbird. She held it there until they were upside down and glanced at Countess Rebecca again who waved. Regina held on tightly and dug the spur in again until they got to the 3rd point before she released pressure and waited for Countess Rebecca's signal. It came quickly and Regina dug the spur in for the final time until they were upright and released it taking a deep breath before turning to look for Countess Rebecca. She saluted her and signaled to fly on to Green Stone. Regina felt the wind blow a tear across her ear. She wept from joy and pride in herself and Waterbird leaning forward to kiss his neck. "You did good Waterbird. Now just stay at altitude for me." She giggled digging both spurs in calling for more speed. The wind began to roar past her ears as the palm trees and the beach flashed underneath her with each pump of Waterbird's wings. Too soon, the tower at Castle Green Stone came into view and Regina turned Waterbird's head to it. As they grew closer to the castle, one by one the other dragons peeled away and Regina pulled back on the reigns to slow Waterbird to land. She knew they would land in the same order they launched so she turned Waterbird's head to the perch and gave the double whistle to land. Waterbird hovered and stretched his back legs and Regina gripped tightly again as he fell forward and began to drink. "No not this time." Regina said urging Waterbird off the perch. As there were only seven perches, Regina knew she had to clear her perch quickly to give room for the next rider and his dragon. Waterbird whistled his protest but stepped off the perch. Regina was first to unbuckle and dismount and a servant took the reigns from her leading Waterbird to a trough. Dust rose up around them as the other dragons hovered before landing two by two on the roof. Count Arthur was the first to greet her as she took a cup filled with the soft cherry wine and sipped it. "Good heavens, you were magnificent Countess Regina. I thought they would break formation when you called for speed but they held perfectly." Arthur said enthusiastically. "Your roll was beyond words. I kept looking back thinking you rolled to the 2nd point too soon but it was perfect." Arthur said slapping her back. The group got quiet as Countess Rebecca made her landing and unbuckled moving quickly to Countess Regina. She wiped a tear from her eye and they all could see the pride she felt in them all. Countess Rebecca raised her glass to Countess Regina. "What a fine rider we have on point. Do we not?" Rebecca exclaimed and the group cheered and she smiled at Regina drinking her wine. "You must keep your eye on me though young countess. I would have slowed you from maximum speed to reserve stamina in our mounts had I been able to get your attention." Rebecca smiled but Regina dropped her head and Countess Rebecca raised her chin immediately. "Do not let one error so minor in its nature spoil your disposition now. Your roll was without exception and I need your spirits high to repeat it exactly so over the ship." Countess Rebecca laughed. "I see no need for another practice at the four point roll unless one of you does. We shall reserve our energy and that of our mounts for the visitors." Countess Rebecca said and walked back to inspect Crimson. "You are indeed impressive beyond words." Count Richard whispered picking up a glass from the table close to Regina. She did not turn to face him but spoke plainly. "Stand back from me Count Richard. I do not choose to name you as friend." Regina said curtly. There was a long moment before Count Richard responded. "If you took offense at my drunken words last night, accept now quickly my apology so our friendship may live." Richard replied and Regina turned to him angrily. "It is not your words that offend me but it is your person that I find utterly repulsive. I warn you Count Richard. Increase the distance between us now or I will call on my true friends to remove you from my presence." Regina said glaring at him and Count Richard smiled uneasily and walked away. Count Cameron and Count Arthur witnessed Count Richard's uneasy withdrawal from Countess Regina and moved to her side seeing her anger. "Do you want me to have words with Count Richard?" Cameron asked softly. "No." Regina said as the smile returned to her face. "If he did not understand my position last night, I am certain he does now." Regina grinned. They waited together the appropriate time before

Countess Rebecca summoned them to return to their mounts. The warm sun shone brightly in the east and Regina turned the formation directly into it following the road out of the city.

Commodore Marantz woke early and ate his breakfast with the captain of the army detachment Captain Razor and Ambassador Freeman in his quarters. Captain Manor stood by his side as they ate and talked. "Commodore Marantz what has changed since yesterday that would convince you this fishing village is part of a larger kingdom." Ambassador Freeman asked doubting the possibility. In the year they had been at sea, they had encountered many of these islands with fishing villages close to the sea as this one was. It was a large village but it appeared to be self-sufficient in his view. It had a wall around the city not just the castle and they appeared to depend solely on the sea for all its sustenance. "Come Ambassador and I will show you." Commodore Marantz suggested moving to a window in his cabin facing the island and throwing it open. He turned the telescope and adjusted it. "This is one reason I insist we sit at anchor for a time before sending the long boats out." He said stepping back from the telescope inviting the Ambassador to look. "Do you see that? Yesterday when we set anchor the area between the dock and the city wall was barren. Now there are some 50 cannon and over 300 men encamped there." Marantz said casually. "They could have just repositioned them from inside the city." Ambassador Freeman suggested and Marantz frowned readjusting the telescope. "Tell me Ambassador. Why would a commander move his cannon and his army outside his gates in full view of the ship where I could decimate them with ships cannon?" He asked pointing to the telescope again. "It's a display of power. They will retreat to the city if hostility begins. Can they range the ship from there?" Freeman replied bending to look through the telescope again. "What am I looking at now sir?" Freeman asked impatiently. "Their cannon **can** range the ship from there." Commodore Marantz said confidently and Ambassador Freeman looked shocked and worried. "If they meant to attack they would have done it at dawn." He said dismissively. "You see the raised ground at the gate. It extends southward as far as you can see. **That** Ambassador is a paved highway. I watched at least three convoys bring those cannon and those men to that encampment under the cover of darkness." Marantz reported. A sailor burst through the door frantically. "Commodore Marantz you need to come topside quickly." He reported and the panic showed in his face. Commodore Marantz followed the group through the bulkhead and up the stairs. Several men stood holding binoculars facing south. "It's a giant bird of some kind." One sailor reported nervously and Commodore Marantz took the binoculars from the closest sailor. It was huge and moving quickly directly toward the ship. The light from the sun glistened in a multicolored array streaming in all directions from it distorting his view horribly. "Get all the archers and every man with a musket on deck immediately." Marantz ordered and the deck broke into chaos. "Man the deck guns! Do not fire until I give the command!" Captain Razor shouted. "What kind of beast from hell is this? It's as wide as the ship!" Ambassador Freeman screamed. "It's not one beast. It's ten great birds and they fly in formation." Marantz reported getting a better view of them as they drew near. About 200 paces before they got to the ship, the ominous formation began to roll. Light flashed from their bodies reflected from the sun brilliantly and the formation glided silently over them upside down and Commodore Marantz had full view of the riders before they rolled back upright. "DO NOT FIRE!" Marantz shouted. "We are not under attack!" He added running to the rail to watch the formation finish the roll and bank and turn back to them. "Have your men drop their weapons. I want no incident with these riders." Marantz said shaking Captain Razor out of his trance as he stared at the formation. "Place all weapons on the deck!" Captain Razor shouted. "Show no fear men. Stand tall!" he added and they watched in awe as the riders came right alongside the ship gliding gracefully in perfect formation. All but the first rider sat upright with his hands folded across his chest defiantly. "That sir is no bird!" Ambassador Freeman gasped revealing the panic in his eyes. "That is a formation of ten of those cursed dragons we encountered on the north side of this island. These savages have befriended the underworld!" Freeman charged hysterically. "Calm yourself Ambassador. Look at them." Marantz exhaled deeply admiring them as they circled his ship. Each dragon reflected his own colors radiantly and magnificently and Marantz learned more about them with each pass. He couldn't take his eyes off of them. "They demonstrate discipline and stamina in the number of their turns. Give them a boisterous cheer as you would an ally man!" Marantz shouted and as the formation cruised past again, they shouted with one loud voice. Marantz watched them closely trying to glean as much information as he could from each pass. As they turned a short distance from his perch on the boat he heard a whistle and the formation began to gain speed. By the time they reached the ship they had turned into a blur and flashed past them at tremendous speed. The wind from their wings blew several men on the decks off their feet and Marantz watched in awe as they turned toward the village and landed atop the castle two by two. "Do you still believe this to be the only city in their kingdom?" Marantz shouted enthusiastically to Ambassador Freeman running back down to his cabin.

"What did you observe?" Commodore Marantz asked Captain Razor. "10 riders 8 men 2 women. In formation the lead rider controls. They are tethered to a harness and had no armor and carry no weapon." Razor reported. "And they command by whistling." Marantz added. "They could carry weapons and armor if they chose to. I wonder how many they have but we shall know for certainty soon enough." Marantz said. "You do not seriously plan to attack these people." Ambassador Freeman asked. "I most certainly do but not as you suppose Ambassador. You are going ashore with as much treasure as we can fill 4 long boats with as gifts for them. You will take no weapons but only scholars and scribes. You are to befriend them and learn their language and teach them ours. Set your camp right next to their military encampment. Bend your knee to every man you encounter. I want their impression of us to be of humble men eager to ally with them as brothers. I have but two objectives to serve our king. Conquer whom I can and make an ally of those I cannot." Commodore Marantz concluded. "I would choose them as ally. We have seen the potential of these dragons on the north side of this island. Their scales are like hardened armor and they breathe fire that consumes and enemy at some distance." Captain Razor added and Commodore Marantz pulled at his thick red beard still contemplating the formation. "Yes we have seen this. I am curious as to why their captain did not make demonstration of that ability?" Marantz questioned. "He is a wise tactician. I would not reveal the full potential of my defenses before combat either." Captain Razor suggested. "I venture he has 3 times the army he has revealed to us this day. By the book, a seasoned captain will send one third of his army forward and keep two thirds in reserve." Captain Razor added and Marantz chuckled heartily. "You assume he studied tactics at the same academy as you captain. Regardless, I will know the secrets of this island kingdom. You have skills as a liaison Ambassador. Perhaps they shall become allies." Commodore Marantz suggested. You have one month Ambassador Freeman; to learn their language and secure this allegiance. Go now and prepare." Commodore Marantz said and turned to his 1st mate Captain Manor. He waited until the Ambassador had left. "Let's keep this discussion of conquest between us three. It will better serve our cause if all our men view the inhabitants of this island as potential allies. Go secretly, Captain Manor and send a message home by two pigeons and tell them we have found a great treasure and should send the armada. Commodore Marantz ordered.

Countess Regina whistled twice and Waterbird hovered over the perch atop Castle Sandista lowering his legs and Regina clung tightly to the harness as he fell forward. As Waterbird folded his wings at his side, she unbuckled quickly handing the reigns to a servant as she dismounted full of excitement. Waterbird hissed and whistled at the servant protesting as the servant led him off the perch to another trough. She met Count Arthur as he stepped down from the perch and her enthusiasm overwhelmed her. She embraced him hugging his neck and they laughed excitedly as the other riders made their landing and joined in their embrace and they danced together. Two by two the other riders landed and their celebration increased in intensity until Countess Rebecca joined them with equal enthusiasm. "I believe we have delivered a clear undeniable message this day!" Rebecca shouted and they all shouted in unison. "NOW and FOREVER! A servant with a large bag came to Countess Rebecca and laid it at her feet before whispering in her ear. Rebecca raised her arms over her head and all the riders went to one knee in silence. Rebecca reached in the bag and pulled out the formal sash of the messenger in the color of Sandista pulling it over her head. "Curb your enthusiasm now and gather your thoughts and the memory of all that you have witnessed in the execution of this task. There is a second part to this task that I could not reveal until now." Rebecca said straightening the sash and smoothing it over her chest smiling excitedly. "Come now and retrieve a sash in the color of your city for we have an audience with the Great Father, The supreme council and all the Kings and Queens of the kingdom this very hour here in the throne room." Countess Rebecca announced and each rider came to her to receive his sash. Regina had suspected as much seeing Countess Rebecca dawn the sash as it was only worn in formal ceremony before Royalty. Her nervousness returned as she pulled the sash into place and a servant quickly undid the braid and brushed her hair down over her shoulders. "Follow me know, for we shall give account of all we have seen with regard to the ship and the visitors directly to the Great Father while it is still fresh in our minds." Countess Rebecca said walking to the stairs.

The throne room had been rearranged for their meeting. The rulers of the seven cities sat in grand chairs behind the Great Father on the throne and seven members of the Supreme Council sat at a long table in front of all of them. Ten chairs faced the table where the Supreme Council sat. Countess Regina stood in the doorway behind Countess Rebecca and her hands trembled. Countess Rebecca turned to the riders. "Do as I do and then take a chair at the table." She whispered and turned back facing the assembly. The two trumpeters at the door blew a long blast and all the Chancellors in the assembly looked at them. Regina's knees felt weak and she wished she had eaten breakfast as a servant began to shout. "To the Great Father and his Supreme Council and to the Rulers of the Seven Cities, I present Countess Rebecca of Gardinia Headmaster of the Academy of Messengers." He concluded and all the Chancellors stood and applauded as Countess Rebecca walked quickly forward. Regina watched closely fearing she would miss something as Countess Rebecca dropped to one knee and bowed her head before the Great Father. The seven rulers of the seven cities looked magnificent wearing robes in the color of their city embroidered with gold and silver and wearing jeweled crowns of gold but they paled in comparison to the vision of the Great Father. A large silver torch burned on either side of the throne where the Great Father sat with his hands outstretched over the arms of the throne with a large silver and gold staff in his lap. His robe was brilliant white with wide silver embroidery outlined in black silk down the lapel all the way to his feet. His crown was silver ordained with radiant black onyx stones and his hair was dyed white braided with black silk ribbons falling to his waist in front of him alongside his long white beard. "Rise Countess Rebecca and take council with us." The Great Father said and his voice was warm and soothingly powerful. Countess Rebecca rose up and took a chair facing the Chancellors before the servant began to shout again. "To the Great Father and the Supreme Council and to the Rulers of the Seven Cities, I present Countess Regina of Red Oak." He concluded and the Chancellors applauded again. Regina summoned all her energy and prayed she would not faint walking forward and dropping to one knee as she had seen Countess Rebecca do. "Rise Countess Regina and take council with us." The Great Father said and tears filled Regina's eyes hearing the Great Father utter her name. She got up slowly and took a chair beside Countess Rebecca. Regina looked across the table at the Chancellor sitting across from her that she was sure she had never seen before and he smiled at her. "Breathe young countess." Rebecca whispered and Regina inhaled deeply trying to smile back at the chancellor. One by one the riders in her party were introduced and took a chair until the last chair was filled and the Chancellor across for Countess Regina stood. "All the member being present this council is declared by the Great Father closed and guarded." He said in a loud voice and all the servants departed and the doors to the throne room were closed. "Being suitably closed and guarded each member is warned revelations of topics or substance matter relating to this council outside these walls will be grounds for an accusation of treason against Sons and Daughters of the Great Father." He concluded and sat back down. He and all the Chancellors opened the leather binders in front of them and began to write. "I wish to congratulate you all in the perfect execution of my task to you so far." The Great Father said and the Chancellors again applauded smiling at the riders with admiration before the Great Father tapped the floor with his staff. "Now we shall examine together your account of the task and I beg you reveal to me and the council every minute detail of what you saw, heard or even smelled or felt. Each one of you in turn will tell your tale to me as you would a friend. Reveal your account comfortably without fear and do not let this council intimate you in any way. Share your adventure with us completely and take honor and joy in your telling of it for this will be the last audience you may ever share your tale with. You will never be able to relate this tale to your little brother or sister or your mother or father or anyone you do not see present with us now. If this is understood by you I require you now to respond I do." The Great Father said and all the riders responded. "I DO!" The Great Father surveyed the room. "Who then was on point?" He asked and Regina looked to Countess Rebecca fearful to respond directly to the Great Father. "He is addressing you. Countess Regina." Rebecca said and Regina felt her heart would burst from her chest and she was certain she would faint. "Do you not wish to honor the desires of the Great Father in that I have pleaded with you not to be intimidated by me or the council? I know it must seem odd that I have commanded you all to relate directly to me instead of a councilman or a captain as you are accustomed to. Ten generations have passed since last a ship from another land has anchored on our coast. They brought good and evil to our shores on one ship. They taught the Sons and Daughter much about agriculture and mining and how to renew the forests but they also brought a desire to disband our way of life and rule over us." The Great Father said and looked at Regina sympathetically. He rose from the throne and walked to the Chancellor in front of Regina urging him to stand and when he did he took his chair. Regina bowed her head and gasped for air. "Is your father still living young countess." He asked. "Yes." Regina replied and he laughed softly and warmly. "She finds her voice. What an excellent start." He chuckled and a few of the council chuckled softly also. "Are my eyes so different than his that you cannot look to them when you speak?" He said softly and Regina lifted her head and gazed into his eyes. "Your eyes are green and brown just like my fathers." Regina smiled and felt the warm inviting smile he returned to her. "If you have had occasion to relate an adventure to your father do so likewise with me now. It must have been a grand adventure for you. Tell me now…, what did you see when you first approached the ship?" He asked. "It was anchored by a heavy chain each link the size of a wine barrel from the market. It hung from a window on the second deck and there were three decks below and one above where the men on deck watched us. There were four arms to control the rudder and it sat low in the water. There were three masts and a man was in a basket watching us atop the second mast. I turned to look to Countess Rebecca and she gave me the signal to begin the roll. I did not look back at the ship until we finished the roll on the other side of it." Regina said and the Great Father smiled. "You tell a story well. Keep no detail from me, what did you see as you came about?" He asked and his expression was excited and he showed his intrigue. Regina started to relax feeling more confident. "The first thing I noticed were the men on deck scurrying about. Some had crackers and some long bows and they were taking aim to fire before a man shouted and they began to lay them down on the deck. There were four little cannons mounted on swivels. Two mounted port side and two starboard and they were manned. Only the ten windows below the top deck had cannons in them on either side of the ship, the others were closed save one and there were no cannon in it but you could see crates in a wide storage area on that deck. There were ten men at the wheel house but only two wore hats and they had long curved swords on their belts. One had a red beard and wore a red and black jacket with a white shirt. The other wore a brown uniform as many of the men on deck did but his had gold shoulder boards and he had a black beard. There was one man with them not attired like any other. He wore a blue robe like a councilman. Every time we passed there were more men on deck. I saw three uniforms. The brown uniform was worn by most but many men wore brown shirts and blue britches. A few men wore blue shirts and blue britches. The man with the black beard was always shouting each time we passed except for our sixth pass when they all shouted and cheered at us. They tried to demonstrate courage but I could see they were very fearful of us." Countess Regina concluded. The Great Father smiled at her obviously pleased with her account and nodded. "I knew you had a fine account of you adventure. Do you not agree gentlemen?" He asked and all the Chancellor's put down their pens and applauded. "How old are you young countess?" The Great Father asked as he stood. "I'm 17 sir." Regina replied and The Great Father turned to look at her King. "You must be very proud of her Raymond. She reflects great honor on all of Red Oak." He said returning to his throne as the council continued to applaud. "Countess Regina I want you to be assured, should another detail come to your memory you need only present yourself to King Raymond or any of the Chancellors present to relay it to us no matter how small you may perceive it to be." He said and tapped his staff. "Now which of you took position to Countess Regina's left flank?" The Great Father asked and Count Arthur replied. "I did sir." For the rest of the morning, one by one the riders gave their account of the task and Regina felt exceedingly proud of herself and her companions. The chancellors scribbled hastily to keep up and whispered amongst themselves during the whole ordeal. Every so often one would interrupt and ask a question. After Countess Rebecca gave her account, the Great Father tapped his staff again. "Is there any detail, from any of you, that comes to memory now that you would share?" He asked and no one stirred. "I want to share my immense affection for each of you but remind you. What has been revealed here is to be kept in confidence. I assure you I will not restrain the magistrate from levying the full weight of the law on any man or woman who would violate our confidence." The Great Father said seriously before he smiled broadly again. "I hear you did not breakfast this morning." He laughed. "In the dining hall of this castle you will find a feast prepared, usually reserved for me and the Supreme Council. Today I am the servant of you elite few and I have had it prepared for you all. In addition there is a small gift on your plate for each of you to show our gratitude. Go now and eat before you take the rest of the day to fulfill your own desires for you have done well in fulfilling mine and your kingdoms." He concluded and tapped his staff. "Watch me." Countess Rebecca whispered in her ear as the Chancellor in front of Countess Regina rose. "Having concluded all witness relating to this guarded and closed council this conference is adjourned." The Chancellor shouted and Countess Rebecca rose and kneeled before the Great Father. "You are dismissed with our blessing Countess Rebecca." The Great Father said and Rebecca rose and turned to make her exit. Countess Regina and the other riders followed Rebecca's lead until they all had been dismissed.

As the last of the messengers departed the throne room, the seven rulers of the seven cities moved to the table with the Chancellors. "We have much to discuss." The Great Father said. "Let us take the midday meal here and continue this council in closed session." He commanded signaled to the lead Chancellor. A procession of servants brought trays filled with food and drink filling the table as the Great Father took his place at the head of the table. Once all the food and drink was brought in, the lead Chancellor directed the servants to close the door to the throne room again. They took council arduously for several hours deliberating over all the facts they had about the visitors. "We have two paths in front of us. Make alliance with our visitors or make war and repel them from our shores. I propose we make intricate plans to travel both paths deferring to the latter only by decree of the supreme council should their intentions be revealed to us as evil." The Great Father suggested as he ate. "They will be revealed as evil in time. Men do not risk life and fortune on the vast ocean if not for treasure and conquest." Queen Isabella said calmly. "Conquest need not always be done by violent means. Perhaps these visitors have peaceful intentions merely to expand their understanding of the world and its inhabitants. The dragon riders delivered an aggressive message and they did not respond with an attack. The demonstration was designed to solicit a response and I perceive their response to reveal their intentions peaceful." King Jeffrey replied. "We overwhelmed their ship with the perceived power of the messengers. A skilled warrior will patiently await an opening before he attacks a foe he perceives to be superior. I fear they will seek out and eventually find an advantage if we give them time." Queen Isabella said adamantly. "All things are possible." King Kevin interjected. "Sandista and Archemeius are particularly vulnerable being on the coast but I personally would risk much, cautiously of course, in making a new ally." He added. "Sandista and Archemeius are both sufficient distance from shore and their ships cannon will not range them. I propose we move hastily to refit our ships and reinforce Sandista and Archemeius as we pursue peace fervently with these visitors." King Kevin suggested and many of the council shook their heads in agreement. "This single ship and its occupants can be easily contained but it very well may be the first of a hundred such ships. We should guard carefully what we reveal to them about the kingdom. "Queen Pamela said. "Requiring them to remain on their ship seems inhospitable to me but I would not have them wander aimlessly over the kingdom. I propose we construct an encampment north of the docks at Sandista and restrict their movement to their ship and that encampment for the present." Queen Pamela suggested. "I have an envoy selected and prepared to venture out to their ship on long boats to greet them as we previously discussed." Chancellor Simon reported. "I have three boats, two of which are filled with gifts of various kinds. There is much venison and pork as we discussed since men at sea for a prolonged journey would find these rare delicacies. I will accompany the lead boat with scholars to begin a dialog with them." Chancellor Simon concluded. "You should move hastily at the conclusion of this session to do so Chancellor Simon." The Great Father agreed. "I would propose King Jeffrey oversee our efforts to befriend our guests and make allies of them and all tasks assumed therein and Queen Isabella oversee our efforts to prepare and defend in the event it is necessary." The Great Father commanded and the council nodded in agreement save Queen Isabella. "I accept this task and thank the council for it for it is the defense of the kingdom that concerns me most fervently. I would make my dissent known now for my council would be to burn their ship and imprison their crew before they could reveal our presence to whomever they serve. The longer we wait to eliminate this threat to the kingdom, the more precarious our position becomes." Queen Isabella said with conviction. "Your dissention is noted with respect Queen Isabella. There being two proposals I submit the Supreme Council take vote and decide. Shall we pursue the course the Great Father has suggested or destroy their ship and imprison their crew." Chancellor Simon announced and each Chancellor opened his folder and wrote in it tearing the page from his folder and folding it before handing it to Chancellor Simon. He waited until he had all seven papers before unfolding them inspecting each. "The vote of the council is 5 to 2 to accept the Great Father's proposal. "King Jeffrey will keep us abreast of his progress as will Queen Isabella. I propose now that we all return to our own cities to see to affairs at home." The Great Father said and Chancellor Simon stood. "Before we adjourn, I have one more proposal to the council." Queen Isabella suggested. "I propose the messengers we witnessed execute their task so perfectly today be reconstituted as a combat force and stationed here at the School of the messengers under command of Countess Rebecca. I would desire that they practice their combat tactics north of Sandista in full view of our visitors to perpetuate the deception that this combat force existed prior to their arrival. In addition, this would remove the temptation for the riders to recount their adventure to friends and family at home." Queen Isabella suggested and the council nodded their approval. "Is there dissention by any member of the council requiring a vote?" The Great Father asked and there was none. "Then let it be done so." He said and nodded to Chancellor Simon. "Having concluded all deliberations of this closed and guarded session the High Council of the Sons and Daughters of the Great Father is adjourned." He shouted and the Rulers of all the cities and the all the other members of the council departed the throne room.

Count Arthur sat next to Countess Rebecca in the dining room anxious to share the rest of the afternoon with her. There were many topics he would like to discuss with her but the most pressing on his mind was the secret Councilman Trent and Count Andrew had shared with him. "Crimson grows very close to his day of maturity." Arthur said casually as they ate. "Yes, I fear Count Andrew's first task after he recovers is going to be to release his dragon back to his brothers and sisters in the mountains." Rebecca smiled. "He has discussed his desire that I be his companion bringing two horses to the release point as is our custom." Arthur said cautiously watching her face carefully but she gave no hint of surprise. "You would honor him in doing so. I had presumed his servant Kenneth would perform that task." Rebecca replied continuing to eat. "What will you do with your bonus?" Rebecca asked changing the subject. Each rider had found gold coins in a box on their plate when they arrived. "50 marks is a substantial amount but being that I am to be married to the Maiden Melisa of Archemeius this seventh day, I will probably need it to fulfill her desires with the ceremony." Arthur replied smiling and Rebecca sat her knife and fork down turning to look at Arthur. "I beg you accept quickly my apology for I had forgotten with all the other events on my mind of late." Rebecca smiled broadly. "I suppose you find these tasks a pleasant diversion from planning a wedding." Rebecca suggested with a chuckle. "I look forward to the ceremony but I would leave the planning of it to Maiden Melisa and her servants and friends. Councilman Trent has been a great ally to her of recent." Arthur replied. "Councilman Trent and his wife both love weddings. I know them both." Rebecca smiled. It was becoming apparent to Arthur that Count Andrew had not told Countess Rebecca of his inclusion in their secret. "There is a matter concerning Councilman Trent and Count Andrew that I would discuss with you in private should you avail the opportunity to me." Arthur said sipping from his glass casually and Countess Rebecca showed the first glimmer of concern in her eyes. Before she could respond, a servant whispered in her ear pointing to the stairway. "I shall return quickly to continue our discussion but one of the Chancellors has summoned me. I pray you will wait for me." Countess Rebecca said as she stood and departed.

Count Cameron finished his meal and sipped his coffee admiring Countess Regina at the other end of the table. His thoughts had been consumed all day by the task and the ship and its occupants but now they drifted back to last night and his time with Countess Regina. How quickly she had transformed. Last night, she was a ravishing young woman who had shared with him the most intimate of kisses and this morning she was a champion messenger capable to accomplish any task the men could and he loved both of them. He set in his mind, to invite her to spend the rest of the day with him. He regretted not telling her he loved her too when she had uttered those words to him and was determined to correct his mistake before they parted company today. Countess Regina was laughing heartily with two other riders as Count Cameron approached her. "I never witness so many men so completely filled with fear." Countess Regina laughed. "Well they probably never witnessed a warrior princess on her dragon like you either." Count Arthur chuckled. Cameron put his hand on Countess Regina's shoulder. "I am considering a venture to the market place here to find purpose for my bonus. Would you find pleasure in being my escort Countess Regina?" Cameron asked and Regina grinned. "I must admit these coins burn a hole in my belt and a walk after such a feast is inviting." Regina replied and she took Cameron's hand to stand.

The servants were moving about the table removing the plates as Countess Rebecca returned and urged them to give their table privacy again. "I beg you suffer me a few more moments before you go your own way for I have exciting news for your ears only." Countess Rebecca whispered drawing them all close to the table curiously. "The Great Father and the Supreme Council have reconstituted the ten of us as the first ever combat team of dragon riders." Countess Rebecca whispered excitedly and the riders were all struck speechless. "You are all to be reassigned here at the school under my command." Countess Rebecca whispered and her excitement increased in intensity looking to Countess Regina. "The Garrison Commander himself will preside at the ceremony this very night as the sun sets. You will no longer be addressed as Countess Regina but instead as Lieutenant Regina as he will commission you in the grade of 1st class Lieutenant. I am to receive commission as your Captain." Countess Rebecca smiled. "Oh my God, all of us?" Arthur exclaimed. "What uniform shall we wear?" He asked enthusiastically. "Everything we do from this point forward will be of our own design save the insignia for 1st Lieutenant will be the same. Everything, from our uniform to our weapons even to include our tactics and strategies. We will design and practice them together here at the academy under command of the Garrison Commander at Castle Green Stone." Countess Rebecca said and Arthur looked perplexed for a moment. Count Arthur was considering the impact on his wedding to Maid Melisa on the next seventh day. "So we will all move here to Sandista?" Arthur asked and Rebecca looked to him understandingly. "You may each have one servant bring your belongings and accompany you here immediately at the school. By the end of this seventh day, I will insure that quarters are adequate to shelter those of you with other family concerns. Neither your marriage plans nor your desire to provide luxuriously for your bride need suffer Count Arthur. All of you shall benefit immensely from your increased stature in the Kingdom but a soldier is not royalty and you lose your quarters in the castle and your position in the royal family." Rebecca smiled. "You are not forced to take this commission. I have authority to select a replacement for you if that is your desire." Rebecca added and the group laughed heartily together. "You think there is one of us that would hesitate to accept this honor?" Arthur laughed surveying the room. "Well, save Count Richard. He may find breaking the hearts of all those young admirers in Archemeius to difficult a task." Arthur joked and everyone laughed. "It will be a great sacrifice for me also but I will find comfort somewhere in Sandista I am certain when I dawn the uniform of 1ˢᵗ Lieutenant." Richard said boldly and laughing. Countess Regina just shook her head. "It will not change him." She thought to herself. "I have much to do. Count Arthur, would you escort me to the academy and share council with me about our future?" Countess Rebecca asked and Arthur stood to leave with her. "Think on this today. We receive our commissions and commission also a name for our detachment at sunset. Take council together and we will vote on its name before the ceremony." Countess Rebecca said and her and Count Arthur departed. "We're going to be commissioned as 1ˢᵗ Lieutenants. Do you even know what a 1ˢᵗ Lieutenant draws as salary?" Countess Regina giggled excitely hugging Count Cameron and he returned her embrace enthusiastically. "I do not but I am certain it is more than double that of a messenger." He replied. "Instead of shopping, I suggest we all make haste to the tailor and undertake the task of designing our uniform as I am certain Countess Rebecca and Count Arthur are addressing the issue of quarters at the school." Regina suggested looking at Count Richard and the rest of the riders. "You invite me to assist in this task?" Richard asked her. "As we are to be intimate companions in this new detachment, I chose to forgive you your past indiscretions and pray your personal conduct will rise to honor your new position. I will call you friend and companion Richard if you will only show me respect henceforth in our associations." Countess Regina said holding her hand out to Count Richard. Richard took her hand grinning. "I respect your abilities as a rider. You are *almost* my equal." Richard chuckled teasing her. "It will be hard to disregard your charm as a woman but I will not make the same mistake with you and incur your wrath again." Richard smiled. "I owe this to you and Count Cameron." He added offering his hand to Cameron and Regina felt a burden lifted from her shoulders believing Richard was sincere in his desire to show them respect. He would not pursue her romantically. Together the eight of them found their way to the market place and a tailor to deliberate and design a uniform.

C H A P T E R 7

SKY RAIDERS

Arthur walked silently toward the Academy of Dragon Riders with Countess Rebecca on his arm. The school is a large three story building made of stone and marble. The stables for the dragons separated it from Castle Sandista and it drew water from the same canal as the castle. It has its own kitchen on the second floor and there were 14 rooms on the 3rd floor that were primarily storage rooms with a few classrooms. Even when he was in school, Arthur had never been past the first floor where the dining hall and classrooms were. Servants always brought their meals down to them. Countess Rebecca gathered all the staff into the dining hall and divided them into groups starting to delegate tasks and explain what transformations had to take place. "In addition to everything else, I want the entire third floor cleared of storage and prepared as quarters. Get the engineers started today for it is my desire to have water running and a bath in each of those rooms by the seventh day." Countess Rebecca stated and Arthur could see the look of concern on all the servants faces. "Countess…, 14 rooms cleared and prepared by the seventh? This is a tremendous task. I will need to hire every carpenter and engineer in Sandista." He protested. "Lord Falcon, if you understand what you need, why do you tarry? Do you plan to negotiate with me for more time?" Countess Rebecca asked forcefully. "No Countess, I know that would be a waste of my energy and yours." He replied and departed quickly. Countess Rebecca led Arthur to a storage room on the third floor. "I'm going to make this the room an office and strategy room." She said and climbed a ladder onto the roof. She had to move crates out of the way to get around the huge tub holding the water for the building to get to the north wall. "Do you think we could build two launches on this wall and walk the dragons around the tub if I build perches from the south wall to the tub?" Countess Rebecca asked and Arthur walked to the north wall and looked over. "They would have to bear left and fly behind the buildings but there is ample room to build speed to take flight from here." Arthur replied looking across the open courtyard. "Why build perches here when there are seven atop the castle?" He asked. "I don't want to interfere with the messengers or have them interfere with me." Rebecca replied as she pulled up a barrel and sat down motioning to Arthur to sit also. "You said earlier you needed to speak to me about Councilman Trent and Count Andrew." Rebecca said looking to the hatch to insure they were alone. You should know that Count Andrew is to be a member of this unit and will receive a commission also. The supreme Council wanted ten riders and I will not ride but serve only as your Captain." Countess Rebecca said. "I will not mince words as time is short and new tasks seem to fill our time quickly. Councilman Trent and Count Andrew made me ally with them and you with regard to his task with Crimson." Arthur said and Rebecca dropped her head dejectedly and shook it. "And to what end did they deem it necessary to make you our ally. What position do they propose to fill in your inclusion as everything is assured and complete?" Rebecca asked looking up. "I am a rider, I am a man of some strength and I think fair intelligence. What happens if Count Andrew is injured again as he is now or one of you his other allies? I can learn and support where needed increasing our chance of success. Will Crimson wait if Count Andrew breaks his leg? I am more closely the same size as Count Andrew and the armor should fit me better." Arthur concluded and Rebecca looked at him still disappointed. "Did you coax this alliance from Count Andrew after his accident? Do you have any idea what we and now you risk even if we are successful." She asked. "I am fearfully aware of it but I would turn down this commission before I would retreat from this task and I have desire to do neither." Arthur admitted. "Take me into your confidence and show me the camp." Arthur pleaded. Now Rebecca had a look of surrender on her face as she stood up. "Let's go. Keep silent as we retrieve our mounts." Rebecca said moving to the ladder. "Once airborne, stay close on my tail when we get north of Willow Lake. I have set everything in motion here and I believe our other ally is at the encampment today. This will be a perfect time to visit it while the others are occupied." Rebecca whispered as they walked back to the castle.

Arthur buckled himself into Emerald's harness as Countess Rebecca spoke to a servant explaining their intent. Shortly, she mounted Crimson and they moved to the launching platforms. Rolling the reigns in his hands he whistled and Emerald bounded from the platform and air rushed past his cheeks. He searched the blue skies and found Crimson and Rebecca were heading due west into the mountains. He turned Emerald's head and soon they were closing on Crimson. The sun was high over head and Arthur felt it on his back through the leather vest as they crossed the mountain range. Rebecca took Crimson right to the treetops once they cleared the mountains and Arthur whistled commanding Emerald to follow and relaxed atop him. The smell of the forest filled his nostrils as they cruised effortlessly for a long while. Rebecca turned and yelled to him after they crossed the north river. "Formation flight won't work when I drop down into the trees. Stay close to me Count Arthur!" She shouted and Arthur whistled signaling Emerald to break formation. Rebecca began to slow Crimson and Arthur followed suit as she dove down below the trees. It made Arthur very nervous as they banked between the giant red oaks and Rebecca turned north. He could see they were getting very close to the northern mountain range and they had just turned into a small clearing when he heard Countess Rebecca's double whistle and he did likewise with Emerald. Rebecca urged Crimson into the tree line still heading north on foot and Arthur followed. The path was unclear and they rode for about 200 paces through the dense forest before Arthur saw the shack with the horse tied to a post in front. They unbuckled and dismounted and Rebecca led Crimson straight to a cave with an iron gate. "Chancellor Winston; it's just me don't be alarmed we have a new ally!" She shouted before turning to Arthur. "There's water in the cave but there's only room for one inside. Tie Emerald to that tree and then get him some water." Rebecca said as she and Crimson disappeared into the cave. As Arthur did as she had instructed, a tall man in hunter's attire emerged from the shack carrying a very large pouch and moved quickly to the cave. Arthur followed him in to find the water. "Did you know the dragon blood I dumped behind the shack attracts insects like other blood but they all die when they come in contact with it?" He said and Rebecca looked at him perplexed. "That's very interesting Chancellor. Say hello to Count Arthur our newest ally." She said taking the pouch from him and hanging it on a pole next to Crimson. "Well I don't know why they changed their minds but I'm glad to have the help." Chancellor Winston said as he drove a syringe under Crimson's scales on his neck. Arthur saw a bucket beside the trough for Crimson and filled it to take to Emerald. "That doesn't seem to bother him." Arthur said watching Winston hook up the tubes to take blood from Crimson. "Oh no, he can't even feel it." Winston replied and Arthur took the bucket out to Emerald to drink setting it down in front of him. As he walked back in he inspected the iron gate with its hinges bolted into the side of the cave. It was certainly strong enough to hold Crimson and covered the entire mouth of the cave. As he walked into the cave Rebecca was backing Crimson into a wedge in the cave. "Come look, follow me." She said and disappeared behind Crimson. He walked past Crimson as Winston checked the pouch before he followed him. It got very narrow and then opened up into the shed. "You see, after each ride, Count Andrew will back him into the wedge and he can mount and dismount from the rear." Countess Rebecca said and pulled a chain that led back to the cave. "This is a trap for Crimson's head that keeps him from turning it around." She added. Arthur peered back into the cave at Crimson. "I'm certain you've seen a dragon when it gets really upset. They can certainly thrash about mercilessly when agitated." Arthur said. "Not in the wedge. With the restraints Councilman Trent has developed, I can pin Crimson down where he can't flinch a talon without hurting him in the least." Rebecca replied pointing to other chains that ran through holes and into the cave. "How long do we have to wait to fill the pouch?" Arthur asked sitting down on a stool. "It will take about an hour and last about a week. Do you want to see the Armor?" She asked moving to a large closet against the stone back of the shed. Arthur stood back up and peered over Rebecca's shoulder as she opened the door. The armor hung in the closet by leather straps and Arthur reached by Rebecca and lifted it by the straps. "It's much lighter than it looks." Arthur said admiring it. The hood was attached to the vest the same way the vest was attached to the coat and the gloves were attached to the coat. The mesh of intricately woven tiny tubes between them tied all the brilliant red scales together. A larger mesh tubes tied the britches and boots to the coat. "The scales are the same color as Crimson." Arthur observed. "They weren't when I selected them. It's Crimson's blood that develops the color as well as the strength and all the other features." Chancellor Winston said caressing the scales on the coat. "It will start to fade after a few hours without the blood but it revives quickly." He added. "You should have been a tailor Chancellor Winston. It looks magnificent." Arthur replied. "Crimson is really becoming comfortable in the cave. It will be important as he seeks relief from the torment of his transformation that the cave is a source of familiarity and comfort to him. Repetition in all the tasks is key. I do wish Count Andrew was well enough to make these visits with Crimson. I can mount and dismount in the wedge with him but Count Andrew is more familiar to him. We give him a special treat of bananas and mangos in the wedge each time he backs in and he has become very comfortable with the maneuver." Countess Rebecca said confidently. "Has Count Andrew ridden him wearing the armor?" Arthur asked and Chancellor Winston shook his head yes. "On several occasions; we are completely confident with the performance of the armor during flight. Our biggest challenge is on the ground should Crimson decide to roll to try to unseat Count Andrew once outside the wedge." He said showing his concern in his expression. The Armor will protect Count Andrew from a great deal of heat but if Crimson focuses and attacks with determination, he will burn Count Andrew." He said shaking his head. "How long do we have before Crimson begins his transformation? I have an idea." Arthur said standing to inspect the suit again. "Two maybe three weeks." Rebecca replied curiously. "Can you make another suit in that time? Not another complete suit but only one that I could wear and serve as decoy and distraction should the situation arise." Arthur suggested and Chancellor Winston scratched his head contemplating it. "I may be able to stand with Andrew on the ground and keep control of Crimson retarding his desire to roll." Arthur added and Rebecca nodded. "Not a shield, mind you, for I will need both hands." He concluded and Chancellor Winston opened a chest in the corner of the shack pulling out a coat and britches made with what appeared to be gray dragon scale. "This design was flawed. "We were going to use the pouch filled with blood and secure it to the riders back but that didn't work. In a week I could modify it to fit your task." Count Winston said pulling it up on the table. "You will only have protection from the front so you will never be able to turn your back on Crimson." He warned as he began to pull apart the mesh of tubes on the suit. "You should return now Count Arthur. We should not return to the Castle together. Limiting our time together will aid in guarding our secret." Countess Rebecca said and Arthur smiled pleased that he had found a purpose for himself in their task. "I shall return in seven days at midday to see what progress you have made." Arthur said as they walked out together. "I will be here before midday and hopefully have a good report for you." Chancellor Winston said as Count Arthur buckled himself in to Emerald's harness. He turned Emerald south and walked him through the trees to the clearing before he doubled the reigns in his hands and whistled. Emerald ran full out for several paces before he spread his wings and pumped them frantically and forcefully. Slowly they became airborne and Arthur felt Emerald tuck his legs underneath them just before he reached the treetops. He continued straight south and Arthur looked back over his shoulder trying to remind himself of the terrain features so he could find the clearing again. They cruised right at the tops of the trees heading due south until they got to Willow Lake where Count Arthur committed a fallen tree next to the lake to memory as a reference point and turned Emeralds head due east to follow the shoreline of the lake. He got his bearings again at the north river and continued to follow the shoreline south until he came to the east river. Arthur whistled again calling for more altitude after he turned Emerald east toward the mountains. He sat upright on Emerald enjoying the warm sun and the rush of air over his torso. Emerald whistled contently and banked lazily keeping his course steady moving east into the mountains. The route back to the shack was tricky but Arthur was certain he would find it again as long as the weather held and no one removed the fallen tree by the lake. As he banked through the pass, he turned and there it was again. A giant white dragon hovered directly in front of him blocking his flight path. He whistled calling for maximum speed and they blew by the huge mature dragon just missing him. He looked over his shoulder nervously as the large white beast followed them closing fast. Arthur's heart pounded in his chest as the formidable shadow covered him and Emerald. Arthur dug his heel into Emerald and the rolled and dove away from the shadow and it disappeared once again. "Blast!" Arthur cursed searching the sky behind him but it was clear. He wondered if all white dragons were territorial and aggressive like that. That was now the fourth time a white dragon had pursued and chased him away. On the downward slope of the mountain, Castle Sandista came into view quickly. Arthur pulled back on the reigns slowing Emerald and he made a circle around the city wall. There was an unusual amount of traffic on the highway going and coming to the city. As he pointed Emerald's head to the perch atop the castle he noticed the mass of people scurrying around the Rider's Academy and smiled knowing they were working diligently to meet Countess Rebecca's demands. Emerald began to hover and Arthur held tight to the harness as he stretched his back talons to the perch before falling forward. "I have completed my tasks for the day as has Emerald sir." Arthur said handing the reigns to a servant as he unbuckled and dismounted to go find his comrades.

Count Richard held up the Army uniform displaying it to the other riders in the tailor's shop. "I tell you, we should make only slight modifications to the present army uniform adding only our unit insignia. We can attach the rings to our armor." He suggested and Count Cameron frowned. "Then we will have to wear armor whenever we fly. Our uniform needs to be leather. You can dye it to match the color of the army uniforms can't you?" Cameron asked the tailor. "Most certainly sir, you can have whatever color you like." He replied. "If our uniform is leather, our armor can be lighter." Cameron added. "Speaking of the insignia, what emblem shall we choose?" Regina inquired examining the samples of embroidery the shop keeper had on display. "A dragon of course." Richard replied. "A white dragon with its wings spread and its talons prepared to strike! Like this one." Regina suggested enthusiastically pulling one from its place on display and Richard frowned. "Why not a powerful red dragon breathing fire." He suggested disagreeing with her. "A white dragon will represent honor and purity of purpose and our dragons don't breathe fire. A white dragon stands for justice." Regina said with conviction. "I have many copies of that white dragon but only a few of the red dragon. Red dragons sell faster than the white dragons do." The shopkeeper said and Richard smiled. "See everybody knows red dragons stand for power." Richard chuckled. "I like the idea of a white dragon. It will stand out proudly on our shoulders." Arthur said enthusiastically as he joined the group. "Finally!" Cameron sighed heavily greeting Arthur. "We have been arguing in this shop for hours. Where is Countess Rebecca so we can vote and make an end to this task?" He asked. "She has many tasks yet to occupy her thoughts and her time. I'm certain she will defer to our judgment with regard to the uniform. Regina was growing very frustrated. Even after Arthur's arrival it took several votes and another hour before they all agreed on the dark green leather uniform dyed to match the army uniform and the white dragon for their emblem. They all agreed quickly though to name the unit "SKY RAIDERS" and have it embroidered under the dragon. "We need ten of these uniforms as quickly as you can provide them." Regina told the tailor. "Eleven, our Captain will not fly with us and she has selected Count Andrew of Sandista to join us. You can cut his uniform to fit me as we are of relative size." He said making all the riders very happy. "Now let us get fitted for the army officer dress uniform for tonight's ceremony. Can you finish the name on the insignia and place it in the left shoulder for each of us before the ceremony?" He asked the tailor. "My apprentice and I will need two hours but I need your Captain." The tailor replied. "I'm certain she will present herself to you well before the ceremony." Arthur replied and when they finished their fittings with the tailor, Arthur took them to reveal to them the plans Rebecca had set in motion at the Academy.

Ambassador Freeman stepped into the long boat feeling pretty nervous. It wasn't because this was something new to him because it wasn't. He had been on this ship with Commodore Marantz for almost a year and he had gone ashore first on several occasions to scout out the inhabitants of an island. It wasn't even because they carried no weapons although he might have felt a little more comfortable with a side arm. These people were obviously different than the savages they had encountered previously. He sensed, partly from his observations of them from the ship, that this was an advanced civilization possibly as advanced as his own. He was nervous because he knew Commodore Marantz sought conquest of them by the most expedient means. He would only seek peaceful conquest if he discovered they had the ability to repel an invasion by the whole armada. He secretly wished that would be true but he sincerely doubted it having seen the armada in action before. These people would have no idea of the power that confronted them by examining the ship Commodore Marantz had sailed into their harbor. The cannon on the larger ships of the armada could easily range this city on the shore and would level it in a day if necessary. He sat down in the long boat and surveyed the coast line and the dock that supported their fishing trade with the various vessels tethered to it. The highway that started at those docks ran behind the new military encampment and on south in front of the city wall to its gate. If there were other cities in this kingdom, they must be south of here because that was the only direction the highway went from the dock. Every once in awhile, he saw one of the ominous dragons circle the city and land atop the castle. That would be the first spot the armada would target if it came to war. Ambassador Freeman knew he needed to focus on his task and demonstrate to these people as well as the Commodore that an alliance between them would be preferable to conflict. He had four long boats filled with gold and silver and wine and rum and silk and satin and a hundred other treasures they had captured during their year at sea. He also had a detachment of scholars and scribes who knew language and how to unravel it secrets and learn quickly as well as teach and he had Cpt Manor. Cpt Manor would relay messages from his camp on shore back to the ship and vice versa but Ambassador Freeman had no misgivings about his real duty. He was there to insure Ambassador Freeman's efforts were legitimately and completely in line with the intentions of Commodore Marantz. As they got closer to shore, Freeman could see the men loading cargo on to long boats and counted the men standing around what was obviously the leader of the group and chuckled. "Will you look at that Lieutenant? The contingent they selected to come out to greet us is almost identical to ours. I'll wager those crates are filled with gifts and the men standing around the tall man in the robe are scholars similar to ours." He said and then whispered laughing. "Which one do you think is there spy?" he asked and Cpt Manor snickered. "They all are."

Chancellor Simon watched closely as the four long boats grew closer to their position on shore. He was relieved to see none of the men carried weapons. Their long boats were of comparable design to theirs and he sent four servants to assist each boat in getting to shore safely. He gathered the seven scribes and scholars behind him in two rows as the rest of the servants continued to load the gifts onto their long boats. The tall man in the long hat stepped from the boat first once it met the white sand of the beach and their eyes met for the first time as he drew near. He smiled broadly as Chancellor Simon studied his clean shaved face and he removed the hat and spread his arms kneeling before the chancellor and his party uttering a proclamation in his own tongue as all the men from the boats fell in behind him quickly and also kneeled. "I bid you welcome from The Great Father and all the inhabitants of our island." Chancellor Simon said in a loud voice as the members of his party kneeled behind him. "Lay a rug in front of them and reveal a sample of the gifts to them." Chancellor Simon commanded and the servants scurried to respond quickly. Chancellor Simon moved directly in front of the man with the hat and went to one knee in front of him. "May the God of the Sea and the God of the Land and the God of the air bless this day in our meeting that it may prove profitable to us both." Chancellor Simon said offering his hand to the man in the hat. Slowly he raised his head to meet Chancellor Simon's gaze and took his hand quickly seeing it outstretched to him and grinned broadly speaking in his own tongue again. Then men behind him rose and ran to their boats and began bringing some of the treasure they had brought and laid it out on the rug. The man in the hat pulled one of his men to his side. He looked to Chancellor Simon and stuck out his tongue pointing to it before he pointed to Chancellor Simon's mouth and then held up two fingers. As Simon fixed his eyes on the man he repeated the gesture and he realized he was trying to make a point. Simon mimicked the gesture, pointing to his own tongue and then the man's tongue before holding up two fingers as he had done and the man smiled excitedly pulling the man between them again. This time he pointed to his tongue and then Simon's tongue and then gestured to the man between them and held up 1 finger grinning. Chancellor Simon suddenly realized what he was suggesting and called one of his chief scholars to his side before repeating the gesture the man had performed pointing to his scholar. "He is suggesting he has brought this man to remedy the language barrier between us as I have brought you." Chancellor Simon said to the scholar smiling broadly at the man in the hat before he made a new gesture to him. He put both hands in front of his face doubled into fists and then opened them as he said "Speak!" and the man mimicked his gesture and said the word "Speak!" Chancellor Simon grinned broadly shaking the man's hand enthusiastically and called the rest of his seven scholars and scribes over and they began to intermingle randomly. "Lord Randy bring the carriages." Chancellor Simon shouted and two fast carriages pulled down beside them on the beach as he invited the man in the hat to join him in the carriage. He and one of his men joined Chancellor Simon and he took them the short distance up the beach north of the city and the harbor where construction of the new village was already underway. The four cornerstones and large redwood supports were already in place on two of the buildings and the engineers and carpenters were beginning work on the roof. Carriages were lined up on the road waiting to deliver materials as they stepped from the carriage. Chancellor Simon tapped his chest and pointed to the city. "Home." He said before he put his hand on the man's shoulder and pointed to the buildings being built and said. "Home." He could tell by the expression on both the men's faces that they understood what he meant as they both bowed to him. "Lord Randy take the carriage back and bring everyone here and have the servants prepared a feast for us here so we may dine as the sun sets." Chancellor Simon commanded and Lord Randy moved quickly to do what he was asked. For the rest of the afternoon and late into the night they ate and dined and drank together sharing words from each other's language as the servants worked diligently to finish the roof and three walls on the buildings hanging heavy canvas curtains over the entrance to them facing the ocean. At one point after the meal was finished, the other man that was with the man with the hat took the carriage and escorted the four long boats with the gifts Chancellor Simon had prepared back to his ship but he returned to rejoin them after a time before the sun set over the mountains. Chancellor Simon believed it was an excellent start.

Countess Regina stood proudly between Count Arthur and Count Cameron as she watched Countess Rebecca hurry to join them and take her place beside Count Arthur. The dress uniform she had just acquired from the tailor fit snuggly and she fought to control her enthusiasm that made her heart pound in her chest. Things were happening so fast that she would never have imagined were possible for her. The supreme commander of the army, Commander Dillon and his staff stood in front of her on the platform and his demeanor did not make Regina feel comfortable. He looked angry. "The Great Father and The Supreme Council have made their desires known to me and I have reluctantly concurred." He said brashly. "But I have made my reservations known to them and will do so with you also." He added forcefully. "I understand their desire to represent this unit as a long standing part of the Army to our visitors and not reveal the newness of your existence as a combat unit. However, Officer training at Greenstone Academy takes six full cycles of the moon to finish properly and prepare a worthy **soldier** for the grade of 2nd Lieutenant. I am going to fulfill the Great Father's desire and commission you according to those desires now but you have much to learn about what it means to be an officer in **my** army!" Commander Dillon shouted angrily and then stopped to regain his composure looking at each of the riders in the eye pacing in front of them. For the next six cycles of the moon, half of your day will be devoted to combat tactics with your mounts but the other half will be devoted to officer training conducted by my special staff whom I will leave here with you. Fail to complete a single task they demand of you and I will personally remove this commission as quickly as you have received it." He said staring straight into Countess Rebecca's eyes. "Learn quickly young riders for I and my staff shall treat you as Officer's in my army until you give me cause to treat you differently. When I pin this rank insignia on your shoulder, every son and daughter of the Great Father will expect you to act and present yourself immediately in the same manner as those that completed the Officer Training at Green Stone. My only advice to you now is to fake it until you can make it." Commander Dillon said and smiled for the first time and he waved to one of his staff to join him in front of Countess Rebecca. "Countess Rebecca of Gardinia, by order of the Great Father and the Supreme Council, you are hereby commissioned Captain Rebecca of Gardinia and assigned Commander of the Royal Sky Raiders." Commander Dillon said as he pinned the insignia on her shoulders and saluted her before shaking her hand. Regina felt the emotion welling up inside her as the Supreme Commander addressed Arthur and she began to tremble fighting to control it and suddenly he was standing in front of her smiling. As he reached to pin the insignia on her shoulder, she could feel her breath coming in short gasps as her heart pounded mercilessly in her chest. "Countess Regina of Red Oak, by order of the Great Father and the Supreme Council, you are hereby commissioned 1st Lieutenant Regina of Red Oak and assigned to the Royal Sky Raiders." He said and Regina saluted him before he shook her hand and she felt the tear slide down her cheek as he moved to Count Cameron. One by one until all the riders had received their commission, he repeated the phrase and Regina felt a new kinship with each of them in hearing it. ***Sky Raiders***; that was her unit. Her parents would be so proud. Commander Dillon walked back to the platform and faced them smiling. "You are now brothers and sisters not only in this new detachment but with us all in this most honored position as Officers in the Army and servants to the sons and daughters of the Great Father. May your conduct in this position reflect great credit and honor to yourselves, the army, and the kingdom." He said and looked to Captain Rebecca. "Captain Rebecca, take charge of your unit." He said and Rebecca walked in front of the new raiders and faced the Commander saluting him before she turned around and they all could see the tears on her face also. "Sky Raiders…, DISMISSED!" She shouted and they turned to each other and embraced crying and laughing excitedly at the same time as Commander Dillon and his staff departed.

As they continued to attempt to converse late into the night, Chancellor Simon learned that the man in the hat was called Ambassador Freeman and the other man with him was Captain Manor. He learned, like him, Ambassador Freeman was not a soldier but served a King named Argos from a distant land called Messiria. He learned the other man with a hat and the red beard was called Commodore Marantz and he was the ships captain. He shared wine with the ambassador and sampled the bourbon anxious to advance their understanding of each other and remained with them several hours. Ten beds and ten chairs with two large tables were finally brought to each building before Chancellor Simon decided to retire and make his way back to the castle leaving the seven scholars and scribes to live in the building next to their guests. He left the driver and the carriage in the budding village with his guests feeling certain they understood he meant for them to use it to get back to their long boats whenever they chose to go back to their ship. It was very late as Chancellor Simon returned to the castle and he resigned himself to make his report in the morning before he returned to his guests and he went up to his bedchambers. The engineers and carpenters worked all though the night and erected four buildings of equal comfort with water diverted from the river by large pipes into one of the great tubs behind the four buildings and built fires under it to heat water before it ran into the buildings in smaller pipes. The work force was tremendous and they accomplished a lot that night. A tub for bathing and a sink were in each building at the rear. A privacy room was erected behind each building and a door set to access it from the rear of each building and the sewer ran north a great distance before it turned east and dumped into the sea. As Chancellor Simon disrobed, he stared out his window looking north over the city and could see the fires burning in the new village revealing the workers scurrying about to accomplish their tasks. He knew that these visitors would change things for the kingdom forever and he felt the weight of his responsibilities heavily on his shoulders as he prepared for bed.

It was very early at Castle Archemeius and Count Andrew knew it. There was but the slightest glimpse of light from the new sun beginning to chase the darkness from his window. He was not sleeping well because he spent so much of his day on his back in the cursed bed. His chest was still sore but the pain was fading fast and he felt much better this morning. Lady Karen slept silently next to him between him and the window and he turned his gaze to her. He had not embraced her as wife as of yet and he so longed to do so. She lay with her back to him and he moved closer to her inhaling her sweet perfume and caressed her shoulder following the curve of her side down to her hip under the covers but on top of her nightshirt. He kissed her neck as he gathered the cloth of the nightshirt upward to find the warm bare skin it covered. His hand retraced the journey under the nightshirt lifting her arm slightly to caress the soft flesh of her breast and his passion rose. Lady Karen rolled dreamily to her back and surrendered to his touch and pressed her lips to his. "I thought you asleep." Andrew whispered softly caressing her more firmly and Karen moaned softly. "How sweet to wake from my dream of you and find your tender caress at my breast. Is this the hour my husband finds his desire for me exceeds the pain of his injury?" Karen whispered kissing Andrew's cheek softly. Andrew turned his lips to hers and kissed her passionately as he pulled her hips over his caressing her firmly urging her down onto him until there erotic embrace was complete. "I beg you be light upon my chest and guard yourself as our passion grows and our pleasure will be increased both for you and for me." He whispered as they began to move together. Karen arched her back and rolled against Andrew enjoying the warm sensation growing inside her as she made love to him. "This is the pleasure that fills my dreams." Karen sighed and dropped her mouth to cover his kissing him fervently as her breath became more labored. Andrew's breath also became strained and came in short gasps for air as he explored her back caressing her as far as he could reach. Finally he let the passion overwhelm him and the pain in his chest was completely consumed and forgotten as their embrace exploded into waves of pure pleasure. Karen collapsed against him careful not to put too much pressure on his chest and kissed his neck tenderly. "What magic is this that I find my pleasure in you is increased tenfold now that I call you husband?" Karen giggled still caressing him carefully. "I too am greatly pleased to have you as my wife. I should have drawn you to my side as spouse instead of servant from the beginning." Andrew sighed apologizing to her.e whispH Karen reached to the night stand beside the bed and retrieved the ointment and began to massage it into his chest. "Give no concern to this for I do not. Our days of joy stretch far into the future and I chose to fill my head with those dreams." She smiled and Andrew sat up in the bed looking out the window. The sky was slowly beginning to turn orange and Andrew took a deep breath. "I must find purpose for my day and get out of this bed and this room." He said throwing back the covers moving to the window and Karen protested playfully. "Can you find no reason to remain with me in the bed until your wound heals completely?" She teased languishing in the bed and hugging the pillow tempting him. Andrew grinned and slapped her playfully on the bottom. "I fear we shall return several times today to this bed but I cannot breakfast here one more day. Come now and dress for it is my sincere desire to breakfast in the dining hall and share conversation with whomever we encounter there." He said pulling on his britches and shirt. Karen rose up reluctantly and ran water in the tub to wash before she dressed. "I will go to the office of messengers and see if there is word from Sandista." Andrew said realizing she was going to take some time to get ready for her day. As he walked into the office, the scribes were very busy transcribing and copying scrolls already. "Is that from Sandista?" He asked the servant at the desk and the servant handed him a very large scroll comparative to the others. "You can keep that one sir." He said smiling and Andrew opened it and began to read as he walked back to his room. There was very little about the task he knew the riders had performed. There was a proclamation by Great Father declaring it forbidden for the sons and daughters of the Great Father to venture to the village being erected for the visitors or to make contact with them of any kind. Andrew was anxious to know how the over flight had gone and hear news of it but he understood the reason for secrecy. He went back to the room and sat in a chair reading the news to Karen as she prepared herself. There was a knock at his door and Andrew frowned at her. "See you have taken too long and the servants are arriving with breakfast." He said moving to the door. "It's too early for them." She replied watching him curiously as he opened the door. Andrew stared stunned at the group at the door. Councilman Trent was escorted by Commander Adam, the Captain of the guard for Castle Archemeius and two of his staff. Andrew at first glance feared the worst seeing the Captain of the Guard with Councilman Trent thinking their secret had been revealed. "I must say I am surprised to greet you this early at my door." He said looking to Councilman Trent who was smiling and it reassured him. "I'm certain your surprise will pale in comparison to my own having received this package from the Supreme Council and my instructions from the Great Father." Commander Adam said as Count Andrew let them in. "I will not pretend to understand the reasoning or logic of it but he made my task clear and I am here to execute his desire." Commander Adam said motioning to one of his staff. The lieutenant handed Andrew a complete officer's dress uniform to include the boots. "If these don't fit perfectly they will have to do for the ceremony. Please attire yourself quickly for I desire to breakfast at its conclusion." Commander Adam said casually and Andrew looked to Councilman Trent confused. "I am not an officer. There must be some confusion here other than my own." Andrew replied and Commander Adam looked perplexed. "I assumed you would know more of this than I but the message was clear. I am to commission you as 1st Lieutenant in the Army and present your assignment. Please make haste." The commander said impatiently again waving to Andrew to dress. Andrew began to change still confused. "What do you know of this Councilman Trent?" He asked and the councilman shrugged his shoulders. "Only that I am required as witness." Trent replied. "The Supreme Council has constituted a new detachment to the Army and activated it yesterday at Sandista. They have been ordained The Royal Sky Raiders and my instructions are to give you your commission and your assignment to them." The commander stated and Andrew smiled beginning to understand. "And whom do I report to in Sandista?" He asked dressing more quickly as Commander Adam took a scroll from his other staff member opening it. "You report to the Academy of Dragon Riders to Captain Rebecca of Gardinia as soon as you have recovered from your injuries." He read out loud as Andrew laced his boots. "That would be today!" Andrew replied excitedly as he stood straightening the uniform and Lady Karen frowned at him disapprovingly. "You need more time before you travel. It said after you heal **completely**." Karen protested. "I can suffer a carriage ride at this point. I must return to Sandista and hear firsthand what has developed. I am ready." Andrew replied looking to the commander who took the insignia from his staff member and turned to Andrew. "Count Andrew of Sandista, by order of the Great Father and the Supreme Council, you are hereby commissioned 1st Lieutenant Andrew of Sandista and assigned to the Royal Sky Raiders at Sandista under the command of Commander Dillon at the garrison in Green Stone." He concluded before he saluted Lt Andrew and shook his hand. "Congratulations and good luck." He smiled before he and his staff departed. Andrew still felt stunned as he gazed at his image in the mirror. "Can you believe this Councilman Trent? Those riders must have been extremely impressive in the execution of their task." He said as he inspected the patch with the white dragon on it. "Indeed, but I would not rush to Sandista to join them if I were you. It is a short time until Lt Arthur's wedding to the Maiden Melisa and they all will be here." Trent said. "Show patience my husband. Will you not be of more benefit to them fully recovered?" Lady Karen pleaded with him. "I long for my own bed and my own quarters. See what they have accomplished in my absence. The secret to their success is in Sandista and I cannot bear to remain here and hear of it second hand and piecemeal from the messengers. My place is there to take council with my captain and assist where I can. You are my wife and my medic." Lt Andrew said pulling her to his side with a grin. "Our carriage ride will be slow and pleasurable but we shall leave after we breakfast." He concluded and Lady Karen ceased to argue with him seeing he was determined.

Ambassador Freeman rose early as the sun revealed itself rising slowly over the ocean. The breeze was cool and heavy blowing in from the shore and he washed his face in the warm water from the sink. There was a feast being brought into the large room and fruits and meats of various sorts covered one of the tables in the center. Cpt Manor handed him a hot cup of coffee and he sipped it. "They are working their slaves mercilessly on the construction of this village for us." Cpt Manor said sipping his own coffee. "These are indeed great craftsmen." Freeman replied walking to the canvas curtain and pushing it open. "The building next to us where they stay has a full kitchen in operation already this morning and they have all but completed all four buildings they started last night." Cpt Manor said showing his respect for their diligence. "Do you really think these men slaves or mere craftsmen called upon to perform this task?" Freeman asked gazing at the progress of the budding village. "If they are not slaves, this is indeed a wealthy kingdom for it would take a great sum of money to pay all these craftsmen. "Did you observe, there is a toilet behind each building and a sewer carrying the waste far north of us and hot water to each building? They are even building a fountain centered in the village." Cpt Manor added. "If they keep this pace up, we will be able to barracks every man from the ship here by week's end." Cpt Manor said sitting down at the table to eat. "They pursue a peaceful alliance fervently. Do they not? I fear they would defend their kingdom with equal enthusiasm." Ambassador Freeman said as he sat to join him. "I have yet to see a woman." Cpt Manor commented. "A wise choice I also would make. I'm certain they will guard against alliances of that nature for some time." Ambassador Freeman chuckled. "The men have been at sea for near a year. It would not take them long to form alliances even with the language barrier." Cpt Manor snickered. "A circumstance I'm sure they have considered and is the reason for their absence." Freeman said as Cpt Manor stood. "Their guards restrict our movement to here and the ship. I would certainly like to get a look at what is on the other side of the wall to the city." Cpt Manor said as he walked beyond the curtain and gazed toward the city. "Be patient and I'll bet as they learn to trust us we will have our tour of the city and more." Freeman replied. "I am returning to the ship to make my report to the Commodore. What hour do you suppose the Chancellor will return to you?" Cpt Manor asked. "I feel his curiosity with us is equal to mine with him and would imagine he will appear early."Freeman replied and Cpt Manor nodded his head before moving quickly to the carriage. The trip to the longboats was short and there were several sailors from the ship standing watch over them as he arrived and they snapped to attention seeing him dismount from the carriage. He boarded one of the boats and the sailors took him to the ship. Captain Razor greeted him as he boarded and he saluted him and they walked together to the commodore's quarters. e askedHH

"I have had no discovery of their defenses beyond what we have already seen but their craftsmanship at construction of the village they are providing to us is nothing short of amazing." Cpt Manor reported and went into great detail describing all he had observed since they arrived. "You and the Ambassador are doing very well to this point." Commodore Marantz said lighting his pipe. "I have examined the gifts they presented to us and they reveal very little about their kingdom beyond the facts about the various game they hunt and their advanced agriculture. I want you to work to this end quickly because like you I am curious what is beyond the wall. Pick one of the scholars that learns their language the quickest and give him my task as spy. I require a survey of the city in no more than seven days. Send him in under the cover of darkness not through the gate but over the wall. He must return before sunrise each trip and if he fails to do so you must make report of his absence to the Chancellor. Tell him if he is caught, he is to plead that having been at sea for a year he was overcome with his desire for female companionship and we will deny prior knowledge of his pursuits. He should beg them for his life and asylum expressing his belief that we will imprison him for his deeds. He should by no means tell them he fears for his life if returned because I want them to believe we abhor killing as a civilization. Tell him if he is successful, I shall reward him beyond his imagination." Commodore Marantz concluded puffing his pipe and stroking the red beard. "I will not move all the men from the ship into the village but I will allow more and more men to venture into it. For now, I want only you few interacting with these people in the most humble manner. Captain Razor and I will present men to you from time to time that demonstrate their ability to reflect this humble nature. It is imperative we have no incident of discourse and certainly no violence." Marantz said emphatically. "Tell me now of Ambassador Freeman's demeanor. Does he seek a peaceful alliance as fervently as I supposed?" Marantz asked with a grin. "Yes sir, as you assumed he is convinced and strives heartfelt into peaceful deliberations with the Chancellor. It is I who will find their weakness for you so that you may deliver this kingdom into the hands of King Argos." Cpt Manor smiled as the Commodore went to his window to gaze at the city. "I feel it in my bones Cpt Manor. This is a very wealthy kingdom and we need only find the appropriate chink in their armor to place our swords and make you and I very wealthy men also. He sighed blowing smoke out his window.

Having made his report to King Jeffrey, Chancellor Simon walked to the stable and boarded the smaller city carriage that would take him to the new village just north of the city wall to Sandista. His breakfast with the king had been short but he had delivered all the information on their progress with the visitors he had hoped to. The king had decided to allow the visitors to tie their ship at the dock to make it easier for them to come and go and this was the message he would attempt to relate to them. There had been some dissension in the city council as many of those who made their living fishing employed women in close proximity to the docks and they were banned from interacting with the visitors but the king's desires won out. The beach would be open again for the women and children to play in the shallow surf there once the long boats were gone so they were appeased. The sun rose right over the top of the new ship in the harbor as Chancellor Simon's carriage turned out of the gate heading north. The new military encampment was quiet as the men there went about their duties having had their breakfast cleaning the cannons and their weapons. Almost all the long bowmen had been replaced with shoulder crackers and they seemed an ominous force. Overhead, a messenger soared and prepared to make his landing atop the castle. The guards at the entrance to the new village saluted his carriage as he passed and one of them peered in to inspect the carriage before he proceeded to the building housing his ten scholars. Five of them lay in their beds sleeping and Chancellor Simon felt pleased to see his instructions were being followed. He wanted the dialog with the visitors to be continuous until all the scholars were conversing freely. He was certain this was the best way to shorten the period necessary to learn each other's language. He didn't care what they talked about as long as they talked. He spoke briefly with one of the scholars preparing to retire and was pleasantly amazed at the progress they were making. As he walked to the building where the visitors were housed, the fast carriage pulled up and Cpt Manor dismounted. "Good morning Cpt Manor." He said bowing to him and the Lieutenant smiled and bowed to him also. "Good morning Chancellor Simon." He replied as Simon offered his hand. "Did you sleep on the ship?" He asked pointing to the ship. "Or did you sleep here?" He continued pointing to the building and Cpt Manor looked at him puzzled for a moment. "I sleep here." He replied after considering his words. "I breakfast Commodore Marantz. Now speak Ambassador Freeman. You come." He added proudly grinning broadly. Chancellor Simon felt exceedingly pleased with himself and the progress they were making. It was evident to him all the members of the landing party were making a concerted effort to learn and speak his language and that demonstrated to him their peaceful intentions. He followed Cpt Manor in past the hanging canvas and greeted Ambassador Freeman who offered him coffee. For the rest of the day he stayed with them breaking down their language barrier as he delivered the decree from King Jeffrey about their ship. It seemed to please them immensely and at one point Ambassador Freeman sent the Lieutenant to inform Commodore Marantz. As eager as he was to learn their language and discover their culture, Ambassador Freeman seemed even more determined to learn his and seemed most insistent that they speak the language of the sons and daughters of the Great Father when they took council. This alone showed great respect as far as Chancellor Simon was concerned and he set his focus to teach him all he could.

Lt Arthur was excited to breakfast with his companions in the new unit designated the Sky Raiders. It was just the type of adventure he had dreamed of for himself. He was still overwhelmed by his good fortune and could not wait to begin formulating tactics and strategies and put them into training exercises with his friends. "We are going to have classes taught by the Commander's special staff in the mornings before we begin to create and execute our combat tactics." Cpt Rebecca said as they ate. "Be diligent and attentive in these classes for I believe the commander is sincere in his desire to have us assimilate properly into the officer ranks. We will begin combat tactics discussions after the midday meal so give no thought to them and focus with fierce determination on the morning classes." Cpt Rebecca warned them. The first class they had after breakfast was military history and they all realized how tedious the instruction was going to be immediately. "I fear it will take a great deal of focus indeed to suffer through these lectures and obtain the favor of these verbose professors to achieve a passing grade." Lt Arthur whispered to Lt Regina as they awaited their next instructor. Lt Regina giggled in agreement. "Write everything down he says so you can regurgitate it on the exam at week's end." Regina suggested and Arthur nodded acknowledging her wisdom. They had 3 classes prior to the midday meal. History, discipline and military customs and their basic officer training was underway. It seemed like a long morning to them all before they could escape the classroom and take refuge in the dining hall.

"We do not want to fight on the ground." Cpt Rebecca said once they had returned to the classroom. "Getting your mount to attack a target on the ground will be easy. Keeping him airborne during the attack may prove more troublesome. Our first tactic should be to teach our mounts to hover over a target and pick it up. Fly to an adequate altitude and then drop it. We already have the long whistle as a command to attack. Teach your mount to drop with a four count whistle and we will consider this tactic mastered." Cpt Rebecca said and Lt Arthur interrupted. "We were attacked once in the valley of cats by wild boars and Emerald picked up one of the boars as we made our escape. I got him to drop the boar by giving him the commands to bank left and then right very quickly." Arthur suggested and Cpt Rebecca shook her head in agreement. "A wild boar is considerably lighter than a man in armor. I have had the servants set up practice dummies made from seed bags weighing 200 lbs just north of the wall in our training area. They are bound in leather but will unravel if you let your mount tear at them with his teeth so my council is to guard against this as we practice. Let us go now and secure our mounts to practice there. I want everyone in full armor. We will train as we fight. We will land on the north wall and take turns making a run at the dummies." Cpt Rebecca said as she moved to the ladder to the roof. She stopped on the ladder and turned grinning at the riders. "Make certain when you give the command to attack that you have your mounts head turned to a dummy and not one of my servants." Cpt Rebecca laughed before proceeding up to the roof. Cpt Rebecca was convinced it must have been an ominous sight to the men in the new village to witness ten dragons perched on the wall. One by one the raiders dove from the wall and attempted to get their mounts to pick up the dummies. At first every dragon would hover and land on the dummy trying to rip it open with its sharp talons and long canine teeth and the raider would have to struggle to get airborne again. The servants had prepared 10 targets and spent a great deal of time repairing them as the afternoon progressed. By the end of the afternoon, a few of the young dragons were getting the idea of simply picking their target dummies up and dropping them from altitude but it was a tedious task. A dragon is a very intelligent beast in comparison to other animals and Cpt Rebecca felt it was a good idea to have them sit on the wall and observe each other. Sweat poured from under Lt Regina's Armor. The hot humid weather was taking its toll and she resigned herself to carry water with her next time. Waterbird was not doing well and Regina was struggling with him powerfully. "Come on now Waterbird, I just want you to pick it up." She said as they dove from the wall and took flight. As he soared across the open field, she turned his head to a dummy and gave the long whistle. Waterbird flew straight to his target and hovered lowering his back legs and grasping the heavy leather bag. Regina whistled for more altitude as soon as he grabbed hold but Waterbird lowered his head landing on the dummy and ripped it open with his teeth. "No no no!" Regina cried pulling at the reigns until she got control of his head again. They bounded across the field and Regina got him airborne again returning to the wall. "Blast! Waterbird, why won't you listen." She shouted feeling very frustrated and Waterbird turned his head whistling and growling in protest. They kept up their training until the sun began to set behind the western mountain range and everyone was exhausted by the time they retreated to the new perches atop the academy and retired. "Treetop is picking up ok. I just can't get him to drop on command yet." Lt Daniel said. Lt Regina was frustrated and tired as they returned their armor to the closets on the roof. "I just can't get Waterbird to pick one up. He just wants to fight on the ground." Lt Regina said shaking her head in disgust. "Waterbird is the youngest. Have patience with him Regina. He will get it." Cpt Rebecca reassured her and Regina looked at her perplexed. "Why can't we just fight on the ground?" She asked disgruntled. "We will be attacking formations of soldiers. Your best ally in combat is going to be speed and distance. A moving target is hard to hit. If you land, every archer and shoulder cracker is going to train his weapon on you. We will be much more effective if we stay airborne." Cpt Rebecca concluded. "Well I certainly hope Waterbird does better tomorrow." Lt Regina pouted. "Maybe if we carry fish and treat them when they are successful." Lt Anthony suggested as he removed his armor. "We could carry them in our pouches." He added. "I think that's an excellent idea. I'll have the servants retrieve some for tomorrows training. For now we should dine and retire. I want clear heads for the morning classes as well as the afternoon." Cpt Rebecca stated as she made her exit toward the dining hall.

Lt Andrew stood from his table in the dining hall as he saw Cpt Rebecca and the raiders come in. They all were dripping in sweat and obviously exhausted but Cpt Rebecca smiled broadly seeing him. He saluted her when she drew near and she reluctantly stopped short and returned his salute. The pain in his chest throbbed from the long carriage ride even though Lady Karen had just reapplied the ointment. "I am most assuredly surprised to see you here." Cpt Rebecca said shaking his hand enthusiastically. "I beg you all refrain from embracing me for I am not healed as far as I thought before leaving Archemeius this morning." He admitted forcing a smile as he greeted each raider. "Your training must be rigorous. You all smell wonderful." Lt Andrew joked and they all chuckled as they took seats at the table. Lt Andrew felt exceedingly pleased to finally be in their company and could barely eat as he listened to them share their experience of the first day of training. "The quarters in the Academy are as of yet unfinished but you must let me escort you and reveal their progress." Lt Arthur said with a grin smiling at Lady Karen. "We have my quarters in the castle so there is no rush." Lt Andrew replied. "I will give you my notes from the classes this morning so you will be well received by our verbose university lecturers." Lt Arthur chuckled rolling his eyes and Cpt Rebecca frowned at him. "You make light of these instructors and they may make your shoulders lighter in return. I would guard my thoughts and my tongue for they could remove you to 2nd Lieutenant and retain you in the unit." Cpt Rebecca warned speaking seriously. Lt Arthur had not considered that and his new concern showed on his face as he finished his meal. "Do you have any idea how I would abuse you as your superior." Lt Regina laughed and everyone did. "I will have to be diligent to see that situation does not present itself." Lt Arthur chuckled raising his glass to Regina playfully. After the meal, Arthur escorted Lt Andrew and Lady Karen on a tour of the Academy building and he revealed all the progress they were making. He walked them into one of the storage rooms being converted into quarters. "These rooms are huge." Lady Karen gasped holding onto Andrew's arm. "They will make fine quarters. I have instructed the servants to divide one like this into three rooms one being a parlor the second a bed chamber and the third smaller room as a privacy room with the bath and sink and a mirrored desk for Maid Melisa's comfort." He said proudly. "I could give instruction to these same servants to convert this room likewise for you and Lady Karen." Arthur smiled. "Could this be true?" Lady Karen giggled excitedly. "What good fortune I have found marrying a man of such standing in the Royal Family." She added cheerfully. "Your perception is not correct my wife." Lt Andrew said sadly realizing her misgivings. "I **had** standing in the Royal family while a messenger and I have increased my wages with this commission but an officer holds no standing in the Royal family. That is why we are moving here from my quarters in the castle. I will have but one servant now. Lord Kenneth will continue with me paid by the military command." He concluded almost apologetically to Lady Karen and she stared at him confused. "You think me disappointed by this change in status and consider it some lower standard?" She asked smiling at Andrew. "I am filled with pride for you and me also as you wife. My desire is for you and our circumstance exceeds my most intimate dream." Lady Karen smiled kissing Andrew's cheek. "I would share your bed if it be in the stables." She whispered giggling and Andrew looked to Arthur. "Instruct the servants to do so as you have suggested and if you are not too weary join us in my quarters to drink wine and go over your notes from the classes this morning before we both retire." Lt Andrew suggested and Arthur agreed.

So for the next two days, the raiders trained having class in the morning and working with their mounts in the afternoon. Lt Andrew healed quickly and set his mind to ride Crimson by midday of the Seventh day to attend the wedding of Lt Arthur and Maid Melisa in Archemeius. By the sixth day, all the raiders had their mounts successfully picking up the heavy dummies and flying to altitude before releasing them with few exceptions. The visitors moved their ship to tether at the dock and more and more men came ashore. Chancellor Simon was growing more confident as his efforts with the scholars progressed beyond his expectations. Queen Isabella was taking a personal interest in her task to oversee defenses. Work at the docks at Archemeius proceeded at a fervent pace as they refit 10 fast ships with heavy cannon keeping them docked and anchored close to Archemeius and out of sight. The whole of the kingdom bore the burden of the expense for upgrading their defenses and engineers and carpenters from every city began working at Castle Greenstone and Castle Archemeius. The seventh day was by tradition a day of rest and the scholars and scribes returned to the city as everyone laid down their tools to enjoy the day. Ambassador Freeman and Cpt Manor spent the day aboard their ship to advise and take council with Commodore Marantz.

"We have discovered much about their culture and I have made assumptions about their civilization that I would share with you." Ambassador Freeman began addressing the Commodore. "7 is a number of significance with them socially, religiously and functionally. Their calendar is divided into seven seasons instead of months named for seven gods who are servants to their high god who created all things. They call him "Idos" and the first 3 weeks of their year is set aside to celebrate him. The season of Idos begins three weeks prior to the spring equinox. They believe Idos created all things in these 3 weeks. All the other seasons last 7 weeks. The season of "Orig" who is the god of life follows "Idos". The season of "Ratton" who is the god of the sun follows "Orig". Then comes the season of "Terrat" the god of the earth followed by "Atmon" the god of the sky. The last three seasons are "Aquino" the god of the sea, "Astral" the god of the stars, and finally "Lumirus" the god of the moon. This is the government of their God "Idos". The seven gods of the seasons serve Idos in governing the earth and the city we see inside those walls has a government that mimics it identically. They call the head of the city government King and he has seven counselors but I think this kingdom consists of seven cities each with a king and his court of seven. I have further heard them speak of a Great Father and I would wager he is the head of a central government with his own council of seven. I believe this city they call Sandista is merely a fishing village and does not give an accurate assessment of their kingdom. Their most powerful and wealthy cities are beyond the mountains and the road we have seen will lead us to a path through the mountains somewhere south of here." Ambassador Freeman concluded. "What do you make of these dragons?" Commodore Marantz asked Cpt Manor. "We have watched 10 stand on the wall and train as a combat unit but there are many more flying to and from the castle as they train. The men wear armor and they are ferocious warriors able to fight on the ground and in the air but we have still not seen them burn their targets as the dragons we saw previously do. It is either a brilliant tactical decision not to reveal their real power to us or they are taming a breed of dragon that does not breathe fire." Cpt Manor reported. "Well let us hope it is the latter. If each city has a similar defense that would mean we face 70 dragons over 200 cannon and 3000 men should we decide to wage war and that could very well prove a formidable force if the dragons breathe fire. And if Ambassador Freeman is correct in his assumption the other cities may have even more defenses. If your spy is ready, I submit we send him tonight well after sunset and see what result we get." Commodore suggested and the men agreed.

The morning of the Seventh Day came and while everyone else was relaxing, Lt Arthur knew he had a busy day in front of him. He dressed in the new heavy leather raider uniform and found Lt Andrew in the dining hall with Lady Karen his wife. He had his appointment with Chancellor Winston at the secret encampment at midday and as Lt Andrew was determined to ride Crimson today, they set in their minds to ride together. "Well at least if he is determined to ride, he will have you to look out for him. I will take a fast carriage to Archemeius to attend your wedding." Lady Karen said grinning broadly as they finished their breakfast. You certainly are in good spirit for someone with a long carriage ride in front of them." Lt Arthur chuckled. "I told her I would have and exciting surprise for her if she would bring our gifts." Lt Andrew said giving her a brief kiss affectionately. "Why don't you let her carry your dress uniform as she will have mine for your ceremony?" Lt Andrew suggested and they walked together back to Arthur's quarters to retrieve it. "You have certainly outdone yourself helping me get these quarters ready for Maid Melisa." Arthur said looking to Lady Karen. "All I really did was stock her bathing room with the luxuries a woman would want." Karen replied. "Nonsense, you can see your hand in each room. I appreciate another woman's point of view and I know Melisa will too." He grinned and hugged her appreciatively. "Well you have a long ride ahead of you. We should get you on your way." Lt Arthur said smiling as they walked her to the stables and Lt Andrew kissed her goodbye. "How is your wound today? Are you certain you are ready to ride?" Arthur asked and Andrew shrugged his shoulders throwing his arms in front of him. "It has healed quicker than I first imagined but there is still some pain. I just hope Chancellor Winston is already there when we get to the camp." Lt Andrew admitted as they climbed the ladder to the roof. Lord Kenneth already had Crimson and Emerald at the perch atop the academy when they arrived. "You follow me in case I fall off." Lt Andrew chuckled before he walked Crimson to the new launch platform and whistled leaning forward on him. Crimson dove from the platform and spread his wings quickly pumping twice before banking behind the buildings on the square. It was a trickier take off than from atop the castle but Crimson was getting used to it. He looked over his shoulder as he whistled for more altitude and turned Crimson westward. He saw Lt Arthur and Emerald bank right behind him as he sat up to enjoy the rush of air over his face. The new sun was at his back and it felt good to be back on Crimson even with the lingering pain of his injury. They cleared the mountains quickly and Lt Andrew banked Crimson leisurely cruising right at treetop level over the forest. The smell of the redwoods filled his nostrils as Lake Willow came into view and he banked and turned Crimson's head again. In short order he found his reference point and dove down into the trees turning northward. He checked his rear again for Lt Arthur as the clearing came into view and they landed with Arthur and Emerald right behind him. He unbuckled from the harness as he walked Crimson into the trees and Crimson whistled approvingly as if he was happy to be back at the camp. Lt Andrew dismounted gingerly careful not to irritate his chest as they got to the cave and he opened the gate walking Crimson inside. He smiled seeing Chancellor Winston's horse was there. Crimson turned in the cave needing only the slightest encouragement to back into the wedge and Andrew hooked the links to the harness before allowing Crimson to drink from the trough. He walked around Crimson and into the shack. "1st Lieutenant Andrew, what a pleasant surprise to see you. How does your injury fair?" Chancellor Winston asked with a grin as he shook his hand. "I will be ready at our appointed time but there is still some pain." Lt Andrew said as Lt Arthur came in the door joining them. "How is your progress on my armor?" Arthur asked and Chancellor Winston moved to the closet opening it. It was a dull grey but complete with hood, gloves, britches and boots. Chancellor Winston took the second pouch from the closet and headed for the cave. "If it changes colors, as I suspect it will when I pump the blood to it, we will successfully have prepared two sets of armor." Winston said disappearing into the cave and Arthur followed him. "This won't drain Crimson of too much energy?" He asked watching Winston tap into the syringes. "No this is very little blood respective to Crimson's size. He may be a little light headed for an hour or so since I am taking two pouches but dragons regenerate blood pretty quick and we feed him treats as we recover his blood." Winston concluded with a smile. "Crimson loves his fruit treats. Don't you boy?" He chuckled tapping the young dragon on his side and Crimson whistled again. They walked back into the shack to wait for the pouch to fill. "By this time tomorrow, your armor should be as red as Lt Andrew's." Winston said confidently. While they waited, Arthur tried on the armor. It was heavy but snug and comfortable and surprisingly flexible. "You see the back is open so it will be imperative that you face Crimson at all times when you assist Lt Andrew." Winston warned him and Arthur shook his head acknowledging Winston. It took two hours to fill both pouches and then they waited another hour to give Crimson sufficient time to recover before leaving the camp. Once airborne, they flew straight south across the plain and directly over Gardinia before Lt Andrew turned Crimson toward the mountains north of Archemeius. It was drawing close to the fifth hour of the afternoon before they saw the top of Castle Archemeius. Lt Arthur imagined Maid Melisa and the wedding party would be fit to be tied as the wedding was but two hours away. "We better find your wife and get changed. I imagine there may be some trepidation at our late arrival." Lt Arthur stated as they unbuckled and moved quickly down the stairs. Lady Karen met them on the sixth floor and grabbed both their arms pulling them to Arthur's old room. She looked absolutely ravishing in a long gown made of dark green and black silk but her face burned red. "Do you have any idea how worried we were? What could you possibly have been doing on your wedding day that would allow me to arrive here before you?" Lady Karen barked at them pushing them into the room. "Both of you get dressed immediately and take your places in the Grand Hall. I have to go try and calm down Maid Melisa for she has been at wits end not knowing your whereabouts. Be quick about it. You have not heard the last from me on this subject." Lady Karen said angrily slamming the door. "This is not a good start I guess." Lt Arthur said gnashing his teeth as he changed quickly.

CHAPTER 8

A GIFT

Maid Melisa was in her quarters pacing in front of the window. The long green and black silk gown dragged the floor behind her. "It's ridiculous he leaves all the planning and arrangements in my hand and he can't even arrive in time for a rehearsal." She snapped at Lady Erin who followed her trying to keep the long cape off of the ground. Lady Ann burst into the room. "I have witnessed their landing. Lady Karen escorts them presently to attire themselves." She panted having run down from the roof. Melisa breathed a long sigh of relief. "We should all make our way to the presentation room while they dress." She said turning to the door. It had been a long day for Melisa. She had dealt with the problem of flowers and chairs for their guests and a myriad of other situations that the groom or his best man usually handle while trying to prepare for the ceremony herself. She tried to understand his lack of involvement in the preparation blaming it on his new commission and the formation of the new unit in Sandista. She knew he was not fond of ceremonies but this was their wedding and she thought he would take a little interest in it. Once in the room, Lady Ann helped her with the headdress and the dark green veil that would cover her face. The last part of the week had gone very slow without him to help her but now things were beginning to happen very fast. The Grand Hall was filled with people wishing to witness the spectacle of a Maiden of the Crown getting married to a young officer in the newly formed Royal Sky Raiders. It was difficult to sit in the silk dress without messing it up so Lady Erin had found her a tall 3 legged stool that she had slipped under the multilayered folds of the dress and she sat her bare bottom on it letting the dress trail behind her unwrinkled. Her and her mother along with Lady Karen, Lady Erin and Lady Ann sat sipping cherry wine waiting for the ceremony to begin. Her mother had been her only confidant save her servants in the absence of her maid of honor and the rest of the wedding party. She looked to her now and was amazed at her strength and calm demeanor. "Shall we let our anger with your groom and his best man smolder even into the ceremony?" Her mother said softly with a grin. He is here!" she shouted cheerfully giggling and raising her glass. "You should let your joy at this event chase all thoughts of sorrow from your head and your heart. In a moment he shall pull you into his embrace and call you his wife destroying all cares with his promised kiss." Her mother grinned and Melisa knew she was right toasting her cheerfully with the wine. A few moments passed before her father stuck his head between the heavy curtains and smiled at her proudly. "It is time." He said softly holding his hand out to her mother and everyone left her alone in the presentation room. A final moment for her to reflect on her life and her decisions that had led her to this point as the orchestra began to play. Her mother was right and all the petty frustrations of preparation seemed to fade away as her excitement filled her. She peered through the curtain watching Lady Karen escorted by Lt Andrew moving up the isle to join the rest of the party already in position on the stage and stepped out. Her eyes became transfixed on Arthur looking so powerfully handsome standing alone to the right of Councilman Trent awaiting her. His new uniform was white with red and blue accents on the lapels and a gold saber hung at his side barely visible under the white cape that hung all the way to the ground. She smiled thinking to herself, "He is prettier than I am." Two young girls stood on either side of her and picked up the train of silk that followed her as the orchestra changed the serenade to the bride's processional and she began to move forward slowly. As she passed each row of guests they stood and showered her with flower pedals and the orchestra added new instruments to the serenade until the music filled the Grand Hall powerfully as she walked up the short stairs to the stage and took Arthur's arm. Councilman Trent's words seemed somehow distant and foreign as she stared into Arthur's eyes still transfixed on him. His eyes were filled with tears as he lifted her veil and she heard Councilman Trent ask him. "Is this the woman you have chosen to make your proposal to?" He said in a loud voice. "It is." Arthur said softly and Councilman Trent turned to her. "Is this the man that you have chosen and will you here now his proposal?" He asked. "It is and I will." She replied and Councilman Trent turned back to the crowd. "Are there those present that would witness this proposal?" The councilman asked and the whole of the Grand Hall echoed "We Will!" and he turned back to Arthur. "What proposal do you make sir?" Councilman Trent asked. "I propose that you, Maiden Melisa of Archemeius accept matrimony with me, Lieutenant Arthur of Archemeius and that we live as husband and wife until death do we part." Arthur concluded smiling nervously at Melisa. "And what responses have you to his proposal." Councilman Trent asked looking back at Melisa. "I accept his proposal without reservation and pledge my love and devotion to him until death we do part." Melisa replied and Councilman Trent opened his arms facing the crowd. "I present Lieutenant Arthur of Archemeius having made his proposal and The Maiden Melisa of Archemeius having accepted the same proposal and declare them legally ordained in marriage until death overcomes them." Councilman Trent announced and Melisa and Arthur kissed as the orchestra began again and the crowd roared to their feet breaking the silence in the Grand Hall. The party closed in on them and they all laughed together boisterously celebrating their official union. Melisa's joy overwhelmed her and she felt relieved not only at being married finally to Arthur but also that the ceremony and this week was over. Slowly they made their way to the dining hall to open their wedding gifts before dining. King Thomas and his wife even made an appearance and congratulated them but declined the invitation to dine with them not wanting to impose on their celebration and intimidate their guests. Lt Andrew pulled Lord Jerome and Lord Kenneth aside as they opened the presents and revealed the secret he and Lt Arthur had planned for their new wives. "Oh my god!" Jerome exclaimed. "How magnificent this night will be for them." He added and Andrew smiled. "Yes as a messenger I was banned from this activity but as an officer in this new unit, I get to make the rules so I will need you and Lord Kenneth to carry the gifts and their things in the fast carriage back to Sandista at first light tomorrow." Andrew chuckled and they agreed enthusiastically.

Once the presents were all opened Lord Jerome and Lord Kenneth cleared them away as the kitchen staff began to bring out their wedding feast. Lady Karen and Maid Melisa were already on their 3rd glass of the cherry wine and Arthur noticed. "I would caution you both to guard against too much wine and food as it may spoil the surprise Lt Andrew and I have for you after the meal." Arthur smiled and Melisa looked at him thoroughly confused. "If there is a night that a woman should not have to curb her desire for wine, one would assume it to be her wedding night." Melisa protested vehemently. Arthur sat back in his chair and grinned broadly. "Have it your way but I will not suffer your complaints as we fly back to Sandista tonight under the moonlight on Emerald together." He chuckled and Melisa and Karen both gasped in surprise. Melisa looked deep into Arthur's eyes to judge the seriousness of his statement. "To this day, you have told me it is forbidden for you to take a passenger on Emerald." She replied in stunned surprise and disbelief. "And that was true while I remained a messenger but now I am an officer in the Army and have full authority to execute my practices with Emerald as I desire." Arthur replied leaning forward to kiss her. "This is our gift to you to be first to test our mounts stamina to carry two passengers from Archemeius to Sandista but you will have to change. I fear this silk will not fair well on the ride." Lt Andrew laughed and kissed Lady Karen who was equally shaken by the news. The servant had just set a plate in front of both of them and Karen looked to Maid Melisa. "My excitement has slain my appetite. How do I eat in anticipation of what I now know is to come." Lady Karen giggled. "You should eat something. It will still take us a fair amount of time to get to Sandista for we shall rest the mounts in Greenstone for a time." Arthur advised her and both girls took several bites from their plates and looked to him giggling. "There we are done with the meal." They laughed together hilariously. "Are you certain this is the path you want to pursue this night? Do you have no desire to embrace Councilman Trent and your other friends on the dance floor and fulfill the celebration here?" Arthur asked sincerely. "I know that all my friends will be slightly disappointed at our departure be it now or in several hours but if my excitement overwhelms my reason, so be it! This will be a fantasy fulfilled that I thought impossible and I will not hesitate or give you cause to deliberate and change your mind." Melisa laughed and took Lady Karen's hand exceedingly excited as they stood together. "What garment should we choose? A shirt and britches with boots, I would assume. We go to change quickly. Shall we wait in my quarters for you to retrieve us or meet you on the roof?" Melisa asked bubbling over with enthusiasm. "Bid farewell to our friends before you depart to appease their disappointment modestly and we will meet you on the roof. Take care and time to let your enthusiasm fade somewhat for an excited stomach makes a bad traveling companion in flight." Lt Andrew warned both of them and both girls went quickly to say farewell to their friends. Arthur and Andrew ate quickly and apologized to their friends. "I did not consider that their reaction would be this severe or I would have delayed in revealing it to them." Arthur said regretfully to all his friends. "Give no thought to it. New brides and grooms always leave the feast early for one reason or another." Councilman Trent laughed. "Be satisfied I will drink my share of this wine and yours." He added with a chuckle hugging his wife.

Maid Melisa and Lady Karen disrobed quickly as Lady Ann looked on searching quickly to find them both appropriate attire. "Do you know how many times I begged Andrew to take me with him and the favors I promised him if he would." Lady Karen giggled as she changed. "I cannot believe they are going to take us. This has got to be the best wedding present ever given or received on the island." Melisa said still excited and turned to see Lady Ann in tears. "Lady Ann, why do you weep so?" Melisa asked moving to embrace her. "I do not wish to spoil your pleasure in this moment and I am angry with myself at delaying my confession to you but I will not be following you to Sandista." She admitted crying uncontrollably. Melisa lifted her chin and kissed her cheek feeling sudden sorrow engulf her completely. "But Lady Ann...., why?" Melisa pleaded. "I have tried to tell you since you got the news of Lt Arthur's assignment but could not find words and now it is the eleventh hour and I must. My family and my fiancé beg me to stay. It is my love for you that restrained me from a timely decision but I cannot leave them." Lady Ann cried ferociously and Melisa began to weep also as they sat down on the bed. "You are certain this is what you must do?" Melisa asked and Lady Ann nodded regretfully. "Oh god what will I do without my confidant and friend." Melisa wailed weeping powerfully into her neck. Melisa lifted Lady Ann's chin again as they wept and pressed her lips to hers in a sweet kiss. "I had suspicions that you might not come with me knowing your close ties with your family and new fiancé but I ignored them praying I would not loose you." Melisa admitted tearfully kissing her again. "I will come visit you in Sandista and you must seek me out whenever you return to Archemeius. My heart is so heavy at this decision." Lady Ann cried embracing Melisa passionately. Melisa pulled an onyx ring from her finger and slipped it on Lady Ann's finger. "We shall always be most intimate friends for I shall stand with you at your wedding as you have done for me and bounce your children on my knee." Melisa cried and Lady Ann embraced and kissed her again before standing. "I must depart now." Lady Ann said wiping the tears from her face. "I will not rain on your pleasure any longer with my tears. I have fallen deeply in love with you and Arthur but as painful as this goodbye is, I know it is the right path for me. Be cheerful as you receive Lt Arthur's gift for it will hurt me deeply to consider I have stolen that pleasure from you. There will always be an embrace for you both in my heart. I love you Melisa." Lady Ann smiled through her tears and turned quickly to run out the door. Lady Karen joined Melisa sitting on the bed and Melisa wept on Lady Karen's shoulder for a long while. Melisa stood and walked to her sink to wash her face. "Why is it pain and pleasure mix so dramatically in my life. Do you experience this whirlwind also in your comings and goings Lady Karen?" Melisa asked fighting with her emotions as she stared out her window into the darkness. "I do." Lady Karen replied moving to her side. "I chose to embrace the pleasures enthusiastically and they help me extinguish the pain. My father died a few years ago but he used to tell me there are many different colored dragons living in each of us. The one that grows the biggest and strongest is the one we chose to feed." Lady Karen said softly and Melisa turned to look in her eyes. "Your father's wisdom lives yet…, inside of you." Melisa replied embracing her again. "Let us go make our fantasy come true and embrace this pleasure earnestly leaving sorrowful morning to another hour in our lives." Lady Karen said letting her excitement show on her face again. "Yes…, this is the right path for me and for you." Melisa replied focusing on her expectations for the rest of the night as they moved quickly to the roof.

As they exited the stairway onto the roof, Andrew and Arthur were already there tending to Crimson and Emerald. "You will wear this vest and these britches and heed my council most earnestly." Arthur said as he held up the heavy leather vest and Melisa slipped her arms into it before sitting to pull on the britches. Both had sturdy rings weaved into the sides under her arms on the vest and on her thighs on the short leather britches. Melisa watched Andrew helping Lady Karen as Arthur pulled the laces on the vest very tight. "Listen to my words closely both of you." Arthur said very seriously turning Melisa's head to look in her eyes. There are two times when you must very cautious and prepared with your posture. The first is when we launch as our mount will fall from the roof a great distance before beginning to fly. Lean hard against me and hold on tight for he will jerk violently when he pumps his wings to climb. The second is when we land. Again you must hold very tightly to me for he will hover as he lowers his back legs and then he will fall forward catching himself with his front legs. It is another violent jerk at the end of the ride but if you will endeavor to stay tight against me, we will be better served." Arthur said looking to Andrew to see if he was ready. "We will mount first and buckle in and then you may mount behind us and we will buckle you in." Arthur said looking back at Melisa. The vest and britches were very tight on her and restricted her breathing as she watched Arthur climb onto the perch and buckle in. Her heart was racing pounding in her chest as she inspected Emerald in his harness. She had seen him in the harness many times before but this was much different. She was betting her life that the harness would keep her attached to the huge beast. Emerald turned his head back and looked directly at her and whistled and growled as she took Arthur's hand to climb on behind him. Just getting to this point was very exciting. "Emerald does not approve of me." Melisa said and Arthur laughed. "If he did not approve, you would be on the ground. He was merely saying hello." Arthur chuckled. There was no saddle and she could feel the massive muscles of the young dragon against her back side as they flexed adapting to her weight. Arthur hooked a clip into the ring on her left side and attached it to his own before pulling he leg up next to his and hooking another short leather strap from her thigh to his. "Move up tighter to me." He said turning to his right to hook the strap there from her side to his. Another short strap from her thigh to his and then he tugged the slack from the strap on his side pulling Melisa very tight against his back. She wrapped her arms around his chest and held on snugly. She felt Arthur turn his head and gazed up at him nervously. "Are you ready?" He smiled confidently and Melisa just shook her head feeling the panic rise inside her. The straps seemed suddenly very thin and small as Arthur urged Emerald toward the launch platform. Melisa looked at Crimson and Andrew was moving him to the other platform as Lady Karen clung to his back. Their eyes met and Melisa waved to her excitedly seeing the intense apprehension in her face also. "Hold on Melisa!" Arthur scolded her. "Remember what I said. "Your first launch will be terrifying. Just hold on and trust me. When I whistle, Emerald will jump." Arthur said as they reached the end of the platform. Melisa wrapped both arms around Arthur and squeezed. "I'm ready." She said and Arthur leaned forward and whistled. Emerald bound from the platform and Melisa felt both her and Arthur rise up off Emerald as they began to fall. She would have screamed as the air began to rush past her face but suddenly Emerald spread his wings and pumped them hard and she and Arthur slammed back down onto Emerald's back with a thump. She felt the straps tighten between them and the harness as they turned skyward and Emerald accelerated. The pressure was extremely intense so that Melisa could not find breath to scream even though her mind called for one frantically. Then just as suddenly, Emerald ceased pumping his wings and they were gliding. "You can relax now." Arthur called to her over the roar of the wind past her ears but her arms would not respond as she gripped Arthur as hard as she could. She felt Arthur sit up straight and slowly her panic subsided and she loosened her death grip on his chest. She opened her eyes and saw the tops of the trees flashing past underneath them. There was a full moon overhead and the stars twinkled brightly filling the cloudless sky. Melisa had to force herself to breath and she giggled hysterically as Arthur held his arms out mimicking Emerald as they flew. Arthur turned his head and their eyes met. "Fly with us Melisa!" He shouted flapping his arms and she released his chest and cautiously held her arms out to each side. The sensation was more powerful than anything she had ever experience and Emerald banked gently left and then rolled back up straight again before another gentle bank to the right and back upright again. "Yes! Oh my god I love this, I'm flying." Melisa shouted as the ocean came into view over the trees. "Hold on. We're going to turn!" Arthur shouted gathering the reigns in his hands and Melisa grabbed his chest again. As they got over the shoreline, Emerald began to bank left and then she saw Arthur turn his head with the reigns and gently they turned to follow the shoreline. "Melisa!" She heard Lady Karen's voice shout to her and she turned to head to see Lady Karen waving to her frantically so she waved back. Crimson pulled right in so close behind them she could have reached out and touched his head. She was having so much fun and she giggled uncontrollably. She heard Andrew shout "Hold on!" And he whistled several times before Crimson began to accelerate past them leaving them behind. Suddenly, he turned straight up climbing high above them before looping over and Melisa could hear Lady Karen scream with excitement. "Do you want to do that?" Arthur shouted and Melisa gripped him tightly again. "Yes I do!" She shouted and Arthur leaned forward and whistled. Emerald pumped his wings ferociously and the wind in Melisa's ears began to roar again. Slowly Emerald turned skyward with his wings outstretched and he kept turning and Melisa felt her body press hard into Emerald's back and against Arthur until they were upside down. An ecstatic scream jumped from her mouth uncontrollably and she felt the weightless feeling as they rolled completely over and came back upright again cruising right beside Crimson and Andrew and Lady Karen. Melisa fought hard to catch her breath laughing uncontrollably again as she and Lady Karen shared their enthusiasm waving to each other. Arthur took her hands and guided them to the straps on Emerald's harness below her thighs. "Hold on here and we will roll!" Arthur shouted and Melisa gripped them tight eager for the next trick. Slowly Emerald turned on his side in flight and Melisa giggled excitedly before he turned again and they were upside down. Another short high pitched screech escaped her lips as he rolled again twice quickly and they were back upright. Melisa sides were starting to hurt, she was laughing so hard and she watched Andrew execute the trick as Lady Karen had the same response. Crimson and Emerald seemed to soar effortlessly as they dove down to treetop level and then back to altitude again several times. Too quickly, it seemed to Melisa, Arthur pointed and she could see Castle Greenstone on the horizon. She breathed in the heavy ocean air holding her arms out again completely relaxed enjoying the ride. "Remember what I said about landing. He's going to hover and then fall forward so hold on tight." Arthur said as they circled the castle and Melisa grasp the front of Arthur's vest with both hands. Arthur pointed Emerald's head directly at a perch and whistled and they descended slowing down as they approached the perch. Emerald pumped his wings frantically as he lowered his back legs and then fell forward and Arthur and Melisa lurched forward awkwardly but the straps kept them from tumbling forward. Emerald immediately began to drink from the trough as Arthur unbuckled them from the harness and each other. Arthur jumped from Emerald and held his hand out to Melisa as she jumped down and discovered too late that she had no strength in her legs. She fell down on her bottom still holding Arthur's hands and laughed hysterically. Unconsciously, she had been gripping Emerald so tightly with her legs, there was no strength left in them. "My legs are no longer with me!" She giggled and felt the air around her disturbed as if a whirlwind was upon them and turned to see Crimson land on the perch next to them. Lady Karen's broad grin turned to a look of concern as their eyes met for Arthur was leaning over her laughing because Melisa could not stand. "Why are you sitting? Did you fall?" Karen asked as Andrew unbuckled them. "You'll see!" Melisa giggled as Andrew dismounted and held his arms out to Karen. She took his hands jumping from Crimson and collapsed falling on her bottom with a look of surprise on her face. The four of them burst into uncontrollable laugher again and Melisa rolled to her side clutching her ribs from the pain her laughing was causing. It was a couple of minutes before she could feel her legs and stand again and Arthur helped her to her feet and they all walked to the dining hall together. Arthur ordered them all a glass of cherry wine. "The confusion as to why you prefer the sky to the earth has been resolved in my mind." Melisa said exuberantly taking a large gulp from her glass. "The loop after the exhibition of speed was almost too much pleasure to bear." Karen echoed her friend's enthusiasm. "We will let them rest for a half hour or so. A dragon does not sweat as a man does but releases heat from his mouth and in his urine only so they need lots of water after a hard run." Andrew said. "How do you fair Andrew? Is your wound still bothersome?" Arthur asked and Andrew chuckled. Between the ointment, Lord Peter's elixir and the wine, I hardly notice it." Andrew laughed and they all did. Melisa was particularly enthralled by her experience and repeated its memory over and over again in her head reliving her joy in it. "I wonder what Emerald is thinking as he flies?" She uttered to no one in particular and Arthur put his arm around her. "You have a new fondness for him now that you have visited his domain." Arthur said knowingly. "I am glad. For now your appreciation for the bond between us will be more to your understanding." Arthur said kissing her forehead. Melisa looked into Arthur's eyes knowing exactly what he meant. She had felt herself becoming a part of Emerald as they flew and realized how that sensation must grow each time Arthur and Emerald fly. "Do you suppose Emerald feels the bond as strongly as you when you fly?" She asked. "I am certain of it. The more we fly, the less energy I need to bend his will to mine and I begin to sense his mood and his desires through his expressions to me. I know when he is displeased and when he finds pleasure in our tasks by his tone and his whistle. A dragon will learn his personality from his rider. That is why it is wise for us to guard our emotions in their presence. This new unit is filled with new and complicated tasks and I fear my frustration corrupts Emerald at times." Arthur stated regretfully. "Yes, I have witnessed this in Crimson also. I hold my anger in check in failure and Crimson is quick to learn but if I release my frustration in word or deed, he too will lose focus." Andrew reported flatly and Arthur shook his head. "You see Lt Regina is young and prone to frustration and anger quickly and Waterbird is last among us. We should share this observation in council with all the raiders as the opportunity presents itself." Arthur said nodding to Andrew. "This bond that grows between Emerald and me; I have felt this with a horse but it is tenfold in intensity with Emerald." Melisa said sincerely. "Yes, a horse has intelligence but it is not comparable to that of a young dragon. I swear to you, Emerald reads me quicker and more accurately than I read him." Arthur chuckled and they all did.

"Are we done with tricks or are there more? It would be pleasurable to me just to glide under the stars to Sandista from here." Melisa sighed and Arthur smiled at her leaning forward and undoing his spurs with a grin. "I shall share with you the complete rapture that is known only to a rider if you dare." He whispered lifting Melisa's boot into his lap. Melisa's eyes grew wide watching him strap the spurs on her boot and she reached to restrain him feeling her heart would jump from her chest. "Oh no Arthur. It's not possible. We will fall from the sky as a rock." Melisa whispered as fear overcame her. "You want to feel the bond with him completely. Trust me in this experience for I will see no harm comes to us and your pleasure will be tenfold in its execution." Arthur said softly persisting in his attempt to fasten the spurs to her boots. "Please Arthur!" Melisa pleaded vigorously. "I have not one minute of training from the academy and you were there three cycles of the moon perfecting your skill. It is not possible." She protested but Arthur continued until he had both spurs fastened tightly to her boots. "Most of the time at school was for Emerald not me. You have a gentle touch. It will serve you well and these tasks are simple beyond your fears. One whistle and he will fly. Whistle twice and he will land. Pull his head left and bear into his side with the left spur and he turns left. It is the same to turn right. Just relax on him when he is going the right way." Arthur said confidently. "You will not believe me if I tell you how exhilarating it is to control him." Arthur whispered excitedly. "Those are not all the commands between Emerald and you." She argued. "No but they are all you will need for a safe journey to Sandista. We have but this one opportunity at this adventure. Take it Melisa and embrace boldly this moment of pleasure." Arthur said and Melisa kissed him trembling with nervous anticipation. She looked to Lady Karen to see if she would rebuke her or give her cause to reject this crazy notion but she had her feet in Andrew's lap and grinned broadly at her having already accepted the spurs on her boots. "Idos guard over your reckless children." Melisa prayed and turned up her glass finishing her wine and slamming it on the table. "If Emerald is willing and does not bite me, we shall fly to Sandista." Melisa said grinning nervously as they stood and walked to the stairway.

The spurs jingled noisily as she walked onto the roof. The wine was not working. It should have been calming her nerves but she was shaking harshly. "Relax Melisa. I will be right behind you." Arthur said reassuring her as she climbed up on top of Emerald who turned his head and whistled sharply at her. "See he feels your fear. Breath deep and relax to embrace your new friend." Arthur said softly but firmly and Melisa tried as he buckled them both in. Her chest hurt her heart was pounding so hard inside it. "Take the reigns and hold them loosely and evenly on both sides so you can turn his head smoothly." Arthur said and she rolled the reigns in her hands until they were even. "Now turn his head to the launch platform and push both spurs gently against his sides." Arthur said and

Emerald began to walk when she did so. "Now when we get to the end of the ramp, he will not jump until you whistle but be certain you are ready for he will go quickly when you do. Hold the harness with both hands." Arthur warned her and she leaned forward clutching the harness with all her might until Emerald stopped at the edge of the platform. "Take a deep breath before you whistle and hold it as he jumps." Arthur said and Melisa was unsure she would be able to whistle her mouth felt so dry. She inhaled as deeply as she could and wet her lips and whistled one time and Emerald leaped from the platform hurling toward the ground. Melisa was certain she was about to die watching the ground come up to them quickly when Emerald suddenly extended his wings and she was pressed forcefully into his back as they turned skyward heading for the stars. The moon reflected brilliantly on the ocean as they gained both speed and altitude heading directly out to sea and Emerald abruptly leveled out and was gliding leisurely. "Breath Melisa and relax." Arthur shouted from behind her and she exhaled feeling the blood rush back into her head before releasing her death grip on the harness and sitting up straight. As she began to breath, she realized from the tingling in her face and blurred vision that she had been mere seconds from passing out. "A very light touch now Melisa. Turn his head left and caress him with the left spur." Arthur shouted and Melisa did so very gently and Emerald banked and turned. "When he's going the way you want him to, just relax." Arthur shouted again and Melisa got him aligned with the shore before she gave him back his head and relaxed her heal in his side. "See I told you the gentle touch is all you need." Arthur laughed and Melisa began to feel extremely comfortable on top of Emerald as the tingling faded and her vision cleared. The moon seemed unnaturally bright as she took in the view all around her. The white sand of the beach on her left melted into the tree line magically under the mystical glow of the full moon. The breakers on the ocean rolled lazily onto the shore glistening under the moon surrounded by a million winking stars in the clear sky above her. She sat very secure on the muscles of Emerald's back and it felt rather sensuous as the muscles caressed her each time Emerald pushed the air behind them with his wings. There were no hard scales on Emerald's back or the back of his neck but only thick soft fur covering the massive muscles. Emerald was an array of extreme sensations and she leaned forward embracing his neck and patted and stroked him as she would a horse. Emerald raised his head and whistled approvingly. She pressed her face and her breasts into the soft velvet of his warm skin and inhaled his scent deeply and the thick aroma no longer seemed strange or unpleasant to her senses. The light from the full moon sparkled brilliantly off the waves of the sea and caught her eye again as they broke against the white sand of the beach below them. She saw giant turtles heading back out to sea as they streaked past and Emerald glided and banked softly following the shoreline. Melisa thought the earth and sky were mingling into an exotic tropical dream. The cool ocean breeze rushing over her face was a tantalizing contrast to the warmth radiating from the soft skin of Emerald's back and nuzzled her cheek into him. She felt Arthur's weight against her and his hands were at her sides teasing their way underneath her breasts. Her mind swam dreamily from exotic to erotic as she imagined the pleasure of combining Arthur's intimate embrace with the warm powerful sensuality she felt against Emerald's back. Melisa turned her head and searched the starlit sky and found Crimson gliding below them to the left and heard Lady Karen giggle excitedly. Karen sat upright on Crimson with her arms outstretched as Crimson banked leisurely left and then right. Now Arthur's hands caressed her intimately as she surrendered to his touch but she watched Crimson closely fearful Lady Karen and Andrew would witness their embrace. She surmised they were both enthralled in their own pleasure since neither of them turned their gaze to her. After a time of languishing in Arthur's caress, Melisa leaned back against Arthur and turned her head straining against the leather straps to kiss him. "Would you expose my desire for you to our friends?" She called to Arthur speaking close to his ear. "I had thought this to be a onetime event but now my mind is filled with schemes to repeat it privately." Arthur said chuckling in her ear as they both watched Crimson. Melisa blushed and giggled as Arthur's hands moved boldly again to caress her intimately. Melisa pulled his hands away again giggling. "Cease your attack lieutenant for there is no path to victory in these restraints for you or for me." She laughed as she banked with Emerald and turned his head to pull closer to Crimson hoping it would deter Arthur from further teasing her. It took them close to an hour to get to Castle Sandista and they all laughed and giggled together enjoying the ride. Melisa became most comfortable in her command of Emerald and he responded to her perfectly. "Circle the city following the wall north. We will land on the new perches atop the academy." Arthur said and Melisa guided Emerald's head to do so. "Pull back on both reigns and point his head to a perch as we approach the academy to slow him down." Arthur said and Melisa was pleased at how well Emerald followed her lead. "You focus on a perch and Emerald will also before you whistle twice quickly." Arthur said and Melisa turned his head and gave the command. "Hold on!" Arthur warned again as Emerald began to hover and reached with his back legs finding the perch before he fell forward and they jerked to a stop. A servant took the reigns from Melisa immediately grinning at her broadly. "That's right, I flew this dragon here!" Melissa said proudly grinning back at the servant as Arthur unbuckled them. Now Melisa was not going to repeat the dismount from before, and she cautiously found her stance as Arthur helped her from Emerald and smiled confidently proud of herself as she melted into Arthur's embrace. She had not been with Arthur since that first night they stole together and that was all that filled her head now. "Shall we retreat to the inn and celebrate as intimate friends with more wine and reveal our joys in this day to one another." Andrew suggested taking Lady Karen to his side playfully. "We shall not join you." Melisa sighed softly. She felt intoxicated and weak from the wine and the ride with Arthur teasing her the way he had. "I am undone from the pleasure of this gift from my husband and it is my desire to mount pleasure upon pleasure quickly." Melisa said blushing wildly hearing the bold admission escape her lips. They were all shocked briefly until Andrew broke the silence. "I am the dull one for certain." Andrew chuckled. "The excitement of the day eclipsed the true joy of the day in my pursuit of pleasure with you both. This is your wedding night." He grinned and pulled Lady Karen backing to the ladder. Arthur pulled away from Melisa's embrace. "Wait here for I possess one more surprise for you." Arthur whispered and rushed to Andrew and Karen before they escaped. He whispered to Andrew who grinned and nodded to him before looking to Melisa. "I pray the sun finds you content and satisfied and we can breakfast together." Andrew grinned and they turned to climb down the ladder as Arthur rejoined her.

Melisa's face was still burning with embarrassment at the way she had revealed her desire to Andrew and Karen. "I pray you forgive me quickly for embarrassing you in the presence of our friends and that servant. I know not what possessed me to speak so crudely." Melisa whispered earnestly remorseful and Arthur pulled her into an embrace. "I would not desire your silence on any topic. I pray that every desire of your heart flows freely from your lips so that I may embrace them and fulfill them quickly. If there is embarrassment to be borne, I will suffer it gladly to know your heart completely." Arthur whispered and kissed her tenderly. Melisa wondered momentarily why they were not moving to the ladder and she grinned. "Why do you hesitate so to deliver me to our new quarters? Do you not know I long to see what arrangements you have made for us?" Melisa smiled. "It is good that I discover early in our marriage my ineptitude at deceiving you even moderately." Arthur laughed. "I am certain it will save me from your scorn in the future." He chuckled taking her hand and leading her to the ladder. "Soon there will be a stairway here and we will have no use for this ladder." He said helping her down into the storage room. Melisa followed him to a curious door with a barred window in it. Arthur opened the door and they went inside and Arthur closed the door and locked it behind them. Melisa surveyed the room and found it very appealing. The colors were all dark green and brown reminding her of the colors of Archemeius. The heavy curtains on the windows began to sway in the breeze as Arthur opened the window in their front door and Melisa looked at him amazed. "This will keep the rooms from becoming too hot even into midday." Arthur smiled proudly and Melisa fell against him reveling in the steady breeze that flowed through the window in the door. "Are you an engineer too?" Melisa giggled and so did Arthur. "No but I have friends that are." He replied and Melisa turned her head to the north wall where there were two doors and she heard water running through the one that was open. "What is that sound?" Melisa whispered moving toward the door. "It is your bath." Arthur replied as she stepped into the smaller room. On the west wall was a large window and the breeze blew the curtains over a huge tub set in stone and the north wall was also completely stone where water streamed gently from the rocks into the tub resembling a waterfall. "These valves regulate the waters temperature." Arthur said pointing them out on the wall. There were shelves beside the valves stacked with an assortment of towels and bottles of bath oils and various other bottles. Against the east wall was a large mirrored desk with the toilet beside it. "I planned this room for you. Does it please you?" Arthur whispered hopefully as Melisa placed her hand under the stream of warm water filling the tub from the little waterfall. Melisa's emotions overwhelmed her and her eyes filled with tears of joy as she turned to face Arthur. "You must cease this sweet attack Arthur." She wept rushing to embrace him. "What have I done and how will I become worthy of this love you rain down on me mercilessly." She cried kissing his neck and Arthur lifted her chin to bring her eyes to his. "You gave me all that I have ever desired when you accepted my proposal." He smiled and pressed his lips to hers in a tender kiss. Melisa trembled in his arms but managed get her hands between them and worked the laces on his vest. "This tub is too large and I will surely get lost in it if you will not be my escort." Melisa whispered pleading with him. "Do you not wish to see your bedchamber?" Arthur smiled softly as Melisa backed to the tub pulling Arthur with her playfully and stepping into it under the streaming water. She let the warm water flow over her hair pulling Arthur tight against her and kissing him passionately. "It is my desire to let that pleasure follow this one." Melisa whispered seductively in his ear pushing the vest down his arms as the water cascaded over them. Slowly her passion rose as she removed one by one each item of clothing until there was no barrier between his desire and hers. "What a perfect place for this mirror." Melisa sighed breathlessly as she watched their image in it and Arthur pressed her against stone wall and made love to her as the water washed over them both. Melisa bit his neck and whispered in his ear confessing each sensation she felt from his erotic embrace and encouraging him until the intensity she felt was too great and she moaned pleasurably as her satisfaction was completed in wave after wave of explosive passion. She kissed his neck as they sank down together into the tub and Arthur poured the bath oil over her as they bathed together. Arthur reached and turned the valves as the water filled the tub and Melisa found a large sponge and began to wash Arthur's body kissing each limb gently. "It is my turn to shower you with adoration and reveal the secrets of the chamber of Maidens." Melisa whispered and for the rest of the night she set her mind to reveal all and let Arthur experience all she knew of the secrets known only to a Maiden to the Crown. Now Arthur was completely overwhelmed with pleasure at all Melisa revealed to him that night and he thanked all the gods for leading him to Melisa.

So it was for the next two weeks, life in the kingdom of the seven kings went on as normal. Fishing boats came and went at Sandista harbor and contact between the fishermen and the sailors was cordial but brief. The new village north of Sandista grew and Commodore Marantz sent more and more of his men ashore to dwell there. Chancellor Simon and his scholars and scribes worked diligently with Ambassador Freeman and the group from the ship to learn each other's language and customs but the restrictions to the visitor's movement remained between the village and the ship.

Queen Isabella was very busy moving about the kingdom shoring up each city's defenses and the refit of the 10 fast schooners was completed adding 10 cannons to each of them. They remained hidden off the coast near Archemeius harbor. Maid Melisa continued her studies at the academy at Sandista and the scholars there sent a report to her professor in Archemeius each 5th day by fast carriage. Captain Rebecca continued her training with the Sky Raiders and they elected to carry the crossbow as their weapon as reloading the shoulder cracker in flight proved troublesome. The engineers developed a bomb for them from a hallowed out coconut that would explode and burn on impact. Captain Rebecca selected Count Mitchell of Sandista to receive his commission and replace Lt Andrew as Crimson's day of maturity drew near. The Great Father and the Supreme Council received a report each day and were pleased with Chancellor Simon's progress. There was talk within the council of allowing Commodore Marantz and Ambassador Freeman to journey to Castle Paternus to meet with the Great Father if the progress continued peaceable.

C H A P T E R 9

✳

CRIMSON'S TRIAL

"**Y**ou cannot delay any longer." Lord Kenneth said sorrowfully standing beside Crimson as Lt Andrew looked on. The days' training with the Sky Raiders was done and Lord Kenneth prepared to take Crimson to the stables. "The membrane covering the glands on both sides is wafer thin and will rupture any day. We must make the trip tomorrow to the mountains and release him." He added feeling the pain he was certain he shared with Lt Andrew. "I will go at midday tomorrow but Lt Arthur will accompany me with the horses for our return." Lt Andrew sighed sadly. "As you wish sir, I know Lt Arthur shares your grief as I do. He will serve you well on this dreadful journey." Lord Kenneth said as he led Crimson away to the stables. Lt Andrew walked nervously to the new stairway to go down to his quarters before the dinner meal and Lt Arthur and Captain Rebecca met him there. "I would take council with you both in my quarters." Captain Rebecca said and they followed her to her door. "Tomorrow is the sixth day. If luck is with us, Crimson will rupture tomorrow or on the Seventh Day and we will have no need for explanation as to your absence." Captain Rebecca whispered cautiously after closing the door. Lt Andrew looked to both of them contemplating an excuse if that did not happen. "If he does not rupture, Arthur can return and say I decided to take refuge in the forest to grieve my loss in solitude." Lt Andrew said and Captain Rebecca nodded. "You should tell everyone at dinner tonight that is your desire and it will be more believable to them." Cpt Rebecca suggested. "I will release Lt Arthur from training tomorrow so he may depart with the horses and I will fly with you at midday after classes. I have sent the message to Chancellor Winston and he will be at our camp by midday I am certain. We should all go down to dine separately." Cpt Rebecca whispered and they departed one by one. Lt Andrew walked to his quarters and went directly to the bathing room to wash his face and hands before dinner. Lady Karen watched him with tears in her eyes knowing what she thought was about to transpire. "It is tomorrow then. Is it not?" She asked seeing the nervous sadness in his face and she ran to him embracing him. "I am so sorry for you and for Crimson." She cried and kissed him. "I desire to grieve his loss in solitude after I release him tomorrow. I think I will go hunting in the forest north of Lake Willow for a few days alone." Andrew said holding her close to him. "I will saddle a horse and be your companion in grieving for him if you desire." Lady Karen suggested and Andrew kissed her again. "No. I will do this alone and return to you absent of grief. Come with me to dine now for the day has been long and I desire to eat and retire early to share an intimate embrace with you as the moon begins his journey." Lt Andrew smiled at her and they departed to the dining hall.

The morning class seemed long and tedious to Lt Andrew and he could not focus nervous at the thought of his secret task. As the last instructor from the special staff of the commander finished, Cpt Rebecca took the podium. "There will be no training this afternoon. It is my desire that you rest your mounts leaving them to the stables in honor of Crimson and the task we all dread that Lt Andrew must perform today. I invite you all to come to the perches and say farewell to Crimson on his last day as a mount for the Sky Raiders." Cpt Rebecca said sorrowfully before leaving for the stairway. There were many tears and much sorrow on the roof as each Raider cried on Lt Andrew's neck but it was the sight of Lady Karen that brought Lt Andrew's tears streaming from his eyes. "You know my love for you is eternal." He cried and kissed her knowing it was highly possible he would not survive this task but he could not reveal it to her. He and Cpt Rebecca mounted and buckled in and he waved to them all before giving the command and Crimson dove from the platform. "I can scarce imagine the pain he feels forced to release Crimson back to the mountains today." Lady Karen said and Cpt Richard nodded and embraced her tearfully. "At least he has found his true love in you to comfort him in his mourning. His sorrow will be shortened knowing he has a bright and full future with you to return to." Richard said and Melisa smiled at him. "Why do not pursue a bond with a woman of this nature Count Richard. You obviously see the value in it." Melisa asked and Richard turned his eyes to the sky and watched Cpt Rebecca and Andrew as they turned north. "I am certain the true desire of my heart is beyond my reach." Richard admitted sorrowfully and Melisa and Karen smiled realizing it was Cpt Rebecca he referred to. "Maybe if you focused as much energy toward the pursuit of true love as you do to your frivolous exploits you could find a path to your heart's desire." Karen suggested and kissed his cheek. "I fear our circumstances and my history are both barriers that will never be breached to this end." Richard replied and Melisa leaned forward and also kissed his cheek. "True love will breach any barrier Richard but if you never venture down this path it most certainly will evade you." Melisa whispered in his ear.

Lt Andrew turned Crimson's head slowly northward. He could feel a difference in the way Crimson flew as if he was irritated by something. Rebecca flew on Emerald right at his side as they cruised over the mountains. As they got to the forests edge, they turned north to follow the cliffs past where the road met the tunnel to Castle Paternus. It was important for them to continue up that road for a brief while in case they were observed. No one traveled the road north into the mountains anymore save those escorting a dragon rider who was releasing his mount. Then they banked west and dropped down into the trees heading to the camp. They found the clearing and landed together before walking the young dragons into the trees to the north. Lt Andrew was happy to see there were three horses tied outside the small shelter as he dismounted and walked Crimson into the cave. He backed Crimson into the wedge securing him with the harness as he drank. Crimson kept spitting the water back out and shaking his head and Andrew knew one of the membranes covering the glands had probably ruptured and the fluid was leaking out into his mouth. He petted his neck comforting the young dragon. "It's going to be painful but we're going to do this together." Andrew said and Crimson whistled the sharp tone he knew to be his expression of disapproval. Lt Andrew walked through the crevice into the shack. "We got here just in time. One of the glands is leaking into his mouth and he doesn't like it." Andrew said and everyone looked tense. "When the second one breaks he is going to like that even less." Chancellor Winston said. "That's when they go into a frenzy but we are betting it will only last a day or maybe two until they learn to control the glands. The pain however will continue each time they spew the liquid until the skin inside the mouth calluses over and that, I fear, may take a week but I'm only guessing." He admitted regretfully.

Andrew leaned against the wall putting his head against his arm and wept. It was the stress at leaving Lady Karen and not telling her. It was the danger of prison if they were discovered. It was the fear of the end of his career as a rider and the end of his bond with Crimson and it was the pain he knew was just beginning for Crimson and for him. He did not fear death. It was the pressure of all his trials coming to fruition in this moment that forced the water from his eyes and Arthur and Rebecca empathized with his pain and fell on his shoulders and wept with him. Chancellor Winston gave them space moving to the stove and setting plates and cups on the table. "I took liberty to fix our dinner." Chancellor Winston said softly after several moments. "I will make and end to this blubbering. There will be no place for self-pity in the execution of this trial. It will serve us well to focus on our task diligently." Lt Andrew said wiping his face and filling his lungs as he sat down at the table with his friends. "The more contact you have; the more Crimson can feel your presence with him during his trial the better for our cause. Crimson must not feel abandoned in his hour of pain." Rebecca said with conviction as they ate. Arthur looked to Rebecca after they had finished. "I told my wife I would stay with Andrew as he grieved if he would let me. I will need my Captain's approval to miss the training." Arthur pleaded with her and Rebecca nodded. "I will make excuses for you both but I must return." Rebecca said regretfully as she stood. They walked out together and no words passed between them as Rebecca embraced them in turn and mounted Emerald buckling in. Arthur thought to himself watching her that she was a woman of substance and worthy of any man's admiration and desire. "Cpt Rebecca. Why have you never married?" He asked and Rebecca smiled at the compliment. "My two favorite men recently married….., but I will find another someday." She laughed and turned Emerald's head south toward the clearing.

The light was fading quickly in the thick forest that surrounded them as they entered the shack and Chancellor Winston lit a torch. They could hear Crimson growl and spit and whistle in the cave and it was unnerving to them all. "I am going to comfort him just to let him know we are still here." Andrew said when he couldn't take anymore. "We agreed you would wear the armor from this point forward." Winston said stopping him and Andrew looked at him pained and frustrated. "It is just one gland. I'll use the armor when he issues fire." He replied squeezing through to the wedge. Crimson strained against the chains that held his head and arched his head spitting and growling in anguish. Andrew climbed onto his back and stroked the soft skin on his neck as he had done so many times before. "I feel your pain my friend you are not alone." He said and for a brief second he felt Crimson relax. Then suddenly without warning he bucked violently throwing Andrew against the wall of the cave and almost stepped on him as a huge stream of fire burst free in front of them. Andrew scrambled toward the shack. "Drop the main harness!" he shouted as Crimson began to flail wildly and Andrew was pushed into the shack forcefully by Crimson's tail. The light from another blast of flame filled the cave as Andrew heard the huge iron rods release the stones holding the heavy main harness. Crimson's cries of agony were torture to his ears as he looked back in seeing Crimson pinned awkwardly on his side and he filled the cave in front of them with another tremendous blast of flame. Fear consumed Andrew's judgment and Crimson struggled against his restraints mightily but they were too much for him. Andrew rushed into the shack and started cranking the lever to the main harness. "We have to let him up. He fell on his side." Andrew shouted but Winston charged him and knocked him down. "No! We have to keep him pinned regardless. He will tear that harness to pieces with his talons if we lift it now!" Winston shouted and Andrew knew he was right. "Andrew sat and wailed tearfully. "He's on his side. We may have broken his wing." He said dejectedly pleading with Winston. "If we did then we killed him but we must follow our plan. Get into your armor and go suffer with your friend." Chancellor Winston commanded as the light from Crimson's flame lit up the cave again. Quickly Andrew moved to the closet and threw on the armor before returning to the cave. Crimson writhed recklessly against the heavy netting that crushed him against the floor and he tossed his head from left to right and blasted great streams of flame in front of him. Andrew cursed himself at their first failure seeing Crimson on his side. They had mistakenly assumed he would be able to climb onto Crimson's back and show him comfort in a familiar position to both of them. Now he had to lie on Crimson's side to reach the soft thick skin of his back and insert the syringe under the armor. The first thing he noticed was the trough in front of Crimson's head was on fire above the waterline. "Fill the trough again and bring me a bucket of water." Andrew yelled noticing that the leather on Crimson's harness that held his head was also on fire. Arthur came in quickly with the bucket and handed it to Andrew and he threw it over Crimson's head extinguishing the harness. Winston pulled the lever in the shed releasing water into the trough. Crimson dropped his head into the trough and gulped water but sprayed another long stream of fire as soon as his head cleared the trough. "If that harness breaks, it's all over." Arthur shouted taking the bucket back into the shack returning quickly to deliver it to Andrew. He sat it down seeing the harness was not burning. Tears ran down Andrew's cheek as he tried unsuccessfully to comfort and calm Crimson.

The pain must have been tremendous for Andrew had never seen Crimson this frantic before for such a long period of time. Andrew stroked his back and talked to him. "This is just the way to maturity my friend. It will not last." He cried as Crimson struggled. Crimson turned his head as far as he could hearing Andrew's voice and Andrew saw wild strained panic in his eye but he knew Crimson could see him. "Yes my brother! I am with you to the end." Andrew wailed and Crimson blasted another stream of flame recklessly catching the harness on fire again. Andrew grabbed the bucket and dowsed Crimson's head extinguishing the harness and called to Arthur to fill it again. For hour after hour, Crimson struggled blasting streams of flames and growling and moaning miserably to the point of exhaustion. It was all Andrew could do to stay with him. More than once he contemplated drawing a sword and ending Crimson's suffering and his own. Just before first light, Crimson collapsed laying his head beside the trough and Andrew wept fiercely praying that the ordeal was over. He felt Arthur's hand on his back and lifted his head to see the cup he held for him. Arthur had his armor on and whispered softly. "Winston said this is a good sign. It means he's learned to close the glands and control the excretion of fluid if he can sleep." Andrew drank the soft cherry wine quickly and lay back against Crimson to try to get some sleep himself. Andrew could hear the rain falling outside the cave as the sun came up. It was well into the morning before he felt Crimson stir below him. "How is my friend this morning?" Andrew said and Crimson raised his head looking back at him with one eye. He growled angrily and blasted a stream of fire and the panic returned to his eye. "No! Don't let it control you." Andrew commanded but Crimson started to struggle violently again and Andrew reached to his back stroking and speaking softly. "Winston! Give us food in the trough!" Andrew shouted and bananas and pineapples fell into the trough after a short time. Crimson snapped them up quickly and then drank the water before turning to look at Andrew again. This time he whistled approvingly and Andrew burst into tears of joy. "There's my friend. We're going to make it." Andrew laughed through his tears. He stroked and scratched and patted and kissed Crimson's back speaking softly to him feeling the young dragon relax accepting the position. "Arthur come and bring me a new harness for his head." Andrew shouted and Arthur appeared quickly in his Armor behind him. "I will have to change that harness on his head before we fly." Andrew said and Arthur looked worried. "Shouldn't we give him more time?" Arthur suggested cautiously. "I want to get him on his feet quickly but I can sit on his neck now and change it and maybe he won't set me on fire." Andrew replied and took the harness from Arthur moving slowly up Crimson's neck. He continued to stroke Crimson's neck until he got up to his head. "You're not going to burn me are you my friend." Andrew said softly working quickly to replace the burnt harness before Crimson even realized his head was free. No sooner had he clipped the restraints back onto the harness, Crimson let loose with a long blast of flame and Andrew jumped back. "No Crimson!" he shouted reaching to find the skin on his neck again.

"He has to do that." He heard Chancellor Winston say from behind Arthur as Crimson blasted another stream of fire. "The glands won't callus over unless he uses them but it's going to take several days." He added and Andrew went back to stroking Crimson's back and he quit. "I want to get him back on his feet." Andrew pleaded and Winston nodded. "I agree. If he controls his panic, we can move forward more quickly. Just stay behind him Lt Andrew." Winston warned and moved back into the shack. Andrew heard the crank and the metal gears and the tension on the main harness began to fade. He removed the syringe from Crimson's neck and slowly it rose as Crimson began to right himself and get to his feet. Winston kept cranking until it was back against the ceiling again. Andrew went to the other side and inspected Crimson carefully. "Give him some more fruit Chancellor Winston, I think he's ok." Andrew said excitedly and he climbed back on top of him and patted his back and scratched him. "God I'm so glad that's over." Andrew said. "We don't know that." Winston said chastising him. "We have no idea what he will do when you give him his head." He added and Andrew restrained his enthusiasm. "I am sure you are right Chancellor. We should give him several hours to get acclimated to his new condition." Andrew said. "Hours? I think you should wait until tomorrow at least." Winston suggested and Andrew frowned at him patting Crimson as he blew another blast of fire and growled unpleasantly. "My part in this venture is not just to ride but assess Crimson's progress as I am the one who has formed a bond with him." Andrew said firmly. "I will wait until mid afternoon but I assure you we will be ready today. I know this animal and we can control his panic through this pain now." Andrew said emphatically. Chancellor Winston shook his head heading back into the shack. "I'm fixing us a midday meal." He called to them as Andrew reinserted the syringe in Crimson's neck. Arthur watched in amazement as Crimson blasted another stream of fire into the far wall of the cave.

He looked at Andrew and the realization of what they had accomplished suddenly hit them and they embraced and laughed heartily. "We should not get to excited yet. There is a long path to get Crimson to fire on command and Chancellor Winston has a point. We should embrace patience to see our task completely successful. I am uncertain what trials confront us on our first flight." Andrew said as Winston brought in a plate for him. It had almost stopped raining as they ate the midday meal and afterward Arthur and Andrew tossed items in front of Crimson encouraging him to set them on fire when they gave the verbal command "FIRE". They could both tell the sensation Crimson felt when he released a stream of flame was extremely painful but he was slowly getting the idea about the command. When Chancellor Winston came back to them, Andrew gave him a demonstration of Crimson's progress. Andrew threw a basket in front of Crimson and after giving the command several times, Crimson set it to blaze and Andrew gave him a banana smiling proudly. "You see I know Crimson and he is ready for the next step. Arthur go around through the shack and open the gate." Andrew said confidently and Winston shook his head again. "I fear this is too early but I will submit to your judgment." Winston said following Arthur into the shack. Andrew leaned forward and unhooked the restraints on Crimson's head and tightened the reigns in his hand to prevent the young dragon from turning his head to him. He took a deep breath as he heard the iron gate open. "Winston thinks we are premature. Let's go prove him wrong." Andrew said and dug both spurs in urging Crimson forward.

As Arthur opened the gate Chancellor Winston exited the shack carrying two buckets. "You better go get water too. I have no guess as to how many fires he will start before he gets airborne." Winston said watching the entrance to the cave. As Crimson emerged from the cave they stood a safe distance away. "Take him out quickly Lt Andrew but make it a short flight." Arthur shouted to him and Andrew nudged him southward again. Crimson whistled and growled irritably and then blew a long stream of flame into the thick forest. "Quickly Lt Andrew or we won't be able to stop the fires." Winston shouted heading for the burning brushes. Arthur watched as Andrew leaned forward and whistled. Crimson began to run full out and before he disappeared into the trees he could see they were airborne. Arthur ran to where the chancellor had dumped his bucket and dumped his on the fire also and they beat the rest of the fire down with the broom Arthur had brought. He looked up once they had the fire out but Arthur knew he wouldn't be able to see anything through the thick trees.

They went back to the shack for another glass of the cherry wine and they waited. They waited for an hour and Lt Arthur began to get nervous. "Does that man not know the meaning of short?" Arthur said walking out to the path. He stared down it for a long while and then walked back to the horse tied at the shack. The light was starting to fade as he mounted the horse and Winston mounted his beside him. "Where shall we search?" Winston asked equally concerned. "I'm just going to the clearing where he should land." Arthur replied and they rode there together. They waited there in the middle of the clearing searching the sky until the light faded completely and the stars came out. "My god Andrew where are you!" Arthur shouted in frustration into the sky and his eyes filled with tears fearing the worst. "We should go back to the shack and pray for his safe return tomorrow." Chancellor Winston suggested. Arthur looked at him and sat down in the tall grass. "You go to the shack and if he finds you first come fetch me but he will surely find one of us soon." Arthur said and he turned his tear stained eyes back to the sky as Winston rode back to the shack.

C H A P T E R 1 0

THE END OF NEGOTIATIONS

Ambassador Freeman sipped the cherry wine staring out over the village and the ocean. The stars were beginning to reveal themselves from behind the clouds that drifted to the west behind him. It had been raining all day but the clouds seemed to be chasing the sun and the brisk clean air filled his lungs. He felt very satisfied with the progress he and his group were making in the village. He had even received an invitation from their leader for him and the Commodore to have an audience with their Supreme Council. He had told Chancellor Simon how honored they were and promised him an answer tomorrow. It was a tremendous opportunity and he was certain the Commodore would finally leave the ship and join him when he heard it. Cpt Manor had gone back to the ship right after the dinner meal to deliver his report and the good news of the invitation. As he sipped from the glass, the fast carriage pulled up in front of him and he smiled at Cpt Manor as he dismounted. "That was indeed a quick trip. Was the Commodore pleased at our invitation?" He asked and Cpt Manor grinned but Ambassador Freeman felt uneasy at his demeanor. "He was very pleased. So much so; that he wants you to return to the ship to discuss with him tomorrow's activities." Cpt Manor said holding the door to the carriage for him. "Right now?" Ambassador Freeman asked bewildered. "He was insistent on it." Cpt Manor replied and Ambassador Freeman set down the cup and moved to the carriage. "I swear, I do not understand the Commodore's aversion to coming ashore himself." Ambassador Freeman sighed taking a seat in the carriage. It was a very short ride to the ship now that it was at the dock and Ambassador Freeman dismounted and walked with Cpt Manor to the Commodore's cabin. The men on the ship were unusually busy securing cargo on the ship as if they were preparing to set sail. Commodore Marantz dismissed the sailor that was with him as they entered and looked to Cpt Manor. "Did you have any trouble?" He asked and Cpt Manor shook his head no as the Commodore poured a glass of wine and offered it to Ambassador Freeman. If Cpt Manor's demeanor had made him uneasy, the Commodore's demeanor scared him. "What is happening Commodore?" He asked taking the glass from him nervously. Commodore Marantz stroked his red beard smiling at him. "Ambassador Freeman, you have performed magnificently in your task and I congratulate you. I have 10 men, not counting yourself of course, that speak their language fluently. I understand their culture and traditions adequately and even more important their capabilities. I have an excellent map of Sandista and a fairly good map of the rest of the island and the 7 other castles." He said putting his arm over Ambassador Freeman's shoulder. "What you have accomplished is no less than spectacular. You are going to be a very wealthy man but your task is complete." The Commodore smiled at him and Ambassador Freeman felt the blood rush from his face feeling faint. "I have much more to do. We are on the brink of complete success in our attempt to secure a peaceful alliance with them." Freeman said. "YOUR ATTEMP!" Commodore Marantz shouted at him. "My goals have always been clear to me!" He said adamantly. "Conquer those I can. Make alliance with those I can NOT! I have never had an advantage such as this thanks to you!" He said confidently. "I beg you sir. There is no need for bloodshed. In another week or two we could negotiate trade agreements that would surely benefit both our kingdoms." Ambassador Freeman pleaded with him but Commodore Marantz merely scoffed at him. "And why would I deliver a mere trade agreement to King Argos when in the same amount of time I can deliver the whole of this kingdom and all the wealth therein?" He boasted waving his hand over a partial map of the island that revealed the location of the seven cities except Archemeius. Mistakenly, the map identified Paternus as the seventh city. "I have some authority here. I demand that you delay your attack until the Armada arrives and I can speak directly to the fleet commander." Ambassador Freeman said brashly but nervously and Commodore Marantz chuckled. "As we speak, the scholars you have taught our language are being murdered in their beds. They will not be discovered until daybreak. When I have all my men back on board, we set sail secretly to join the Armada which awaits me on the north side of the island. The attack begins at Dawn." The Commodore replied dismissively. "Oh and as for you speaking directly to the fleet commander....., you just did." Commodore Marantz said proudly looking to Cpt Manor. "We better secure the Ambassador in his quarters. I fear he does not have the stomach for war." Commodore Marantz ordered and Cpt Manor took the Ambassador's arm. "You better kill me Commodore. I intend to make full report of this to King Argos!" Ambassador Freeman shouted at him and Commodore Marantz smiled at him. "Don't tempt me." He replied waving his hand and Cpt Manor took him away.

Chancellor Simon was awakened early by the sound of shouting in the hallway and then a servant was pounding on his door frantically. It was still dark in his room. "Chancellor Simon, the King awaits you on his balcony. He commands you come quickly!" The servant shouted and Chancellor Simon leapt from his bed running to the door throwing it open. "On his balcony!" The servant repeated breathlessly and turned to depart running to the stairs. Chancellor Simon dressed quickly and headed for the balcony. Every torch in the castle was lit and guards and servants ran past him moving quickly in each direction. King Jeffrey was putting on his armor as Chancellor Simon came to the balcony. "It appears Queen Isabella was right and we have been deceived. Give the chancellor your report again." He said nervously looking to a guard. "The ship is gone. The village is empty and Lord Bartholomew and all the other scribes and scholars have been slain in their beds." The guard said and a heavy cloud of disbelief and fear overwhelmed Chancellor Simon. "This cannot be! Ambassador Freeman is a man of peace!" Chancellor Simon gasped. "Well your man of peace murdered every one of your friends before he departed." King Jeffrey stated pulling the chancellor to the wall and pointing out to sea. It was still dark and the sun had not yet begun to fill the horizon with light. There was a row of torches on the ocean just before the horizon to the north and east that seemed unending. "Those are not the lights of his ship but a horde of ships heading for our harbor. I sent a messenger out to count them. I have ordered the evacuation of the city of all women and children to Castle Greenstone. Where is Captain Rebecca?" King Jeffrey shouted and Cpt Rebecca stepped forward bowing to him. "I am here sir." She replied. "You take your Sky Raider's and attack their lead ship as soon as there is light enough. We must deplete their numbers before their cannon come into range." King Jeffrey said strapping on his sword and Commander Ryan of the castle guard grabbed her arm. "Cpt Rebecca, stay well above them for their decks will certainly be filled with archers and shoulder crackers. Use the coconut bombs and focus on the lead ship until it burns sufficiently before going to the next ship." He said and Cpt Rebecca saluted and ran for the academy. A messenger came running to the balcony as Rebecca departed and bowed to King Jeffrey. "I count 51 ships." The messenger said gasping for air and King Jeffrey fell backwards into his chair dejected. He looked around the balcony at his seven councilmen seeming stunned as if his heart had failed. "That's over 10 thousand men." He sighed heavily looking to Commander Ryan. "Send all the messengers out to alert the kingdom and pull the infantry and archers behind the city wall. The cannon will engage as soon as they have range." Commander Ryan ordered and turned to gaze out to sea over the balcony. "Close the city gates when the last of the women and children have departed." He shouted turning back to the King and Chancellor Simon. "You should make your escape to Castle Greenstone now. Your insight may prove useful in the defense of the rest of the kingdom." King Jeffrey said filling his chest with air. "You give my apologies to Queen Isabella for doubting her and tell the Great Father we remain at Castle Sandista to our best." Chancellor Simon could see in the kings eyes he understood that staying was suicide. He was tremendously angry at being deceived and at the murder of his friends and servants. "I will stay by your side and revenge the blood of my court!" He pleaded as tears filled his eye and King Jeffrey removed his crown and handed it to him. "You will do as I have commanded taking my carriage and deliver this crown to the Great Father. If I survive this day, I will retrieve it with honor through blood. If I perish I will die knowing I did my best to preserve this crown for another son of the Great Father." He said proudly and Chancellor Simon reluctantly followed a servant to the King's fast carriage to depart for Greenstone.

Cpt Rebecca ran up the stairs atop the academy where the rest of the Sky Raiders awaited her. She threw two bags filled with the coconut bombs across Emerald's back and began to fasten it down. "We have our task. Sandista is under attack!" She shouted angrily. "Take as many bombs as you can carry and follow my lead. We go to set the lead ship on fire first. Attack what I attack but stay clear of their archers. We will attack in single file. I want you all to return here for this battle will be a long one and we will fight as a unit." She said mounting Emerald. She walked Emerald to the launch platform and one by one the Sky Raiders took to the air. There was a orange red tinge to the horizon and Rebecca knew there was less than an hour to 1st light. She circled the castle allowing all the Sky Raiders to join her and briefly thought of Arthur and Andrew as she turned toward the first light on the ocean. She climbed high into the sky before turning north toward the lead ship. She reached back into the bag and grabbed one of the coconut bombs and tore away the safety chip as she turned Emerald into a dive straight at the ship. It was a wide easy target and Rebecca released the bomb before turning Emerald back skyward. She looked back over her shoulder in time to see her bomb hit in the middle of deck and burst into flames. The new fire on the ship revealed the enormity of the vessel and she could see the sailors scurry to extinguish the fire as another bomb exploded and then another adding to the blaze and to the confusion. Nine bombs found their mark on the deck and Cpt Rebecca was extremely pleased as she reached for a second coconut and pulled away the safety chip. This time she dove at the rear of the ship before releasing her bomb again and turning Emerald back skyward. She was surprised that there was no one firing at them from the deck and the second fire grew quickly as more of the Sky Raiders dropped their bombs. Cpt Rebecca counted quickly in her head. She had 10 coconuts in each bag giving her 20. As she realigned Emerald heading for the front of the ship, she calculated they could attack the first 7 ships before they had to return to resupply. She wished the coconut bombs were more powerful but knew they would have to be bigger and then they would carry less. As she looked down the line of ships, she thought how time consuming this task was and cursed for not beginning sooner. She adjudged the first ship was burning out of control as they had not been able to extinguish the first fire and turned Emerald to the second ship. She looked over her shoulders at the other Raiders flying tight behind her. The light from the morning sun was turning the sky grey with streaks of orange as she dove Emerald toward the center of the ship. The deck of the ship crackled and popped as she released the bomb and Cpt Rebecca realized they were firing at her from the deck as she turned back skyward. She was certain she was too high for their weapons as she watched the bomb explode on the deck and the sailors began to scramble. As she reached for the next coconut and turned Emerald toward the back of the ship, the ocean around them lit up brightly blinding her for a second and then she heard the tremendous explosion on the first ship and then another of equal intensity. As she looked a great hole was revealed in the side of the ship and it began to lean dramatically to one side. Cpt Rebecca focused on her task, dropping another bomb but she could hardly contain her elation at their success. Again and again the Sky Raiders dived on the ships as the sun rose over the ocean but the ships kept creeping further into the harbor. It became more evident to Cpt Rebecca how limited their success was as one by one the heavy ships moved into the harbor and began to fire their huge cannons. The cannons of the garrison on the shore did not stand a chance as the larger ships cannons with their increased range decimated the encampment quickly. As Cpt Rebecca dropped her last bomb she could see the futility in what they were doing. They had sunk four ships and damaged three others but they kept coming. Cpt Rebecca turned Emerald back toward the city determined to resupply and return to do as much damage as she could. They were not beginning to launch the long boats yet and that puzzled Cpt Rebecca but she knew when they did that Emerald would be able to attack and sink those with his talons if they could withstand the fire from the shoulder crackers. She watched as one of the ships that was shaped much different and had no sails was being towed by another ship even closer to shore. Cpt Rebecca landed and dismounted quickly as Emerald drank. Again she thought of Andrew and Arthur and how badly they could use them now especially Crimson if they had been successful. Emerald protested as she climbed back up, wanting to drink more and Cpt Rebecca knew they would have to rest the young dragons soon but now was not the time. As she urged him toward the launch platform she heard a tremendous explosion and looked to see a gaping hole in the city wall. Then in a horrific series of explosions the wall and the castle and the whole of the city began to crumble. Cpt Rebecca whistled and Emerald dove just before a cannonball demolished the launch platform behind her. Emerald circled around to the safety behind the buildings on the west side of the city and Rebecca looked over her shoulder to see the stream of Sky Raiders that followed her. She could only count seven as she circled around back toward the Academy. The disaster she witnessed broke her heart and her spirit. The city wall facing the ocean was a mass of rubble and most of the soldiers that had taken shelter behind it were dead or wounded. The only thing left of the wall was the gate and the two towers with their cannons and they continued to fire out to sea sporadically. There were no long boats but only the oddly shaped ship with oars coming from its sides closing on the shore. The cannon fire from the ships had stopped and only the cannons from the gates towers continued to splash cannonballs close to the ominous ship. The Castle was riddled with holes and the sixth floor where the King's quarters were had collapsed. As she banked around the castle her horror was increased tenfold and she cried out tearfully as she saw Waterbird lying in the rubble atop the roof of the academy. Cpt Rebecca was uncertain what to do as she circled the city a second time but the one ship moving toward the shore seemed to be the obvious target at the moment. She looked back at the ships at sea and they were beginning to launch their longboats as she turned Emerald's head toward the oddly shaped ship and grabbed a coconut bomb. Abruptly, before she could attack, the front of the huge vessel dropped open and a horde of wild beasts that she had never seen before began to pour out of it. They were black and brown and ran on four legs sprinting toward the city in the shallow surf. Each was as big as a small bear but leaner and faster looking very muscular and howled as they ran. Cpt Rebecca dropped her bomb in the middle of the pack with little effect and Emerald circled around the castle again still uncertain of what to do. As she flew over what was left of the academy, she saw Lightning on the only perch left standing. "Blast!" She cursed banking hard and tight to circle the academy. Lt Cameron had broken formation and landed when they went by the first time and she hadn't noticed. She located him kneeling over Lt Regina in the stables who had obviously fallen from the roof when Waterbird was killed. She watched him pick her up moving back into the Academy. Rebecca looked back over her shoulder and saw the wild beasts streaming through the wall and they began to rip the wounded soldiers to pieces as they spread out through the city like a swarm of locusts. She pointed Emerald's head toward a beast heading for the academy and whistled the command to attack and they swooped down and picked up the beast turning skyward. The beast growled and bit at Emerald's talon's ferociously until they got high enough and they dropped him. Cpt Rebecca pulled a bomb from her bag and dove back at the entrance to the academy. The other Sky Raiders followed her lead but she saw the horde of beast streaming into the academy as Lt Cameron emerged on the roof moving quickly to Lightning. She hovered above the entrance and began throwing the bombs at the entrance killing several dogs and collapsing the wall until the entrance was blocked. Rebecca looked back to the other side of the roof and Cameron was in trouble. There were 6 of the beasts on the roof and every time a raider snatched one another came up the stairs. Lt Regina was unconscious against what was left of the wall with Cameron standing over her with his sword drawn stabbing at two of the beasts. Lightning was fighting ferociously with the other four. Rebecca whistled twice as she unbuckled from Emerald and she rolled off the front of him as he landed and drew her sword. She whistled again for him to attack but he was already ripping at one of the beasts on Lightning. Rebecca jumped high into the air and came down on one of the beasts attacking Cameron and slashed hard killing it in one blow. As she spun around beside Cameron, they stabbed at the other beast until it fell dead. "Pick her up!" Cpt Rebecca yelled as Emerald and Lightning killed the other beasts ripping them to pieces and Rebecca jumped back onto Emerald buckling in quickly. "Give her to me!" She waved her arms frantically as another beast came up the stairs and Lightning attacked it killing it quickly. Cameron laid Regina's limp body in front of Rebecca who looked into his eyes before he mounted Lightning. She could see the pain and the anger in his eyes that she felt in her whole body. "We're going to Greenstone. There's nothing left here." She shouted to him and then moved Emerald to the wall and whistled. She circled the city inside the walls and witnessed the horror that had become Sandista first hand. The wild beast swarmed across the city killing anything that moved. She could hear the screams of agony from the towers at the gate as those cannons went silent. Tears rolled down Cpt Rebecca's face as she saw the mass of long boats stream onto the shore unmolested and she turned Emerald's head north toward Castle Greenstone.

The ride to Castle Greenstone was the longest ride in Chancellor Simon's memory. The highway was crowded with refugees from Sandista but they moved to the side when they saw the King's carriage approaching. The Maiden Terea, King Jeffrey's wife, sat across from him with her two small children close at her side and she was weeping uncontrollably. Two of her servants sat at his side. They shared no words during the entire trip. Chancellor Simon's mind was filled with anger and disillusionment at his judgment of Ambassador Freeman. It was unbelievable to him that a man could be so treacherous as to preach peace so adamantly in one moment and execute murderous destruction in the next. It was most evident to Chancellor Simon; these were evil men with no equal in his memory. As they made the turn down the ramp at Greenstone and up to the front of the Castle, Chancellor Simon looked at the crown in his lap covered in the ceremonial cloth and wept for King Jeffrey again. As he entered the council chambers, Commander Dillon was the first to address him angrily. "Why does King Jeffrey not sent word of the nature of the battle and what reinforcements he desires?" Commander Dillon shouted. "Where is the Great Father?" Chancellor Simon asked solemnly. "He is in route from Paternus. Answer my question man!" Commander Dillon shouted and Chancellor Simon uncovered the crown holding it out with trembling hands as his tears fell. Commander Dillon and the entire chamber fell to their knees knowing what this meant. He walked to Queen Isabella and put his hand on her shoulder as she wept. "He begged me deliver a message to you." He said and Queen Isabella looked up. "He asked me to deliver his apology for doubting your judgment with these treacherous men and he asked me to deliver his family into your hands to insure their safety." He said tearfully and turned to Commander Dillon. "King Jeffrey and his staff knew at the onset of the battle that there was no time for your army to reinforce them and that you would be slaughtered on the highway to Sandista if he summoned you. There were 51 ships and they were in the harbor before I lost sight of Sandista beginning their bombardment. The Sky Raiders were dispatched to sink as many as they could before 1st light but I have no report of their success. I am certain they made it ashore with the bulk of their army." Chancellor Simon concluded sorrowfully. Commander Dillon ordered 4 messengers be put to the task of monitoring the battle at Sandista and one launched every hour to make the round trip to Sandista and back. He and his staff and Queen Isabella and her council debated frantically over the course of action to take at the invasion and the Great Father and the Supreme council joined them just after the midday meal. They delivered the dire report to the Great Father and Chancellor Simon presented him with the crown and King Jeffrey's last words for him. It was several hours later before Cpt Rebecca and the Sky Raiders made their landing atop Castle Greenstone.

CHAPTER 11

AMANDA

The sun was setting over the mountains behind what was left of Sandista as Commodore Marantz stepped from his ship onto the dock. "Have your handlers rounded up all the war dogs from the city yet Cpt Manor?" he said as he joined him in the one fast carriage they had captured. "They have but they found something of a surprise." He replied with an ominous grin. "There is a small group in the north of the city that discovered a group of women in a cellar and the handlers restrained the war dogs from killing them to present the women to you." Cpt Manor said smiling at him as the carriage began to roll toward the city gate. Commodore Marantz smiled back at him pulling at the red beard. "How many women are there?" He asked. "Maybe six but they are young none of them being over 20 years." Cpt Manor replied. "You go to them and choose the fairest of these women for you and I to enjoy tonight and leave the rest for the handlers to do with as they will for the war dogs carried the battle today and I would share this pleasure with them." He laughed as they pulled in front of the castle. As they walked together into the castle, there were sailors and soldiers moving throughout the battered castle and one of them met them at the stairs. "There are grand rooms up these stairs and the water still flows to many of them. The Commodore may bath in comfort and sleep well tonight." He said excitedly and led the two of them up the stairs to one of the rooms. It was the King's chambers. "You see now the problem with these people." The Commodore smiled moving to the window of the undamaged room. "They devoted all their energy to the pleasure of life with little concern for its defense. Go now and gather my staff in the dining hall and we will feast on our spoils and make plans for the next city. When you have made my command known, go quickly to fetch this woman to me for I will have complete fulfillment in this night of conquest and pleasure after we set our plans for the morning. Find one that pleases you and I am certain I will find pleasure in her also." He smiled turning the valve above the tub to fill it with warm water. "Do not trouble yourself to make haste to return for the meeting for I will appraise you of our plan in due course." He added undressing and Cpt Manor departed leaving a guard at his door.

The east wall of the city was in rubble but the north and west were virtually undamaged save the dead body occasionally found lying in the street. Cpt Manor rode the carriage to the spot where the soldier said they found the women and dismounted in front of a handsome wooden house. There were several handlers in front of the house each with two or three dogs on chains. They were barking and pulling against the handlers who restrained them. The chief handler for the war dogs met him in the doorway with two of the dogs on a chain and they were growling at a group of women and a small boy bound with ropes cowering in the corner. Cpt Manor walked to them and inspected each one and they wept dramatically afraid. "Why have you spared this boy?" He asked the handler. "The women guarded him and we thought him possibly a prince and may have use to the Commodore for diplomacy." He replied and as Cpt Manor examined the women, one with long blonde hair caught his eye. "We have no use or need for the boy. Take them all outside and I will give you a lesson in diplomacy." Cpt Manor said and they stood them all and walked them out in front of the house into the road. Cpt Manor pulled the boy away from the women several paces and pulled out his dagger. He looked at the boy and spoke to him in his own language as he cut the ropes on his hands and feet. "Are you a fast runner boy?" He asked smiling wickedly at the child who looked up nervously and shook his head no. "Then this is a very sad day for you for running is your only hope." Cpt Manor replied and the boy looked at him full of fear. "RUN BOY!" Cpt Manor shouted and the boy dashed away as Cpt Manor nodded to the handlers and they released their dogs. The young boy did not get 10 paces away before one the dogs knocked him to the ground and he screamed horrifically. The other dogs joined in quickly and the women watched as they tore huge chunks of flesh and meat from the boy until he quit screaming and then quit struggling and collapsed on the road but the dogs continued to tear at him until they had ripped off his legs and arms and shook them in their teeth fighting over them. The women collapsed on the ground wailing and screaming and Cpt Manor knelt before them speaking in their own language again as the handlers regained control of their dogs. "Who will be next?" He said poking his dagger at them threateningly and he lifted the young blonde girls chin looking into her eyes. "Ah but maybe one of you could save all the others from my beasts." He smiled and the young girl just stared at him terrified clinging to another girl. "Shall I spare them or do we continue with my sport?" He asked pulling her to her feet as he cut her ropes.

Amanda was the oldest of the girls being 19. She had been left in charge of her father's house and all the children as her parents and theirs had left the city yesterday for a shopping tour in Archemeius. They were all in the basement that morning and had not heard the call to evacuate the city as her father's house was secluded in the far northwest of the city. By the time she had discovered the danger and ran with her charges to the front gate it was too late and they all had witnessed the city wall fall on the infantry. She had brought them all back to her father's house to hide in the basement. Amanda struggled fiercely to control her panic from what she had just witnessed. The other girls were her lifelong friends and the boy had been her best friends little brother. "What must I suffer?" She trembled feeling sick and afraid. "Pleasure." Cpt Manor replied smiled broadly touching her hair. His smile was ugly and threatening from Amanda's perspective. "I will take you to the Commodore and if you can please him and me, I promise to release you and all your companions to run back to your countrymen tomorrow. We need to send them a message and you will make the perfect messengers. But I warn you, if either the Commodore or I find your conduct less than completely satisfying tonight, you and all your companions will find yourselves playthings for my dogs at first light." Cpt Manor warned her lifting her chin with his dagger again. Amanda was petrified with fear and trembled and shook crying desperately as Cpt Manor pulled her into his embrace. The handlers began to gather the war dogs and put the chains back on their collars. "What is your name girl?" He asked more softly. "Amanda!" She screamed still crying uncontrollably. "Do you love your friends Amanda? Will you agree with me to give them a chance at life and escape from all this?" He asked calmly and Amanda looked back at her friends. She knew how she responded to him would determine whether her and her friends lived or died horrifically as the small boy had. The echo of the small boys screams was still in her head. Her arms were shaking so dramatically she could barely control them as she put them around Cpt Manor's neck. "What will become of my friends when I leave with you?" She asked fighting her emotions. "I will leave them here in the safety of this house guarded by my handlers until you have secured their release." Cpt Manor replied casually. He knew she was terrified but he liked her change in demeanor. "Show me with a kiss you understand and convince me now I will have more pleasure in your living than watching you die." Cpt Manor whispered in her ear and Amanda pulled all her strength together and delivered a kiss as she surrendered to his embrace. She prayed it would be enough to save her friends. Cpt Manor was well pleased with the soft passion of Amanda's kiss as it had been some time since he had experienced the tenderness of a woman's body under the caress of his hands. He was hard pressed not to take her for himself where they stood. Reluctantly, he pulled her lips from his as the handlers chuckled and laughed. Amanda knew that he was lying and feared that they would kill her friends as soon as she lost sight of them. "I beg you sir, if you find pleasure in my kiss, give me but a moment with my friends to convince them to surrender as I have before we depart. They are all young and have not known a man but I am not confused at what you intend for them this night in my father's house. I fear there is no message for my countrymen and you do not intend our release at first light. In a few words, I will convince them to deliver the passion you desire rather than resistance and we will all live to reap the benefits of the night ahead and none of us suffer death." Amanda whispered still trembling dramatically in Cpt Manor's embrace. Cpt Manor was amazed and impressed at the young girl's perceptiveness. He looked at her and smiled contemplating the benefits to him and all his men to have a brothel in their newly captured city so soon. "Your wisdom exceeds my expectations. Take your companions back into your father's house and perhaps if pleasure exceeds resistance as you have suggested, we will make a new bargain and this may become a safe haven for you and all your friends. I will give you 5 minutes with them." He smiled and Amanda looked to her terrified companions as Cpt Manor handed her his dagger to cut their ropes. She thought for a brief moment to cut his throat but she knew that would be certain death for her and her friends so she forced a dreadful smile at him moving quickly to her friends. Cpt Manor looked to his chief handler and spoke in his own tongue again so she would not understand. "The Commodore is well pleased with you and all your handlers in the conduct of this most successful battle. He was so pleased that he wants you and your handlers to be first to reap the pleasure of this find. I will take the blonde girl for the Commodore but the rest I will leave in this house for you and your handlers to indulge yourselves. If you find resistance in them at first take your pleasure forcefully but leave them alive and unbroken for it is the Commodore's desire to make this house a brothel for all his army to enjoy once you have had your fill of them tonight. Tonight is for you and the handlers only by the Commodore's decree. The blonde girl makes their new path in life clear to them and if I guess right you will find them more submissive to your pleasures. Have someone clean up this mess before she exits the house. I would not have this vision of her house be the last she takes back to the castle tonight." He said smiling at the chief handler. "Take the war dogs to the stables beside the castle and secure them all there before you bring your men back to the brothel but keep them guarded. The Commodore would not suffer their escape lightly." He warned him and the chief handler laughed and saluted appreciatively before departing.

Amanda cut the ropes on all her friends and they moved quickly into the house and fell on the couch and the floor weeping. "Listen to me quickly Elisha for there is a way that we might live and not perish this night." She said to her best friend who crawled to her on the floor trying to pull the dagger from her grip. "I beg you, give me the dagger so I can end my life now." Elisha wept. "This is not the council your mother or father would give you nor will I." Amanda said pleading with her and wrestling the dagger from her. "They would tell you to do whatever was required to hold onto life. Elisha, I love you all and I implore you. Our fate is tragic but it need not end in our death and our parents would not wish it so. If we let these men have their way with us and give ourselves willingly it will be an abomination to all of us but we will **live**." Amanda pleaded with her looking to the other girls. "Look at me!" She shouted moving from one girl to the next quickly lifting their eyes to hers. "One day we will be discovered and rescued and revenge will be taken on these men but tonight each one of us must convince whoever comes to lie down with us that we possess the only thing that they value us for now in abundance. This is our only path to life for the coming days. I know that none of you has been with a man and may feel now that death is a better choice but I beg you all consider my words for I and all those that truly love you would not consider it so." Amanda pleaded returning to Elisha's side. They were all horribly terrified and trembling. Amanda took a deep breath intent on being an example to them as to how to survive. "Whoever comes to you, be whatever he wants you to be and submit to him willingly as if he were your one true love. It may be that you will secure your own life and that of all of us. I tell you now if one of us resists or does not strive to satisfy them completely we are all in jeopardy." Amanda said forcefully and she took heart that they listened to her now attentively. "I would not wish this true for myself or you or even my worst enemy but it is our new reality for a time and to survive we must suffer it and find comfort in each other. Do not fail me Elisha for I would present you alive to our families and make this but a tragic memory some years from now if we can but suffer it now and survive." Amanda said embracing her and kissing her tenderly. Elisha was but a year younger than her and wiped her tears from her eyes. "Amanda is right." She replied looking to the other girls remorsefully. We have no choice but surrender until we are rescued or find a way of escape for all of us. One day they will pay for what they did to my brother and all of us but tonight I will do what is necessary to survive and bear witness to that day as all of us must do." She said and began to embrace all the younger girls. "Take no shame in whatever evil falls to you or they force on you and convince them your pleasure is equal to theirs and you will survive." Elisha whimpered as they all wept and embraced below the couch. Amanda stood reluctantly satisfied she had convinced them and seeing that Elisha was in agreement with her plan. "I must leave but I am certain they will return me to you in the morning. I beg you all, do what you must so that I will find you alive when I return." Amanda whispered and Elisha hugged her and kissed her before she departed.

Amanda set her mind to her task wiping the tears from her eyes as she approached the fast carriage where Cpt Manor waited. She handed him back the dagger and he smiled at her. "You are surprising wise for your age and it gives me cause for concern." He said as helped her into the carriage. "I am but a young girl, 19, who knows what value you place with me and my friends. I pray that you will return me to them if I perform well and you will think it wise to keep me alive so that you may revisit tonight's pleasure at your leisure in the future." Amanda said as Cpt Manor took his seat in the carriage across from her. Amanda's whole body was still shaking but she moved to his side as the carriage began to roll. "I have known the pleasure of a boy before from this city but you are not a boy." Amanda said trying to sound inviting to him. "I will not resist you. Will you share now your name with me?" Amanda whispered laying her head on his shoulder. "My name is Cpt William Manor and as much as I find your aggressiveness appealing to me, I promised to deliver you un-violated to Commodore Marantz. If I unwrap my present before I deliver it to him; it will not be as well received."

Cpt Manor smiled pushing her hands into her lap. "I am going to take you to the Queen's quarters at the castle. There you will bath and chose a gown from her wardrobe you feel will be appealing to him. You will be the last conquest of the day for the Commodore and I recommend you surrender to him as quickly and as easily as this city did today." Cpt Manor explained as they pulled in front of the castle. He walked her quickly into the castle and up the stairs and every guards jaw dropped as they passed them. They got to the quarters of the King's wife who he had assumed was queen and Cpt Manor ushered her in. The quarters were large being three rooms in one with a parlor and a dressing room with large closets containing many gowns and a separate bathing room with a balcony off of it. There was a door that led to the King's bedchamber off the parlor room. A strong fire burned in the fireplace in the wall between the bedchamber and the parlor. Amanda had never imagined a more beautiful room in her life but her astonishment was stifled by her fear for herself and her friends. "Did I not tell you the pleasure would not be mine alone." Cpt Manor said smiling at her again. "You have precious little time before I present you to the Commodore. I suggest you use it wisely. When next I open this door, I expect to present the most voluptuous flower in the city to my Commodore." He said before he had words with the guard and closed the door. She ran quickly to the balcony but it was so high. She cried staring down at the ground covered with guards. Even if she did escape, she would not be able to bear the death of all her friends. What would she tell their parents. She had no choice. She moved to the bathing room and started the warm water filling the tub and removed her gown. She poured lilac scented oil into the tub as it filled and ran to the closet to find a gown. Amanda's whole body trembled uncontrollably from the horror she had witnessed and she stopped and gritted her teeth to control her panic. She must focus on this task to save her friends. There were so many gowns and they were all beautiful but one red silk flowing gown caught her eye above the rest. As she laid it across the chair beside the tub, she couldn't help but feel a sharp pang knowing what certainly lay ahead tonight for her friends at the hands of the ruffians that were the handlers. She felt a little guilty that she had been chosen to feed the desires of the senior officer because she was certain he would not be as cruel to her. Whatever trauma she suffered would most assuredly be less than theirs. She submersed her head in the tub and washed quickly and took two large towels to dry her body and her hair wrapping one around her waist. What did he mean by a precious little time? It would take a long time to dry her hair and she went to the fireplace to brush it out. She would be doing none of this if she wasn't convinced that her body was the only weapon she could use against them to secure a future for her and her friends. Cpt Manor had told her. If she failed, they would all be adjudged as useless and fed to those beasts and Amanda was determined not to let that happen to her friends regardless of what she had to endure. Her hair finally dried after some time in front of the fire and she adorned herself with the finest jewels the King's wife had and sprayed herself with lilac perfume. She looked at herself in the mirror adjusting her long blonde hair and clipping a braid in both sides of her head. She felt half naked already in the thin red silk gown as the neckline dipped low leaving her breasts partially exposed in the middle but she knew this was what a man found appealing.

"It is good to have the power over life and death." Amanda heard from behind her and it startled her and she turned quickly to face him. There stood a tall man with a neatly trimmed red beard holding a glass of wine in one hand with his other on the hilt of his saber at his side. "It is no wonder that they kept their women from us if they are all as lovely as you." He said softly. "You speak my language." Amanda said nervously as she assessed her visitor presuming him to be the Commodore. "I find conquest easier if I first learn to communicate with my adversary." The Commodore replied smiling at her. This was not what Amanda expected at all. Commodore Marantz seemed very polite and cordial as a gentleman. She was unsure of what to do next as she stood frozen in place in front of the mirror. "Am I your adversary?" Amanda asked still puzzled by his demeanor and he chuckled pleasantly. "In a manner of speaking; yes you are. You see I plan on winning your heart by giving it what it desires within reason." He smiled and Amanda was even more confused by her circumstances. She started to tremble again and turned her back to him facing the mirror and dropping her head in her hands. "Do you like that gown?" He asked taking a step closer to her gazing at her image in the mirror. She lifted her eyes looking at him in the mirror and herself. "It is of no consequence, what I think of the gown if it pleases you Commodore." Amanda replied and he frowned at her. "Do not be coy with me Amanda. If you seek a bond with me, answer my inquiries simply and honestly." He said still smiling. "Do you like the dress or not." He repeated casually. A bond? What was he talking about? "I do." Amanda replied curtly. "What pleases you about this dress that you would select it above all the others in her closet?" He asked and he ran his hand over the thin silk covering her back touching her softly for the first time. "I like the color and the way it feels against my skin. It invites the touch of a man's hand as you do now." Amanda replied fighting the tremendous urge to run away and Commodore Marantz chuckled and removed his hand. "You have to add the words that you think I want to hear." He laughed. "The color is a great compliment to you and I am even certain you like the feel of silk against your skin for your breasts reveal your excitement at the caress of the soft material I am certain is foreign to them but your heart does not long for my touch." He giggled. "I fear you would prefer to see my hand wither and fall from my arm rather than caress you in this moment." He grinned and chuckled and Amanda was thoroughly bemused. This was like a parlor game that she heard royalty play in lighthearted fun and flirtation. Could it be that he did not know the horror she had experienced today. This could not be possible but he addressed her as a man beginning a courtship between two new friends. "I do not know this game. Perhaps my adolescence hides the meaning of it from me. Do you truly pursue my heart's desire?" She asked looking into his eyes pitifully backing away. "Within reason." He replied still grinning. Now Amanda was still fearful but angry. "Do you not know that today I bear witness to your war dogs tear my youngest companion to pieces in front of my eyes at the command of your Lieutenant simply because he was a boy and not a girl and by this action he made a decree in your name, enticed me to your bed and my friends into debauchery with your handlers? Is this how men win women's hearts in your kingdom?" Amanda asked tearfully and Commodore Marantz did look surprised and suddenly disappointed. His jaw tightened under the beard and he clinched his fists. "This is what you witnessed?" He gasped and recoiled from her. "Cpt Manor's tactics are many times crude and crass and oft times regrettable but he has proven to be a great asset to me. I am sorry for your friend. It was not necessary." He said and Amanda judged his demeanor to be sincere seeing a tear form in his eye as his anger grew. He slammed his fist on the desk. "I have the power over life and death but I cannot change the past or revoke a decree made in my name by my Captain." He continued struggling for his words as his anger grew and Amanda was frightened. "He should never have made such a decree. This was not my command to him! If we want our men taken prisoners treated fairly we must treat our prisoners with respect also." He spoke as if someone else was in the room. He grimaced and gritting his teeth and then he looked at Amanda remorsefully. "But I will make you this promise. I must let the decree he made in my name stand for the handlers but this is the only night your friends will have to suffer this indignity. I will bring them to the castle at first light to live here in safety with you under watch of my personal guard." He promised gripping his sword again until his knuckles turned white. Amanda's fear waned realizing his anger was not with her but his captain and she grew hopeful. "I must go to dine with my officers and you will accompany me. Cpt Manor and all my officers must have a demonstration from me of how I expect them to treat our prisoners. I know you have suffered much at the hands of my men and your friends suffer still but if you will suffer me this dinner it will serve me well in securing their respect for your friends and any other prisoners we take in the future." He pleaded with her and again Amanda searched his eyes and found only sincere remorse and determination to remedy her circumstances and those of her friends. "I will be escort to you at dinner but I still do not understand. Why can you not intervene for the safety of my friends now?" Amanda pleaded nervously and carefully knowing it was dangerous to confront him improperly and incur his wrath. "Because he made the decree in my name!" He sighed deeply and regretfully shaking his head no. "He is my second in command and if I rebuke him now it will spread through my whole army as a plague and destroy the very structure of my command. As much as it pains me, I cannot revoke his decree." He admitted and Amanda searched deep into his soft green eyes and judged he was pleading honestly with her. The Commodore rubbed his forehead and his eyes fell to her feet. "I am certain even if I could, it is already too late as the handlers would not have delayed to make haste to the house and fulfill their own lustful desires for them having been at sea for so long." He said and took her hands softly in his as if to apologize. "There are but 12 handlers and I know many, if not all of your friends, will know a man for the first time in this night but they will be left unbroken and alive and I will speed them to the safety of your side tomorrow." Commodore Marantz replied sorrowfully and Amanda thought it wise to be his escort and prayed his sincerity was genuine so she took his arm to go down to the dining hall.

The guard at the door snapped to attention as they exited the room. In the stairwell, Cpt Manor met them. "I was coming to see if you were joining us for dinner." He smiled speaking in the language Amanda understood and then he and Commodore Marantz began to converse in their own language. Amanda watched the smile fade from Cpt Manor's face as the conversation intensified and he looked at Amanda several times and each time the expression was more worried. They appeared to argue bitterly for a time before Cpt Manor's demeanor showed his surrender to the Commodore's demands and he departed without a another word to her. "Cpt Manor will not be joining us for dinner. I sent him to your father's house to insure that all the handlers understand what the word gentle means tonight." He said to her still showing his disappointment in his face. "Thank you." Amanda said squeezing his arm hoping that would make the night a little less horrific for her friends. At dinner she could understand none of the conversation other than what she and the Commodore had. He introduced her to the bourbon they had brought from the ship and it slid warm down her throat as nothing she had ever tasted before. Commodore Marantz appeared to Amanda as a very gentle man who was sincerely mortified by his captain's actions. He told her how the dragons had attacked his fleet and he was forced into war as he was seeking diplomacy. She was so hopeful he was being sincere with her. Her fear of him began to turn into something else as she watched him interact with his men. His soft disposition and his pleasant demeanor were in harmony with her growing affection for him personally. The music they played after dinner and even the instruments were something very new to her but it was exciting and enticingly different. He introduced her to all his officers and Amanda knew this was important to the Commodore to instill his desire for the fair treatment of prisoners as he had said earlier. Everyone else was having a good time and Amanda felt herself getting caught up in the festive mood and she let her anxieties fade with each little glass of the bourbon. He was making her the center of attention and they even shared a dance together as all the other men applauded and watched them smiling broadly at her. All the men admired him and sought his approval and Amanda was finding herself wanting more and more for him to find favor with her also. Slowly she was convinced he could be her salvation as well as her friends. Amanda had never been treated as royalty before but she certainly felt like a princess now. She even met one of the scholars who also spoke her language and the Commodore invited him to sit on her other side and she laughed as he made comical descriptions of all the officers. Cpt Manor came back late in the evening and took a seat across from them. He said something to the Commodore who smiled approvingly and nodded. "Give her your report for I am sure she has been worried." The Commodore said in her language and Cpt Manor leaned forward. "All the handlers have retired and your friends sleep comfortably in their beds with the Commodore's personal guards outside their door. It appears you have found a piece of the Commodore's heart I did not recognize until tonight." He whispered and Amanda could see the resignation in his eyes as he sat back in his chair admiring her and smiling sympathetically. She couldn't imagine more joyful news being delivered in that moment. "Would you like to take account of them for yourself?" Commodore Marantz suggested and he stood offering her his arm. Her legs were unstable from the drink as she took his arm and he lead her to a large room. There a guard raised a torch and Amanda could see Elisa and all her friends sleeping soundly on mats on the floor in front of a fireplace. Now Amanda moved to run to them and embrace them but the Commodore restrained her and held his finger to his lips. "Shhh.., let them sleep tonight and you can confront them in the morning." He suggested and she squeezed the Commodore's arm and pressed her lips to his as she turned to face him. She was intoxicated by the Commodore and the drink. "My joy is complete for you have given comfort to the desire of my heart." Amanda whispered gratefully wanting desperately to believe their ordeal was over. She looked deep into his green eyes and felt a warm romantic force engulf her whole body. Commodore Marantz was unlike any other man she had ever met. He was powerful but gentle and patient with her. He commanded respect and admiration from all the other men around him and he was extremely handsome. His lips were soft and enticing and his hands were not course but drove her passion intensely when he caressed her. He was just the kind of man Amanda had dreamed she would fall in love with some day. "Can I tell you a secret?" She giggled leaning her head on his shoulder and nuzzling against him as they walked back to the hall. "I felt guilty when I first saw you because of the desire I felt for you seeing how handsome you are and I **did** consider you my adversary. After all you have done for me and my friends my guilt has faded leaving only my desire to thank you and share your intimate embrace in gratitude for the kindness you have shown us." Amanda whispered and pressed her lips to his kissing him passionately. Oh how she loved his lips on hers. The only thing warmer in her mouth was the bourbon which he presented to her now after each kiss. It became as a game to them and she laughed more with each kiss and each drink. Commodore Marantz pulled away from her lips and stroked her hair smiling at Cpt Manor before speaking to him in their language so she would not understand. "Conquest is magnificent in any venue. As I said before; tonight I will make love to this young beauty and rest my head between her breasts to sleep completely satisfied that she would cut your throat tonight if you came in meaning to do harm to my person. At first light I will wake and make love to her again as a husband going off to work and the smell of her will be on my hand as I go forth to conquer another of her cities." He smiled and winked at Cpt Manor. "As I dress for battle, as I promised, you will come in and have your way with her and I will watch to judge your prowess and skill in the Kings bed." He laughed softly and Cpt Manor nodded approvingly sipping his wine to hide his chuckle. "Then you will return her to her father's house and join me on the battlefield taking charge of the ground forces as I sail with the fleet in your support. Do not kill them for I intend to add to their number with each city I conquer." Commodore Marantz smiled as he stood and helped his intoxicated escort to her feet. "You should have allowed me to bring her friend, the brown haired girl, Elisha." Cpt Manor whispered with a chuckle. "She is not as voluptuous as this one but she responds well to a stiff rod and seems to relish more than one at a time. The four of us would have been great sport this night." He said with a broad grin. "Do not tempt me to delay our advance for this indulgence." Commodore Marantz sighed pulling Amanda next to him caressing the curve of her hip through the thin silk of the dress as she leaned against him. "We will have time for more exotic games with them after I conquer another of her cities." He smiled and Captain Manor nodded. "I think I will return and take her friend for myself for the rest of the evening." He smiled as he took Amanda's hand and kissed it. "We should send the Queen's wardrobe with her in the morning as few of her friends have a garment that has not been torn to shreds. The handlers found great sport in relieving them of their attire forcefully since we did not allow them to beat them." Cpt Manor smiled and the Commodore nodded his agreement. Amanda was curious at their conversation, thinking she had heard Elisha's name but her desire for the Commodore grew too intense feeling his caress tease below her breast and she dismissed it anxious to retire with him to the privacy of the bedchamber. "Goodnight Cpt Manor. I shall see you tomorrow." Amanda giggled softly and smiled at him oblivious to their conversation. "I am looking forward to it." Cpt Manor replied in her own language and smiled watching the Commodore sweep her off her feet carrying her toward the stairs. "I am completely undone by you." Amanda whispered in his ear. "I by no means ever dreamed I would feel such pleasure or deep desire for you in our meeting." Amanda breathed heavily as he carried her in his arms and she kissed his neck languishing in feel of his beard on her cheek. "If this be our only night together, I pray our passion will live in your memory and mine forever." Amanda whispered. "I have many more surprises for you as I reveal my heart to you Amanda and I pray each will draw your heart closer to mine with their exposure and this will be but the first of a thousand nights we share our passion." Commodore Marantz whispered softly as he carried her into the King's bedchamber and the guard closed the door behind them.

C H A P T E R 1 2

✳

DEFENSE AND REGINA'S SURRENDER

Cpt Rebecca bound from Emerald and assisted two servants in pulling Lt Regina's body from her mount. There was much shouting and confusion on the perches as Cpt Rebecca knelt beside Lt Regina and screamed for a medic. The wind swirled ferociously around them as the other Raiders made their landing. Lt Regina had a severe gash on the back of her head and the skin fell loose bleeding badly and her arm was twisted unnaturally at her side. Cpt Rebecca saw Regina's blood covering her own boot and leg armor and when she looked back at Emerald she could see the trail down his side that Regina had left during their flight. She was deeply concerned with Lt Regina's condition as her heart beat faintly and she had lost a lot of blood. Two servants quickly placed her on a litter at the command of the medic and rushed her down the stairs and Lt Cameron helped them pleading hysterically with the medic to do something. Chancellor Simon grabbed Cpt Rebecca's arm turning her to face him as they made their way down the stairs. "You must come with me and give your account to the Great Father." He said pulling her hurriedly toward the council chambers and away from the others. Cpt Rebecca stepped in the chamber and she realized her right leg and boot were soaked with Lt Regina's blood. Disillusionment and fear clutched her chest making it hard to breathe and she was fatigued beyond memory. "Please Cpt Rebecca, tell us how the battle fairs at Sandista." The Great Father said fearing the worst from his previous reports. Cpt Rebecca raised her eyes to his and shook her head remorsefully. "All is lost at Sandista. I fear King Jeffrey is dead and I pray no one attempted to take refuge in a hidden part of the city for wild beasts run free there killing what they can discover." Cpt Rebecca sighed and the gathering around her gasped in disbelief. "Those are what Ambassador Freeman called their war dogs. They release them in front of their infantry to scatter and confuse their enemy." Chancellor Freeman explained. "They will gather them together again before they occupy the city or make another assault." He added. "The walls to the city facing seaward are no more save the gate which was still closed." Cpt Rebecca continued. "I saw over a hundred horsemen unloading on the dock and moving to the north of the city and cannon being unloaded on the beach. There were too many men to count on the beach waiting to enter the city. They did not lose a single man save those on the four ships we sank. Our cannon never got range and our infantry and archers perished under the crumbling walls and the intense barrage of cannon fire from the ships. I lost Waterbird, one of the Sky Raiders mounts, while we attempted to resupply as the sky was saturated with cannon balls. They do not pursue us but rather take possession of Sandista as I made my retreat. There was nothing more I could do to advance our cause so I brought my wounded here." Rebecca said remorsefully in conclusion and the Great Father came to his feet. "We do not judge your actions harshly but rather commend you for your extraordinary effort and also those of the Sky Raiders. We pray for Lt Regina and her recovery and mourn the loss of her companion Waterbird and also King Jeffrey and all his subjects." The Great Father said opening his arms to Cpt Rebecca and inviting her to his embrace. Rebecca dropped her head on his shoulder and wept and the Great Father wept with her for a matter of some moments and the chamber remained silent.

"We have not been idle here. Thank Idos for Queen Isabella and her plan." The Great Father said. "We have suffered a terrible defeat this day at the hands of a most diabolical and evil people but I tell you as assuredly as the sun will rise we will avenge this treachery and cleanse our shores of this abomination!" The Great Father shouted with conviction and determination in his voice. He turned to Commander Dillon pulling Cpt Rebecca under his arm as if he needed her for support. "Their arrogance will be their undoing and we shall implement the Commander's plan for defense. Where the highway narrows against the cliffs on the way to Archemeius, we build a barrier of fire with troughs filled with oil so it will burn for a complete cycle of the moon if necessary and draw them toward us here at Greenstone. The fire must burn from the ocean to the cliffs for as far as you can see on the road westward and they will have no choice but to turn north into the forest. There we shall kill them and in the open fields. Our archers and our cannon will have the advantage for they will not be able to engage our walls until they clear the forest." The Great Father said confidently and looked at Cpt Rebecca. "You, Cpt Rebecca will no longer be addressed as Captain but Commander and your lieutenants are now captains for we have a plan for the defense of Archemeius that I am placing on your shoulders and those of your captains. Every man woman and child in Archemeius is gathering coconuts to make more bombs for your raiders and I have drafted every messenger in the kingdom to Archemeius under your command. You will teach them the tactics of your raiders and begin an assault on their fleet at first light. Instead of 10 you will command 70 and each of your captains will lead 5 to 7 raiders to seek out and destroy their fleet before it can reach Archemeius. The ten fast schooners will assist you under the command of Admiral Lance from the dock at Archemeius. We will construct barriers in the open field between the forest and the city wall to slow their advance and our cannon and shoulder crackers and our archers will kill them there. When they retreat our cavalry will pursue and slaughter them completely without mercy before we take back Sandista. The battle will be long and bloody but I pray Idos will deliver our enemies into our hands with this plan." The Great Father said as the crowd roared their approval.

He raised Commander Rebecca's chin and looked into her eyes. "You and your captains will have but a few hours to train all the messengers with the bombs so their efforts will be adequate?" He said calmly and Commander Rebecca felt new confidence flow from his eyes to hers and her spirits were lifted by his demeanor. "It will take but a matter of hours if they are gathered together in one place for me and my raiders to address them." She replied drawing a deep breath and standing erect to answer him. He turned his gaze to Commander Dillon who stepped toward Commander Rebecca and spoke to her. "That is well received for all the messengers gather tonight in Archemeius. I want you and your Captains to sleep well tonight here at Greenstone. I have retained a small group of four messengers to keep watch on our enemy and they will report on their advance. It is my belief they will wait until first light or even later to begin their march and you will have sufficient time to train your force at Archemeius if you depart at first light." He said and the Great Father stroked her hair as he would his daughters as Commander Dillon continued. "Go now and brief your captains and eat well so that you may sleep well. Choose your words carefully so that you may instill confidence in your captains that will resonate to all the dragon riders." He said encouraging her. Rebecca looked deep into the Commander's experienced eyes and fell on one knee before him. "You are an inspiration to me and to my captains also and they fear you as a son fears his father. My words will fall faintly on their ears compared to those I know you would express to them boldly from experience. I beg you dine with me and my captains this night and deliver your confidence to them and lift their hearts as only a man can do with another man." Commander Rebecca pleaded with him. Commander Dillon was greatly moved by Commander Rebecca's words and he saw for the first time both the tremendous strength she possessed as a leader and the misguided doubt she had because she was a woman and he dropped to one knee in front of her and cupped her face with his powerful hands. "I **will** dine with you and your captains but I have words for you before we depart the Great Father's presence." He said lifting her eyes to his. "There is no officer in the entirety of my army I perceive as your equal in the command of these men. Your captains follow you with a devotion that cannot be taught at my academy so let us not count that as loss to you now. If they perceive me as father, they most assuredly recognize you as mother and I tell you that is the stronger bond with men. Your closeness to your captains clouds your assessment of their opinion of you as their leader. Do not underestimate their faith in you or any command you give to them because you are a woman. Stand firm in your decisions and show confidence in their abilities and they will expend the last ounce of their energy to execute any task you give them. Lastly be assured that both I and the Great Father have no reservations with your selection as commander of this unit or any other. You are Commander Rebecca of Gardinia and Commander of the Sky Raiders the most deadly force in the Kingdom of the Seven Kings." Commander Dillon said boldly smiling as he took her hands and lifted her to her feet. He pulled the insignia of commander from his pocket and replaced the ones on her shoulders. "Go now to your captains Commander and send for me when you are ready to dine and I will bring the new insignias for all your captains. Whatever you require, my staff will provide to you. You need only ask." He said and Commander Rebecca saluted him proudly and shook his hand. "There is one thing I am certain I need. My tactics and all my decisions will be better quality if I have a confidant to debate my ideas with as you do with your staff. Your staff are colonels and majors and I would promote one of my captains to perform duties of similar nature in this new fleet and have a superior position to my captains if that seems a wise choice to you and the Great Father." Commander Rebecca suggested and Commander Dillon smiled broadly signaling to one of his staff. "Having one of your raiders as your staff seems the only logical choice and I am certain no member of the supreme council would argue this wisdom. I leave his selection entirely up to you." He replied placing in her hand the insignia of a major in the Army.

Lt Cameron stood at the top of the bed and held Lt Regina's head in place as the medic had instructed him. Her forearm was twisted and crushed and the medic took hold of it and looked at all the raiders that held her. "Are you ready?" He asked looking to Cameron who shook his head yes. He jerked it quickly and turned it back as it should have been. Lt Regina's eyes flashed fully open and she screamed in agony and thrashed trying to get away. "I've got you Regina." Cameron said dropping his cheek to hers and she passed out again from the intense pain. His tears spilled from his cheek to hers and she felt cold. There was a heavy bandage wrapped around her head where the medic had sewn the huge gash above her ear closed. "That should do it. The bones are back in place and I just need to splint her arm." The medic said sighing heavily taking four redwood planks and wrapping her arm in them. Then he took a blade and placed it under Regina's vest and cut through it with a long steady stroke from her waist to her neck and then cut both shoulders of the vest away before he did the same with her shirt and laid them back exposing her torso completely to inspect it. He then placed the blade in the waist of Regina's leather britches and cut them all the way down to her ankle on one side before cutting open the other leg of the britches and peeling them back leaving her completely exposed to him to inspect. "We need to roll her on her good arm and you pull her leathers and the rest of her clothes away." The medic said pointing to Lt Richard before he looked at Lt Cameron. "I need to examine her back. You keep her head turned even with her body as they roll her on her side." He added and Lt Anthony and Lt Daniel grabbed her and turned her slowly to her side as Lt Richard gently pulled the scraps that were her uniform away. The medic wiped the blood off her back before he grabbed a hook needle to sew up a long cut on her back just above her hip. He pulled a 3 inch splinter of wood from the gash and showed it to Lt Cameron. "Looks like she hit the fence pretty hard." He said as he began to sew the gash shut. Regina moaned incoherently and pitifully. "Don't let her start thrashing around again if she comes to." The medic said and Regina moaned more loudly beginning to struggle against them. "We need more hands on her until I finish." The medic said and Lt Samuel and Lt Mitchell rushed in to help. Lt Samuel put his hands against Regina's chest and Cameron looked at him. "Find somewhere else to hold her." He said angrily and Lt Samuel moved to grab her arm. Regina's eyes flashed open wide and she screamed in agony again arching her back trying to pull away from the medic as he stitched her back. Cameron kneeled down looking into her eyes. "It's ok Regina. You're with a medic but you have to lie still for us." He said softly and Regina panted and looked into his eyes confused. "What are you doing to me Cameron?" She gasped looking past him to the other raiders in panic and extreme pain and she strained to free herself again. "LIEUTENANT REGINA! Quit fighting us and let the medic finish!" Cameron shouted and Regina's eyes focused on him and seemed to clear. "God it hurts so bad Cameron." She said and he could see the tears form pools in her eyes and stream down her cheeks. "Where do you hurt Lt Regina?" The medic asked pausing his task at her back. "My arm and my back and my head." Regina replied turning her eyes to look down her frame as all the raiders held her. "Where the hell are my clothes? Regina gasped. "Get your hands off me!" She said beginning to strain against them again. "We can't do that yet until the medic finishes closing up your back Regina just try to lay still. I have to keep your neck straight." Cameron said and she quit fighting and stared up at him in pain. "Just hurry up then." She gasped angrily and the medic went back to work on the gash on her back. Regina grimaced and strained trying not to jerk as the medic stabbed her with the needled and pulled the thread tight to close the gash. Regina hovered at the edge of consciousness but each stab of the medic's needle brought sharp pain shooting up her back to her head. "I better not hear one stupid comment from any of you after he's done." Regina exclaimed angrily and the Raiders holding her down chuckled. "I'm serious you bastards!" She chastised them and grimaced tensing all her muscles before crying out as the medic put another stitch in her back. "God damn how big is this cut!" Regina asked as the pain subsided slightly and she realized it was Richard's hand she squeezed tightly. "One more." The medic replied and Regina tensed and fought hard not to cry out kicking her feet hard as he made the final stitch. "Is that it?" Regina gasped sucking air into her lungs forcefully. "I just need to clean it up and cover it." The medic replied and Regina strained to look at him. "You need to cover me before you do that and all you other sons of bitches need to get out of my room!" Regina shouted angrily. The raiders began to file out as the medic covered her with a light blanket but Cameron continued to hold her head. "Why do you hesitate? Do you think I hold you in higher esteem than them? Get out!" Regina said angrily pulling the blanket over her breasts with her good hand and Cameron looked nervously to the medic. He was still holding her head as the medic had told him. "Ok Lt Regina give me just a second." The medic said as he pulled a neck brace from a closet and put it around her neck before leading Cameron to the door. "She's embarrassed. That's why she's angry and that's a good sign. She's strong even with all the blood she lost. The good news is she's going to recover and I would wager her anger with you all will subside before her wounds heal." The medic said and Cameron sighed heavily and turned to see Commander Rebecca had heard their conversation. "Can I go in and address her?" She asked the medic. "By all means Commander, she just needs rest and fluids now. We can find her a bed here in the castle in about an hour." He replied as Cameron's mouth fell open staring at her shoulder boards after hearing the medic call her Commander. She saw Cameron's expression and looked to him before entering Regina's room. "You take the other raiders to the dining hall and I will explain when I get there." She said and closed the door behind her.

Regina had her good arm over her face and she wept partially from the physical pain and partially from the humiliation she felt. "Do you know what happened?" Commander Rebecca said pulling a chair close to Regina. "Yes, those bastards stripped me naked to set my arm and stitch up my back." Regina replied weeping loudly. "No mam, I did that." The medic replied handing her a glass with medicine in it. "Drink this. It will help with your pain and make you sleep. It was my choice to cut off your uniform. Serious wounds can hide under clothing and I needed to find them all quickly. I promise you it is a required procedure and absolutely necessary. I am sorry it embarrassed you but I won't apologize for doing it." The medic said and Commander Rebecca shook her head. "And you find no favor in my eyes either!" Regina said angrily. "That's not what I was asking. Do you even know where you are?" She smiled and Regina looked puzzled. "A room in the castle somewhere." Regina replied still frowning at the medic. "What castle?" Commander Rebecca asked and Regina looked at her completely perplexed. "Sandista." She replied and Rebecca shook her head no. "You're in Castle Greenstone. I brought you here after the explosion on the roof at the academy. Do you remember that?" She asked and Regina just closed her eyes after drinking the contents of the glass. "I landed on the perch and dismounted to go get more bombs and then suddenly I was here in pain and naked with every ones hands all over my body." She said weeping again. "I can't believe Cameron let them do that to me." She said and Commander Rebecca looked at the medic. "She took a real stiff lick to the head. It will be some time before she has all her faculties and reasons and processes information properly again." He said and Regina frowned at him again. "I process what you and Cameron did to me as inexcusable and I find your incessant chatter irritating." Regina said angrily beginning to cry. "She will get back to normal." The medic said and Regina pointed to the door. "Make yourself useful now and bring me something to drink." Regina said sharply and he frowned back at her and departed to get her some wine. "I have a bone to pick with Cameron also." Rebecca said taking Regina's hand. "It was **he** that broke formation to find you and bring you back to the roof so we could make our escape." Rebecca said and Regina just stared blankly back at her. She didn't remember any of this. "You fell from the roof into the stables and Cameron carried you back to the roof before the dogs could get to you and we all fought them but it was Cameron who saved you." Rebecca smiled softly. "I should bring charges against him for breaking formation in combat but I admire his results enough to refrain from that course." Commander Rebecca said and Regina looked at her confused as she tried to remember something or anything after she landed. "Cameron rescued me?" Regina asked and wept pulling her good hand over her eyes. "Where is Waterbird?" She asked fearfully moving her hand to cover her mouth as the vision of the explosion on the roof filled her head. Rebecca began to weep with her as she shook her head no. "Oh my god…., Waterbird is gone." Regina sobbed and they cried together for some time and Rebecca knew Regina's physical pain was in no way comparable to the loss she felt in Waterbird's death. They wept together and Rebecca stayed with her for a long time as the medicine the medic brought her did it's job and put her to sleep.

It was hours before Regina awoke again from the pain in her back and her arm. The medic inspected her wounds and gave her more to drink. "We are unique in this Army and in this unit and I believe Idos selected us both for tasks we will have to perform because we possess these unique qualities." Commander Rebecca said looking at Regina with admiration. "I need for you to heal quickly Regina. I need you to overcome not only these physical wounds but put also your emotional loss behind you." "Things change quickly Regina and I need those that have lived this experience close to me. I am no longer a captain of a squadron but now have become a commander of many squadrons and I need you by my side." She said and Regina shook her head. "What use shall I be to you as I can barely walk and will certainly not be able to fly for some time?" Regina sighed heavily not seeing her own value to her commander. "I will not fly with these squadrons but will be on a ship with Admiral Lance and I will need my staff with me to council with me as the battle progresses." She said pulling from her pocket the insignia she had received from the Supreme Commander. "I need **you** Regina to be at my side." She said handing Regina the insignias and she stared at them in disbelief. "You think more aggressively than I at times and you are not afraid to confront me when you perceive I am in error. And you know all the limitations and all the positive traits of each of my captains which makes you and invaluable asset as I…., or we decide how to deploy them. I need **you** Regina, barring the medic's refusal, to fly with me on Emerald to Archemeius and plan with me its defense." She concluded and Major Regina fought her tears filling her lungs proudly and sat up in the bed. "There is nothing commander, that will keep me from your side and witness these ships burn under our attack." She said boldly and Rebecca smiled and hugged her gently so as not to aggravate her wounds. "I must depart now for I take dinner with our new captains and also with the Supreme Commander. I would see you rest for the ride tomorrow will certainly test this medic's skill in your stitches." Commander Rebecca said and Major Regina protested. "Will I not eat also this night? Is this first council with our captains and the Supreme Commander of so little importance that your staff need not be present? I think I can execute one flight of stairs to dine with our unit in this hour. I beg you, find me a uniform or I will execute those stairs naked for all the captains have seen me so this day already and I fear you will suffer more embarrassment than I as I expose myself to the Supreme Commander." Major Regina demanded and broke into a grin as Commander Rebecca chuckled and called to a servant at the door. She instructed him to find the uniform before turning back to Major Regina. "Are you certain you have the strength to dine with us?" She asked and Major Regina's smile grew broad. "Would you deny me this pleasure to see the faces of our captains as they contemplate their new circumstances with me as their superior after the indignation I suffered under their clammy hands here earlier? I am certain this will thwart any juvenile jest or comment I may have suffered them before." Major Regina laughed through her pain and Commander Rebecca did also. It was but a short time before the servant returned with the uniform and Commander Rebecca helped her into it. Regina felt light headed and had to sit on the bed for a time after she got dressed and the medic came back in and handed her a glass of the soft cherry wine. "What is this? How may I inspect your wound in that uniform and where do you think you're going." He said curtly. "Be silent!" Major Regina barked at him. "I am dining with the Supreme Commander in the dining hall. You may escort me if you wish but be silent! It is my desire to refrain from exposing my limitations to him and you will be silent or I will feed you to a dragon." Major Regina said brashly as Commander Rebecca stifled a laugh. There was a look of reluctant resignation on the medic's face. "What is your name sir?" Major Regina said more calmly as she gulped the cherry wine he had brought her. "I am Lord Paul the chief medic here at Castle Greenstone." He replied and Regina could see the concern on his face. "I know your only concern is for me as a patient but I also have new responsibilities that I am concerned about." She said as she gathered her strength. "I need for you to get me to a table in the dining hall for a short dinner with my men and then I will retire and you can check my wounds and reinforce what you think is pertinent. At first light, I will mount a dragon to travel to Archemeius and you will be done with me." Major Regina said and Lord Paul's face showed his deep concern as he shook his head no. "I beg you Major, there is no way you can fly to Archemeius without pulling every stitch from your back. You would have to wear a brace of significant proportion to immobilize that area and still you risk having to redo what I have done in Archemeius." He reported insistently and Major Regina smiled at him. "Then I suggest after I retire you dedicate your time to preparing this brace because I **will** fly to Archemeius tomorrow even if I have to suffer new surgery when I arrive." She replied and Lord Paul saw the resolve in her eyes and reluctantly surrendered to her demands.

The three of them left the room together and Lord Paul had two servants carry Major Regina in a chair down the stairs to the dining hall. Major Regina would have preferred to try to walk but she compromised with Lord Paul accepting his advice. All the Raiders stood and stared in stunned silence as the two servants set her chair at one end of the table beside Lt Cameron's and Commander Rebecca sat across from her. "You can take your seats." Commander Rebecca said but Lt Cameron remained standing and protested still stunned at Regina's presence and glared at Commander Rebecca. "Are you kidding me? Why do you suffer her to dine with us? She cannot yet stand. Her place is in bed!" Lt Cameron said angrily and Regina stood slowly turning to face him and Cameron noticed her insignia for the first time. "Who gave you this task to decide what I was capable of? Take your seat as the Commander has ordered." Major Regina said calmly and Lt Cameron fell backwards into his chair with his mouth open in surprise. "We have a new and most difficult task in front of us and it would serve us all well if each of you would focus to remedy your own limitations to meet this new challenge. Every dragon rider in the kingdom is headed for Archemeius as we dine. Commander Rebecca has been chosen to command this new fleet with the responsibility of the defense of Archemeius. The Supreme Commander will be here shortly and he is determined to make each of you captains of your own squadron under her command. Guard your tongue in his presence and do not give us cause to recommend a replacement for any of you in this new position." Major Regina said looking down at Lt Cameron as Commander Dillon appeared in the stairway. The Raiders all stood again as Commander Dillon took his chair at the head of the table with Commander Rebecca on his right and Major Regina on his left. "You may take your seats." Commander Dillon said and everyone sat down. "Have you briefed the mission?" He asked Commander Rebecca. "Major Regina was doing so as you came in." Rebecca replied and Commander Dillon turned to her. "Please continue Major." He said as a servant brought him a glass of wine and Regina stood back up and she felt a little more nervous speaking in front of Commander Dillon now. "While the citizens of Archemeius gather coconuts and make the bombs for us, we will divide all the dragon riders into seven groups of seven and each one of you will lead them. We must teach them how to safely deploy the bombs and our attack methods. Commander Rebecca and I will be on a ship with Admiral Lance and direct the attack from there. We will engage the enemy ships as soon as we locate them and you will fly from the castle at Archemeius out to your target with your squadron and then to us on the ship before returning to Castle Greenstone to rest your mounts and resupply. We will continue this tactic until we sink every last ship or the battle turns and a new tactic is required. Once the threat from the enemy fleet is vanquished we will begin to deploy you in support of Commander Dillon and the ground forces. When we get to Archemeius at first light, Commander Rebecca will speak to all the dragon riders before we divide them into squadrons. Once we do…, those men belong to you and you will be responsible for their health, welfare, safety and training. You will have but a few hours to mold them into an effective squadron to deliver our bombs. Emphasis safety with the bombs and discipline in flight and we will defeat this enemy and return 56 Sky Raiders to Archemeius in victory." Major Regina concluded before she took her seat. Commander Dillon smiled at Major Regina as he stood to address the Raiders.

"The council and I and the Great Father have serious concerns about the battle tomorrow. We do not know what forces will return to their ships. Things change quickly once an engagement begins. There fleet may scatter once they learn of your numbers and you may have to pursue them well into the day tomorrow. We are building a barrier on the road to Archemeius to force them into the forest and into our trap in the forest south of Greenstone. Any number of problems may arise and force us to adjust our plans for the defense of the kingdom." He said as he began to walk around the table. His presence was an ominous one as Commander Rebecca was right and they all feared him as a son fears his father. "Things change quickly you will learn. The unit that I was the most concerned with a week ago has become least of our concerns today and it is because of you men and women sitting here." He said placing his hands on Commander Rebecca's shoulders. Regrettably, Sandista fell quickly under the cannons of their armada. You Sky Raiders had the only success against this evil horde and I am certain if we successfully divide their power we can defeat them. I am thoroughly convinced you will not allow one cannon ball to find a home in Archemeius if you can train your squadrons to fight as you did at Sandista." He said as he continued to walk around the table looking into each of the Raider's eyes. "The only way that success is guaranteed in battle is by your diligent, aggressive, disciplined pursuit of it. Be an inspiration to your men as you are to me." He said as he laid the insignia of captain in front of each one of them. "I am an old soldier and did not seek or expect to find this battle in my destiny but here it is." He said and his tone turned aggressive and angry. "Tomorrow I will gird up my loins and draw my sword and I will stand in the gate to Greenstone and shout to my enemy, HERE AM I, and I will not sheath my sword until every dog and every man who has violated my kingdom lies dead at my feet and King Jeffrey of Sandista is revenged. If there be men here that will stand with me let them rise to their feet and accept this commission to captain in my army." Commander Dillon said angrily and every Raider took to his feet and changed his insignia quickly as Commander Dillon returned to stand behind his chair. "I leave you with this last piece of council. "I have placed the defense of Archemeius and possibly the whole kingdom squarely on the shoulders of your Commander and now you also. I will fight tomorrow without fear for Archemeius for I know you all." He said raising his glass to them. "Drink with me now for the next time I toast you it will be in the council chambers in Sandista!" He said raising his glass and Cpt Cameron shouted. "NOW AND FOREVER!" and everyone responded, "NOW AND FOREVER!" before they turned up there glasses and drank them empty before Commander Dillon departed.

Major Regina knew she was going to fall dead asleep as soon as she finished the meal and she ate quickly. Her arm and her back hurt terribly and her head just felt numb under the bandage. She glanced at Cpt Cameron several times during the meal but he was avoiding eye contact with her and she assumed it was because she had chastised him so harshly earlier. The only one that made eye contact with her was Cpt Richard and she knew the thoughts behind his eyes by the grin on his face. It seemed nothing was going to deter his amorous demeanor toward her so she just grinned back at him. "If you are finished, I will call the servants." Lord Paul said and Major Regina waved him off. "Cpt Richard; would you be opposed to helping Cpt Cameron escort me to my quarters so I can retire." She asked and she saw Commander Rebecca smile at her from the corner of her eye. "Yes mam, it would be my pleasure." Cpt Richard replied as he stood and walked to her side. Cpt Cameron looked at her puzzled before he stood and they lifted her chair to follow Lord Paul. She stopped them before they took a step. "I want to apologize to you all for my anger with you earlier." She said with a grin. "I am certain this is the only unit in the army where all the officers have seen their Executive Officer naked and I pray we will limit any discussion about my anatomy to that select group of officers." Major Regina said ginning and everyone chuckled as they departed. As they arrived in the quarters Lord Paul had selected for her, the two captains set her down and she moved to the bed to sit as Lord Paul began to undo the lace work on the back of her vest. "Do you think I selected you randomly to be my escorts?" Regina asked and they turned to look at her and Cpt Richard was smiling. "I did not. Both of you have amorously pursued me to this point and I would address this issue with you now. Cpt Richard please wipe the smile off your face for you will find quickly that I mean to be serious." She said and he nodded agreeably. She looked at him intently. "To this point I have dismissed your flirtations as a flaw in your personality that I could tolerate. In this recent change in our circumstances, I must warn you that you risk the rank you have so rightly attained if I perceive your demeanor toward me to be anything short of completely professional." She said glaring at Cpt Richard. "Do you understand me Cpt Richard?" She asked curtly. "Yes mam. I was sincere previously when we made peace on this subject." He replied. "Do you have a question in this matter for I make this statement for your benefit. I will not tolerate any foolishness from you and it would be unwise of you to think I will not act at the slightest provocation from you." She said emphatically and the smile was completely gone from his face when he responded. "No mam, I will not jeopardize my position or yours in this matter. I assure you now, I value your respect and friendship to highly. If you mistake my jovial demeanor for flirtation, I will cease that in your presence also." He replied and Major Regina just stared at him for a long moment to emphasize her point as Lord Paul pulled up her shirt to look at the wound. She grimaced as he pressed against the bandage. "I have complete faith in your abilities as a Raider, have faith in my judgment and we will get along fine. You are dismissed Cpt Richard." She said and he saluted her before he departed.

Regina's back was a stinging mass of pain under the bandage and her arm was throbbing. "I'm going to leave this bandage for tonight and I will change it before you depart tomorrow." Lord Paul said and handed her another glass half filled with the potion. "Drink all of this before you retire or you will not sleep well." He warned and walked to the dresser to pour her some more of the cherry wine as she drank the first glass. Regina made an ugly face after she swallowed the contents of the glass. "Why do your potions always taste so nasty?" She asked and looked to Cameron. "Will you help me with my boots Cameron?" She asked purposely addressing him informally and he knelt before her and worked the laces. Regina's breath came short and she wanted to lie down feeling now the pain in her head. "Was that message for me also?" Cameron asked looking glum and dejected. "Are we finished Lord Paul for I need to speak to Cpt Cameron alone." Regina said and he handed her the glass of wine taking the empty one from her before he left. She was disappointed when Cameron didn't rise to embrace and kiss her for she was certain he was merely waiting for them to be alone. She just watched him for a few seconds as he undid the laces in her knee high boots. "Who am I to you Cameron? Is it my wounds that make me repulsive in your eyes now or do you reject me because of the insignia on my shoulders?" Regina asked and the pain in her arm and back were beginning to throb even more. "Commander Dillon was right. Things change quickly." He replied sorrowfully as he pulled her boot off and began to work the laces on the other. Regina's eyes filled with tears as she watched him. Had his feelings toward her truly changed? "Are you choosing now to cease our romantic pursuits?" Regina asked cautiously and Cameron raised his eyes to hers. "A week ago you were the cute young girl who had beaten me in the race of the messengers and stolen my prize and my heart with your adolescent ways and your reckless curiosity. Today you are my superior and a true and proven leader of men. As I listened to you speak at dinner, I realized you have flown past me as a dragon at maximum speed passes a fast carriage. How could I possibly hope to compete and win your heart in our present circumstances?" Cameron admitted as he pulled the other boot off and stood up. Regina was struggling to assess whether it was her injuries or his words that caused her the most pain. "My destiny seems set in stone before me now and I am fearful of it." She sighed. "I by no means have chosen either this position with this insignia or the man that I have fallen in love with." Regina sighed heavily. "Do you perceive me so adolescent and reckless that I cannot separate my private desires from my professional ones for I would not assume this of you? I have confessed my love for you Cameron but you have never done likewise. Maybe Commander Rebecca was right and there is more in common between her and I than I perceived earlier. I cannot make you love me Cameron. I will understand and respect your choice if you feel our circumstances have drawn a barrier between us that you choose not to breach. As for me, this is my private room and I beseech you now to go to the door and either leave me to pursue my professional desires or lock the door and return to my bed." Regina demanded as a tear ran down her cheek. Cameron looked sorrowfully into her face and she saw his eyes fill with tears also as he turned to walk slowly to the door. Regina fell back against her pillow unable to sit up straight any longer. The pain was too great and she cried as Cameron stood at the door for a long moment. She closed her eyes in pain that seemed to throb from the center of her being and out through her whole body and cried. "Please don't leave me Cameron." She moaned and there was another long moment before she heard the door lock. She felt the bed move and opened her eyes to see Cameron's face. "I cannot. Are these words what you require of me?" He whispered and pressed his lips softly to hers. "I love you beyond what my words can express." He whispered and kissed her again as Regina felt half of her pain dissolve in his kiss. "You give me scarce few opportunities to reveal my heart to you. So let me reveal my secret that no other man or woman that I call friend knows of me now." He said and kissed her sweetly before sitting up and struggling quickly out of his boots. His urgency and his quickness were surprising to her and she giggled as he slid under her covers naked and pulled them over her also. He kissed her again but before she could begin to get lost in his sweet kiss he disappeared below her and she giggled again nervously as he struggled to remove her leather britches. Regina lay on her side and her good arm as she could not take the pressure on her back where her stitches were. As he came back up and kissed her neck pulling her vest and shirt away carefully, she moaned pleasurably and whispered in his ear. "Are you going to take my flower from me this night?" She sighed and he whispered back to her. "And you will take mine for that is my secret." He smiled and kissed her tenderly and she smiled. "You are a bad liar for I have heard you share tales of your romantic conquests with Richard when you thought I was not listening." She teased him and kissed him playfully. "No I am a good liar for he believed my tales." He smiled and his hands felt like magic against Regina's bare skin as he caressed her and kissed his way to her breast and suckled at them both in turn. Regina's passion grew strong and her hips moved against him involuntarily as her heart pounded and her breath became labored. "Cameron how will they whisper if we do this?" She asked having no desire to stop the momentum he had begun. "They will whisper whether we do this or not for all the riders have born witness to my desire for you but I promise you this tale I will not share with anyone." He replied and Regina pulled his hair with her good hand forcing his lips back to hers and kissed him ravenously before whispering in his ear again. "I fear I cannot support your weight on my back but I beg you now cease teasing with me and find a sheath for your sword in me quickly." Regina panted and Cameron pulled her leg at the knee up and over his hip and pushed forward until he found his mark. Regina moaned and bit his shoulder softly as she felt Cameron begin his erotic journey. He stopped and they lay together not moving once he had completed his voyage and Regina trembled against him in the intense pleasure. "If there is truth in the tales of Richard and our friends the first time is for me and you will find your pleasure the second time. If you find pain in what I do I will stop." Cameron whispered breathlessly kissing her shoulder. "My god Cameron, do as you please but stop talking." Regina gasped unable to imagine a sensation more pleasurable than what she felt with him now. He made love to her slowly and gently. He was concerned for her injuries and was taken completely by surprise when she gripped him forcefully and found her pleasure before he did and he smiled pleased with himself in his first performance before his own passion overtook him and the moment was pure magic and extreme pleasure to them both. Cameron did not move as they caught their breath but lay still until her passion and his subsided. "Shall we stay like this and wait for your desire for me to return. I find this position with you most comfortable even with my injury and could sleep the entire night with your cheek on my breast." Regina sighed feeling completely satisfied and Cameron laughed. "The potion is working well on you." He chuckled and Regina looked into his eyes smiling. "You really think a potion has put this smile on my face." She giggled and kissed him. It was a short time before his passion for her grew again and they made love a second time before sleep overcame them and they drifted away in each other's arms.

It was a serious discussion Commander Rebecca was having with the Raiders after Cpt Richard returned to their table and she scarcely noticed the large group of women that rushed to her. It was Lady Karen and Maid Melisa with their servants and they were in a panic. "I beg you Commander, tell us quickly where we may find Arthur and Andrew." They pleaded tearfully and sorrow filled Rebecca's eyes again. "I cannot reveal them to you for I know not where they are. Arthur took horses to meet Andrew in the pass where he would release Crimson. I gave them both leave to share Andrew's time of mourning for the loss of his mount and they have not returned to me nor did I expect them." Rebecca lied to them and it pained her to do so. "I believe they camp in safety north of lake willow unaware of what has transpired and will return here before the sun sets tomorrow." Rebecca said trying to reassure them. "I fear some evil has overcome them for evil certainly is having its way with us all on this island presently. We barely escaped from Sandista and have heard terrible reports from that city that it has fallen completely to the invaders." Maid Melisa cried fiercely afraid. "Take heart in my words for I assure you neither Arthur nor Andrew were witness to the tragedy at Sandista and there is no path save through Green Stone for them to return there. You will surely meet with them before I do if you will but wait here patiently." Commander Rebecca said as she stood and embraced them both. They accepted her council and departed and Rebecca prayed what she had advised them was correct. She was very tired and seeing them had brought only more concern to her frazzled mind so she departed also for her quarters. Rebecca had a last glass of cherry wine poured for herself and settled into her nightgown and her bed but her concerns filled her head spinning around not allowing the fatigue she felt to pull her into slumber. She was worried about Regina but she was also envious of her for at least she had Cameron and smiled knowing she would sleep well in his company tonight. There was Arthur and Andrew on her mind for she would have gone to the shack to see their progress but there was no opportunity for that in this circumstance and she had no clue to their situation. Her task tomorrow would be tremendous and the words she would have to prepare to address this new unit failed to take form in her head. She thought about how she would divide the men into squadrons and what tasks she must give them and then there was knock at her door. Rebecca threw back the covers and walked to the door fearful she would not escape from the demands on her and find sleep. She opened the door to find Cpt Richard in his nightshirt looking worried and exhausted as she was and she allowed him to enter. He walked past her to the center of her room as she closed the door and turned to face him. "I cannot find sleep for my concerns for tomorrow swirl around in my head exploding like bombs from one concern to the next." He admitted staring at the floor. "I contemplated all these things in my quarters unable to sleep and it came to mind that you also must have a great number of demons that chatter unmercifully in your head as I do." He said cautiously and looked up her. Rebecca looked at him quizzically knowing Richard well and had a hopeful suspicion of his reason for his presence now in her room but she was shocked at his boldness and did not believe her suspicions possible. In truth she was glad to see him. "Am I a medic? Did you come here thinking I had some potion to aid in your search for slumber?" She asked nervously fearful of his response and confused in her own mind as to why she did not dismiss him quickly now. Now Richard turned and moved closer to her and she backed against the door. "I know you may consider me a delinquent child and see my reasoning as juvenile and absurdly ridiculous or even crazy but I know what potion gives me the most peaceful slumber and if you would drink from this cup with me we both may find slumber." Richard said stepping closer to her as she pressed against the door searching for the handle behind her back. "Have you lost your senses?" Rebecca whispered harshly and Richard suddenly embraced her and pressed his lips to hers pushing her forcefully against the door as his hands began to caress her firmly gathering her nightshirt upward to find the bare skin of her hips. Rebecca dropped the cup of wine on the floor as she felt the tremendous rush of passion spring wildly from his embrace into her whole body. It was Richard's bold aggressiveness that was her undoing. She struggled hard in her head to push him away and do the only thing she knew was right but her hands would not respond to the logic in her mind and she fell against the door finding the lock and turning it. In an instant Richard's hands were on her under the nightshirt and Rebecca ceased to struggle against his attack returning his kiss passionately. "I swear to you Richard if rumors of this visit find ears we are both finished." Rebecca gasped and Richard did not reply but instead carried her quickly to the bed and made love to her ferociously and forcefully and Rebecca cried tears of ecstasy at the extreme pleasure they found together. All of her anxieties fell victim to Richard's passion and each was vanquished one by one with each thrust of his sword until he set them on fire deep inside her and they exploded and burned into wave after wave of exotic pleasure. In the end, he rolled to her side and pulled her comfortably against him gazing into her eyes and kissing her softly as passion retreated from them. Now logic began to chase her passion of Richard from her mind. She knew she might suffer extreme consequences tomorrow for this indiscretion. They did not debate further the wisdom of the moment and merely fell into blissful slumber together and Rebecca smiled cuddling tightly against him to leave the consequences of their actions for tomorrow.

Torches burned brightly all across the city of Archemeius and Chancellor Trent and many of the servants worked well into the night finding quarters to house all the messengers as they arrived and making temporary stables to accommodate their mounts. Only a few slept in the city as most gathered coconuts and brought them to the craftsmen in the courtyard to be fashioned into the bombs they would need and those were stacked into neat piles of 20 all around the courtyard. A great convoy of wagons of all sizes brought barrels of oil from every city all night long to the narrow path where they would build the barricade of fire. The convoys curled around the troughs that the engineers fitted with long pipes that would feed the oil to them. When lit it would become an impenetrable wall of fire over a quarter of a mile long from the ocean to the cliffs in the north. A single troop of cavalry camped and waited by the oil reserves to cut down any band that attempted to circumvent the barrier and brave the deep waters along the coast there. It was part of the defense plan Queen Isabella had planned weeks ago. Admiral Lance retired early having prepared and briefed his men on the 10 fast schooners as to their mission.

In Green Stone the work also continued all night. The distance from the highway atop the city wall to the edge of the forest was 200 paces and in that open field they dug trenches to fill with oil and erected barriers to slow down the enemy advance. They destroyed the highway to Sandista and the wall where it met the forest and every cannon in the kingdom was set wheel to wheel on the highway to Archemeius and behind the wall so they could fire over it and engage whatever presented itself in the open field. 100 men on horseback filled the city and there were 500 infantry with longbows and shoulder crackers to stand with the cannon and defend the walls. Commander Dillon stood with his staff at the balcony facing south watching the progress in the open field below. Only he and his immediate staff knew the reality of what they faced. The messengers flew continuously from Castle Greenstone to Sandista and back to deliver him the reports on his enemy and they were massive in their numbers. He was out number 10 to 1 and his only chance was to catch them in the open field and not allow their cannon to get within range of his wall. He knew his enemy would adapt once they discovered his defenses and he must be prepared for an extended war. He must fight for control of the forest in front of him and not allow his enemy to deploy cannon on this side of it. He just prayed they had not discovered Archemeius for if they redeployed to ships to sail around the barrier before the Sky Raiders could attack, he would be forced to abandon a second city. There had been no probes or no advance units not even a ship on the sea and this told him he was probably right about their command. They were arrogant and confident after their easy victory at Sandista and most likely expected to march unchallenged to their next conquest. Commander Dillon prayed that was true for the kingdom was ill prepared for war as they had not been invaded in many lifetimes and none of his countrymen had any experience in combat or any notion of the horror that they faced tomorrow. At least he knew they would not surprise him again as he had good track of them with his messengers. He would send his cavalry into the forest tonight to watch for spies on the road and they would camp there and he would use them to draw their whole army to him tomorrow if his plan worked. He gave command to one of his staff before he retired to his quarters to get a few hours of sleep before sunrise.

C H A P T E R 1 3

BATTLE PLAN

The sky was turning orange out the window as Amanda awoke feeling the Commodore caress her gently from behind and she rolled sleepily to face him. She kissed him and searched under the covers to find him completely awake and moaned pleasurably as he pulled her on top of him. She smiled pleasantly sitting up on him and looked down at him and those beautiful green eyes. "Shall I be captain of your ship and steer us to our next port of pleasure." Amanda whispered and he put his hand behind her neck and pulled her lips to his. "It is morning and time for me to reveal more of my heart to you my love." He said and reached with his other hand and pulled Cpt Manor's head between them and he kissed him also as he joined them in the bed. She looked in sudden horror as Cpt Manor had only his white shirt on as he turned smiling at her and she was terrified at his sight and struggled to withdraw but the Commodore caught her pulled her back between them on her back. "Now Amanda, remember our bargain and show me no resistance." Cpt Manor chuckled and she began to cry looking at the Commodore. "You promised safety for me and my friends." She wailed horrified. "And I still may. Their fate is still in your hands." He chuckled rising above her pushing her legs apart. "Have you no pity for me." Amanda sobbed knowing it was futile to resist them and the Commodore laughed. "How can you ask me that? Do you not see that I love you so much that I share my most intimate friend with you?" He chuckled and Amanda closed her eyes and tried to go far away in the back of her mind to escape what they did to her.

Commodore Marantz buckled his sword around his waist and inspected his image in the mirror to insure his uniform was straight before looking back to the bed. Cpt Manor had not nearly found an end to his pleasure with Amanda and the Commodore grinned. "I think bringing her friends to the castle with her was an excellent idea William. I do so enjoy watching you with her." He snickered and walked to the door. "Join me on the docks when you have had your fill. I go to check on the progress with the damaged ships after I breakfast." He said and departed for the dining hall. His commanders all rose as he approached the table and he waved them off. "Keep your seats." He said cheerfully as he took his spot at the head of the table. "Shall we wait for Cpt Manor." One of his staff asked and he waved his empty hand as he ate. "We shall speak with him shortly. He is preoccupied with another task for me. What do you have for me?" He said and one of his commanders stood. "We found a dragon dead atop the academy behind us. It was definitely one of the ones they used for combat." He said and the Commodore smiled. "Good that leaves them 8. Have you found an answer for this force? I certainly don't want to trade four ships for every dragon." He said and the commander shook his head no. "If they stay at altitude to drop these bombs we cannot range them with the deck cannons. They are too small. The only solution is to leave bowmen or riflemen on the ships to engage them and still they can avoid them." He replied and the Commodore shook his head no. "I'm not going to do that. We're going to turn inland to attack the other six cities anyway. I am going to bring the fleet south for fire support should this next city be in range for them but after today we shall depend solely on our mobile artillery. What number do we travel with?" He asked and another Commander stood. "I have 80 operational and rigged for travel sir." He replied and the Commodore frowned. "Where are the other 20 sir?" He asked. "They were on one of the ships that sank but the good news is the water is shallow and we can retrieve them." He replied and the Commodore nodded. "I guess we will march with 80 then and what report from my cavalry is there?" He continued and another officer rose. "I have 300 resting north of the wall here. What is the order of battle sir?" The Commander asked and the Commodore wiped his chin. "I want a formation of tens with the infantry in front followed by the war dogs and then the cannons followed by the cavalry. The cannon can stay on the highway. They will move easier there until we get to this next city. Tell me how my war dogs fair this morning." He said finishing his breakfast and washing his beard. "I still have almost 400. We did not lose but 10 in this city and I have good news for we have twelve new pups this morning." His chief handler reported. "Excellent sir, find a place for the pups and their mothers in the stables here and you can march with the rest." The Commodore said smiling broadly. "I thoroughly suspect we have defeated the bulk of their army already and they will surrender quickly once they see our numbers." He said confidently. "What is the status of the damaged ships?" He asked his first mate. "Three require a new mast and cannot sail. They are at the dock making repairs and we will have them back in a week's time." He replied and the Commodore stroked his beard. "I think I will just take 40 with me. Leave the rest here at the dock to assist in repairs. That will give you seven crews repairing the three damaged ships. I want to return the fleet to King Argos as soon as I can load it with as much treasure as I can. Tell them to make haste with repairs for this conquest may not take a full week." He said as he stood. "Well gentleman, let us go find this next city and take possession of it for King Argos!" He shouted and they drank a toast before heading for the beach and the dock.

Commander Rebecca woke early feeling Richard exit the bed and her surrender to him weighed heavily on her mind as she watched him now standing at her window his image outlined by the orange glow of the coming dawn. It was still very dark in her room but she could tell Richard was in deep contemplation looking out her window in his nightshirt. "Which of your demons has returned to cause you so much concern so early?" Rebecca whispered and Richard turned and knelt by her head. She could barely make out the features of his face as he spoke. "You are my commander on this side of the door or the other and I will do nothing to place you or I in jeopardy but I confess to you now truly. You are also the commander of my heart and I would refrain from seeking an intimate embrace in any bed but this one at a word from you. I fear my amorous history may taint the sincerity I express to you now." He whispered and Rebecca felt his lips deliver a sweet kiss briefly to which she did not respond. "I have dreamed of a night such as this in frustration thinking you beyond my station but my heart has ached for you secretly and I must reveal it to you now. I beg you tell me now before I depart? Does true love blossom in your heart as it does in mine?" Richard pleaded delivering another sweet kiss before awaiting her response. There were many concerns as to why Rebecca had to dismiss him now. She was his commander and 8 years his senior. It would be certain suicide to her career and his if she was discovered having an affair with one of her captains and she had a tremendous responsibility in front of her. This was not the time to start even a legitimate and professionally acceptable romance. But there was one concern that outweighed all of those. From the first time Rebecca had seen Richard she had fought with her romantic attraction to him fiercely in her heart being severely jealous of his romantic exploits and his words now were like music to her ears. "We will have scarce few opportunities to water this blossom. Give me your promise and I will give you mine." Rebecca replied and this time when Richard kissed her she returned his kiss passionately. "It will suffice for me to know that this flower exists." He whispered excitedly kissing her again quickly. Test me Rebecca for I will turn my eyes from you when we meet in public and wait patiently for a sign from you to return to this intimacy." He added and Rebecca pulled him forcefully back into bed with her. "I will inquire in your presence if you think it might rain and this will be the sign between us and you will know that it is my desire for you and this intimate kiss." Rebecca whispered and they made love again this time softly and tenderly and Richard smiled when Rebecca's pleasure was fulfilled and he whispered in her ear. "I will pray for an opportunity to deliver this pleasure to you a thousand times but I fear if I do not depart quickly the sun will reveal to the world our love for each other and we shall both suffer." He whispered and retreated reluctantly disappearing across the room and Rebecca heard him close the door.

Commander Rebecca rose quickly after Cpt Richard departed and lit a lamp and washed herself and began to dress. She fought the grin on her face as she chased the memory of her embrace with Richard from her head. Was her love for Richard real or had they let their emotions run recklessly free because of the dire circumstances. She had no time to seriously contemplate her feelings and knew she must put it out of her thoughts. She had to get all the Raiders to Archemeius as soon as possible this morning and she dressed quickly. She heard a knock at her door and called out. "Enter for it is unlocked." Lord Paul came in holding a reinforced vest in his arms accompanied by two servants carrying baskets of fruit and bread. "I assumed you would not go down to breakfast so we prepared these." Lord Paul said as one of the servants presented a basket to her. She took a banana and a roll and the other servant poured her a glass of the soft cherry wine. "This is what I designed for Major Regina." He said holding up the vest that had strips of redwood laced onto the vest. "I will go to wake her now and I hope it will afford her some protection for her wound." Lord Paul said backing out the door. "Tell her to meet me on the roof." Rebecca called to him and she grabbed another banana sticking it in her pocket as she headed for the stairs.

The roof was already crowded with servants and dragons on every perch and Commander Rebecca moved to Emerald and inspected his harness before she pulled the banana from her pocket and gave it to him. Emerald swallowed it quickly and whistled contently as she sat down on the perch to wait for the Raiders. One by one they made their appearance in the stairwell and moved to their dragons and Commander Rebecca acknowledged each one but stayed sitting and drinking her wine. Finally, Major Regina and Cpt Cameron approached her escorted by Lord Paul. Major Regina was wearing the vest and she didn't look happy as Rebecca stood up. "I feel like a crate of fruit." Major Regina said sarcastically and Rebecca chuckled looking to Cpt Cameron. "You may leave now. Go ahead of us and insure that there is a medic and sufficient help to unload our crate of fruit in Archemeius." She giggled and Cpt Cameron snickered and moved to Lightning and buckled in. He turned and waved one more time as Lightning came to the edge of the launch platform and Cpt Cameron whistled before they disappeared over the edge of the wall. "Well let's get you loaded." Commander Rebecca said and they stacked crates next to Emerald so that Major Regina could climb up easily onto his back. Commander Rebecca climbed up in front of her and buckled in as Lord Paul buckled Major Regina's legs with a clip. "I cannot clip the vest for that will cause too much stress each time you bounce and the vest may cause damage to her wound." Lord Paul reported. "Well I guess we'll have to avoid rolls then." Commander Rebecca smiled at Regina before she rolled Emerald's reigns in her hand and urged him toward the launch platform. "You know the launch and the landing are going to be the most traumatic." Rebecca said and Regina wrapped her arms around Rebecca's waist. "I'm ready." She sighed and Rebecca whistled. Rebecca felt the vest against her back as they leaned forward trying stay against Emerald as they fell. When he spread his wings and turned skyward, there was a sudden jerk and then more pressure than Rebecca expected against her back as Emerald pumped his wings and gained altitude. When he leveled off, the pressure subsided greatly and Rebecca felt the blood run down her hip from where the vest had cut her. "Crap now I'm injured too." Rebecca thought and cursed herself for not thinking to put padding between her and Regina. "Are you ok?" Rebecca shouted to Regina as she turned Emerald's head toward Archemeius. "I'm fine." Regina replied as they sat up straight on Emerald and Rebecca reached back to feel the cut on her back. There was nothing she could do now but she held up her hand to show Regina the blood. "The vest cut me. I don't know what we can do different when we land but we need keep it away from my back." She shouted to Regina and she felt her scoot back and maneuver around behind her before she put both arms around her and scooted back against her back. "Is that better?" Regina asked close to her ear. "I can't feel it anymore." Rebecca shouted in reply. "I got rid of it." Regina said and Rebecca jerked her head to look at her. "You need that!" She said and Regina smiled. "I hope you're wrong because it's gone now." Regina replied and Rebecca just shook her head and they rode in silence the rest of the way. Commander Rebecca flew low over the road and there was still a long convoy of wagons carrying barrels of oil from all the cities to the narrow pass. The pass was crisscrossed with troughs and the convoy snaked between them. Rebecca could see the pipes that would feed the oil into the troughs and the engineers were there still connecting them. The troop of cavalry on the other side of the pass stood and saluted them and cheered as they saw the Raiders approaching and Rebecca made Emerald bank left and then right quickly to wave back at them. The castle at Archemeius came into view quickly and Rebecca felt Regina tighten her grip around her waist. She pulled back on Emerald's reigns and whistled twice and Emerald slowed and began to hover above the perch before he found it with his back legs. Rebecca leaned forward and braced herself. There was no way to avoid the sudden jerk as they fell forward and Rebecca was relieved when Emerald came to a stop and started drinking. Commander Rebecca recognized Lord Peter as the medic that assisted Cpt Cameron who was unbuckling Major Regina. "What happened to your vest?" Cpt Cameron asked showing his serious concern. "It cut into the Commander's back and I dumped it." Major Regina shouted pointing to Commander Rebecca's back. Lord Peter looked at Major Regina sternly. "You're in my house now Major and you will do as I tell you. Lay face down on the stretcher and they will take down stairs." He ordered and looked quickly at Commander Rebecca's back as she unbuckled. "You can walk but you won't escape my needle with that cut. Follow the stretcher and your Major." He said helping her off of Emerald. "Cpt Cameron; We will follow shortly. You and the Raiders go down to the courtyard and form up all the messengers into a formation of seven rows making sure they are evenly matched. I do not want all the tall messengers in one row or the fat ones or the old ones or the young ones…., you see what I mean?" She asked and Cpt Cameron nodded before they separated and left Commander Rebecca and Major Regina with Lord Peter. "This is not so bad as I thought." Lord Peter said after he pulled away Commander Rebecca's vest and shirt. "The skin is cut but the muscle is not. I can close this with a few stitches." He said as he poured a cool potion over her cut and cleaned it. As Lord Peter took his needle and began to stitch her wound closed, Regina stared at Rebecca in amazement. "Does that not hurt?" She asked Rebecca who lay on the stretcher beside her. "I feel nothing for that part of my back is numb." Rebecca replied. "How is this possible? When Lord Paul closed my wound the pain was tremendous." Regina asked and Lord Peter raised the bottle with the potion. "Did you by chance have cross words with Lord Paul because sometimes he forgets the numbing potion when he is agitated?" Lord Peter giggled and Major Regina just stared at him. "That sorry bastard." Major Regina stated as Lord Peter moved to her and peeled back the bandage to inspect her cut. "Well at least his work has held on your flight. I will place new bandages on both of you and you can get to work here shortly." Lord Peter said after he checked Major Regina's head and arm. He handed Regina a glass filled with cherry wine and medicine. "You still need lots of fluids Major. If you overextend yourself, you may feel faint again. I want to see you with a glass in your hand for the rest of the day and no heavy wine or beer just water or the soft cherry wine." He said smiling at her and he finished with them both before they headed for the courtyard.

Commander Rebecca stepped from the castle escorted by Major Regina whose splinted arm was in a sling and her head was bandaged with a red bandana that she chose to cover and disguise her wound. The men were in formation as Commander Rebecca had ordered and all became silent as they stepped in front. "Let me speak to them." Major Regina whispered to Commander Rebecca and she nodded to her approvingly. "Show confidence." Rebecca whispered back and Regina looked to the captains. "Pick for yourselves a row of messengers and go stand in front of them and face me." Major Regina said quietly to them and they did as she commanded. When they had done so she looked at the formation but she could not see them all for she was too short. "Sit down!" Major Regina shouted and the messengers began to take a seat in the grass but Regina's face turned red with anger for they responded to her casually and she could see that some of them contemplated her position and considered her unworthy. "That was pitiful! You move as old women unworthy of the position that has been granted you this day. **On you feet!**" Major Regina shouted forcefully and they all stood back up quickly. "You are all to be trained and learn the difference between a mere messenger and a Sky

Raider!" Major Regina shouted and began to move among them looking each in the eye. The first lesson is when an officer gives a command, do not contemplate. To live, you must respond quickly and do exactly what he commands without contemplation. Now, SIT DOWN!" Regina shouted ferociously and all the men fell to their seats save one who looked at Major Regina with contempt as he took his seat slowly and Regina rushed to his side and glared at him. "Depart from my sight and return to your mother's breast to tell your parents the little girl chased you away finding you too weak to become a Sky Raider!" Major Regina shouted chastising him and he looked around to the others as he stood to protest and Major Regina drew her sword laying it at his throat. "I will not debate with you boy but I will stain this grass with your blood before I allow an impertinent child to invade my ranks." She said angrily with complete conviction and reluctantly he retreated back into the castle. Major Regina kept a firm grasp on her sword as she moved back to the front of them and stared boldly into their eyes. "As a young child, my father taught me to hunt and the bleeding of prey is not foreign to me. I have hung many a boar in a tree and cut his throat and I learned to relish the meaning of it. But like you I have never imagined a man as my prey. This evil that has come to our shores is filled with men unlike us and they are practiced at war!" Major Regina shouted raising her sword to them. "They will split you open and move to the next man without a second of contemplation and I have seen it." Regina said demonstrating a slash with her sword. "Which one of you has seen a man try to push his entrails back into his chest or heard a man's horrific scream as he burns to death?" Regina asked as she replaced her sword in her belt. "I have…., and so have your captains." She said remorsefully and then turned to them and grinned wickedly. "And we long to see it again." Regina said gritting her teeth. "But I would not have you fall victim to this horror so I warn you now. I lost my mount on the ground. Stay in the air and when your captain gives you a command do not think but act quickly. In a moment I will have your captain take charge of you." Major Regina said walking to a pile of bombs and picking up two and she pulled the safety chip from it and threw it high in the air and it landed in the fountain in front of them all sinking to the bottom. "They serve no purpose in the water." Regina said and pulled the safety chip on the second one and threw it high landing it on the grass several paces from them and it burst into flames covering a good ten paces and the men gasped. "They are designed for a ship so be diligent and follow your captain to insure your efforts are not futile." She said and walked among them again. "Discipline; your captain will be your god today for he holds the power of life and death for you in his hands and all **you** must do is hear him and obey to live. **On you feet!**" Major Regina shouted and all the messengers rose quickly as she moved in front of Commander Rebecca and drew her sword again to salute her and Rebecca smiled proudly at her. "I will add only this to what the Major has said." Commander Rebecca shouted. "The ships you will see today laid waste to Sandista destroying it completely without mercy. I challenge you now…, sink them all and learn the battle cry of the of the most powerful force on the Island of the Seven Kings for you are the pride and the sword of the Great Father. You are Sky Raiders and this is our island NOW AN FOREVER!" Commander Rebecca shouted pulling her sword over her head and they all responded loudly NOW AND FOREVER!" Major Regina stepped back in front of her and saluted. "Have the captains take charge and teach them our tactics. Make sure they understand the safety chip. I would not see any of them burst into flames before they find a target." Rebecca smiled and Regina saluted turning to face them. "Captains take charge of your squadrons!" She shouted and saluted and all the captains saluted and took their raiders to the stacks of bombs to begin. "I am going to meet with Admiral Lance on the ship." Commander Rebecca said and Regina nodded. "I am going to replace that boy with one of the messengers Commander Dillon kept for himself so Cpt Richard will not be shorthanded. After I do that I will have a word with each captain before I join you aboard ship shortly." Major Regina said and she headed for the castle. "Where is your water you promised the medic you would carry today?" She called to Regina. "I will get some in the castle!" Major Regina replied as she walked away.

CHAPTER 1 4

✳

THE WAR

It was not a great distance to the docks at Archemeius but Commander Rebecca took a carriage to save time. "Return now and bring the Major to me when she is ready." She said to the driver. There was only one fast schooner at the dock so she assumed it was the Admiral's and went quickly to it. Admiral Lance was a heavy set man in his mid 40s and sweat poured over his face. "The cannons are hard work." He said wiping his brow. "We just finished loading the extra powder and I was helping." He smiled. "Our schooners are faster than their giant war ships but we have but five cannon on each side and they have 30. We can harass them and we can distract them but it will take me forever to sink one on my own even if I can keep away from his broadside." The Admiral admitted. "It would seem speed and position are tactics we share." Commander Rebecca said. "Do you have any report on our adversary?" She asked. "Not of yet; I expect a messenger anytime." He replied looking to the horizon. "What is your plan for attack Commander?" He asked. "As soon as the captains have finished training with the bombs, they will begin the raids on their ships. Each captain will seek out this vessel first so we can control the attack. Once the Major joins us, I would suggest we set sail and take a position south of Green Stone so we can respond quickly. We have bombs in Green Stone and Archemeius so we can resupply from whichever is quickest. Initially the Raiders will attack as a single force to maximize the impact but the subsequent attacks will be sequenced so I can keep Raiders in the air at all times." Commander Rebecca concluded and moved to the rail to look out at the ocean. "You wish you could fly with them don't you?" Admiral Lance said. "I do....., but somebody has to do this too." She replied and the Admiral handed her a cup. "Well, I'm ready to sail whenever the Major arrives. Here's to victory. Idos be with us." He smiled raising his cup to her. She saw the flash of light over the ocean and new immediately it was the reflectionHHHHHH of the sun off of a yellow dragon. It was a messenger and he was traveling at maximum speed directly toward them. In an instant, he was hovering beside them and Commander Rebecca fought to maintain her balance as the wind swirled around them from the wings of the hovering young dragon. "Their fleet just got underway moving south from Sandista." He shouted. "The whole army is on shore marching on the road." He added. "Go now and report to Major Regina in the courtyard in Archemeius. Land in the courtyard. Give her your report and tell her you want to fly with Cpt Richard as a Sky Raider. Tell her I said she should make haste to join me for we sail quickly." She shouted at him and his eyes brightened before he whistled and departed north to the castle. She didn't know whether Major Regina had replaced the lost man in Richard squadron yet but it made no difference. Commander Dillon would not need him anymore. "They are starting very late. It will be 6 hours and well into the day before they can turn west." Commander Rebecca said turning to Admiral Lance. "I do not think they are prepared for our reception. Commander Dillon was right. They are arrogant and fool hearty and I hope they stay that course." He replied turning to his 1st Officer. "Prepare to make sail when you see a carriage approaching." He said and the man replied "As you command sir."

Cpt Manor looked to the east out to sea and could barely make out Commodore Marantz's flag ship as they sailed next to them just off shore. The ships sailed two by two and stretched far in front of him and behind him. He took a sip from his canteen wishing it was wine and not water. They had already been on the road for four hours and the sun was beating down mercilessly. "This road is much longer than we expected. Send a cavalry troop forward to discover how much further we must march. If it is much further, I will stop and rest the infantry to take a meal." He said and one of the men with him turned on his horse and went to do his bidding. In a moment the cavalry troop galloped past him and disappeared up the road. "The men's spirit is high sir. You will not see them falter in the attack." One of his officers said. "Your men are well trained but I live for action. These long road marches are not in my nature." Cpt Manor replied. An hour went by before the cavalry troop returned and the officer rode up to him. "You have another hour before the road turns east and then follows a river north into the forest. The road hugs the mountain and becomes a wall with the road on top of it." He reported. "Good, we will wait at the forest edge for Commodore Marantz to join us. He was right again." Cpt Manor laughed pulling out his canteen. There next city is just beyond the forest by our map and he will want to march with us. Did you meet any resistance at all?" Cpt Manor asked disappointedly. "The forest seems quiet but we only went in a short distance." He replied and Cpt Manor shook his head. "I almost wish they did have an army left but I imagine Commodore is probably right about that too. When we get to the wall and turn north I want 5000 men west of the wall and the rest will stay on the road and move to the east of the wall as it moves away from the mountain. Keep the artillery on the road and the war dogs and the cavalry can follow them." He commanded and they departed to set his plan. "That road may have been constructed this way to force you to do exactly this and divide your army." One of his staff suggested and Cpt Manor looked at him frustrated. "Have you seen anything from these people that would make you think they have a mind toward defense?" He asked and waved him off dismissing his suggestion. He sent a rider to the shore to signal Commodore Marantz and as they turned north and the forest began, 2000 men dropped over the wall to the east and they all set up to eat and refresh themselves. A short time later, a long boat touched the shore and Commodore Marantz met Lt Manor on the beach. He briefed the Commodore as to what he had done as they walked to the edge of the forest and a tent to eat in comfort.

As they ate a runner came to the tent. "Sir there are ships on the horizon." He said and they all scurried to the beach and pulled binoculars to survey the ocean nervously. "There they are." Commodore Marantz exclaimed and began to chuckle. "It seems I was wrong. There must be another city west of here and look Cpt Manor; they've sent their navy out to greet us." He laughed. "Ten schooners, god I should have stayed on the ship but we have a perfect vantage point from here don't we William?" He laughed. Send the Cavalry up the beach to see what prize has birthed this navy." He chuckled and one of the officers scurried away. "Those are fast schooners. Do you think they are trying to pull the fleet away from us?" Cpt Manor asked watching them. "Nope I don't....., I think that's all they have and they're choosing to use them rather than just surrender." The Commodore replied and turned to face Cpt Manor. "I want you to send three riders under a white banner north up the road. Tell them these are my terms of surrender. That they lay down their arms and deliver to me the remaining Kings of this kingdom and I will promise them no more blood will be shed." He said. "Oh and tell them I sank their navy as I am certain by the time they get there I will have." He added laughing. "We get to see what kind of sailors I have." He chuckled again as he turned to see his fleet turn aggressively toward the schooners. Cpt Manor departed to dispatch the messengers north and then suddenly the sky above the schooners began to flash with brilliant reflections of green and red and blue lights and the horizon was filled with the lights all heading toward the fleet. As they grew closer to the fleet, he suddenly realized it was the sun reflecting off the scales of those damnable dragons but there was not seven, as he had suspected but it seemed closer to seventy. He watched in horror as they climbed high above the fleet and began to dive down onto it and he could see the first seven ships start to smoke and burn. "Signal the fleet to disperse!" he shouted running forward toward the shore in a panic. "Good god, why have they hidden these from me until now!" He screamed and he felt helpless as he watched the sky rain fire down on his fleet. He fell to his knees and watched and his anger grew seeing each ship try to find the best wind and make sail to escape but the dragons were relentless in their pursuit and the fire from the sky seemed unending. There was no way the ships could outrun the dragons and he prayed that they did not have sufficient bombs to set fires on the whole fleet. His flag ship was at the rear and it appeared to be successfully making its retreat but Commodore Marantz counted 28 ships burning out of control after a little more than an hour. Cpt Manor returned to his side just before the entire cavalry came rumbling back to him on the beach. "Did you find the city?" He asked his cavalry commander as he dismounted. "I did not." He huffed and grabbed a stick to draw in the sand. "There is a narrow pass between the ocean and the cliffs here." He pointed out. "The pass, for as far as you can see to the west, is on fire and burns 20 feet in the air." He reported and dropped the stick. "You couldn't ride around it in the surf?" The Commodore asked indignantly. "There is no surf sir but only rock and deep water. We would be swept out to sea or picked off easily by marksmen further up before we could gain any advantage." He replied and in that moment they heard a terrified blood curdling scream and when they looked up there were three dragons carrying something in their talons high above them. As the dragons released what they carried the screams grew louder and they realized what the dragons had dropped were the three men Cpt Manor had sent north under the white banner. They hit the ground with a terrible thud and their screaming was silenced.

"We have their answer regarding surrender. This is where they want us to be Commodore." Cpt Manor said as the dragons that were attacking the fleet began to stream over their heads heading northward. "I would urgently recommend we retreat back to the dock and evaluate our losses." Cpt Manor said and he was extremely afraid watching wave after wave of dragons pass over his head. "You want me to surrender 10 thousand men to an island people that can't possibly number 10 thousand men women and children? I will not retreat!" He shouted angrily. "I will however, kill every man and every boy and every male child on this abominable island before I leave!" Commodore Marantz shouted turning back to his cavalry. "You ride up that rode and bring me back a report I can use as to what lies between me and this city." He shouted and the cavalry commander gathered all the horsemen together putting some of them on the road but many of them traveled north also but on the west side of the road in the forest. He could not get horsemen east of the road as it was too high. There were sailors coming ashore, some burned badly but all of them had abandoned their ships. There was chaos all around the Commodore and he could not see a ship on the ocean that was not burning save the 10 fast schooners. Then he heard the rumble of cannon fire to the north and long rifles cracked in the ocean air. After a time, his cavalry commander returned and grabbed a stick after he dismounted. "The forest is maybe 5 miles and it opens to a field which is maybe 200 yards from their wall. The walls to the castle are twenty feet high as the road is here. They have cannon lining the wall hub to hub and they cover the open field to the forest edge. We can rush the wall and breach it but we will lose a lot of men in the open field if we don't knock that wall down first and silence those cannon. Our cannon have greater range but we cannot deploy them in the forest." He concluded handing the stick to the Commodore. "Then we will cut the forest down!" Commodore Marantz said. "If we have to work all night, I want a swatch through the forest cut so that I can line 40 cannon side by side and be in range for their wall. I want the other 40 right behind them so I can turn the castle to rubble once the wall is gone. We can blast the remaining trees down in front of us once we can range the wall. Bring all the infantry back on this side of the road and set every man's hand to an axe. Put ropes and chains to the trees and let the horses pull them up. I don't care how you do it. Just get my cannon in range of their wall by morning!" Commodore Marantz yelled and they dispersed to set each man to his task. "Why do you think they're not using the dragons against the ground forces?" Cpt Manor asked and Commodore

Marantz looked at him frustrated by his question. He paced back and forth in the sand, his anger burning in his face. "Come on William. I pay you to ask questions we don't have answers for yet. They know the long rifle will bring one down if they are in range. That's obvious and the bombs they have work well against structures but they'd have to be damn good shots to hit a man and that is ineffective anyway." He said looking out to the ships burning on the sea. "Those bastards were damn effective against the fleet though. I should have sent the fleet to sea." He said shaking his head in disgust. "I should have known there were more than 10 of them. What I would give to have 10 of those dragons in the armada." He cursed kicking the sand in his futility. "When we find their commander, I want him alive." He said as he watched a group fly over his head and out to sea. "I would wager you a gold piece to a rock; he is on one of those schooners." Cpt Manor said as they watched the schooners sail between the burning war ships in pursuit of his fleet.

"God this is terrible. We're going to lose them before I can get another squadron on them." Commander Rebecca protested in frustration. "Show some faith Commander. They can't escape my fast schooners. Where are they going to go?" The Admiral laughed. The Raiders were setting the warships on fire and the schooners would sail in an finish them off with a well placed volley to the stern of the big ships. "Give me 10 degrees to port and prepare to fire Mr. Reynolds!" He shouted jumping to the port side of the ship. "We're just not as effective one squadron at a time. I need to mass them again to finish them off quickly but I'm going to lose daylight before I can do that." She admitted. "They are running to the dock at Sandista. I'll bet you anything that's where they're going." Maj Regina said as another squadron came overhead and she recognized Lightning separate from the group and swoop down beside their ship. "Port guns ready sir!" Mr. Reynolds shouted as Commander Rebecca leaned over the starboard side to yell at Cpt Cameron. "Take your squadron back to Greenstone now and wait until all the squadrons are rested. Then come find me in Sandista harbor and bring all the raiders." Commander Rebecca shouted. "Port guns stand by!" Admiral Lance shouted. "Port Guns..., FIRE!" Admiral Lance shouted and the air cracked with a thunderous roar that shook the whole ship and they watched as the side of the huge warship splintered and broke open and then the sky lit up around the warship and there was another even more tremendous explosion on the ship and it began to lean to one side. "God that is so cool." Major Regina shouted as Cpt Cameron rose back up above them and turned Lightning's head toward Greenstone. "That one is headed for the bottom. Reset the mast Mr. Reynolds. We're headed north again!" Admiral Lance called. "By your command, north it is sir!" Mr. Reynolds replied. "I wish you would relax just a little Commander Rebecca. Your plan is working perfectly, certainly beyond my expectations." He said with a smile. "We have to sink them all Admiral. That's my charge. We cannot let one of them escape!" Commander Rebecca said and her anxiety was evident in her voice. She walked to the front of the ship and watched the horizon and the small dot she knew was a warship. She looked back at the Admiral and pointed northward and he smiled again. "I see him commander. That's where we're going." He chuckled and his frivolity was no comfort to Commander Rebecca. "Ten degrees left rudder Mister Reynolds!" He shouted. "By your command, ten degrees left rudder!" Mr. Reynolds responded. They sailed for an hour closing steadily on the Warship before she saw them. There were 10 ships in close proximity to the dock at Sandista. Two were actually tied to the dock as best she could tell. She looked back south and saw the twinkle of lights reflecting the sun and knew it was the Raiders. "That's our boys. Right on time." Major Regina said with a proud grin. "You get us in close Admiral Lance." Commander Rebecca said and suddenly there were more than 50 Raiders hovering overhead and Cpt Richard swooped in beside their ship this time. "Commander Dillon sent a message!" He shouted. "Don't sink the flagship but capture it." He added and Commander Rebecca frowned. How the hell was she going to do that? She and Maj Regina had been keeping count of the warships. "That's the last of them Cpt Richard! Now go finish this!" She shouted and moved to the front of the ship with the Admiral and Major Regina. "How do you capture a ship?" She asked the Admiral and he just shook his head. "I know not. I only learned this day how to sink one." He replied and they watched together as the shadow of the raiders moved over the fleet of warships as an ominous cloud high above them and then one by one each captain led his squadron in a dive toward a ship and they dropped their bombs before returning to the ominous cloud. Commander Rebecca was now most concerned with the flagship and she watched it move behind the other ships where the bombs were beginning to feed great plumes of black smoke. "What is he doing?" Major Regina asked as the flag ship did not turn but crashed forcefully into the dock and a great section of it collapsed under the weight of the ship as the sailors began to dive into the water. "My god they will sink it themselves in their recklessness! Bring us alongside the flagship Mr. Reynolds!" Admiral Vance yelled. "By your command sir!"

Mr. Reynolds replied. "Signal the fleet we are going in." Make ready the port cannon!" Admiral Vance shouted as he drew his sword. "We're going to sail right through them Commander. I pray your raiders have them sufficiently distracted and one of their bombs does not find us." He shouted and Commander Rebecca drew her sword and moved to her side. As they moved precariously between two of the warships the Raiders continued to rain the bombs mercilessly on all the ships around them and sailors splashed into the water from all of them. None of the cannons fired but the ship to their port side erupted in a tremendous explosion and splinters of burning wood and smoke enveloped them as Commander Rebecca was knocked to the deck. She pulled herself back to her feet and for a moment could see nothing. As the smoke cleared, she could see Admiral Lance helping Major Regina back to her feet and she looked up. Their main sail had a hole in it and was on fire. "10 degrees left rudder Mr. Reynolds!" Admiral Lance shouted urgently looking also to their main sail. "By your command, 10 degrees left rudder sir." Mr. Reynolds replied and as she looked over the bow of their ship the flagship came into view. The dock creaked and the heavy timbers exploded under the weight of the massive warship as the wind in her sails pressed her against the dock. Another section of the dock collapsed and the flagship move forward crushing the wood under her bow. Admiral Lance swung his sword and slashed one rope and then another and the burning main sail fell into the sea on the port side as they pulled next to the flag ship. All the sailors on the schooner grabbed hooks with rope and tossed them at the flagship pulling them alongside. "You stay with Mr. Reynolds until we secure her." Admiral Lance shouted as more of the schooners came along side the warship and Admiral Lance and all the sailors climbed the ropes onto the flagship. The heavy timbers of the dock exploded again as another section of the dock fell under the weight of the massive warship and it jerked forward. Two of his sailors lost their grip on the ropes and fell into the water. Admiral Lance and his sailors moved quickly to the main sail of the flagship and cut it down and the cracking timbers of the dock fell silent as the flagship finally stopped. A great cheer rose up from the flagship as Admiral Lance appeared above her smiling broadly. "Take this to him." Mr. Reynolds said and he handed her a banner as she turned her eyes to him. She stuffed it into her vest and grabbed the rope as Mr. Reynolds helped her climb until Admiral Lance could grasp her arm and pull her up. There was no one on board save her and the Admiral and his sailors as he led her to the main mast. "Tie it here." He said grinning broadly holding the narrow white rope out and Commander Rebecca clipped the latches from the banner onto it. Together her and Admiral Lance pulled at the rope and raised the banner to the top of the mast as the sailors screamed and cheered. As they tied it off, Rebecca's excitement and relief overwhelmed her and she too screamed and laughed hysterically and she danced with Admiral Lance under the banner of Sandinista they had raised on the flag ship.

Amanda pushed passed the terrified guards to get to the window in time to see the banner raised to the top of the ship at the dock. A feeling of complete elation filled her body as she watched the dragon riders land on the beach and encircle the sailors there as they fell down prostrate in the sand before them. "We're being rescued!" She screamed and turned to Elisha and the other girls who cowered on the Kings bed. One of the guards drew his sword mumbling something in his own language before he grabbed Amanda by her hair and threw her to the ground and raised his sword to kill her. The interpreter Commodore Marantz had left with them fell on top of Amanda and screamed at the guard and they argued. Reluctantly the guard released his grip on Amanda's hair and she scurried back to Elisha and her friends on the bed. "I convinced him they would not spare our lives if they found you dead." The interpreter said nervously. "I have spared your life now spare mine also as we return you to your countrymen." He said as he opened the door to the bedchamber. "Go and we shall follow." He said and his whole body trembled waiting for her to move. Elisha was the first to rise and she took Amanda's hand and one of the other girls and they departed holding tightly to each other and the 5 guards and the interpreter followed close behind them. They moved quickly over the rubble of the wall looking back at the guards still fearful of what they might do following them so close. They saw Admiral Lance with Commander Rebecca and Major Regina on the beach with the sailors and moved quickly toward them. As they approached the guards moved among them and in front of them and Amanda was scared again that her and all her friends might perish this close to being rescued and she huddled tightly to Elisha and the girls. Then suddenly the guards dropped their swords and their daggers and fell on their faces in front of Admiral Lance and his group. Admiral Lance and Commander Rebecca and all who stood there surveyed the women behind the guards. They stood huddled together dressed in royal gowns but all could see the terror in their faces and they felt pity for them imagining what they had suffered. "We return to you the prisoners we captured and you see they are unharmed so I plead with you, spare our lives also." The interpreter cried but before Admiral Lance could reply, Elisha ran forward and swooped up one of the swords the guards had dropped. She plunged it into the interpreters back. As he screamed in agony all the girls rushed forward grabbing a sword or a dagger and as Admiral Lance looked on stunned, the girls attacked and killed all the guards and the interpreter and no one moved to stop them. When they had finished and the last guard lay dead, they ran and fell at Admiral Lance's feet and kissed them and Rebecca's and Major Regina's also and they all fell to their knees in the sand and wept together for a time.

The sun was setting and the breeze from the ocean was blowing dark clouds in from the east. "It's going to rain tonight." Commander Dillon said turning away from the window to face Queen Isabella. He was tense because he knew what his enemy was doing and he had no recourse to stop them. By tomorrow they will have cut away enough of the forest to deploy their cannon in range of the city wall where his only defense to the city stood in wait. He knew once that wall fell, the horde of cavalry and infantry would follow the war dogs and rush through the city like water through a broken dam. "I want you to lead the women and children to Castle Paternus tonight and tell the Great Father how we stayed to defend the kingdom." Commander Dillon said remorsefully and the blood rushed from Queen Isabella's face as she stared at him in disbelief. "Have you lost faith in the sons and daughters of the Great Father and in Idos also and in his promise that we shall dwell in safety?" Queen Isabella replied and Commander Dillon turned his eyes to her feet. "I see only the futility in my own strength to stand against this evil and wish not to see our women and children fall prey to them before my eyes. Perhaps Idos will deliver you from them another day as we will assuredly thin their ranks but I do not see victory in my efforts much beyond first light." He replied and in that moment a messenger broke into his chambers shouting. "Sandista is ours once again and their fleet is no more! The Sky Raiders return victorious and are landing in the city square as we speak." He concluded and a cheer of joy rang up in the chambers that spread mightily through the castle and the whole city. The news lifted Commander Dillon's spirit but it did not vanquish the dread in his heart and he turned back to the window to gaze south. "Bring Commander Rebecca to me so that we may take council and I may hear her report." He said and Queen Isabella came to his side at the window. "Why is you countenance still low? Do you not perceive that Idos has delivered his sword into your hands to strengthen your Army?" She asked with concern and Commander Dillon looked into her eyes and gathered his strength. "I am a warrior that has never known war before this week but I know his sword and its limitations. The Sky Raiders have fought bravely and will do so again but I will not withdraw my council to you in regard to the women and children and I pray you make haste to act on it quickly." He said with complete conviction. Queen Isabella put her hands on his shoulders. "You are the Commander of the Army and I have never questioned your wisdom nor will I do so now. I will heed your council and evacuate the city this night as you desire. We shall march to Castle Paternus and sing a prayer for you and all that remain as we march that Idos shall deliver them into your capable hands." Queen Isabella said and kissed his cheek before she departed.

Commander Rebecca looked over Cpt Richard's shoulder as they began to hover over the perch at Castle Green Stone. She was extremely proud of all the Sky Raiders and what they had accomplished and she watched Cpt Cameron and Major Regina land on the perch beside them. They all rushed to assist Major Regina once both dragons came to a stop and began to drink and Rebecca turned to her captains. "You two go now quickly and insure all the mounts and our men also are well fed and find comfort for I know not what council we shall hear with the Commander. We may be pressed right back into the battle or find rest for a time. Gather all into the dining hall and we shall join you there shortly to reveal to you all that the Commander's desires from us." Commander Rebecca said. Lord Paul met them as they headed for the stairway. "How do your wounds fair?" He asked Major Regina moving quickly to her side. "My wounds throb with a dull pain and I would have more of your elixir but you and I will have words when time permits me." She said frowning at him and slapping his hands away from her splinted arm. Lord Paul had heard of Major Regina's discovery of his neglect to administer the numbing agent as well as Commander Rebecca's injury and he knew that meeting was not going to be pleasant. "I will await you outside the Queen's chambers to inspect your wounds and answer for my indiscretion with you." He replied handing Major Regina a vial of the elixir of pain killer. Major Regina swallowed a healthy gulp of the elixir and gritted her teeth at the foul taste before handing it back to him as they made their way to the Queen's chambers.

e HeAs Commander Rebecca entered the Queen's chamber, Commander Dillon turned from the window to greet her and she could see the stress in his face. "The joy of your victory proceeds you Commander. Give me your report and lighten my heart." He said forcing a smile at her. "Admiral Lance stands guard over 100 sailors we captured and three of their ships. Among these is the flagship which has only minor damage. The other two were at the dock and they were repairing them so we did not see cause to sink them. Sandista's banner flies over the castle again but the city is empty save 6 women we found they had taken prisoner. Their report to me and to Admiral Lance also was one of horror and debauchery including the murder of a small child and acts of a nature I would not repeat committed by even the commander of this evil horde. Admiral Lance stands guard between these women and the sailors for they would surely take vengeance upon them all given opportunity." Commander Rebecca concluded and Commander Dillon gritted his teeth in disgust and anger. "Send word to Admiral Lance to build gallows on the docks to accommodate 50 men at a time and He shall know tomorrow whether he shall hang these men and take to the sea or rejoice with us in victory. I may choose to let these women execute the order if they are to be hanged." Commander Dillon said and one of his staff departed. "What plans do you have for the Sky Raiders for we have sufficient supplies to rain fire into their camp and they will find no rest this night if that is your command?" Commander Rebecca suggested and Commander Dillon shook his head no. "They do not seek rest this night but work diligently to cut down the forest and move their cannon into range of our wall by 1st light. You would not find targets for your bombs to deter them sufficiently from this task but I fear a fire in the forest would but hasten their advance. I would rather keep you in reserve and well rested to meet the challenge that only the light of the new day may reveal to us." Commander Dillon said and turned back to gaze out the window. "Take pride in your victory today Commander as I do and try to find slumber for you and your men for tomorrow will be a great test to us all." He said and Commander Rebecca would have saluted him but he did not turn back to her before she departed.

A small fire burned in front of Commodore Marantz's tent and he sat on his saddle looking across it at Cpt Manor. The loss of his fleet weighed heavily on his mind and was keeping him awake as his anger raged at his mistakes to this point in the battle. His Cavalry Commander rode up to the fire and dismounted. "I took a troop and rode the wall in the west and it circles back to the city. There is no one on that wall or the road there. Another highway turns west through the forest and where it meets the wall the forest is thin and a great plain begins. If I could get cannon into that plain, we could flank the city and attack it's walls from two sides." The Cavalry Commander said excitedly. "Could you protect the artillery with your troop?" Commodore Marantz asked and Cpt Manor shook his head. "We should not divide our Army again. See how we paid a severe price the last time." He suggested. "You lack boldness in planning for battle William. I will not embrace tameness because of a past failure and flanking them will limit my losses in the attack. You go also with the troop and take 40 cannon and 200 infantry. At dawn's first glimmer knock down the highway and rush through to join me and attack their city wall from behind. If all goes well, the war dogs will do the work for us and we can preserve our infantry again for another city." He smiled and Cpt Manor rose reluctantly. "I want 300 infantry for I do not trust completely this report." Cpt Manor said as he saddled his large white stallion. "You can take 300 if that's what you want William." Commodore Marantz chuckled. "You know we probably lost our whores to that commander of the dragons today." Cpt Manor sighed heavily tightening his stirrups. "We shall visit them again and many more like them before I bring an end to their resistance." Commodore Marantz said as Cpt Manor mounted his stallion. "I shall speak to you next in their city square." Cpt Manor said and saluted him before he departed and it began to rain. Commodore Marantz pulled his saddle into his tent and laid across it watching the rain roll in from the ocean in the moonlight. He was less worried about the attack on the city tomorrow knowing he had an opportunity to flank them and he fell asleep quickly listening to the gentle rain against his tent.

Cpt Cameron ate heartily and laughed out loud hearing his new squadron share the tails of their victory today. He was much more than proud of them. He knew now this was what he was destined to do and he grinned at Cpt Richard who sat across from him with his squadron. "We should carry shoulder crackers instead of this crossbow. Their range is much better." One of the Raiders in Richard's squadron said and Cpt Cameron scoffed. "And what will you do when you lift the shoulder cracker in battle and find the ball has fallen out from bouncing at your side? How long will it take you to reload it?" Cpt Cameron laughed. "We could carry several and turn them upright so the balls will not dislodge in flight." The young raider replied and Cpt Cameron laughed even harder. "How many will you carry, 10? And what will I do for you when you bank quickly and one or more of them discharges and blows your arm or your head off." Cpt Cameron replied and all the raiders laughed leaving the one who suggested it embarrassed. Cpt Cameron stood and pulled the crossbow from his back and loaded it. "I can carry 40 arrows for my crossbow on my person and I can load it while flying." He said and took aim at a painting of a man on horseback across the dining facility. He pulled the trigger and let the arrow fly and it found it's mark in the center of the man's chest and Cpt Cameron replaced the crossbow on his back as the men cheered. "The crossbow is the perfect weapon for a Sky Raider if he is the master of it." Cpt Cameron said and returned to his seat. "On your FEET!" Major Regina shouted as she led Commander Rebecca into the dining hall and the sound of the chairs sliding against the wood floor echoed in the room as the Raiders jumped up and silence fell over the room. Commander Rebecca fought to control her emotions as her pride in all of them surged though her chest creating pressure behind her eyes. She moved quickly to the head table and stood for a moment surveying the room. "Let me have my captains at this table and the rest of you take your seats." She said and the men there scurried to leave as she and Major Regina sat down. A servant brought the glasses and plates of fish and venison. "I cannot begin to express to you how proud Queen Isabella, Commander Dillon and his staff were of all of you." Commander Rebecca said once they had all joined her and Richard stood. "Queen Isabella leads all the women and children to Castle Paternus tonight." Cpt Richard interrupted her and Rebecca looked at him distraught by the interruption and she put her hand on Major Regina's shoulder to restrain her. "Do you suggest that we join her Cpt Richard?" She asked and Cpt Richard blushed red realizing his error as he sat back in his chair. "I merely meant to share with you what we had witnessed." He said apologetically. "I'm fairly certain the Commander briefed me thoroughly but please go ahead if you have something else to share." Commander Rebecca said curtly and Cpt Richard felt like he was back in class with her again and speaking out of turn. He shook his head no and looked back at his plate. "Good. We have a time of rest and I want you all to insure your men use it wisely. I know not what our next task is but I want fresh mounts and fresh minds. Check all quivers and resupply the bombs tonight. Their spirits are high and I want that same spirit to ride with them tomorrow regardless of our task. I want every raider by his mount one hour before 1st light. When you return to your men, reinforce how proud all of us are of them and how they have lifted everyone's spirit with their success today. Do you have any questions for me?" Commander Rebecca said trying to project confidence and professionalism as she looked to each of them. When she looked back at Cpt Richard he smiled proudly at her. "Do you think it will rain all night?" He asked not changing the expression on his face but Rebecca felt a twinge of a smile knowing the true nature of his question and their secret code. "I will not concern myself with the rain tonight as Major Regina and I shall share quarters in the castle. Make certain you and all your men find shelter also out of the weather and stay by their sides tonight. If there is nothing further, you are dismissed." She repliede He and all the captains stood and saluted her before returning to the tables with their men. "That was stupid question." Regina whispered to her. "Did Richard think you meant for them to sleep in the rain?" Regina scoffed. Rebecca looked to Major Regina after she finished her meal and saw her yawn dramatically and rub eyes. "Your medicine is working well. We should retire Regina." Commander Rebecca said softly and Major Regina shook her head no. "I have energy left to see that your orders are executed." Regina replied. "To what purpose?" Commander Rebecca replied. "Give them reigns to show faith in them also and come with me now to retire." Rebecca suggested and Regina looked to surrender to her will and smiled before she rose and faced the Raiders. "On your FEET!" She shouted and the clatter of chairs resounded in the dining hall again as Commander Rebecca rose and Regina followed her out of the hall. As they departed Major Regina shouted again. "What motto do we embrace?" and the whole room responded. "NOW AND FOREVER!" and Major Regina said "You may retire" as they disappeared into the stairway and the Raiders all sat down.

Amanda stood in the archway to Castle Sandista and watched the rain falling on the rubble that had been the city wall. Her heart felt heavy and numb but her anger toward the invaders still burned in her head. The sound of the soft rain falling all around her was soothing to her and her friends as they all stood under the archway but the pain was still very real to all of them. "Do you hear that?" Elisha suddenly asked pulling away from her and running out into the rain. Amanda ran out next to her concerned deeply for Elisha because she had suffered more loss than any of them. She stood there with her for a moment and all the other girls followed them. "I hear nothing Elisha. We should not stay out in the rain." Amanda said and Elisha looked at her smiling as if possessed. "You do not hear that child?" Elisha asked before she broke from her and ran to the side of the castle toward the stable. "Elisha wait!" Amanda called to her but she kept running and Amanda ran after her as the other girls followed. Amanda was afraid for all of them. The city was abandoned but she feared some evil might still reside there. Then as she caught up to Elisha, she heard it too. The playful giggle of a child came from the stable. "You see, you hear him too." Elisha said excitedly grabbing Amanda's hand and pulling her into the stable. Amanda gasped in shock as she stared at the scene in front of her in the middle of the stables. There was Elisha's little brother surrounded by 10 little black puppies and he giggled excitedly lifting them to his face and kissing them. Two mother dogs lay passively at his side and did not move as Elisha ran to her brother and embraced him. "There you are!" He said as Elisha cried and kissed him passionately. "How is this possible?" Amanda cried as tears of joy filled her eyes and she fell to her knees beside them. "Caleb how did you get here?" Amanda wept and he just stared up at her confused for a moment. "I fell asleep in your basement and I had a bad dream. A man woke me up and I was afraid for you were all gone but he told me not to be afraid because he had a present for me and soon you would find me. He brought me here and he gave me these puppies and look you have found us now also as he said." Caleb laughed holding one of the puppies up to Amanda. "Where is this man?" Amanda asked looking nervously around the stables. "I know not for I turned my head from him for but a moment and when I turned back he was gone." Caleb replied and Amanda wept dramatically pulling at his shirt to inspect him but could find no scar or scratch on him anywhere. "It is a gift from Idos. He has heard my prayer and returned my brother to me." Elisha wailed joyfully and they all shared an embrace with Caleb and sang together the song of praise to Idos their mothers had taught them in their youth.

Darkness lay heavily over the whole city of Green Stone as Commander Dillon stared out the window to the south. He had ordered all torches extinguished and he had been there all night just listening to the rain and the faint sounds from his enemy in the forest. Periodically, he had fired his cannon into the darkness praying to Idos to guide the balls to his enemy. The sounds of destruction had grown louder as the night progressed but now there was only darkness and silence and he knew that meant their cannon were in range of his wall. Behind him stood all his staff and Commander Rebecca as he prayed for a solution to the evil out his window. Slowly the sky began to turn orange at the horizon and Commander Dillon drew his sword and lit a torch illuminating the chamber. He looked at all their faces before he thrust the torch and his sword out the window and shouted. "HERE AM I!" And every voice in the castle began to scream. "HERE AM I! HERE AM I! HERE AM I!" as torches were lit all over the city. Then suddenly they heard the sound of massive cannon fire to the west and Commander Dillon ran to that window to see the flashes of light in the distance and he turned quickly to Commander Rebecca. "They move to flank us!" He shouted. "Take your Sky Raiders and go to greet them!" Commander Dillon shouted and she and Major Regina bolted from the room. Outside the door, Commander Rebecca grabbed Major

Regina by the shoulders. "Make haste to our captains and have them meet me in the sky to the west. I pray for your forgiveness one day but I cannot remain on the ground in this battle and I cannot take you with me with your arm." Rebecca said and she could see the pain in Regina's face. "You kept Emerald for yourself secretly." She gasped as Rebecca kissed her. "Now and Forever Rebecca." Regina whispered in her ear before they parted and Rebecca ran up the stairs to the roof. Rebecca checked Emerald's harness quickly and the bags on each side loaded with bombs before she buckled in and urged him quickly to the ramp. A great rumble of cannons roared in the forest and in the dim light she could see the trees splinter and begin to fall at the forests edge. They were going to clear their field of fire by shooting down the remaining trees between them and the open field. Rebecca whistled and Emerald dove from the wall as she leaned forward to meet the pressure as Emerald spread his wings and pumped them powerfully heading skyward. She circled the city and watched as the other Sky Raiders took to the air. Cpt Richard and Cpt Cameron pulled alongside her and their squadrons were right behind them as she turned Emerald's head westward. "Whatever is in front of us must die!" Commander Rebecca shouted as she pulled the crossbow from her back and an arrow from her quiver and loaded it. "Speed Captain, it will be a lucky shot that finds you at 50 miles per hour!" She shouted and looked up to see the line of cannon and infantry that followed the Cavalry. She guided Emerald low to the ground and called for maximum speed and the wind began to roar in her ears as she took aim at the lead rider with her crossbow. She pulled the trigger and fired before she blew over the enemy line and it erupted into cracks and pops as they returned fire. As she pulled back on the reigns and banked with Emerald she watched but a few of the cavalry fall from their horses. One of Sky Raiders did not bank and turn but continued on straight at maximum speed. It was one of Cpt Anthony's men and as she watched him disappear she felt the pain in her chest from her first loss. She knew it was the cannon they must stop so she pulled to altitude and grabbed a bomb. She set Emerald at a hover well out of their range and began to hurl the bombs in their path. She cursed under her breath as she watched each one burst into flame and the driver just steer around the fire. No matter how hard she tried, she couldn't find the right second to release the bomb. They just weren't practiced at hitting small moving targets. The infantry had formed into ranks so she hurled a few into them but they again avoided any real damage by moving away from the flames. She stayed at altitude trying to find a solution as she watched the Sky Raiders make their high speed attacks but it seemed less than hopeful. They just weren't thinning them out fast enough and then she saw one of the Raiders hit the ground at high speed and the rider separated from his dragon and both of them rolled horrifically to their deaths in cloud of dust. If they were going to stop the cannons they were going to have land and fight on the ground and try to let the dragons destroy the cannons. It was the only way she could see that they might even have a chance but the infantry was going to be able to target and kill them easily once they gave up their advantage in the air. As she surveyed the battlefield and was making preparations to dive again, a glimmer of light to the north caught her eye. As it drew near she recognized the familiar sparkle of the sun off a dragon's scales and it was not just one dragon but two and they were traveling at high speed toward the battle. To her amazement, they swooped low toward the infantry and set their course for the center of the formation and Commander Rebecca gasped with joyous surprise as both of them blew a line of fire into the formation and it panicked and began to disperse in all directions. The red dragon banked and turned to deliver another stream of fire on the infantry but the white dragon flew toward her. It was the most glorious and ominous sight she had ever witnessed. The white dragon pulled next to her and hovered. On him sat a rider adorned in brilliant dragon scale armor that glistened white in the new sun equaled only by the scales of his dragon. The dragon whistled approvingly as the rider pulled back his helmet to reveal it was Arthur and she stared with her mouth open. "Stay clear of Crimson for he has not yet learned control fully." He shouted. "This is Arch Angel." He added as he pulled the helmet back down and dove back down toward their enemy before Commander Rebecca could utter a word. The field below had become chaos as men and horses ran in all directions and all the raiders began to chase them and pluck the men from the ground carrying them high into the air and dropping them. The men on the carts pulling the cannons, released the cannons in an effort to gain more speed in their escape and Commander Rebecca saw the man on the white stallion bolt at high speed back toward the hole they had made in the wall. She whistled at Emerald and turned his head toward the white horse as she dove. He rode quickly with two other riders at his side and they turned in their saddles and fired at her as she drew near but missed. Rebecca turned Emerald's head to the back of the man on the white stallion and gave the command whistle to attack. She saw the panic and fear on his face for only a brief moment before Emerald slammed against him and his horse toppled forward as the young dragon dug his talons into the rider. Rebecca pulled Emerald sky ward and he pumped his wings ferociously as they climbed and the man let out a blood curdling scream of agony and fear. She banked back around at altitude and dove toward the other riders as Emerald released the man and he fell to his death still screaming. She turned Emerald's head to the other rider and repeated the commands plucking him also from his horse and climbing to altitude before releasing him. The third rider jumped the debris at the wall and disappeared into the forest as Commander Rebecca turned Emerald to return to where the battle was. The Raider's were making quick work of their enemy now as one by one they swooped in, securing a man in the talons of their dragons and lifting them high into the air before releasing them to their fall to their death. She surveyed the battlefield and found Cpt Arthur had landed beside a cannon. Crimson and what she assumed was Cpt Andrew hovered close by spewing fire toward each cannon in turn and she turned Emerald's head toward Arch Angel and gave him the command to land. Arthur pulled back the helmet again as he saw Commander Rebecca land and approach him. "Arthur..., I have many inquiries that I would make of you but this is but a small portion of the force that attacks us and they lay siege to the gates of Green Stone as we speak. I beg you and Andrew come with us now and see what course we shall take to defend the castle!" She shouted and turned Emerald's head giving him the command to fly quickly before Arthur could respond.

The new sun was completely above the horizon now as Commander Rebecca flew at altitude above the enemy. They were still out of range of the cannon on the wall and a massive horde stood in wait behind their own cannons. As she banked and turned toward the castle the enemy cannon roared a thunderous explosion and she watched the huge wood and iron gate to the city splinter and collapse. Arthur and Andrew dove down on the enemy cannon in front of them and spewed fire as far as they could setting fire to many of the cannons and the infantry behind them and the cannon began to explode. The mass of infantry was but a few paces behind their cannons and many of them fired on Arthur and Andrew with their shoulder crackers. The Armor that Arthur and Andrew wore saved them from real damage but the intensity of the fire drove them backwards. She saw there was no chance the two dragons could stand against the thousands of soldiers and Commander Rebecca would have called them back fearful that the horde would envelop them but there was no time. Something was happening. Commander Rebecca looked to the sky as it slowly began to turn dark. She watched as the light slowly departed from the sun. It was the moon moving in front of the sun. Emerald and all the dragons made haste to land in the open field behind Arthur and Andrew and she could do nothing to stop him. All the dragons lay down on the field facing south and spreading their wings on the ground as the earth below them began to tremble and then shake mightily. In the failing light, they witness the earth begin to rise up in front of Arthur and Andrew and they all were very afraid. A great pillar of stone pushed its way up from the earth some 30 paces above them and then one by one seven smaller pillars rose up on each side of the center one some 20 paces high stretching from the wall in the east to the wall in the west before complete darkness fell over them all. Not even a star twinkled in the sky but only the torches on the castle behind them gave some light to the field where they lay. Rebecca tried fervently to get Emerald to move but he would not. He lay still as if dead and then Rebecca also froze as she witnessed a single star shine in the dark sky and it grew brighter as she watched it come to them from the east. As it grew closer, they could see it was an enormous golden dragon and the light that emanated from him was so intense they had to turn their eyes from him as he circled and landed atop the pillar with his back to them. Then slowly he spread his massive wings and a great stream of unending fire erupted from his head into the forest on the other side of the pillars and screams of torturous agony echoed on the other side of the pillars out of their sight and they all trembled at the awesome power of the golden dragon. And then seven lesser silver dragons appeared atop the seven lesser pillars and bowed facing the Golden Dragon in the center as he turned and faced the castle. Again the earth trembled below their feet so dramatically Rebecca feared it would fall away and they all would plunge into a bottomless pit. Slowly in the intense light he transformed into the image of a man before them and the light faded and they could look upon him. "I am Idos and a thousand years have passed since my people have seen my face." He spoke softly but his voice was in every man and woman's ear distinctly. "The thousand years of safety I promised has come to an end and I am well pleased with my people for they have kept my government and have done well in my eyes. Two lessons you have learned this day, one of peace and one of war. In peace, you have embraced the sword of Idos completely and I will strengthen the bond between my people and my sword removing the seven days of pain in his maturing. In war, you have born witness to the evil in the hearts of the men in the earth who have embraced gods of their own imaginations. My commandment to you is eternal that you love one another as I love you but this day I set a new commandment before you. Return your cities to their former glory and strengthen them but go forth from this island and spread my truth to the all the kingdoms in the earth for there are yet seven continents in the earth and I will deliver each into the hand of the ruler you choose. Seek peace patiently but carry my sword with you and have no fear for I am Idos the creator of all things and I will never forsake you or abandon you." He concluded and he began to transform back into a golden dragon before he spread his wings and all the dragons on the pillars flew after him into the sky.

The stars began to shine again and a mighty wind blew briefly from the ocean as the light returned to the sun. Emerald moved underneath Commander Rebecca as he rose to his feet and she turned his head to an open spot in the field and gave the command to fly nervously. He ran briefly before he spread his wings and pumped them gracefully taking to the air. Commander Rebecca turned his head and banked over the great pillar that had risen from the earth and a feeling of great joy filled her heart as she viewed the sight on the other side of the pillars. The forest was gone. The whole valley had sunk down and the waves crashed softly onto a new beach that extended from the mountains in the east to the mountains in the west and only the highway remained. Commander Rebecca circled and landed quickly filled with excitement as Commander Dillon emerged from the castle with all the men of the army into the open field and they stared in amazement at the pillars of stone. Commander Dillon climbed up part way on the pillar to address the Army. "Today you bear witness that it was not by our own hands but by the hand of Idos that we were delivered from our enemies." He said and looked to the Sky Raiders. "Go quickly now to all the cities of the Great Father and spread the news of what you have seen this day for we shall declare and set aside this as the day of Idos for all generations to remember how he delivered us from disaster." Commander Dillon shouted and the crowd of men roared and cheered in their victory. Commander Rebecca gathered all the captains and dispersed each to a city with his squadron to accompany him and she and Major Regina were left with Commander Dillon. "What lies beyond these pillars?" Commander Dillon asked her as he had seen her fly over them earlier as he departed the castle. "The forest there is no more and our highway circles a great bay with a white sand beach between it and the pillars." Rebecca reported and tears filled the Supreme Commander's eyes. "And what evidence of our enemy did you find?" He asked cautiously. "There is none sir for the sea has washed every trace of them from our presence. It is as if they were never there." Commander Rebecca said and Commander Dillon rejoiced and sang and danced with all his men zealously in celebration.

The celebration went on all day as Queen Isabella and all the women of the city returned and people from all across the island came to view the pillars and sing praises to Idos and hear the tale. Before the sun set that day, the entire field was filled so that there was not a place to stand and Commander Rebecca gathered her captains in the dining hall and they celebrated together with Cpt Arthur and Cpt Andrew also away from the people. "Please tell us now how you found success in your task with Crimson." Commander Rebecca pleaded and Cpt Andrew kissed Lady Karen before he rose to tell his tale. "You know now that our plan was not my secret alone but that of Chancellor Trent and Chancellor Winston in alliance with Commander Rebecca and Cpt Arthur." He stated and they applauded each one of them and cheered. "I departed from the shack to test my bond with Crimson for what I planned to be a short flight but in returning Crimson would not land. The trauma he had experienced in the cave was so intense he trembled and fought me each time I attempted to make a landing there so I gave him his head to see where he would go. He took me into the mountains in the north and found a cave behind a waterfall and I slept on his back that night in the cave. When I awoke in the morning, I was very afraid for there in the cave sleeping next to us was Arch Angel and when he awoke he inspected me on Crimson's back and my fear subsided as he whistled approvingly and nuzzled me. He became a comfort to Crimson in his pain and they whistled and purred together as long lost friends as Crimson learned control of his flame. When we left the cave I flew back to the clearing and Arch Angel followed us but this time I got him to land and Cpt Arthur was there to greet us." Cpt Andrew concluded and Cpt Arthur stood up keeping his hand on Maid Melisa's shoulder. "If Cpt Andrew was afraid when he first saw Arch Angel, it is safe to say I was petrified." Arthur laughed and everyone did. "I ran....., fearing one or both of them would certainly set me on fire." He chuckled. "But Andrew called to me and I found my nerve to approach them cautiously. I know now that Arch Angel has pursued me all these years in our passing because he did not want to sever our bond and now it is like we were never apart." Cpt Arthur said and all could see the emotion in his face. I went back to the shack and retrieved a harness for him and set my mind to fly with Cpt Andrew until Crimson's days of pain were fulfilled. It wasn't until we decided to fly north of Lake Willow that we discovered what evil was transpiring here." Cpt Arthur concluded and the group applauded them all and cheered as Arthur kissed Melissa again and sat down. There was a blast of trumpets and then they could hear music from the orchestra coming in the doors to the balcony in the south. They all moved to the balcony together with their drinks and peering over the side they could see the orchestra had set up on the balcony below them and everyone was dancing in the open field and celebrating under the moonlight. Now Commander Rebecca knew the celebrating was going to last all night. She found Cpt Richard and moved to his side as Major Regina and Cpt Cameron ran over to her excitedly. "Shall we go down together to the field and find a place share an embrace and dance?" Regina said enthusiastically and Rebecca moved against Richard and looked up at the stars. "You and Cameron go ahead, I am tired and I am fearful it might rain." She said smiling staring out across the field. Regina looked quizzically at her and then at the clear sky and shook her head confused as she and Cpt Cameron departed for the field. Now Regina stopped at the stairs and turned back to them. "Are you not coming Richard?" She asked. Now Richard had a peculiar grin on his face as he looked at the sky and then at Regina. "Did you not hear Commander Rebecca? It's going to rain." He smiled and turned back to stare with Rebecca across the wall.

The sons and daughters of the Great Father released their prisoners sending them back to King Argos with their warning on the flagship they had captured but kept for themselves the other ships. For the next year they rebuilt Sandista and strengthened their defenses having learned a great lesson from the invaders. As the Sky Raiders worked and trained with the dragons, they found the promise of Idos was true and their bond with his sword grew mightily. The mountain dragons no longer attacked the sons and daughters of the Great Father unprovoked and they found many treasures previously hidden from them in the mountains. In the spring, Cpt Cameron ventured into the valley of the dragons and secured a single egg to present to Major Regina at her birthday party. During the ceremony it hatched into a beautiful blue baby dragon and Major Regina presented to it a live fish.

THE END

About the Author

Ken Stephenson is 60 and twice retired. He went to high school at Putnam City High school in Oklahoma City and excelled in sports and music. He got married to his high school sweetheart when she got pregnant and went to College on a sports scholarship at McCook, Nebraska but lost it due to a lack of self-discipline. The marriage failed too for basically the same reason and he then joined the Army in 1972 and volunteered for Vietnam. The Army was pulling back from Vietnam then and he didn't get to go but he stayed with the Army and learned how to deal with success and failure. He met his current wife at Manhattan, Kansas and they had three kids. By the time he retired in 1992, he was a decorated Command Sergeant Major of an Artillery Battalion in California but he never went into combat. His entire career with the Army was spent supervising large groups of men in physically demanding tasks. He longed for a change and decided then to work where he was minimally supervised and responsible for no one else. He went into transportation and after 5 years, he bought his own truck and drove nationwide for various companies. In 2004, his first son with his current wife died tragically in a car accident. Towards the end of his truck driving career, he was very successful and spent a short time teaching new drivers before he retired again in 2010. All his life, Ken has been a story teller but only recently has he attempted to write his stories out. He is many times described as a hopeless romantic and now lives in Killeen, Texas where he was born surrounded by his family and six grandkids.